More praise for *Graceling*

A Publishers Weekly Best Book of the Year
An SLJ Best Book of the Year
A Kirkus Reviews Best Book of the Year
A Booklist Editor's Choice

"A brilliant, unforgettable story. I consumed *Graceling* in one sitting, awed by its originality, breadth, and humanity. For a first novel—for any novel—this book is extraordinary."
—Catherine Gilbert Murdock, author of *Dairy Queen*

"Discovering one's true identity and powers is a common theme in young adult literature, but Kristin Cashore, with compelling characters and an ease in combining genres—fantasy, mystery, adventure, romance—develops this theme with enormous freshness."
—*Newsday*

"I can't remember when I last was this impressed by a new fantasy. Kristin Cashore's voice is fresh and fluent . . . the end result is a story that you tear through so that you can immediately start again at the beginning and read it with the care it deserves. A truly spectacular novel."
—Susan Hirschman, founder of Greenwillow Books

KRISTIN CASHORE

GRACELING

HOUGHTON MIFFLIN HARCOURT

Boston   New York

Text set in Adobe Garamond
Maps by Jeffery C. Mathison

The Library of Congress has cataloged the hardcover edition as follows:
Cashore, Kristin.
Graceling/Kristin Cashore.
p. cm.
Summary: In a world where some people are born with extreme
and often-feared skills called Graces, Katsa struggles for redemption
from her own horrifying Grace, the Grace of killing, and teams up with
another young fighter to save their land from a corrupt king.

[1. Fantasy.] I. Title.
PZ7.C26823Gr 2008
[Fic]—dc22 2007045436
HC ISBN 978-0-15-206396-2
PA ISBN 978-0-547-25830-0

Printed in the United States of America
DOM 10 9 8
4500271901

For my mother,
Nedda Previtera Cashore,
who has a meatball Grace,
and my father,
J. Michael Cashore,
who is Graced with losing (and finding) his glasses

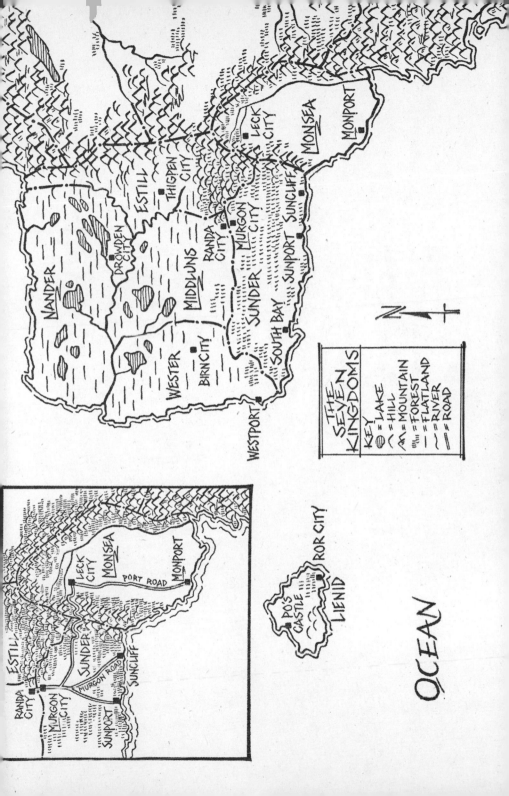

THE SEVEN KINGDOMS

KEY
⊙ = LAKE
⌒ = HILL
ᴧᴧ = MOUNTAIN
ᵐ = FOREST
≡ = FLATLAND
∼ = RIVER
= = ROAD

N

NANDER

ESTILL

DROWDEN CITY

THIGPEN CITY

LECK CITY

MONSEA

MONPORT

MIDDLUNS

RANDA CITY

MURGON CITY

SUNDER

SUNPORT

SUNCLIFF

WESTER

BIRN CITY

SOUTH BAY

WESTPORT

ESTILL

LECK CITY

MONSEA

MONPORT

PORT ROAD

RANDA CITY

SUNDER

MURGON CITY

MURGON ROAD

SUNPORT

SUNCLIFF

POS CASTLE

ROR CITY

LIENID

OCEAN

PART ONE

The Lady Killer

CHAPTER ONE

IN THESE DUNGEONS the darkness was complete, but Katsa had a map in her mind. One that had so far proven correct, as Oll's maps tended to do. Katsa ran her hand along the cold walls and counted doors and passageways as she went. Turning when it was time to turn; stopping finally before an opening that should contain a stairway leading down. She crouched and felt forward with her hands. There was a stone step, damp and slippery with moss, and another one below it. This was Oll's staircase, then. She only hoped that when he and Giddon followed her with their torches, they would see the moss slime, tread carefully, and not waken the dead by clattering headlong down the steps.

Katsa slunk down the stairway. One left turn and two right turns. She began to hear voices as she entered a corridor where the darkness flickered orange with the light of a torch set in the wall. Across from the torch was another corridor where, according to Oll, anywhere from two to ten guards should be standing watch before a certain cell at the passageway's end.

These guards were Katsa's mission. It was for them that she had been sent first.

Katsa crept toward the light and the sound of laughter. She could stop and listen, to get a better sense of how many she would face, but there was no time. She pulled her hood down low and swung around the corner.

She almost tripped over her first four victims, who were sitting on the floor across from each other, their backs against the wall, legs splayed, the air stinking with whatever strong drink they'd brought down here to pass the time of their watch. Katsa kicked and struck at temples and necks, and the four men lay slumped together on the floor before amazement had even registered in their eyes.

There was only one more guard, sitting before the cell bars at the end of the corridor. He scrambled to his feet and slid his sword from its sheath. Katsa walked toward him, certain that the torch at her back hid her face, and particularly her eyes, from his sight. She measured his size, the way he moved, the steadiness of the arm that held the sword toward her.

"Stop there. It's clear enough what you are." His voice was even. He was brave, this one. He cut the air with his sword, in warning. "You don't frighten me."

He lunged toward her. She ducked under his blade and whirled her foot out, clipping his temple. He dropped to the ground.

She stepped over him and ran to the bars, squinting into the darkness of the cell. A shape huddled against the back wall, a person too tired or too cold to care about the fighting going on. Arms wrapped around legs, and head tucked between knees. He was shivering—she could hear his breath. She shifted, and the light glanced over his crouched form. His hair was white and cut close to his head. She saw the glimmer of gold in his ear. Oll's maps had served them well, for this man was a Lienid. He was the one they were looking for.

She pulled on the door latch. Locked. Well, that was no surprise, and it wasn't her problem. She whistled once, low, like an owl. She stretched the brave guard flat on his back and dropped one of her pills into his mouth. She ran up the corridor, turned the four unfortunates on their backs beside each other, and dropped a pill into each mouth. Just as she was beginning to wonder if Oll and Giddon had lost themselves in the dungeons, they appeared around the corner and slipped past her.

"A quarter hour, no more," she said.

"A quarter hour, My Lady." Oll's voice was a rumble. "Go safely."

Their torchlight splashed the walls as they approached the cell. The Lienid man moaned and drew his arms in closer. Katsa caught a glimpse of his torn, stained clothing. She heard Giddon's ring of lock picks clink against itself. She would have liked to have waited to see that they opened the door, but she was needed elsewhere. She tucked her packet of pills into her sleeve and ran.

THE CELL GUARDS reported to the dungeon guard, and the dungeon guard reported to the underguard. The underguard reported to the castle guard. The night guard, the king's guard, the wall guard, and the garden guard also reported to the castle guard. As soon as one guard noticed another's absence, the alarm would be raised, and if Katsa and her men weren't far enough away, all would be lost. They would be pursued, it would come to bloodshed; they would see her eyes, and she would be recognized. So she had to get them all, every guard. Oll had guessed there would be twenty. Prince Raffin had made her thirty pills, just in case.

Most of the guards gave her no trouble. If she could sneak up on them, or if they were crowded in small groups, they never knew what hit them. The castle guard was a bit more complicated, because five guards defended his office. She swirled through the lot of them, kicking and kneeing and hitting, and the castle guard jumped up from his guardhouse desk, burst through the door, and ran into the fray.

"I know a Graceling when I see one." He jabbed with his sword, and she rolled out of the way. "Let me see the colors of your eyes, boy. I'll cut them out. Don't think I won't."

It gave her some pleasure to knock him on the head with the hilt of her knife. She grabbed his hair, dragged him onto his back, and dropped a pill onto his tongue. They would all say, when they woke to their headaches and their shame, that the culprit had been a Graceling boy, Graced with fighting, acting alone. They would assume she was a boy, because in her plain trousers and hood she looked like one, and because when people were attacked it never occurred to anyone that it might have been a girl. And none of them had caught a glimpse of Oll or Giddon: She had seen to that.

No one would think of her. Whatever the Graceling Lady Katsa might be, she was not a criminal who lurked around dark courtyards at midnight, disguised. And besides, she was supposed to be en route east. Her uncle Randa, King of the Middluns, had seen her off just that morning, the whole city watching, with Captain Oll and Giddon, Randa's underlord, escorting her. Only a day of very hard riding in the wrong direction could have brought her south to King Murgon's court.

Katsa ran through the courtyard, past flower beds, fountains, and marble statues of Murgon. It was quite a pleasant courtyard, really, for such an unpleasant king; it smelled of grass and rich soil, and the sweetness of dew-dripped flowers. She raced through Murgon's apple orchard, a trail of drugged guards stretching out behind her. Drugged, not dead: an important distinction. Oll and Giddon, and most of the rest of the secret Council, had wanted her to kill them. But at the meeting to plan this mission, she'd argued that killing them would gain no time.

"What if they wake?" Giddon had said.

Prince Raffin had been offended. "You doubt my medicine. They won't wake."

"It would be faster to kill them," Giddon had said, his brown eyes insistent. Heads in the dark room had nodded.

"I can do it in the time allotted," Katsa had said, and when Giddon had started to protest, she'd held up her hand. "Enough. I won't kill them. If you want them killed, you can send someone else."

Oll had smiled and clapped the young lord on the back. "Just think, Lord Giddon, it'll make it more fun for us. The perfect robbery, past all of Murgon's guards, and nobody hurt? It's a good game."

The room had erupted with laughter, but Katsa hadn't even cracked a smile. She wouldn't kill, not if she didn't have to. A killing couldn't be undone, and she'd killed enough. Mostly for her uncle. King Randa thought her useful. When border ruffians were stirring up trouble, why send an army if you could send a single representative? It was much more economical. But she'd killed for the Council, too, when it couldn't be avoided. This time it could be avoided.

At the far end of the orchard she came upon a guard who was old, as old, perhaps, as the Lienid. He stood in a grove of yearling trees, leaning on his sword, his back round and bent. She snuck up behind him and paused. A tremor shook the hands that rested on the hilt of his blade.

She didn't think much of a king who didn't retire his guards in comfort when they'd gotten too old to hold a sword steady.

But if she left him, he would find the others she'd felled and raise the alarm. She struck him once, hard, on the back of the head, and he slumped and let out a puff of air. She caught him and lowered him to the ground, as gently as she could, and then dropped a pill into his mouth. She took a moment to run her fingers along the lump forming on his skull. She hoped his head was strong.

She had killed once by accident, a memory she held close

to her consciousness. It was how her Grace had announced its nature, a decade ago. She'd been a child, barely eight years old. A man who was some sort of distant cousin had visited the court. She hadn't liked him—his heavy perfume, the way he leered at the girls who served him, the way his leer followed them around the room, the way he touched them when he thought no one was watching. When he'd started to pay Katsa some attention, she had grown wary. "Such a pretty little one," he'd said. "Graceling eyes can be so very unattractive. But you, lucky girl, look better for it. What is your Grace, my sweetness? Storytelling? Mind reading? I know. You're a dancer."

Katsa hadn't known what her Grace was. Some Graces took longer than others to surface. But even if she had known, she wouldn't have cared to discuss it with this cousin. She'd scowled at the man and turned away. But then his hand had slid toward her leg, and her hand had flown out and smashed him in the face. So hard and so fast that she'd pushed the bones of his nose into his brain.

Ladies in the court had screamed; one had fainted. When they'd lifted him from the pool of blood on the floor and he'd turned out to be dead, the court had grown silent, backed away. Frightened eyes—not just those of the ladies now, but those of the soldiers, the sworded underlords—all directed at her. It was fine to eat the meals of the king's chef, who was Graced with cooking, or send their horses to the king's Graced horse doctor. But a girl Graced with killing? This one was not safe.

Another king would have banished her, or killed her, even if she was his sister's child. But Randa was clever. He could see that in time his niece might serve a practical purpose. He sent her to her chambers and kept her there for weeks as punishment, but that was all. When she emerged, they all ran to get out of her path. They'd never liked her before, for no one liked the Graced, but at least they'd tolerated her presence. Now there was no pretense of friendliness. "Watch for the blue-eyed green-eyed one," they would whisper to guests. "She killed her cousin, with one strike. Because he complimented her eyes." Even Randa kept out of her way. A murderous dog might be useful to a king, but he didn't want it sleeping at his feet.

Prince Raffin was the only one who sought her company. "You won't do it again, will you? I don't think my father will let you kill anyone you want."

"I never meant to kill him," she said.

"What happened?"

Katsa sent her mind back. "I felt like I was in danger. So I hit him."

Prince Raffin shook his head. "You need to control a Grace," he said. "Especially a killing Grace. You must, or my father will stop us seeing each other."

This was a frightening notion. "I don't know how to control it."

Raffin considered this. "You could ask Oll. The king's spies know how to hurt without killing. It's how they get information."

Raffin was eleven, three years Katsa's senior, and by her young standards, very wise. She took his advice and went to Oll, King Randa's graying captain and his spymaster. Oll wasn't foolish; he knew to fear the quiet girl with one eye blue and one eye green. But he also had some imagination. He wondered, as it had occurred to no one else to wonder, whether Katsa hadn't been just as shocked by her cousin's death as everyone else. And the more he thought about it, the more curious he became about her potential.

He started their training by setting rules. She would not practice on him, and she would not practice on any of the king's men. She would practice on dummies that she made out of sacks, sewn together and filled with grain. She would practice on the prisoners that Oll brought to her, men whose deaths were already decreed.

She practiced every day. She learned her own speed and her own explosive force. She learned the angle, position, and intensity of a killing blow versus a maiming blow. She learned how to disarm a man and how to break his leg, and how to twist his arm so severely that he would stop struggling and beg for release. She learned to fight with a sword and with knives and daggers. She was so fast and focused, so creative, she could find a way to beat a man senseless with both arms tied to her sides. Such was her Grace.

In time her control improved, and she began to practice with Randa's soldiers—eight or ten at a time, and in full suits of armor. Her practices were a spectacle: grown men grunting and clattering around clumsily, an unarmed child whirling and diving among them, knocking them down with a knee or a hand that they didn't see coming until they were already on the floor. Sometimes members of the court would come by to watch her practices. But if she caught their gaze, their eyes would drop and they would hurry on.

King Randa had not minded the sacrifice of Oll's time. He thought it necessary. Katsa wouldn't be useful if she remained uncontrolled.

And now in King Murgon's courtyard, no one could criticize her control. She moved across the grass beside the gravel paths, swiftly, soundlessly. By now Oll and Giddon must almost have reached the garden wall, where two of Murgon's servants, friends of the Council, guarded their horses. She was nearly there herself; she saw the dark line ahead, black against a black sky.

Her thoughts rambled, but she wasn't daydreaming. Her senses were sharp. She caught the fall of every leaf in the garden, the rustle of every branch. And so she was astonished when a man stepped out of the darkness and grabbed her from behind. He wrapped his arm around her chest and held a knife to her throat. He started to speak, but in an instant she had deadened his arm, wrenched the knife from his hand, and thrown the blade to the ground. She flung him forward, over her shoulders.

He landed on his feet.

Her mind raced. He was Graced, a fighter. That much was clear. And unless he had no feeling in the hand that had raked her chest, he knew she was a woman.

He turned back to face her. They eyed each other, warily, each no more than a shadow to the other. He spoke.

"I've heard of a lady with this particular Grace." His voice was gravelly and deep. There was a lilt to his words; it was not an accent she knew. She must learn who he was, so that she could know what to do with him.

"I can't think what that lady would be doing so far from home, running through the courtyard of King Murgon at midnight," he said. He shifted slightly, placed himself between her and the wall. He was taller than she was, and smooth in his movements, like a cat. Deceptively calm, ready to spring. A torch on the path nearby caught the glimmer of small gold hoops in his ears. And his face was unbearded, like a Lienid.

She shifted and swayed, her body ready, like his. She didn't have much time to decide. He knew who she was. But if he was a Lienid, she didn't want to kill him.

"Don't you have anything to say, Lady? Surely you don't think I'll let you pass without an explanation?" There was something playful in his voice. She watched him, quietly. He stretched his arms in one fluid motion, and her eyes unraveled the bands of gold that gleamed on his fingers. It was enough. The hoops in his ears, the rings, the lilt in his words—it was enough.

"You're a Lienid," she said.

"You have good eyesight," he said.

"Not good enough to see the colors of your eyes."

He laughed. "I think I know the colors of yours."

Common sense told her to kill him. "You're one to speak of being far from home," she said. "What's a Lienid doing in the court of King Murgon?"

"I'll tell you my reasons if you'll tell me yours."

"I'll tell you nothing, and you must let me pass."

"Must I?"

"If you don't, I'll have to force you."

"Do you think you can?"

She faked to her right, and he swung away, easily. She did it again, faster. Again, he escaped her easily. He was very good. But she was Katsa.

"I know I can," she said.

"Ah." His voice was amused. "But it might take you hours."

Why was he playing with her? Why wasn't he raising the alarm? Perhaps he was a criminal himself, a Graceling criminal. And if so, did that make him an ally or an enemy? Wouldn't a Lienid approve of her rescue of the Lienid prisoner? Yes—unless he was a traitor. Or unless this Lienid didn't even know the contents of Murgon's dungeons—Murgon had kept the secret well.

The Council would tell her to kill him. The Council would tell her she put them at risk if she left a man alive who knew her identity. But he was unlike any thug she'd ever encountered. He didn't feel brutish or stupid or threatening.

She couldn't kill one Lienid while rescuing another.

She was a fool and she would probably regret it, but she wouldn't do it.

"I trust you," he said, suddenly. He stepped out of her path and waved her forward. She thought him very strange, and impulsive, but she saw he'd relaxed his guard, and she wasn't one to waste an opportunity. In an instant she swung her boot up and clipped him on the forehead. His eyes opened wide with surprise, and he dropped to the ground.

"Maybe I didn't have to do that." She stretched him out,

his sleeping limbs heavy. "But I don't know what to think of you, and I've risked enough already, letting you live." She dug the pills out of her sleeve, dropped one into his mouth. She turned his face to the torchlight. He was younger than she'd thought, not much older than she, nineteen or twenty at most. A trickle of blood ran down his forehead, past his ear. The neck of his shirt was open, and the torchlight played along the line of his collarbone.

What a strange character. Maybe Raffin would know who he was.

She shook herself. They would be waiting.

She ran.

THEY RODE HARD. They tied the old man to his horse, for he was too weak to hold himself up. They stopped only once, to wrap him in more blankets.

Katsa was impatient to keep moving. "Doesn't he know it's midsummer?"

"He's frozen through, My Lady," Oll said. "He's shivering, he's ill. It's no use if our rescue kills him."

They talked about stopping, building a fire, but there was no time. They had to reach Randa City before daybreak or they would be discovered.

Perhaps I should have killed him, she thought as they thundered through dark forests. *Perhaps I should have killed him. He knew who I was.*

But he hadn't seemed threatening or suspicious. He'd been more curious than anything. He'd trusted her.

Then again, he hadn't known about the trail of drugged guards she'd left in her wake. And he wouldn't trust her once he woke to that welt on his head.

If he told King Murgon of their encounter, and if Murgon told King Randa, things could get very tricky for the Lady Katsa. Randa knew nothing of the Lienid prisoner, much less of Katsa moonlighting as rescuer.

Katsa shook herself in frustration. These thoughts were no help, and it was done now. They needed to get the grandfather to safety and warmth, and Raffin. She crouched lower in her saddle and urged her horse north.

CHAPTER TWO

IT WAS a land of seven kingdoms. Seven kingdoms, and seven thoroughly unpredictable kings. Why in the name of all that was reasonable would anyone kidnap Prince Tealiff, the father of the Lienid king? He was an old man. He had no power; he had no ambition; he wasn't even well. Word was, he spent most of his days sitting by the fire, or in the sun, looking out at the sea, playing with his great-grandchildren, and bothering no one.

The Lienid people didn't have enemies. They shipped their gold to whoever had the goods to trade for it; they grew their own fruit and bred their own game; they kept to themselves on their island, an ocean removed from the other six kingdoms. They were different. They had a distinctive dark-haired look and distinctive customs, and they liked their isolation. King Ror of Lienid was the least troublesome of the seven kings. He made no treaties with the others, but he made no war, and he ruled his own people fairly.

That the Council's network of spies had traced King Ror's father to King Murgon's dungeons in Sunder answered nothing. Murgon tended not to create trouble among the kingdoms, but often enough he was a party to the trouble, the agent of another man's crime as long as the money was good.

Without a doubt, someone had paid him to hold the Lienid grandfather. The question was, who?

Katsa's uncle, Randa, King of the Middluns, was not involved in this particular trouble. The Council could be certain of this, for Oll was Randa's spymaster and his confidant. Thanks to Oll, the Council knew everything there was to know about Randa.

In truth, Randa usually took care not to involve himself with the other kingdoms. His kingdom sat between Estill and Wester on one axis and between Nander and Sunder on the other. It was a position too tenuous for alliances.

The kings of Wester, Nander, and Estill—they were the source of most of the trouble. They were cast from the same hotheaded mold, all ambitious, all envious. All thoughtless and heartless and inconstant. King Birn of Wester and King Drowden of Nander might form an alliance and pummel Estill's army on the northern borders, but Wester and Nander could never work together for long. Suddenly one would offend the other, and Wester and Nander would become enemies again, and Estill would join Nander to pound Wester.

And the kings were no better to their own people than they were to each other's. Katsa remembered the farmers of Estill that she and Oll had lifted secretly from their makeshift prison in a cowshed weeks before. Estillan farmers who could not pay the tithe to their king, Thigpen, because Thigpen's army had trampled their fields on its way to raid a Nanderan village. Thigpen should have been the one to pay the farmers; even Randa would have conceded this, had his own army done the damage. But Thigpen intended to hang the farmers for nonpayment of the tithe. Yes, Birn, Drowden, and Thigpen kept the Council busy.

It had not always been like this. Wester, Nander, Estill, Sunder, and the Middluns—the five inner kingdoms—had once known how to coexist peacefully. Centuries back they had all been of the same family, ruled by three brothers and two sisters who had managed to negotiate their jealousies without resorting to war. But any acknowledgment of that old family bond was long gone now. The kingdoms' people were at the mercy of the natures of those who rose to be their rulers. It was a gamble, and the current generation did not make for a winning hand.

The seventh kingdom was Monsea. The mountains set Monsea apart from the others, as the ocean did for Lienid. Leck, King of Monsea, was married to Ashen, the sister of King Ror of Lienid. Leck and Ror shared a dislike for the squabbles of the other kingdoms. But this didn't forge an alliance, for Monsea and Lienid were too far removed from each other, too independent, too uninterested in the doings of the other kingdoms.

Not much was known about the Monsean court. King Leck was well liked by his people and had a great reputation for kindness to children, animals, and all helpless creatures. The Monsean queen was a gentle woman. Word was she'd stopped eating the day she'd heard of the Lienid grandfather's disappearance. For of course, the father of the Lienid king was her father as well.

It had to be Wester or Nander or Estill who had kidnapped the Lienid grandfather. Katsa could think of no other possibility, unless Lienid itself was involved. A notion that might seem ridiculous, if it hadn't been for the Lienid man in Murgon's courtyard. His jewelry had been rich: He was a noble of some sort. And any guest of Murgon's warranted suspicion.

But Katsa didn't feel he was involved. She couldn't explain it, but it was what she felt.

Why had Grandfather Tealiff been stolen? What conceivable importance could he have?

THEY REACHED Randa City before the sun did, but only just. When the horses' hooves clattered onto the stones of city roads, they slowed their pace. Some in the city were already awake. They couldn't tear through the narrow streets; they couldn't make themselves conspicuous.

The horses carried them past wooden shacks and houses, stone foundries, shops with their shutters closed. The buildings were neat, and most of them had recently been painted. There was no squalor in Randa City. Randa didn't tolerate squalor.

When the streets began to rise, Katsa dismounted. She passed her reins to Giddon and took the reins of Tealiff's horse. Giddon and Oll turned down a street that led east to the forest, leading Katsa's horse behind them. This was the arrangement. A grandfather on horseback and a boy at his side climbing to the castle were less likely to be noticed than four horses and four riders. Oll and Giddon would ride out of the city and wait for her in the trees. Katsa would deliver Tealiff to Prince Raffin through a high doorway in a defunct section of the castle wall, the existence of which Oll kept carefully from Randa's notice.

Katsa pulled the old man's blankets more firmly around his head. It was still fairly dark, but if she could see the hoops in his ears, then others would be able to see them as well. He lay on the horse, a huddled shape, whether asleep or unconscious she did not know. If he was unconscious, then she couldn't think how they were going to manage the last leg of the journey, up a crumbling staircase in Randa's wall where the horse couldn't go. She touched his face. He shifted and began to shiver again.

"You must wake, Lord Prince," she said. "I can't carry you up the steps to the castle."

The gray light reflected in his eyes as they opened, and his voice shook with coldness. "Where am I?"

"This is Randa City, in the Middluns," she said. "We're almost to safety."

"I didn't think Randa the type to conduct rescue missions."

She hadn't expected him to be so lucid. "He isn't."

"Humph. Well, I'm awake. You'll not have to carry me. The Lady Katsa, is it?"

"Yes, Lord Prince."

"I've heard you have one eye green as the Middluns grasses, and the other eye blue as the sky."

"Yes, Lord Prince."

"I've heard you could kill a man with the nail of your smallest finger."

She smiled. "Yes, Lord Prince."

"Does it make it easier?"

She squinted at his form hunched in the saddle. "I don't understand you."

"To have beautiful eyes. Does it lighten the burden of your Grace, to know you have beautiful eyes?"

She laughed. "No, Lord Prince. I'd happily do without both."

"I suppose I owe you my gratitude," he said, and then settled into silence.

She wanted to ask, For what? From what have we rescued you? But he was ill and tired, and he seemed asleep again. She didn't want to pester him. She liked this Lienid grandfather. There weren't many people who wanted to talk about her Grace.

They climbed past shadowed roofs and doorways. She was beginning to feel her sleepless night, and she would not rest again for hours. She replayed the grandfather's words in her mind. His accent was like the man's, the Lienid man's in the courtyard.

IN THE END, she did carry him, for when the time came she couldn't wake him up. She passed the horse's reins to a child crouched beside the wall, a girl whose father was a friend of the Council. Katsa tipped the old man over her shoulder and staggered, one step at a time, up the rubble of the broken stairway. The final stretch was practically vertical. Only the threat of the lightening sky kept her going; she'd never imagined that a man who looked like he was made of dust could be so heavy.

She had no breath to produce the low whistle that was to be her signal to Raffin, but it didn't matter. He heard her approach.

"The whole city has likely heard your approach," he whispered. "Honestly, Kat, I wouldn't have expected you to be capable of such a racket." He bent down and eased her load onto his own thin shoulders. She leaned against the wall and caught her breath.

"My Grace doesn't give me the strength of a giant," she said. "You Ungraced don't understand. You think if we have one Grace, we have them all."

"I've tasted your cakes, and I remember the needlework you used to do. I've no question a good number of Graces have passed you over." He laughed down at her in the gray light, and she smiled back. "It went as planned?"

She thought of the Lienid in the courtyard. "Yes, for the most."

"Go now," he said, "and safely. I'll take care of this one."

He turned and crept inside with his living bundle. She raced down the broken steps and slipped onto a pathway leading east. She pulled her hood low, and ran toward the pink sky.

CHAPTER THREE

KATSA RAN past houses and work shacks, shops and inns. The city was waking, and the streets smelled of baking bread. She ran past the milkman, half asleep on his cart, his horse sighing before him.

She felt light without her burden, and the road sloped downward. She ran quietly and fast into the eastern fields and kept running. A woman carried buckets across a farmyard, the handles hanging from a yoke balanced on her shoulder.

When the trees began, Katsa slowed. She had to move carefully now, lest she break branches or leave boot prints and create a trail straight to the meeting place. Already the way looked a bit traveled. Oll and Giddon and the others on the Council were never as careful as she, and of course the horses couldn't help creating a path. They would need a new meeting place soon.

By the time she broke into the thicket that was their hideout, it was daylight. The horses grazed. Giddon lay on the ground. Oll leaned against a pile of saddlebags. Both men were asleep.

Katsa choked down her annoyance and passed to the horses. She greeted the animals and lifted their hooves, one by one, to check for cracks and gravel. They'd done well, the horses, and at least they knew better than to fall asleep in the forest, so close to the city and such a great distance from where Randa supposed them to be. Her own mount whickered, and Oll stirred behind her.

"And if someone had discovered you," she said, "sleeping at the edge of the forest when you were supposed to be halfway to the eastern border?" She spoke into her saddle and scratched her horse's shoulder. "What explanation would you have given?"

"I didn't mean to sleep, My Lady," Oll replied.

"That's no comfort."

"We don't all have your stamina, My Lady, especially those of us with gray hair. Come now, no harm was done." He shook Giddon, who responded by covering his eyes with his hands. "Wake up, My Lord. We'd best be moving."

Katsa said nothing. She hung her saddlebags and waited by the horses. Oll brought the remaining saddlebags and fastened them in place. "Prince Tealiff is safe, My Lady?"

"He's safe."

Giddon stumbled over, scratching his brown beard. He unwrapped a loaf of bread and held it out to her, but she shook her head. "I'll eat later," she said.

Giddon broke off a piece and handed the loaf to Oll. "Are you angry that we weren't performing strength exercises when you arrived, Katsa? Should we have been doing gymnastics in the treetops?"

"You could've been caught, Giddon. You could've been seen, and then where would you be?"

"You would've thought of some story," Giddon said. "You would've saved us, like you do everyone else." He smiled, his warm eyes lighting up a face that was confident and handsome but that failed to please Katsa at the moment. Giddon was younger even than Raffin, strong, and a good rider. He had no excuse for sleeping.

"Come, My Lord," Oll said. "Let's eat our bread in the saddle. Otherwise our lady will leave without us."

She knew they teased her. She knew they thought her too critical. But she also knew she wouldn't have allowed herself to sleep when it was unsafe to do so.

Then again, they would never have allowed the Graceling Lienid to live. If they knew, they'd be furious, and she wouldn't be able to offer any rational excuse.

They wound their way to one of the forest paths that paralleled the main road and set out eastward. They pulled their hoods low and pushed the horses hard. After a few minutes, the pounding of hooves surrounding her, Katsa's irritation diminished. She couldn't be worried for long when she was moving.

THE FORESTS of the southern Middluns gave way to hills, low hills at first that would grow as they neared Estill. They stopped only once, at midday, to change their horses at a secluded inn that had offered its services to the Council.

With fresh horses they made good time, and by nightfall they approached the Estillan border. With an early start they could reach the Estillan estate that was their destination by midmorning, do their business for Randa, and then turn back. They could travel at a reasonable pace and still return to Randa City before nightfall of the following day, which was when they were expected. And then Katsa would know whether Prince Raffin had learned anything from the Lienid grandfather.

They made camp against an enormous rock crag that broke through the base of one of the eastern hills. There was a chill to the night, but they decided against a fire. Mischief hid in the hills along the Estillan border, and though they were safe with two sworded men and Katsa, there was no reason to attract trouble. They ate a supper of bread, cheese, and water from their flasks, and then they climbed into their bedrolls.

"I'll sleep well tonight," Giddon said, yawning. "It's lucky that inn came forward to the Council. We would've ridden the horses into the ground."

"It surprises me, the friends the Council is finding," Oll said.

Giddon propped himself up onto his elbow. "Did you expect it, Katsa? Did you think your Council would spread as it has?"

What had she expected when she'd started the Council? She'd imagined herself, alone, sneaking through passageways and around corners, an invisible force working against the mindlessness of the kings. "I never even imagined it spreading beyond me."

"And now we have friends in almost every kingdom," Giddon said. "People are opening their homes. Did you know one

of the Nanderan borderlords brought an entire village behind
his walls when the Council learned of a Westeran raiding
party? The village was destroyed, but every one of them lived."
He settled down onto his side and yawned again. "It's heart-
ening. The Council does some good."

KATSA LAY on her back and listened to the men's steady breathing. The horses, too, slept. But not Katsa: Two days of hard
riding and a sleepless night between, and she was awake. She
watched clouds flying across the sky, blotting out the stars and
revealing them again. The night air puffed and set the hill grass
rustling.

The first time she'd hurt someone for Randa had been in
a border village not far from this camp. An underlord of
Randa's had been exposed as a spy, on the payroll of King
Thigpen of Estill. The charge was treason and the punishment
was death. The underlord had fled toward the Estillan border.

Katsa had been all of ten years old. Randa had come to
one of her practice sessions and watched her, an unpleasant
smile on his face. "Are you ready to do something useful with
your Grace, girl?" he called out to her.

Katsa stopped her kicking and whirling and stood still,
struck by the notion that her Grace could have any beneficial
use.

"Hmm," Randa said, smirking at her silence. "Your sword
is the only bright thing about you. Pay attention, girl. I'm sending you after this traitor. You're to kill him, in public, using

your bare hands, no weapons. Just him, no one else. I'm sure we all hope you've learned to control your bloodlust by now."

Katsa shrank suddenly, too small to speak, even if she'd had something to say. She understood his order. He refused her the use of weapons because he didn't want the man to die cleanly. Randa wanted a bloody, anguished spectacle, and he expected her to furnish it.

Katsa set out with Oll and a convoy of soldiers. When the soldiers caught the underlord, they dragged him to the square of the nearest village, where a scattering of startled people watched, slack jawed. Katsa instructed the soldiers to make the man kneel. In one motion she snapped his neck. There was no blood; there was no more than an instant's pain. Most in the crowd didn't even realize what had happened.

When Randa heard what she'd done he was angry, angry enough that he called her to his throne room. He looked down at her from his raised seat, his eyes blue and hard, his smile nothing more than a baring of teeth. "What's the point of a public execution," he said, "if the public misses the part where the fellow dies? I can see that when I give orders I shall have to compensate for your mental ineptitude."

After that his commands included specifics: blood and pain, for this or that length of time. There was no way around what he wanted. The more Katsa did it, the better she got at it. And Randa got what he wished, for her reputation spread like a cancer. Everyone knew what came to those who crossed King Randa of the Middluns.

After a while Katsa forgot about defiance. It became too difficult to imagine.

ON THEIR many travels to perform Randa's errands, Oll told the girl of things Randa's spies learned when they crossed into the other kingdoms. Young girls who had disappeared from an Estillan village and reappeared weeks later in a Westeran whorehouse. A man held in a Nanderan dungeon as punishment for his brother's thievery, for his brother was dead, and someone had to be punished. A tax that the King of Wester had decided to levy on the villages of Estill—a tax Wester's soldiers saw fit to collect by slaying Estillan villagers and emptying their pockets.

All these stories Randa's spies reported to their king, and all of them Randa ignored. Now, a Middluns lord who had hidden the majority of his harvest in order to pay a smaller tithe than he owed? Here was worthwhile news; here was a problem relevant to the Middluns. Randa sent Katsa to crack the lord's head open.

Katsa couldn't say where the notion had come from, but once it pushed its way into her mind, it would not leave. What might she be capable of—if she acted of her own volition and outside Randa's domain? It was something she thought about, something to distract herself as she broke fingers for Randa and twisted men's arms from their sockets. And the more she considered the question, the more urgent it became, until she thought she would blaze up and burn from the frustration of not doing it.

In her sixteenth year she brought the idea to Raffin. "It just might work," he said. "I'll help you, of course." Next she went to Oll. Oll was skeptical, even alarmed. He was used to bringing his information to Randa so Randa could decide what action to take. But he saw her side of it eventually, slowly, once he understood that Katsa was determined to do this thing with or without him, and once he convinced himself that it would do the king no harm not to know every move his spymaster made.

In her very first mission, Katsa intercepted a small company of midnight looters that the Estillan king had set on his own people, and sent them fleeing into the hills. It was the happiest and headiest moment of her life.

Next Katsa and Oll rescued a number of Westeran boys enslaved in a Nanderan iron mine. One or two more escapades and the news of their missions began to trickle into useful channels. Some of Oll's fellow spies joined the cause, and one or two underlords at Randa's court, like Giddon. Oll's wife, Bertol, and other women of the castle. They established regular meetings that took place in secluded rooms. There was an atmosphere of adventure at the meetings, of dangerous freedom. It felt like play, too wonderful, Katsa thought sometimes, to be real. Except that it was real. They didn't just talk about subversion; they planned it and carried it out.

Inevitably over time they attracted allies outside the court. The virtuous among Randa's borderlords, who were tired of sitting around while neighboring villages were plundered. Lords from the other kingdoms, and their spies. And bit by bit, the people—innkeepers, blacksmiths, farmers. Everyone was tired of the fool kings. Everyone was willing to take some small risk to lessen the damage of their ambition and disorder and lawlessness.

Tonight, in her camp on the Estillan border, Katsa blinked at the sky, wide awake, and thought about how large the Council had become, how fast it had spread, like one of the vines in Randa's forest.

It was out of her control now. Missions were carried out in the name of the Council in places she'd never been, without her supervision, and all of it had become dangerous. One careless word spoken by the child of some innkeeper, one unlucky encounter across the world between two people she'd never met, and everything would come crashing down. Her missions would end, Randa would see to it. And then, once again, she would be no more than the king's strongarm.

She shouldn't have trusted the strange Lienid.

Katsa crossed her arms over her chest and stared at the stars. She would like to take her horse and race around the hills in circles. That would calm her mind, tire her out. But it would tire her horse as well, and she wouldn't leave Oll and Giddon alone. And besides, one didn't do such things. It wasn't normal.

She snorted, and then listened to make sure that no one woke. Normal. She wasn't normal. A girl Graced with killing, a royal thug? A girl who didn't want the husbands Randa pushed on her, perfectly handsome and thoughtful men, a girl

who panicked at the thought of a baby at her breast, or clinging to her ankles.

She wasn't natural.

If the Council were discovered, she would escape to a place
where she wouldn't be found. Lienid, or Monsea. She'd live in
a cave, in a forest. She'd kill anyone who found her and recognized her.

She wouldn't relinquish the small amount of control she'd
taken over her life.

She must sleep.

Sleep, Katsa, she told herself. *You need to sleep, to keep your
strength.*

And suddenly tiredness swept over her, and she was asleep.

CHAPTER FOUR

In the morning they dressed like themselves, Giddon in traveling clothes befitting a Middluns underlord, and Oll in his captain's uniform. Katsa changed into a blue tunic lined with the orange silk of Randa's courts, and the matching trousers she wore to perform Randa's errands, a costume to which he consented only because she was abusive to any dresses she wore while riding. Randa didn't like to think of his Graceling killer doling out punishment in torn and muddy skirts. It was undignified.

Their business in Estill was with an Estillan borderlord who had arranged to purchase lumber from the southern forests of the Middluns. He had paid the agreed price, but then he'd cleared more than the agreed number of trees. Randa wanted payment for the additional lumber, and he wanted the lord punished for altering the agreement without his permission.

"I give you both fair warning," Oll said as they cleared the camp of their belongings. "This lord has a daughter Graced with mind reading."

"Why should you warn us?" Katsa asked. "Isn't she at Thigpen's court?"

"King Thigpen has sent her home to her father."

Katsa yanked hard on the straps that attached her bag to her saddle.

"Are you trying to pull the horse down, Katsa," Giddon said, "or just break your saddlebag?"

Katsa scowled. "No one told me we'd be encountering a mind reader."

"I'm telling you now, My Lady," Oll said, "and there's no reason for concern. She's a child. Most of what she comes up with is nonsense."

"Well, what's wrong with her?"

"What's wrong with her is that most of what she comes up with is nonsense. Or useless, irrelevant, and she blurts out everything she sees. She's out of control. She was making Thigpen nervous. So he sent her home, My Lady, and told her father to send her back when she became useful."

In Estill, as in most of the kingdoms, Gracelings were given up to the king's use by law. The child whose eyes settled into two different colors weeks, months, or on the rarest occasions years after its birth was sent to the court of its king and raised in its king's nurseries. If its Grace turned out to be useful to the king, the child would remain in his service. If not, the child would be sent home. With the court's apologies, of course, because it was difficult for a family to find use for a Graceling. Especially one with a useless Grace, like climbing trees or holding one's breath for an impossibly long time or talking backward. The child might fare well in a farmer's family, working among the fields with no one to see or know. But if a king sent a Graceling home to the family of an innkeeper or a storekeeper in a town with more than one inn or store to choose from, business was bound to suffer. It made no difference what the child's Grace was. People avoided a place if they could, if they were likely to encounter a person with eyes that were two different colors.

"Thigpen's a fool not to keep a mind reader close," Giddon said, "just because she's not useful yet. They're too dangerous. What if she falls under someone else's influence?"

Giddon was right, of course. Whatever else the mind readers might be, they were almost always valuable tools for a king to wield. But Katsa couldn't understand why anyone would want to keep them close. Randa's chef was Graced, and his horse handler, and his winemaker, and one of his court dancers. He had a juggler who could juggle any number of items without dropping them. He had several soldiers, no match for Katsa, but Graced with sword fighting. He had a man who predicted the quality of the next year's harvest. He had a woman brilliant with numbers, the only woman working in a king's countinghouse in all seven kingdoms.

He also had a man who could tell your mood just by putting his hands on you. He was the only Graceling of Randa's who repelled Katsa, the only person in court besides Randa himself whom she took pains to avoid.

"Foolish behavior on the part of Thigpen is never particularly surprising, My Lord," Oll said.

"What kind of mind reader is she?" Katsa asked.

"They're not sure, My Lady. She's so unformed. And you know how the mind readers are, their Graces always changing, and so hard to pin down. Adults before they've grown into their full power. But it seems as if this one reads desires. She knows what it is other people want."

"Then she'll know I'll want to knock her senseless if she so much as looks at me." Katsa spoke the words into the mane of her horse. They were not for the ears of her companions, for them to pull apart and make a joke of. "Is there anything else I need to know about this borderlord?" she asked aloud as she stepped into her stirrup. "Perhaps he has a guard of a hundred Graced fighters? A trained bear to protect him? Anything else you've forgotten to mention?"

"There's no need to be sarcastic, My Lady," Oll said.

"Your company this morning is as pleasant as always, Katsa," Giddon said.

Katsa spurred her horse forward. She didn't want to see Giddon's laughing face.

THE LORD'S HOLDING stood behind gray stone walls at the crest of a hill of waving grasses. The man who ushered them through the gate and took their horses told them that his lord sat at his breakfast. Katsa, Giddon, and Oll stepped directly into the great hall without waiting for an escort.

The lord's courtier moved forward to block their entrance into the breakfast room. Then he saw Katsa. He cleared his throat and opened the grand doors. "Some representatives from the court of King Randa, My Lord," he said. He slipped behind them without waiting for a response from his master and scampered away.

The lord sat before a feast of pork, eggs, bread, fruit, and cheese, with a servant at his elbow. Both men looked up as they entered, and both men froze. A spoon clattered from the lord's hand onto the table.

"Good morning, My Lord," Giddon said. "We apologize for interrupting your breakfast. Do you know why we're here?"

The lord seemed to struggle to find his voice. "I haven't the slightest idea," he said, his hand at his throat.

"No? Perhaps the Lady Katsa could help you bring it to mind," Giddon said. "Lady?"

Katsa stepped forward.

"All right, all right." The lord stood. His legs jarred the table, and a glass overturned. He was tall and broad shoul-dered, larger even than Giddon or Oll. Clumsy now with his fluttering hands, and his eyes that flitted around the room but always avoided Katsa. A bit of egg clung to his beard. So fool-ish, such a big man, so frightened. Katsa kept her face expres-sionless, so that none of them would know how much she hated this.

"Ah, you've remembered," Giddon said, "have you? You've remembered why we're here?"

"I believe I owe you money," the lord said. "I imagine you've come to collect your debt."

"Very good!" Giddon spoke as if to a child. "And why do you owe us money? The agreement was for how many acres of lumber? Remind me, Captain."

"Twenty acres, My Lord," Oll said.

"And how many acres did the lord remove, Captain?"

"Twenty-three acres, My Lord," Oll said.

"Twenty-three acres!" Giddon said. "That's rather a hefty difference, wouldn't you agree?"

"A terrible mistake." The lord's attempt at a smile was pained. "We never realized we'd need so much. Of course, I'll pay you immediately. Just name your price."

"You've caused King Randa no small inconvenience," Giddon said. "You've decimated three acres of his forest. The king's forests are not limitless."

"No. Of course not. Terrible mistake."

"We've also had to travel for days to settle this matter," Giddon said. "Our absence from court is a great nuisance to the king."

"Of course," the lord said. "Of course."

"I imagine if you doubled your original payment, it would lessen the strain of inconvenience for the king."

The lord licked his lips. "Double the original payment. Yes. That seems quite reasonable."

Giddon smiled. "Very good. Perhaps your man will lead us to your countinghouse."

"Certainly." The lord gestured to the servant at his side. "Quickly, man. Quickly!"

"Lady Katsa," Giddon said as he and Oll turned toward the door, "why don't you stay here? Keep His Lordship company."

The servant led Giddon and Oll from the room. The big doors swung shut behind them. Katsa and the lord were alone.

She stared at him. His breath was shallow, his face pale. He didn't look at her. He seemed as if he were about to collapse.

"Sit down," Katsa said. He fell into his chair and let out a small moan.

"Look at me," she said. His eyes flicked to her face, and then slid to her hands. Randa's victims always watched her hands, never her face. They couldn't hold her eyes. And they expected a blow from her hands.

Katsa sighed.

He opened his mouth to speak, but nothing came out but a croak.

"I can't hear you," Katsa said.

He cleared his throat. "I have a family. I have a family to care for. Do what you will, but I beg you not to kill me."

"You don't want me to kill you, for the sake of your family?"

A tear ran into his beard. "And for my own sake. I don't want to die."

Of course he didn't want to die, for three acres of wood. "I don't kill men who steal three acres of lumber from the king," she said, "and then pay for it dearly in gold. It's more the sort of crime that warrants a broken arm or the removal of a finger."

She moved toward him and pulled her dagger from its sheath. He breathed heavily, staring at the eggs and fruit on his plate. She wondered if he would vomit or begin to sob. But then he moved his plate to the side, and his overturned glass and his silver. He stretched his arms onto the table before him. He bent his head, and waited.

A wave of tiredness swept over her. It was easier to follow Randa's orders when they begged or cried, when they gave her nothing to respect. And Randa didn't care about his forests; he only cared about the money and the power. Besides, the forests would grow back one day. Fingers didn't grow back.

She slipped her dagger back into its sheath. It would be his arm, then, or his leg, or perhaps his collarbone, always a painful bone to break. But her own arms were as heavy as iron, and her legs didn't seem to want to propel her forward.

The lord drew one shaky breath, but he didn't move or speak. He was a liar and a thief and a fool.

Somehow she could not get herself to care.

Katsa sighed sharply. "I grant that you're brave," she said, "though you didn't seem it at first." She sprang to the table and struck him on the temple, just as she'd done with Murgon's guards. He slumped, and fell from his chair.

She turned and went to wait in his great stone hall for Giddon and Oll to return with the money.

He would wake with a headache, but no more. If Randa heard what she had done, he'd be furious.

But perhaps Randa wouldn't hear. Or perhaps she could accuse the lord of lying, to save face.

In which case, Randa would insist she return with proof in the future. A collection of shriveled fingers and toes. What *that* would do for her reputation. . . .

It didn't matter. She didn't have the strength today to torture a person who didn't deserve it.

A small figure came tripping into the hall then. Katsa knew who she was even before she saw the girl's eyes, one yellow as the squash that grew in the north, and one brown as a patch of mud. This girl she would hurt; this girl she would torture if it would stop her from taking Katsa's thoughts.

Katsa caught the child's eyes and stared her down. The girl gasped and backed up a few steps, then turned and ran from the hall.

CHAPTER FIVE

THEY MADE good time, though Katsa chafed at their pace.

"Katsa feels that to ride a horse at anything but breakneck speed is a waste of the horse," Giddon said.

"I only want to know if Raffin has learned anything from the Lienid grandfather."

"Don't worry, My Lady," Oll said. "We'll reach the court by evening tomorrow, as long as the weather holds."

THE WEATHER held through the day and into the night, but sometime before dawn, clouds blotted out the stars above their camp. In the morning they broke camp quickly and set out with some trepidation. Shortly thereafter, as they rode into the yard of the inn that kept their horses, raindrops plopped onto their arms and faces. They'd only just made it to the stables when the skies opened and water poured down. Rushing streams formed between the hills around them.

It became an argument.

"We can ride in the rain," Katsa said. They stood in the stables, the inn ten steps away but invisible through a wall of water.

"At the risk of the horses," Giddon said. "At the risk of catching our deaths. Don't be foolish, Katsa."

"It's only water," she said.

"Tell that to a drowning man," Giddon said. He glared down at her, and she glared back. A raindrop from a crack in the roof splashed onto her nose, and she wiped at it furiously.

"My Lady," Oll said. "My Lord."

Katsa took a deep breath, looked into his patient face, and prepared herself for disappointment.

"We don't know how long the storm will last," Oll said. "If it lasts a day, we'd best not be in it. There's no reason to ride in such weather—" He held up his hand as Katsa started to speak. "No reason we could give to the king without him thinking us mad. But perhaps it'll only last an hour. In which case, we'll only have lost an hour."

Katsa crossed her arms and forced herself to breathe. "It doesn't look like the kind of storm that lasts an hour."

"Then I'll inform the innkeeper we're in need of food," Oll said, "and rooms for the night."

THE INN was some distance from any of the Middluns hill towns, but still, in summer, it had decent custom from merchants and travelers. It was a simple square structure, with kitchen and eating room below, and two floors of rooms above. Plain, but neat and serviceable. Katsa would have preferred no fuss to have been made over their presence. But of course the inn was unaccustomed to housing royalty, and the entire family threw itself into a dither in an attempt to make the king's niece, the king's underlord, and the king's captain comfortable. Against Katsa's protests a visiting merchant was moved from his room so that she might have the view from his window, a view invisible now but which she imagined could only be of the same hills they'd been looking at for days.

Katsa wanted to apologize to the merchant for uprooting him. She sent Oll to do so at the midday meal. When Oll directed the man's attention to Katsa's table, she raised her cup to him. He raised his cup back and nodded his head vigorously, his face white and his eyes wide as plates.

"When you send Oll to speak for you, you do seem so dreadfully superior, Your Ladyship," Giddon said, smiling around his mouthful of stew.

Katsa didn't answer. He knew perfectly well why she'd sent Oll. If the man was like most people, it would frighten him to be approached by the lady herself.

The child who served them was painfully shy. She spoke no words, just nodded or shook her head in response to their requests. Unlike most, she seemed unable to keep her eyes away from Katsa's face. Even when the handsome Lord Giddon addressed her, her eyes slid to Katsa's.

"The girl thinks I'll eat her," Katsa said.

"I think not," Oll said. "Her father's a friend to the Council. It's possible you're spoken of differently in this household than you are in others, My Lady."

"She'll still have heard the stories," Katsa said.

"Possibly," Oll said. "But I think she's fascinated by you."

Giddon laughed. "You do fascinate, Katsa." When the girl came around again, he asked her name.

"Lanie," she whispered, and her eyes flicked to Katsa's once again.

"Do you see our Lady Katsa, Lanie?" Giddon asked.

The girl nodded.

"Does she frighten you?" Giddon asked.

The girl bit her lip and didn't answer.

"She wouldn't hurt you," Giddon said. "Do you understand that? But if someone else were to hurt you, Lady Katsa would likely hurt that person."

Katsa put her fork down and looked at Giddon. She hadn't expected this kindness from him.

"Do you understand?" Giddon asked the girl.

The child nodded. She peeked at Katsa.

"Perhaps you'd like to shake hands," Giddon said.

The girl paused. Then she leaned and held her hand out to Katsa. Something welled up inside Katsa, something she couldn't quite name. A sort of sad gladness at this little creature who wanted to touch her. Katsa reached her hand out and took the child's thin fingers. "It's a pleasure to meet you, Lanie."

Lanie's eyes grew wide, and then she dropped Katsa's hand and ran to the kitchen. Oll and Giddon laughed.

Katsa turned to Giddon. "I'm very grateful."

"You do nothing to dispel your ogreish reputation," Giddon said. "You know that, Katsa. It's no wonder you haven't more friends."

How like him. It was just like him, to turn a kind gesture into one of his criticisms of her character. He loved nothing more than to point out her flaws. And he knew nothing of her, if he thought she desired friends.

Katsa attacked her meal and ignored their conversation.

THE RAIN didn't stop. Giddon and Oll were content to sit in the main room and talk with the merchants and the innkeeper, but Katsa thought the inactivity would set her screaming. She went out to the stables, only to frighten a boy, little bigger than Lanie, who stood on a stool in one of the stalls and brushed down a horse. *Her* horse, she saw, as her eyes adjusted to the dim light.

"I didn't mean to startle you," Katsa said. "I'm only looking for a space to practice my exercises."

The boy climbed from his stool and fled. Katsa threw her hands into the air. Well, at least she had the stable to herself now. She moved bales of hay, saddles, and rakes to clear a place across from the stalls and began a series of kicks and strikes. She twisted and flipped, conscious of the air, the floor, the walls around her, the horses. She focused on her imaginary opponents, and her mind calmed.

AT DINNER, Oll and Giddon had interesting news.

"King Murgon has announced a robbery," Oll said. "Three nights past."

"Has he?" Katsa took in Oll's face, and then Giddon's. They both had the look of a cat that's cornered a mouse. "And what does he say was robbed?"

"He says only that a grand treasure of the court was stolen," Oll said.

"Great skies," Katsa said. "And who's said to have robbed him of this treasure?"

"Some say it was a Graceling boy," Oll said, "some kind of hypnotist, who put the king's guards to sleep."

"Others talk about a Graceling man the size of a monster," Giddon said, "a fighter, who overcame the guards, one by one." Giddon laughed outright, and Oll smiled into his supper.

"What interesting news," Katsa said. And then, hoping she sounded innocent, "Did you hear anything else?"

"Their search was delayed for hours," Giddon said, "because at first they assumed someone at court was to blame. A visiting man who happened to be a Graceling fighter." He lowered his voice. "Can you believe it? What luck for us."

Katsa kept her voice calm. "What did he say, this Graceling?"

"Apparently nothing helpful," Giddon said. "He claimed to know nothing of it."

"What did they do to him?"

"I've no idea," Giddon said. "He's a Graceling fighter. I doubt they were able to do much of anything."

"Who is he? Where is he from?"

"No one's said." Giddon elbowed her. "Katsa, come on— you're missing the point. It makes no difference who he is. They lost hours questioning this man. By the time they began to look elsewhere for the thieves, it was too late."

Katsa thought she knew, better than Giddon or Oll could, why Murgon had spent so much time grilling this particular

Graceling. And also why he'd taken pains not to publicize from where the Graceling came. Murgon wanted no one to suspect that the stolen treasure was Tealiff, that he'd held Tealiff in his dungeons in the first place.

And why had the Lienid Graceling told Murgon nothing? Was he protecting her?

This cursed rain had to stop, so that they could return to court, and to Raffin.

Katsa drank, then lowered her cup to the table. "What a stroke of luck for the thieves."

Giddon grinned. "Indeed."

"And have you heard any other news?"

"The innkeeper's sister has a baby of three months," Oll said. "They had a scare the other morning. They thought one of its eyes had darkened, but it was only a trick of the light."

"Fascinating." Katsa poured gravy onto her meat.

"The Monsean queen is grieving terribly for Grandfather Tealiff," Giddon said. "A Monsean merchant spoke of it."

"I'd heard she wasn't eating," Katsa said. It seemed to her a foolish way to grieve.

"There's more," Giddon said. "She's closed herself and her daughter into her rooms. She permits no one but her hand-maiden to enter, not even King Leck."

That seemed not only foolish but peculiar. "Is she allow-ing her daughter to eat?"

"The handmaiden brings them meals," Giddon said. "But they won't leave the rooms. Apparently the king is being very patient about it."

"It will pass," Oll said. "There's no saying what grief will do to a person. It will pass when her father is found."

The Council would keep the old man hidden, for his own safety, until they learned the reason for his kidnapping. But perhaps a message could be sent to the Monsean queen, to ease her strange grief? Katsa determined to consider it. She would bring it up with Giddon and Oll, when they could talk safely.

"She's Lienid," Giddon said. "They're known to be odd people."

"It seems very odd to me," Katsa said. She'd never felt grief, or if she had, she didn't remember. Her mother, Randa's sister, had died of a fever before Katsa's eyes had settled, the same fever that had taken Raffin's mother, Randa's queen. Her father, a northern Middluns borderlord, had been killed in a raid across the border. It had been a Westeran raid on a Nanderan village. It hadn't been his responsibility, but he'd taken up the defense of his neighbors, and gotten himself killed in the process. She hadn't even been of speaking age. She didn't remember him.

If her uncle died, she didn't think she would grieve. She glanced at Giddon. She wouldn't like to lose him, but she didn't think she would grieve his loss, either. Oll was different. She would grieve for Oll. And her ladyservant, Helda. And Raffin. Raffin's loss would hurt more than a finger sliced off, or an arm broken, or a knife in her side.

But she wouldn't close herself in her rooms. She would go

out and find the one who had done it, and then she'd make that person feel pain as no one had ever felt pain before.

Giddon was speaking to her, and she wasn't listening. She shook herself. "What did you say?"

"I said, lady dreamer, that I believe the sky is clearing. We'll be able to set out at dawn, if you like."

They would reach court before nightfall. Katsa finished her meal quickly and ran to her room to pack her bags.

CHAPTER SIX

THE SUN was well on its way across the sky when their horses clattered onto the marble floor of Randa's inner courtyard. Around them on all sides, the white castle walls rose and stood brightly against the green marble of the floor. Balconied passageways lined the walls above, so that the people of the court could look down into the courtyard as they moved from one section of the castle to another and admire Randa's great garden of crawling vines and pink flowering trees. A statue of Randa stood in the center of the garden, a fountain of water flowing from one outstretched hand and a torch in the other. It was an attractive garden, if one did not dwell on the statue, and an attractive courtyard—but not a peaceful or private one, with the entire court roaming the passageways above.

This was not the only such courtyard in the castle, but it was the largest, and it was the entrance point for any important residents or visitors. The green floor was kept to such a shine that Katsa could see herself and her horse reflected in its surface. The white walls were made of a stone that sparkled, and they rose so high that she had to crane her neck to find the tops of the turrets above. It was very grand, very impressive. As Randa liked it.

The noise of their horses and their shouts brought people to the balconies, to see who had come. A steward came out to greet them. A moment later, Raffin came flying into the courtyard.

"You've arrived!"

Katsa grinned up at him. Then she looked closer—stood on her toes, for he was so very tall. She grabbed a handful of his hair.

"Raff, what've you done to yourself? Your hair is positively blue."

"I've been trying a new remedy for headache," he said, "to be massaged into the scalp. Yesterday I thought I felt a headache coming on, so I tried it. Apparently it turns fair hair blue."

She smiled. "Did it cure the headache?"

"Well, if I had a headache, then it did, but I'm not convinced I had one to begin with. Do you have a headache?" he asked, hopefully. "Your hair's so dark; it wouldn't turn nearly as blue."

"I don't. I never do. What does the king think of your hair?"

Raffin smirked. "He's not speaking to me. He says it's appalling behavior for the son of the king. Until my hair is normal again I'm not his son."

Oll and Giddon greeted Raffin and handed their reins to a boy. They followed the king's steward into the castle, leaving Katsa and Raffin alone in the courtyard, near the garden and the splashing of Randa's fountain. Katsa lowered her voice and pretended to focus on the straps that tied her saddlebags to her horse. "Any news?"

"He hasn't woken," Raffin said. "Not once."

She was disappointed. She kept her voice low. "Have you heard of a Lienid noble Graced with fighting?"

"You saw him, did you?" Raffin said, and she swung her eyes to his face, surprised. "As you came into the courtyard? He's been lurking around. Hard to look that one in the eyes, eh? He's the son of the Lienid king."

He was here? She hadn't expected that. She focused on her saddlebags once more. "Ror's heir?"

"Great hills, no. He has six older brothers. His name is the silliest I've heard for the seventh heir to a throne. Prince Greening Grandemalion." Raffin smiled. "Have you ever heard the like?"

"Why is he here?"

"Ah," Raffin said. "It's quite interesting, really. He claims to be searching for his kidnapped grandfather."

Katsa looked up from her bags, into his laughing blue eyes. "You haven't—"

"Of course not. I've been waiting for you."

A boy came for her horse, and Raffin launched into a monologue about the visitors she'd missed while she was gone. Then a steward approached from one of the entrances.

"He'll be for you," Raffin said, "for I'm not my father's son at the moment, and he doesn't send stewards for me." He laughed, then left her. "I'm glad you're back," he called to her, and he disappeared through an archway.

The steward was one of Randa's dry, sniffy little men. "Lady Katsa," he said. "Welcome back. The king wishes to know if your business in the east was successful."

"You may tell him it was successful," Katsa said.

"Very good, My Lady. The king wishes you to dress for dinner."

Katsa narrowed her eyes at the steward. "Does the king wish anything else?"

"No, My Lady. Thank you, My Lady." The man bowed and scampered away from her gaze as quickly as possible.

Katsa lifted her bags onto her shoulder and sighed. When the king wished her to dress for dinner, it meant she was to wear a dress and arrange her hair and wear jewels in her ears and around her neck. It meant the king planned to sit her next to some underlord who wished a wife, though she was probably not the wife he had in mind. She would ease the poor man's fears quickly, and perhaps she could claim not to feel well enough to sit through the entire meal. She could claim a headache. She wished she could take Raffin's headache remedy and turn her hair blue. It would give her a respite from Randa's dinners.

Raffin appeared again, a floor above her, on the balconied passageway that ran past his workrooms. He leaned over the railing and called down to her. "Kat!"

"What is it?"

"You look lost. Have you forgotten the way to your rooms?"

"I'm stalling."

"How long will you be? I'd like to show you a couple of my new discoveries."

"I've been told to make myself pretty for dinner."

He grinned. "Well, in that case, you'll be ages."

His face dissolved into laughter, and she tore a button from one of her bags and hurled it at him. He squealed and dropped to the floor, and the button hit the wall right where he'd been standing. When he peeked back over the railing, she stood in the courtyard with her hands on her hips, grinning. "I missed on purpose," she said.

"Show-off! Come if you've time." He waved, and turned into his rooms.

And that's when the presence in the corner of Katsa's eye took shape.

He was standing a floor above her, to her left. He leaned his elbows on the railing, the neck of his shirt open, and watched her. The gold hoops in his ears, and the rings on his fingers. His hair dark. A tiny welt visible on his forehead, just beside his eye.

His eyes. Katsa had never seen such eyes. One was silver, and the other, gold. They glowed in his sun-darkened face, uneven, and strange. She was surprised that they hadn't shone in the darkness of their first meeting. They didn't seem human. She couldn't stop looking at them.

A steward of the court came to him then and spoke to him. He straightened, turned to the man, and said something in response. When the steward walked away, the Lienid's eyes flashed back to Katsa's. He leaned his elbows on the railing again.

Katsa knew she was standing in the courtyard's center, staring at this Lienid. She knew she should move, but she found that she couldn't.

Then he raised his eyebrows a hair, and his mouth shifted into the hint of a smirk. He nodded at her, just barely, and it released her from her spell.

Cocky, she thought. Cocky and arrogant, this one, and that was all there was to make of him. Whatever game he was playing, if he expected her to join him he would be disappointed. Greening Grandemalion, indeed.

She tore her eyes away from his, hitched her bags higher, and pushed herself forward into the castle, all the while conscious of the strange eyes burning into her back.

CHAPTER SEVEN

HELDA HAD COME to work in Randa's nurseries around the same time Katsa began to dole out Randa's punishments. It was hard to know why she'd been less frightened of Katsa than others were. Perhaps it was because she had borne a Graceling child of her own. Not a fighter, only a swimmer, a skill that was of no use to the king. So the boy had been sent home, and Helda had seen how the neighbors avoided and ridiculed him simply because he could move through the water like a fish. Or because he had one eye black, and the other blue. Perhaps this was why when the servants had warned Helda to avoid the king's niece, Helda had reserved her opinion.

Of course, Katsa had been too old for the nurseries when Helda arrived, and the children of the court had kept Helda busy. But she'd come to Katsa's training sessions, when she could. She'd sat and watched the child beat the stuffing out of a dummy, grain bursting from cracks and tears in the sack and slapping onto the floor like spurting blood. She'd never stayed long, because she always needed to return to the nursery, but still Katsa had noticed her, as she noticed anyone who didn't try to avoid her. Had noticed and noted her, but hadn't troubled herself with curiosity. Katsa had had no reason to interact with a woman servant.

But one day Helda had come when Oll was away and Katsa was alone in the practice rooms. And when the child had paused to set up a new dummy, Helda had spoken.

"In court they say you're dangerous, My Lady."

Katsa considered the old woman for a moment, her gray hair and gray eyes, and her soft arms, folded over a soft stomach. The woman held her gaze, as no one other than Raffin, Oll, or the king did. Then Katsa shrugged, hoisted a sack of grain onto her shoulder, and hung it from a hook on a wooden post standing in the center of the practice-room floor.

"The first man you killed, My Lady," Helda said. "That cousin. Did you mean to kill him?"

It was a question no one had ever actually asked her. Again the girl looked into the face of the woman, and again the woman held her eyes. Katsa sensed that this question was inappropriate coming from a servant. But she was so unused to being talked to that she didn't know the right way to proceed.

"No," Katsa said. "I only meant to keep him from touching me."

"Then you are dangerous, My Lady, to people you don't like. But perhaps you'd be safe as a friend."

"It's why I spend my days in this practice room," Katsa said.

"Mastering your Grace," Helda said. "Yes, all Gracelings must do so."

This woman knew something about the Graces, and she wasn't afraid to say the word. It was time for Katsa to begin her exercises again, but she paused, hoping the woman would say something more.

"My Lady," Helda said, "if I may ask you a nosy question?"

Katsa waited. She couldn't think of a question more nosy than the one the woman had already asked.

"Who are your servants, My Lady?" Helda asked.

Katsa wondered if this woman was trying to embarrass her. She drew herself up and looked the woman straight in the face, daring her to laugh or smile. "I don't keep servants. When a servant is assigned to me, she generally chooses to leave the service of the court."

Helda didn't smile or laugh. She merely looked back at Katsa, studied her for a moment. "Have you any female caretakers, My Lady?"

"I have none."

"Has anyone spoken to you of a woman's bleedings, My Lady, or of how it is with a man and a woman?"

Katsa didn't know what she meant, and she had a feeling this old woman could tell. Still, Helda didn't smile or laugh. She looked Katsa up and down.

"What's your age, My Lady?"

Katsa raised her chin. "I'm nearly eleven."

"And they were going to let you learn it on your own," Helda said, "and probably tear through the castle like a wild thing because you didn't know what attacked you."

Katsa raised her chin another notch. "I always know what attacks me."

"My child," Helda said, "My Lady, would you allow me to serve you, on occasion? When you need service, and when my presence is not required in the nurseries?"

Katsa thought it must be very bad to work in the nurseries, if this woman wished to serve her instead. "I don't need servants," she said, "but I can have you transferred from the nurseries if you're unhappy there."

Katsa thought she caught the hint of a smile. "I'm happy in the nurseries," Helda said. "Forgive me for contradicting such a one as yourself, My Lady, but you do need a servant, a woman servant. Because you have no mother or sisters."

Katsa had never needed a mother or sisters or anyone else, either. She didn't know what one did with a contradictory servant; she guessed that Randa would go into a rage, but she was afraid of her own rages. She held her breath, clenched her fists, and stood as still as the wooden post in the center of the room. The woman could say what she wanted. They were only words.

Helda stood and smoothed her dress. "I'll come to your rooms on occasion, My Lady."

Katsa made her face like a rock.

"If you ever wish a break from your uncle's state dinners, you may always join me in my room."

Katsa blinked. She hated the dinners, with everyone's sideways glances, and the people who didn't want to sit near her, and her uncle's loud voice. Could she really skip them? Could this woman's company be better?

"I must return to the nurseries, My Lady," Helda said. "My name is Helda, and I come from the western Middluns. Your eyes are so very pretty, my dear. Good-bye."

Helda left before Katsa was able to find her voice. Katsa stared at the door that closed behind her.

"Thank you," she said, though there was no one to hear, and though she wasn't sure why her voice seemed to think she was grateful.

KATSA SAT in the bath and tugged at the knots in her tangle of hair. She heard Helda in the other room, rustling through the chests and drawers, unearthing the earrings and necklaces Katsa had thrown among her silk undergarments and her horrid bone chest supports the last time she'd been required to wear them. Katsa heard Helda muttering and grunting, on her knees most likely, looking under the bed for Katsa's hairbrush or her dinner shoes.

"What dress shall it be tonight, My Lady?" Helda called out.

"You know I don't care," Katsa called back.

There was more muttering in response to this. A moment later Helda came to the door carrying a dress bright as the tomatoes Randa imported from Lienid, the tomatoes that clustered on the vine and tasted as rich and sweet as his chef's chocolate cake. Katsa raised her eyebrows.

"I'm not going to wear a red dress," she said.

"It's the color of sunrise," Helda said.

"It's the color of blood," Katsa said.

Sighing, Helda carried the dress from the bathing room. "It would look stunning, My Lady," she called, "with your dark hair and your eyes."

Katsa yanked at one of the more stubborn knots in her hair. She spoke to the bubbles gathered on the surface of the water. "If there's anyone I wish to stun at dinner, I'll hit him in the face."

Helda came to the doorway again, this time with her arms full of a soft green silk. "Is this dull enough for you, My Lady?"

"Have I no grays or browns?"

Helda set her face. "I'm determined that you wear a color, My Lady."

Katsa scowled. "You're determined that people notice me." She held a tangle of hair before her eyes and pulled at it, savagely. "I should like to cut it all off," she said. "It's not worth the nuisance."

Helda put the dress aside and came to sit on the edge of the bath. She lathered her fingers up with soap, and took the tangled hair out of Katsa's hands. She worked the curls apart, bit by bit, gently.

"If you ran a brush through it once every day while you were traveling, My Lady, this wouldn't happen."

Katsa snorted. "Giddon would get a good laugh out of that. My attempts to beautify myself."

That knot untangled, Helda moved to another. "Don't you think Lord Giddon finds you beautiful, My Lady?"

"Helda," Katsa said, "how much time do you suppose I spend wondering which of the gentlemen finds me beautiful?"

"Not enough," Helda said, nodding emphatically. A hiccup of laughter rose into Katsa's throat. Dear Helda. She saw what Katsa was and what she did, and Helda didn't deny that Katsa was that person. But she couldn't fathom a lady who didn't want to be beautiful, who didn't want a legion of admirers. And so she believed Katsa was both people, though Katsa couldn't imagine how she reconciled them in her mind.

IN THE GREAT dining hall, Randa presided over a long, high table that might as well have been a stage at the head of the room. Three low tables were arranged around the perimeter to complete the sides of a square, giving the guests an unobstructed view of the king.

Randa was a tall man, taller even than his son, and broader in the shoulders and the neck. He had Raffin's yellow hair and blue eyes, but they weren't laughing eyes like Raffin's. They were eyes that assumed you would do what he told you to do, eyes that threatened to bring you unhappiness if he didn't get what he wanted. It wasn't that he was unjust, except perhaps to those who wronged him. It was more that he wanted things the way he wanted them, and if things weren't that way, he might decide that he'd been wronged. And if you were the person responsible—well, then you had reason to fear his eyes.

At dinner he wasn't fearsome. At dinner he was arrogant and loud. He brought whomever he wanted to sit with him at the high table. Often Raffin, though Randa spoke over him and never cared to hear what he had to say. Rarely Katsa. Randa kept his distance from her. He preferred to look down on his lady killer and call out to her, because his yelling brought the attention of the entire room to his niece, his prized weapon. And the guests would be frightened, and everything would be as Randa liked it.

Tonight she sat at the table to the right of Randa's, her usual position. She wore the soft green silk and fought the urge to tear off the sleeves that widened at her wrists and hung over her hands and dragged across her plate if she wasn't careful. At least this dress covered her breasts, mostly. Not all of them did. Helda paid her no attention when she gave instructions about her wardrobe.

Giddon sat to her left. The lord to her right, whom she supposed to be the eligible bachelor, was a man not old, but older than Giddon, a small man whose bugged eyes and stretched mouth gave him the appearance of a frog. His name was Davit, and he was a borderlord from the Middluns' northeast corner, at the border of both Nander and Estill.

His conversation wasn't bad; he cared a great deal about his land, his farms, his villages, and Katsa found it easy to ask questions that he was eager to answer. At first he sat on the farthest edge of his chair and looked at her shoulder and her ear and her hair as they talked, but never her face. But he grew calmer as the dinner progressed and Katsa didn't bite him; his body relaxed, he settled into his chair, and they spoke easily. Katsa thought him unusually good dinner company, this Lord

Davit of the northeast. At any rate, he made it easier for her to resist tearing out the hairpins that dug into her scalp.

The Lienid prince was also a distraction, no matter how much she willed him not to be. He sat across the room from her and was always in the corner of her eye, though she tried not to look at him directly. She felt his eyes on her at times. Bold, he was, and entirely unlike the rest of the guests, who carefully pretended she wasn't there, as they always did. It occurred to her that it wasn't just the strangeness of his eyes that disconcerted her. It was that he wasn't afraid to hold hers. She glanced at him once when he wasn't looking. He raised his eyes to meet her gaze. Davit had asked the same question twice before Katsa heard him and turned from the Lienid's uneven stare to answer.

She supposed she would have to face those eyes soon. They would have to talk; she would have to decide what to do with him.

She thought that Lord Davit would be less nervous if he knew there was no chance of Randa offering him her suit.

"Lord Davit," she said, "have you a wife?"

He shook his head. "It's the only thing my estate lacks, My Lady."

Katsa kept her eyes on her venison and carrots. "My uncle is very disappointed in me, because I intend never to marry."

Lord Davit paused, and then spoke. "I doubt your uncle is the only man who finds that disappointing."

Katsa considered his pointy face, and could not stop herself from smiling. "Lord Davit," she said, "you're a perfect gentleman."

The lord smiled in return. "You think I didn't mean it, My Lady, but I did." Then he leaned in and ducked his head. "My Lady," he whispered, "I wish to speak with the Council."

The voices of the dinner guests were lively, but she heard him perfectly. She pretended to focus on her dinner. She stirred her soup. "Sit back," she said. "Act as if we were only talking. Don't whisper, for it draws attention."

The lord settled back into his seat. He raised his finger for a serving girl, who brought him more wine. He ate a few bites of his venison and turned to Katsa once more.

"The weather has been very kind to my aging father this summer, My Lady," he said. "He suffers in the heat, but it's been cool in the northeast."

"I'm happy to hear it," Katsa said. "Is it information, or a request?"

The lord spoke around his mouthful of carrots. "Information." He sliced another piece of venison. "It becomes more and more difficult to care for him, My Lady."

"Why is that?"

"The elderly are prone to discomforts. It's our duty to keep them comfortable," he said, "and safe."

Katsa nodded. "True words, indeed." She kept her face even, but excitement rattled at the edges of her mind. If he had information about the kidnapping of the Lienid grandfather, they would all want to hear it. She reached under the heavy tablecloth and rested her hand on Giddon's knee. He leaned toward her slightly, without turning away from the lady on his other side.

"You're a man of great information, Lord Davit," she said to the lord, or rather, to her plate, so that Giddon could hear. "I hope we'll have the opportunity to speak with you more during your stay at court."

"Thank you, My Lady," Lord Davit said. "I hope so, too."

Giddon would spread the word. They would meet that night, in her own rooms—because they were secluded and because they were the only rooms not traveled by servants. If she could, she'd find Raffin beforehand. She'd like to visit Grandfather Tealiff. Even if he was still sleeping, it would be good to see with her own eyes how he was faring.

Katsa heard the king speak her name, and her shoulders stiffened. She didn't look at him, for she didn't wish to encourage him to draw her into his conversation. She couldn't make out his words; most likely he was telling some guest the story of something she'd done. His laughter rolled across the tables in the great marble hall. Katsa tried to push back the scowl that rose to her face.

The Lienid prince was watching her. She felt that, too. Heat licked at her neck and crawled along her scalp. "My Lady," Lord Davit said, "are you quite all right? You look a bit flushed."

Giddon turned to her then, his face flashing with concern. He reached for her arm. "You aren't ill?"

She pulled back, away from him. "I'm never ill," she snarled, and she knew suddenly that she must leave the hall. She must leave the clatter of voices and the sound of her uncle's laugh, Giddon's smothering concern, the Lienid's burning eyes; she must get outside, find Raffin, or be on her own. She must, or she would lose her temper, and something unthinkable would happen.

She stood, and Giddon and Lord Davit stood with her. Across the room the Lienid prince stood. One by one, the rest of the men saw her standing, and rose. The room quieted, and everyone was looking at her.

"What is it, Katsa?" Giddon asked, reaching for her arm again. So that he wouldn't be shamed before everyone in the hall, she allowed him to take it, though his hand was like a brand that burned into her skin.

"It's nothing," she said. "I'm sorry." She turned to the king, the only man in the room who wasn't on his feet. "Forgive me, Lord King," she said. "It's nothing. Please, sit down." She waved her hand around the tables. "Please."

Slowly, the gentlemen sat, and the voices picked up again. The king's laugh rang out, directed at her, she was sure. Katsa turned to Lord Davit. "Please excuse me, My Lord." She turned to Giddon, whose hand still grasped her elbow. "Let go, Giddon. I want to take a walk outside."

"I'll go with you," he said. He started to rise, but at the warning in her eyes he sat back again. "Very well, Katsa, do what you will."

There was an edge to his voice. She had probably been rude, but she didn't care. All that mattered was that she leave this room and go to a place where she couldn't hear the drone of her uncle's voice. She turned, careful not to catch the eyes of the Lienid. She forced herself to walk slowly, calmly, to the doorway at the foot of the room. Once through the doorway, she ran.

She ran through corridors, around corners, past servants who flattened themselves trembling against walls as she flew by. Finally she burst into the darkness of the courtyard.

She crossed the marble floor, pulling pins from her hair. She sighed as her curls fell around her shoulders and the tension left her scalp. It was the hairpins, and the dress, and the shoes that pinched her feet. It was having to hold her head still and sit straight, it was the infuriating earrings that brushed against her neck. That was why she couldn't stand to spend one moment longer at her uncle's fine dinner. She took off her earrings and hurled them into her uncle's fountain. She didn't care who found them.

But that was no good, because then people would talk. The entire court would speculate about what it meant, that she'd thrown her earrings into her uncle's fountain.

Katsa kicked off her shoes, hitched up her skirt, and climbed into the fountain, sighing as the cold water ran between her toes and lapped at her ankles. It was a great improvement over her shoes. She would not put them on again tonight.

She waded out to the glimmers she saw in the water and retrieved her earrings. She dried them on her skirt, dropped them into the bodice of her dress for safekeeping, and stood in the fountain, enjoying the coolness enveloping her feet, the drifting air of the courtyard, the night noises—until a sound from inside reminded her of how much the court would talk if she were found wading, barefoot and wild haired, in King Randa's fountain. They would think her mad.

And perhaps she was mad.

A light shone from Raffin's workrooms, but it wasn't his company she sought after all. She didn't want to sit and talk. She wanted to move. Movement would stop the whirring of her mind.

Katsa climbed out of the fountain and hung the straps of her shoes over her wrists. She ran.

CHAPTER EIGHT

THE ARCHERY RANGE was empty, and dark except for the lone torch that glowed outside the equipment room. Katsa lit the torches along the back of the range so that when she returned to the front, the man-shaped dummies stood black against the brightness behind them. She grabbed a bow randomly from the supplies and collected handfuls of the lightest-colored arrows she could find. Then she drove arrow after arrow into the knees of her targets. Then the thighs, then the elbows, then the shoulders, until she'd emptied her quiver. She could disarm or disable any man with this bow at night, that was clear enough. She exchanged the bow for another. She yanked the arrows from the targets. She began again.

She'd lost her temper at dinner, and for no reason. Randa hadn't spoken to her, hadn't even looked at her, had only said her name. He loved to brag of her, as if her great ability were his doing. As if she were the arrow, and he the archer whose skill drove her home. No, not an arrow—that didn't quite capture it. A dog. To Randa she was a savage dog he'd broken and trained. He set her on his enemies and allowed her out of her cage to be groomed and kept pretty, to sit among his friends and make them nervous.

Katsa didn't notice her heightened speed and focus, the

ferocity with which she was now whipping arrows from her quiver, the next arrow notched in the string before the first had hit home. Not until she sensed the presence behind her shoulder did she stir from her preoccupation and realize how she must look.

She *was* savage. Look at her speed, look at her accuracy, and with a poor bow, curved badly, strung badly. No wonder Randa treated her so.

She knew it was the Lienid who stood behind her. She ignored him. But she slowed her movements, made a show of taking aim at thighs and knees before she fired. She became conscious of the dirt under her feet and remembered, too, that she was barefoot, with her hair falling around her shoulders and her shoes in a pile somewhere near the equipment room. He would have noticed. She doubted there was much those eyes didn't notice. Well, he wouldn't have kept such stupid shoes on his feet, either, or left pins in his hair if his scalp were screaming. Or perhaps he would. He seemed not to mind his own fine jewelry, in his ears and on his fingers. They must be a vain people, the Lienid.

"Can you kill with an arrow? Or do you only ever wound?"

She remembered his raspy voice from Murgon's courtyard, and it was taunting her now, as it had done then. She didn't turn to him. She simply took two arrows from her quiver, notched them together, pulled, and released. One flew to her target's head, and the other to its chest. They hit with a satisfying thud, and glowed palely in the flickering torchlight.

"I'll never make the mistake of challenging you to an archery match."

There was laughter in his voice. She kept her back to him and reached for another arrow. "You didn't forfeit our last match so easily," she said.

"Ah, but that's because I have your fighting skill. I lack your skill with a bow and arrow."

Katsa couldn't help herself. She found that interesting. She turned her eyes to him, his face in shadows. "Is that true?"

"My Grace gives me skill at hand-to-hand combat," he said, "or sword-to-sword. It does little for my archery."

He leaned back against the great slab of stone that served as a table for the equipment of the archers. His arms were crossed. She was becoming accustomed to this look, this lazy look, as if he could nod off to sleep at any moment, but it didn't fool her. She thought if she were to spring at him, he'd react quickly enough.

"Then, you need to be able to grapple with your opponent, to have an advantage," she said.

He nodded. "I may be quicker to dodge arrows than someone Ungraced. But in my own attack, my skill is only as good as my aim."

"Hmm." Katsa believed him. The Graces were odd like that; they didn't touch any two people in quite the same way.

"Can you throw a knife as well as you shoot an arrow?" he asked.

"Yes."

"You're unbeatable, Lady Katsa." She heard the laughter in his voice again. She considered him for a moment and then turned away and walked down the course to the targets. She stopped at one, the one she'd "killed," and yanked the arrows from its thighs, its chest, its head.

He sought his grandfather, and Katsa had what he sought. But he didn't feel safe to her, this one. He didn't feel quite trustworthy.

She walked from target to target, pulling out arrows. He watched her, she felt it, and the knowledge of his eyes on her back drove her to the back of the range, where she put the torches out, one by one. As she extinguished the last flame, darkness enveloped her, and she knew she was invisible.

She turned to him then, thinking to examine him in the light of the equipment room without his knowing. But he slouched, arms crossed, and stared straight at her. He couldn't see her, it wasn't possible—but his gaze was so direct that she couldn't hold it, even knowing he didn't know she stared.

She walked across the range and stepped into the light, and his eyes seemed to change focus. He smiled at her, ever so slightly. The torch caught the gold of one eye and the silver of the other. They were like the eyes of a cat, or a night creature of some kind.

"Does your Grace give you night vision?" she asked.

He laughed. "Hardly. Why do you ask?"

She didn't answer. They looked at each other for a moment. The flush began to rise into her neck again, and with it, a surging irritation. She'd grown far too used to people avoiding her eyes. He would not rattle her so, simply by looking at her. She wouldn't allow it.

"I'm going to return to my rooms now," she said.

He straightened. "Lady, I have questions for you."

Well, and she knew they must have this conversation eventually, and she preferred to have it in the dark, where his eyes wouldn't unnerve her. Katsa pulled the quiver over her head, and laid it on the slab of stone. She placed the bow beside it. "Go on," she said.

He leaned back against the stone. "What did you steal from King Murgon, Lady," he said, "four nights past?"

"Nothing that King Murgon had not himself stolen."

"Ah. Stolen from you?"

"Yes, from me, or from a friend."

"Really?" He crossed his arms again, and in the torchlight he raised an eyebrow. "I wonder if this friend would be surprised to hear himself so called?"

"Why should he be surprised? Why should he think himself an enemy?"

"Ah," he said, "but it's just that. I thought the Middluns had neither friends nor enemies. I thought King Randa never got involved."

"I suppose you're wrong."

"No. I'm not wrong." He stared at her, and she was glad for the darkness that kept his strange eyes dim. "Do you know why I'm here, Lady?"

"I was told you're the son of the Lienid king," she said. "I was told you seek your grandfather, who's disappeared. Why you've come to Randa's court, I couldn't say. I doubt Randa is your kidnapper."

He considered her for a moment, and a smile flickered across his face. Katsa knew she wasn't fooling him. It didn't matter. He may know what he knew, but she had no intention of confirming it.

"King Murgon was quite certain I was involved in the robbery," he said. "He seemed quite sure I knew what object had been stolen."

"And that's natural," Katsa said. "The guards had seen a Graceling fighter, and you're no other than a Graceling fighter."

"No. Murgon didn't believe I was involved because I was Graced. He believed I was involved because I'm Lienid. Can you explain that?"

And of course she would give him no answer to that question, this smirking Lienid. She noticed that the neck of his shirt was now fastened. "I see you close your shirt for state dinners," she heard herself saying, though she didn't know where such a senseless comment came from.

His mouth twitched, and his words, when he spoke, did not conceal his laughter. "I didn't know you were so interested in my shirt, Lady."

Her face was hot, and his laughter was infuriating. This was absurdity, and she would put up with it no longer. "I'm going to my rooms now," she said, and she turned to leave. In a flash, he stood and blocked her path.

"You have my grandfather," he said.

Katsa tried to step around him. "I'm going to my rooms." He blocked her path again, and this time he raised his arm in warning.

Well, at least they were relating now in a way she could understand. Katsa cocked her head upward and looked into his eyes. "I'm going to my rooms," she said, "and if I must knock you over to do so, I will."

"I won't allow you to go," he said, "until you tell me where my grandfather is."

She moved again to pass him, and he moved to block her, and it was almost with relief that she struck out at his face. It was just a feint, and when he ducked she jammed at his stomach with her knee, but he twisted so that the blow didn't fall true, and came back with a fist to her stomach. She took the blow, just to see how well he hit, and then wished she hadn't. This wasn't one of the king's soldiers, whose blows hardly touched her, even with ten of them on her at once. This one could knock the wind out of her. This one could fight, and so a fight was what she would give him.

She jumped and kicked at his chest. He crashed to the ground and she threw herself on top of him, struck him in the face once, twice, three times, and kneed him in the side before he was able to throw her off. She was on him again like a wildcat, but as she tried to trap his arms he flipped her onto her back and pinned her with the weight of his body. She curled her legs up and heaved him away, and then they were on their feet again, crouching, circling, striking at each other with hands and feet. She kicked at his stomach and barreled into his chest, and they were on the ground again.

Katsa didn't know how long they'd been grappling when she realized he was laughing. She understood his joy, understood it completely. She'd never had such a fight, she'd never had such an opponent. She was faster than he was offensively—much faster—but he was stronger, and it was as if he had a premonition of her every turn and strike; she'd never known a fighter so quick to defend himself. She was calling up moves she hadn't tried since she was a child, blows she'd only ever imagined having the opportunity to use. They were playing. It was a game. When he pinned her arms behind her back, grabbed her hair, and pushed her face into the dirt, she found that she was laughing as well.

"Surrender," he said.

"Never." She kicked her feet up at him and squirmed her arms out of his grasp. She elbowed him in the face, and when he jumped to avoid the blow, she flew at him and flattened him to the ground. She pinned his arms as he had just done, and pushed his face into the dirt. She dug one knee into the small of his back.

"You surrender," she said, "for you're beaten."

"I'm not beaten, and you know it. You'll have to break my arms and legs to beat me."

"And I will," she said, "if you don't surrender." But there was a smile in her voice, and he laughed.

"Katsa," he said, "Lady Katsa. I'll surrender, on one condition."

"And the condition?"

"Please," he said. "Please, tell me what's happened to my grandfather."

There was something mixed in with the laughter in his voice, something that caught at Katsa's throat. She didn't have a grandfather. But perhaps this grandfather meant to the Lienid prince what Oll—or Helda or Raffin—meant to her.

"Katsa," he said into the dirt. "I beg you to trust me, as I've trusted you."

She held him down for just a moment, and then she let his arms go. She slid from his back and sat in the dirt beside him. She rested her chin in her palm, considering him.

"Why do you trust me," she said, "when I left you lying on the floor of Murgon's courtyard?"

He rolled over and sat up, groaning. He massaged his shoulder. "Because I woke up. You could've killed me, but you didn't." He touched his cheekbone and winced. "Your face is bleeding." He stretched out his hand to her jaw, but she waved it aside and stood.

"It doesn't matter," she said. "Come with me, Prince Greening."

He heaved himself to his feet. "It's Po."

"Po?"

"My name. It's Po."

Katsa watched him for a moment as he swung his arms and tested out his shoulder joints. He pressed his side and groaned. His eye was swelling, and blackening, she thought, though it was hard to tell in the darkness. His sleeve was torn, and he was covered with dirt, absolutely smeared from head to foot. She knew she looked the same—worse, really, with her messy hair and bare feet—but it only made her smile.

"Come with me, Po," she said. "I'll take you to your grandfather."

CHAPTER NINE

WHEN THEY WALKED into the light of Raffin's workrooms, his blue head was bent over a bubbling flask. He added leaves to the flask from a potted plant at his elbow. He watched the leaves dissolve and muttered something at the result.

Katsa cleared her throat. Raffin looked up at them and blinked.

"I take it you've been getting to know each other," he said. "It must've been a friendly fight, if you come to me together."

"Are you alone?" Katsa asked.

"Yes, except for Bann, of course."

"I've told the prince about his grandfather."

Raffin looked from Katsa to Po and back to Katsa again. He raised his eyebrows.

"He's safe," Katsa said. "I'm sorry for not consulting you, Raff."

"Kat," Raffin said, "if you think he's safe even after he's bloodied your face and"—he glanced at her tattered dress— "rolled you around in a puddle of mud, then I believe you."

Katsa smiled. "May we see him?"

"You may," Raffin said. "And I have good news. He's awake."

RANDA'S CASTLE was full of secret inner passageways; it had been that way since its construction so many generations before. They were so plentiful that even Randa didn't know of all of them—no one did, really, although Raffin had had the mind as a child to notice when two rooms came together in a way that seemed not to match. Katsa and Raffin had done a fair bit of exploring as children, Katsa keeping guard, so that anyone who came upon one of Raffin's investigations would scuttle away at the sight of her small, glaring form. Raffin and Katsa had chosen their living quarters because a passageway connected them, and because another passageway connected Raffin to the science libraries.

Some of the passageways were secret, and some were known by the entire court. The one in Raffin's workrooms was secret. It led from the inside of a storage room in a back alcove, up a stairway, and to a small room set between two floors of the castle. It was a windowless room, dark and musty, but it was the only place in the castle that they could be sure no one would find, and that Raffin and Bann could stay so near to most of the time.

Bann was Raffin's friend of many years, a young man who had worked in the libraries as a boy. One day Raffin had stumbled across him, and the two children had fallen to talking about herbs and medicines and about what happened when you mixed the ground root of one plant with the powdered flower of another. Katsa had been amazed that there could be more than one person in the Middluns who found such things interesting enough to talk about—and relieved that Raffin had found someone other than her to bore. Shortly thereafter, Raffin had begged Bann's help with a particular experiment, and from that time on had effectively stolen Bann for himself. Bann was Raffin's assistant in all things.

Raffin ushered Katsa and Po through the door in the back of the storage room, a torch in his hand. They slipped up the steps that led to the secret chamber.

"Has he said anything?" Katsa asked.

"Nothing," said Raffin, "other than that they blindfolded him when they took him. He's still very weak. He doesn't seem to remember much."

"Do you know who took him?" Po said. "Was Murgon responsible?"

"We don't think so," Katsa said, "but all we know for sure is that it wasn't Randa."

The stairs ended at a doorway. Raffin fiddled with a key.

"Randa doesn't know he's here," Po said. It was more of a statement than a question.

"Randa doesn't know," Katsa said. "He must never know."

Raffin opened the door then, and they crowded into the tiny room. Bann sat in a chair beside a narrow bed, reading in the dim light of a lamp on the table beside him. Prince Tealiff lay on his back in the bed, his eyes closed and his hands clasped over his chest.

Upon their entrance, Bann stood. He seemed unsurprised as Po rushed forward; he only stepped aside and offered his chair. Po sat and leaned toward his grandfather, looked into his sleeping face. Simply looked at him, and did not touch him. Then Po took the man's hands and bent his forehead to them, exhaling slowly.

Katsa felt as if she were intruding on something private. She dropped her eyes until Po sat up again.

"Your face is turning purple, Prince Greening," Raffin said. "You're on your way to a very black eye."

"Po," he said. "Call me Po."

"Po. I'll get you some ice from the vault. Come, Bann, let's get some supplies for our two warriors."

Raffin and Bann slipped through the doorway. And when Katsa and Po turned back to Tealiff, the old man's eyes were open.

"Grandfather," Po said.

"Po?" His voice rasped with the effort of speaking. "Po." He struggled to clear his throat and then lay still for a moment, exhausted. "Great seas, boy. I suppose I shouldn't be surprised to see you."

"I've been tracking you down, Grandfather," Po said.

"Move that lamp closer, boy," Tealiff said. "What in the name of Lienid have you done to your face?"

"It's nothing, Grandfather. I've only been fighting."

"With what, a pack of wolves?"

"With the Lady Katsa," Po said. He cocked his head at Katsa, who stood at the foot of the bed. "Don't worry, Grandfather. It was only a friendly scuffle."

Tealiff snorted. "A friendly scuffle. You look worse than she does, Po."

Po burst into laughter. He laughed a lot, this Lienid prince. "I've met my match, Grandfather."

"More than your match," Tealiff said, "it looks to me. Come here, child," he said to Katsa. "Come to the light."

Katsa approached the other side of the bed and knelt beside him. Tealiff turned to her, and she became suddenly conscious of her dirty, bloody face, her tangled hair. How dreadful she must look to this old man.

"My dear," he said. "I believe you saved my life."

"Lord Prince," Katsa said, "if anyone did that, it was my cousin Raffin with his medicines."

"Yes, Raffin's a good boy," he said. He patted her hand. "But I know what you did, you and the others. You've saved my life, though I can't think why. I doubt any Lienid has ever done you a kindness."

"I'd never met a Lienid," Katsa said, "before you, Lord Prince. But you seem very kind."

Tealiff closed his eyes. He seemed to sink into his pillows. His breath was a drawn-out sigh.

"He falls asleep like that," Raffin said from the doorway. "His strength will come back, with rest." He carried something wrapped in a cloth, which he handed to Po. "Ice. Hold it to that eye. It looks like she's cracked your lip, too. Where else does it hurt?"

"Everywhere," Po said. "I feel as if I've been run over by a team of horses."

"Honestly, Katsa," Raffin said. "Were you trying to kill him?"

"If I'd been trying to kill him, he'd be dead," Katsa said, and Po laughed again. "He wouldn't be laughing," she added, "if it were that bad."

It wasn't that bad; or at least Raffin was able to determine that none of his bones were broken and that he'd sustained no bruises that wouldn't heal. Then Raffin turned to Katsa. He examined the scratch that stretched across her jaw, and wiped dirt and blood from her face.

"It's not very deep, this scratch," he said. "Any other pains?"

"None," she said. "I don't even feel the scratch."

"I suppose you'll have to retire this dress," he said. "Helda will give you a terrible scolding."

"Yes, I'm devastated about the dress."

Raffin smiled. He took hold of her arms and held her out from him so that he could look her up and down. He laughed.

"What can be so funny," Katsa said, "to a prince who's turned his hair blue?"

"You look like you've been in a fight," he said, "for the first time in your life."

KATSA HAD five rooms. Her sleeping room, decorated with dark draperies and wall hangings that Helda had chosen because Katsa had refused to form an opinion on the matter. Her bathing room, white marble, large and cold, functional. Her dining room, with windows looking onto the courtyard, and a small table where she ate, sometimes with Raffin or Helda, or with Giddon when he wasn't driving her to distraction. Her sitting room, full of soft chairs and pillows that Helda, again, had chosen. She didn't use the sitting room.

The fifth room used to be her workroom, but she couldn't remember the last time she'd embroidered or crocheted, or darned a stocking. She couldn't remember the last time she'd worn a stocking, truth be told. She'd turned the room into a place for the storage of her weapons: swords, daggers, knives, bows, and staffs lined the walls. She'd fitted the room with a solid, square table, and now the Council meetings were held there.

Katsa bathed for the second time that day and knotted her wet hair behind her head. She fed her dress to the sleeping-room fire and watched its smoky demise with great satisfaction. A boy arrived who was to keep watch during the Council meeting. Katsa went into the weapons room and lit the torches that hung on the walls between her knives and bows.

Raffin and Po were the first to arrive. Po's hair was damp from his own bath. The skin had blackened around his eye, the gold eye, and made his gaze even more rakish and uneven than it had been before. He slouched against the table with his hands in his pockets. His eyes flashed around the room, taking in Katsa's collection of weapons. Po was wearing a new shirt, open at the neck and with the sleeves rolled to the elbows. His forearms were as sun darkened as his face. She didn't know why she should notice. She found herself frowning.

"Sit, Your High Majestic Lord Princes," she said. She yanked a chair from the table and sat down herself.

"You're in fine temper," Raffin said.

"Your hair is blue," Katsa snapped back.

Oll strode into the room. At the sight of the scratch on Katsa's face, his mouth dropped open. He turned to Po and saw the black eye. He turned back to Katsa. He began to chuckle. He slapped his hand on the table, and the chuckle turned into a roar. "How I would love to have seen that fight, My Lady. Oh, how I would love to have seen it."

Po was smiling. "The lady won, which I doubt will surprise you."

Katsa glowered. "It was a draw. No one won."

"I say." It was Giddon's voice, and as he entered the room and looked from Katsa to Po, his eyes grew dark. He put his hand to his sword. He whirled on Po. "I don't see where you come off fighting the Lady Katsa."

"Giddon," said Katsa. "Don't be ridiculous."

Giddon turned to her. "He had no right to attack you."

"I struck the first blow, Giddon. Sit down."

"If you struck the first blow then he must have insulted you—"

Katsa jumped up from her seat. "That's enough, Giddon—if you think I need you to defend me—"

"A guest to this court, a total stranger—"

"Giddon—"

"Lord Giddon." Po had risen to his feet, and his voice cut through hers. "If I've insulted your lady," he said, "you must forgive me. I rarely have the pleasure of practicing with someone of her caliber, and I couldn't resist the temptation. I can assure you she did more damage to me than I did to her."

Giddon didn't take his hand from his sword, but his grimace lessened.

"I'm sorry to have insulted you, as well," Po said. "I see now I should've taken greater care of her face. Forgive me. It was unpardonable." He reached his hand across the table.

Giddon's angry eyes grew warm again. He reached out and shook Po's hand. "You understand my concern," Giddon said.

"Of course."

Katsa looked from one of them to the other, the two of them shaking hands, understanding each other's concern. She didn't see where Giddon came off feeling insulted. She didn't see how Giddon had any place in it at all. Who were they, to take her fight away from her and turn it into some sort of understanding between themselves? He should've taken more care of her face? She would knock his nose from his face. She would thump them both, and she would apologize to neither.

Po caught her eyes then, and she did nothing to soften the silent fury she sent across the table to him. "Shall we sit?" someone said. Po held her eyes as they sat. There was no trace of humor in his expression, no trace of the arrogance of his exchange with Giddon. And then he mouthed two words. It was as clear as if he'd said them aloud. "Forgive me."

Well.

Giddon was still a horse's ass.

Sixteen Council members attended the meeting, in addition to Po and Lord Davit: Katsa, Raffin, Giddon, Oll, and Oll's wife, Bertol; two soldiers under Oll's command, two spies who worked with him, three underlords of Giddon's rank, and four servants—one a woman who worked in the kitchens of the castle, one a stable hand, one a washerwoman, and one a clerk in Randa's countinghouse. There were others in the castle involved with the Council. But most nights, these were their representatives, along with Bann, when he could get away.

Since the meeting had been called to hear Lord Davit's information, the Council wasted no time.

"I regret I can't tell you who kidnapped Prince Tealiff," Davit said. "You would, of course, prefer that type of information. But I may be able to tell you who didn't. My lands border Estill and Nander. My neighbors are the borderlords of King Thigpen and King Drowden. These borderlords have worked with the Council, and some of them are in the confidence of Thigpen's and Drowden's spies. Prince Raffin," Davit said, "these men are certain that neither King Thigpen nor King Drowden was involved in the kidnapping of the Lienid."

Raffin and Katsa caught each other's eyes.

"Then it must be King Birn of Wester," Raffin said.

And so it must, though Katsa couldn't imagine the motive.

"Tell us your sources," Oll said, "and your sources' sources. We'll look into it. If this turns out to be true information, we'll be that much closer to an explanation."

THE MEETING did not go on long. The seven kingdoms had been quiet, and Davit's news was enough to occupy Oll and the other spies for the time being.

"It would help us, Prince Greening," Raffin said, "if you'd allow us to keep your grandfather's rescue a secret for now. We can't guarantee his safety if we don't even know who attacked him."

"Of course," Po said. "I agree."

"But perhaps a cryptic message to your family," Raffin said, "to say that all's well with him . . ."

"Yes, I think I could fashion such a message."

"Excellent." Raffin clapped his hands on the table. "Anything else? Katsa?"

"I've nothing," Katsa said.

"Good." Raffin stood. "Until we hear some news, then, or until Grandfather Tealiff remembers more. Giddon, will you take Lord Davit back to his rooms? Oll, Horan, Waller, Bertol, will you come with me? I wish a moment. We'll take the inner passage, Katsa, if you don't mind a parade through your sleeping room."

"Go ahead," Katsa said. "It's better than a parade through the corridors."

"The prince," Raffin said. "Katsa, will you take the prince—"

"Yes. Go on."

Raffin turned away with Oll and the spies; the soldiers and the servants said their good-byes, and departed.

"I trust you've recovered from your illness at dinner, Katsa," Giddon said, "if you've been starting fights. Indeed, it sounds as if you're back to your normal self."

She would be civil to him in front of Po and Lord Davit, though he laughed now in her face. "Yes, thank you, Giddon. Good night to you."

Giddon nodded and left with Lord Davit. Po and Katsa were alone. Po leaned back against the table. "Am I not trusted to find my way through the halls by myself?"

"He meant for me to take you through an inner passage-way," Katsa said. "If you're seen wandering around the hall-ways of Randa's court at this hour, people will talk. This court will turn the most mundane thing into something to talk about."

"Yes," he said. "I believe that's the case with most courts."

"Do you plan to stay long at the court?"

"I should like to stay until my grandfather's feeling better."

"Then we'll have to come up with an excuse for your presence," Katsa said. "For isn't it generally known that you seek your grandfather?"

Po nodded. "If you agreed to train with me," he said, "that might serve as an excuse."

She began to put out the torches. "What do you mean?"

"People would understand," he said, "if I stayed in order to train with you. They must see that in our view, it's a valuable opportunity. For both of us."

She paused before the last torch and considered his proposal. She understood him completely. She was tired of fighting nine or ten men at once, fully armored men, none of them able to touch her, and she always tempering her blows. It would be a thrill, a pure thrill, to fight Po again. To fight him regularly, a dream.

"Wouldn't it seem as if you'd given up the search for your grandfather?"

"I've already been to Wester," he said, "and Sunder. I can travel to Nander and Estill under the guise of seeking information, can't I, using this city as my base? No city's more central than Randa's."

He could do that, and no one would have reason to question it. She put out the last torch and walked back to him. Half of his face was lit by the light in the hall outside the door. It was his gold eye, his blackened eye, that was illuminated. She looked up at him and set her chin.

"I'll train with you," she said. "But don't expect me to take more care of your face than I did today."

He burst into laughter, but then his eyes sobered, and he looked at the floor. "Forgive me for that, Katsa. I wished to make an ally of Lord Giddon, not an enemy. It seemed the only way."

Katsa shook her head with impatience. "Giddon is a fool."

"He reacted naturally enough," he said, "considering his position."

He brought his fingertips to her chin suddenly. She froze, forgetting the question she'd been about to ask, regarding Giddon, and what in the Middluns his position should be. He tilted her face to the light.

"It was my ring."

She didn't understand him.

"It was my ring that scratched you."

"Your ring."

"Well, one of my rings."

It was one of his rings that scratched her, and now his fingertips touched her face. His hand dropped, returning to his side, and he looked at her calmly, as if this were normal, as if friends she'd only just made always touched her face with their fingertips. As if she ever made friends. As if she had any basis for comparison, to decide what was normal when one made friends, and what was not.

She was not normal.

She marched to the doorway and grabbed the torch from the wall. "Come," she said. For it was time to get him out of here, this strange person, this cat-eyed person who seemed created to rattle her. She would knock those eyes out of his face the next time they fought. She would knock the hoops from his ears and the rings from his hands.

It was time to get him out of here, so that she could return to her rooms and return to herself.

CHAPTER TEN

H<small>E WAS</small> a marvelous opponent. She couldn't get to him. She couldn't hit him where she meant to, or as hard as she wanted. He was so quick to block or to twist, so quick to react. She couldn't knock him from his feet, she couldn't trap him when their fight had devolved into a wrestling match on the floor.

He was so much stronger than she, and for the first time in her life, she found her lesser strength to be a disadvantage. No one had ever gotten close enough to her for it to matter, before this.

He was so finely tuned to his surroundings, and to her movements; and that was also part of the challenge. He always seemed to know what she was doing, even when she was behind him.

"I'll grant you don't have night vision if you'll grant you have eyes in the back of your head," she said once, when she'd entered the practice room and he'd greeted her without looking round to identify her.

"What do you mean?"

"You always know what's happening behind you."

"Katsa, do you never notice the noise you make when you burst into a room? No one flings doors open the way you do."

"Perhaps your Grace gives you a heightened sense of things," she said.

He shook his head. "Perhaps, but no more than your own."

He still got the worst of their fights, because of her flexibility and her tireless energy, and mostly because of her speed. She might not hit him how she wanted, but she still hit him. And he suffered pain more. He stopped the fight once while she grappled to pin his arm and his legs and his back to the ground and he hit her repeatedly in the ribs with his one free hand.

"Doesn't that hurt?" he said, gasping with laughter. "Don't you feel it? I've hit you possibly twelve times, and you don't even flinch."

She sat up on her heels and felt the spot, below her breast. "It hurts, but it's not bad."

"Your bones are made of rock. You walk away from these fights without a sore spot, while I limp away and spend the day icing my bruises."

He didn't wear his rings while they fought. He'd come without them the first day. When she'd protested that it was an unnecessary precaution, his face had assumed a mask of innocence.

"I promised Giddon, didn't I?" he'd said, and that fight had begun with Po ducking, and laughing, as Katsa swung at his face.

They didn't wear their boots, either, not after Katsa accidentally clipped him on the forehead. He had dropped to his hands and knees, and she saw at once what had happened. "Call Raff!" she'd cried to Oll, who watched on the side. She'd sat Po on the floor, ripped off her own sleeve, and tried to stop the flow of blood that ran into his dazed eyes. When Raffin had given him the go-ahead to fight a few days later, she'd insisted they fight barefoot. And in truth, she had taken more care of his face since then.

They almost always practiced in front of an audience. A scattering of soldiers, or underlords. Oll, whenever he could, for the fights gave him so much pleasure. Giddon, though he always seemed to grow grumpy as he watched and never stayed long. Even Helda came on occasion, the only woman who did, and sat with wide eyes that grew wider the longer she sat.

Randa did not come, which was pleasant. Katsa was glad of his tendency to keep her at arm's length.

They ate together most days, after practicing. In her dining room, alone, or in Raffin's workrooms with Raffin and Bann. Sometimes at a table Raffin had brought into Tealiff's room. The grandfather was still very ill, but company seemed to cheer and strengthen him.

When they sat together talking, sometimes the silver and gold of Po's eyes caught her off guard. She could not become used to his eyes; they muddled her. But she met them when he looked at her, and she forced herself to breathe and talk and not become overwhelmed. They were eyes, they were only his eyes, and she wasn't a coward. And besides, she didn't want to behave toward him as the entire court behaved toward her, avoiding her eyes, awkwardly, coldly. She didn't want to do that to a friend.

He was a friend; and in the final few weeks of summer, for the first time in her life, Randa's court became a place of contentment for Katsa. A place of good hard work and of friends. Oll's spies moved steadily, learning what they could from their travels to Nander and Estill. The kingdoms, amazingly, were at peace. The heat and the closeness of the air seemed to bring a lull to Randa's cruelty as well, or perhaps he was merely distracted by the flood of foods and wares that always washed into the city from every trade route at that time of year. Whatever the reason, Randa did not summon Katsa to perform any of his nasty errands. Katsa found herself daring to relax into summer's end.

She never ran out of questions for Po.

"Where'd you get your name?" she asked him one day as they sat in the grandfather's room, talking quietly so as not to wake him.

Po wound a cloth wrapped with ice around his shoulder. "Which one? I've got lots to choose from."

Katsa reached across the table to help him tie the cloth tight. "Po. Does everyone call you that?"

"My brothers gave me that name when I was little. It's a kind of tree in Lienid, the po tree. In autumn its leaves turn silver and gold. Inevitable nickname, I guess."

Katsa broke a piece of bread. She wondered if the name had been given fondly, or if it had been an attempt by Po's brothers to isolate him—to remind him always that he was a

Graceling. She watched him pile his plate high with bread, meat, fruit, and cheese and smiled as the food began to disappear almost as fast as he'd piled it up. Katsa could eat a lot, but Po was something else altogether.

"What is it like to have six older brothers?"

"I don't think it was for me what it would be for most others," he said. "Hand fighting is revered in Lienid. My brothers are great fighters, and of course I was able to hold my own with them, even though I was small—and eventually surpass them, every one of them. They treated me like an equal, like more than an equal."

"And were they also your friends?"

"Oh yes, especially the younger ones."

Perhaps it was easier, then, to be a Graceling fighter if one was a boy or in a kingdom that revered hand fighting; or perhaps Po's Grace had announced itself less drastically than Katsa's had. Perhaps if Katsa had six older brothers, she would also have six friends.

Or maybe everything was different in Lienid.

"I've heard the Lienid castles are built on mountain peaks so high that people have to be lifted up to them by ropes," she said.

Po grinned. "Only my father's city has the ropes." He poured himself more water and turned back to the food on his plate.

"Well?" Katsa said. "Are you going to explain them to me?"

"Katsa. Is it too much for you to understand that a man might be hungry after you've beaten him half to death? I'm beginning to think it's part of your fighting strategy, keeping me from eating. You want me weak and faint."

"For someone who's Lienid's finest fighter," she said, "you have a delicate constitution."

He laughed and put his fork down. "All right, all right. How can I describe this?" He picked his fork up again and used it to draw a picture in the air as he spoke. "My father's city sits at the top of this enormous, tall rock, tall as a mountain, that rises straight up from the plains below. There are three ways up to the city. One is a road built into the sides of the rock, that winds around and around it, slowly. The second is a stairway built into one side of the rock. It bends back and forth on itself until it reaches the top. It's a good approach, if you're strong and wide awake and don't have a horse, though most who choose that route eventually tire and end up begging a ride from someone on the road. My brothers and I race it sometimes."

"Who wins?"

"Where's your confidence in me, that you need to ask that question? You would beat us all, of course."

"My ability to fight has no bearing on my ability to run up a flight of stairs."

"Nonetheless, I can't imagine you allowing anyone to beat you at anything."

Katsa snorted. "And the third way?"

"The third way is the ropes."

"But how do they work?"

Po scratched his head. "Well, it's fairly simple, really. They hang from a great wheel that sits flat, on its side, at the top of the rock. They dangle down over the edge of the rock, and at the bottom they're attached to platforms. Horses turn the wheel, the wheel pulls the ropes, and the platforms rise."

"It seems a terrible amount of trouble."

"Mostly everyone uses the road. The ropes are only for great shipments of things."

"And the whole city sits up in the sky?"

Po broke himself another piece of bread and nodded.

"But why would they build a city in such a place?"

Po shrugged. "I suppose because it's beautiful."

"What do you mean?"

"Well, you can see forever from the edges of the city. The fields, the mountains and hills. To one side, the sea."

"The sea," Katsa said.

The sea put an end to her questions for a moment. Katsa had seen the lakes of Nander, some of them so wide she could barely make out the opposite shore. But she'd never seen the sea. She couldn't imagine that much water. Nor could she imagine water that rocked, and crashed against the land, as she'd heard the sea did. She stared absently at the walls of Tealiff's small room, and tried to think of it.

"You can see two of my brothers' castles from the city," Po said. "In the foothills of the mountains. The other castles are beyond the mountains, or too far to see."

"How many castles are there?"

"Seven," Po said, "just as there are seven sons."

"Then one is yours."

"The smallest one."

"Do you mind that yours is the smallest?"

Po chose an apple from the bowl of fruit on the table. "I'm glad mine is the smallest, though my brothers don't believe me when I say so."

She didn't blame them for disbelieving. She'd never heard of a man, not even her cousin, who didn't want as large a holding as he could have. Giddon was always comparing his estate to that of his neighbors; and when Raffin listed his complaints about Thigpen, he never neglected to mention a certain disagreement over the precise location of the Middluns' eastern border. She'd thought all men were like that. She'd thought she wasn't like that because she wasn't a man.

"I don't have the ambitions of my brothers," Po said. "I've never wanted a large holding. I've never wanted to be a king or an overlord."

"No," Katsa said, "nor have I. I've thanked the hills countless times that Raffin was born the son of Randa, and I only his niece, and his sister's daughter at that."

"My brothers want all that power," he said. "They love to get wrapped up in the disputes of my father's court. They actually revel in it. They love managing their own castles and their own cities. I do believe sometimes that they all wish to be king."

He leaned back in his chair and absently ran his fingers along his sore shoulder.

"My castle doesn't have a city," he said. "It's not far from a town, but the town governs itself. It doesn't have a court, either. Really it's just a great house that'll be my home for the times when I'm not traveling."

Katsa took an apple for herself. "You intend to travel."

"I'm more restless than my brothers. But it's so beautiful, my castle; it's the most wonderful place to go home to. It sits on a cliff above the sea. There are steps down to the water, cut into the cliff. And balconies hanging over the cliff—you feel as if you'll fall if you lean too far. At night the sun goes down across the water, and the whole sky turns red and orange, and the sea to match it. Sometimes there are great fish out there, fish of impossible colors. They come to the surface and roll about—you can watch them from the balconies. And in winter the waves are high, and the wind'll knock you down. You can't go out to the balconies in winter. It's dangerous, and wild.

"Grandfather," he said suddenly. He jumped up and turned to the bed. Informed that his grandfather had awoken, Katsa thought wryly, by the eyes in the back of his head.

"You speak of your castle, boy," the old man said.

"Grandfather, how are you feeling?"

Katsa ate her apple and listened to them talk. Her head was full of the things Po had said. She hadn't known there were sights in the world so beautiful a person would want to spend an age staring at them.

Po turned to her then, and a torch on the wall caught the gleam of his eyes. She focused on breathing. "I have a weakness for beautiful sights," he said. "My brothers tease me."

"Your brothers are the foolish ones," Tealiff said, "for not seeing the strength in beautiful things. Come here, child," he said to Katsa. "Let me see your eyes, for they make me stronger."

And his kindness brought a smile to her face, though his words were nonsense. She went to sit beside Grandfather Tealiff, and he and Po told her more about Po's castle and Po's brothers and Ror's city in the sky.

CHAPTER ELEVEN

"How far is Giddon's estate from Randa City?" Po asked her late one morning. They sat on the floor of their practice room, drinking water and resting. It had been a good session. Po had returned the day before from a visit to Nander, and Katsa thought the time apart had been good for them. They came together again with a new sharpness.

"It's near," Katsa said. "In the west. A day's journey, perhaps."

"Have you seen it?"

"Yes. It's large and very grand. He doesn't get home often, but he still manages to keep it well."

"I'm sure he does."

Giddon had come to their practice today. He'd been the only visitor, and he hadn't stayed long. She didn't know why he came, when it always seemed to put him in a bad humor.

Katsa lay on her back and looked up at the high ceiling. The light poured into the room from the great, east-facing windows. The days were beginning to shorten. The air would crispen soon, and the castle would smell of wood burning in the fireplaces. The leaves would crackle under her horse's hooves when she went riding.

It had been such a quiet couple of weeks. She would like a Council task—she'd like to get out of the city and stretch her legs. She wondered if Oll had any news about Grandfather Tealiff yet. Maybe she could go to Wester herself and poke around for information.

"How will you answer Giddon when he asks you to marry him?" Po asked. "Will you accept?"

Katsa sat up, and stared at him. "That's an absurd question."

"Absurd—why?" His face was clear of its usual smiles. She didn't think he was teasing her.

"Why in the Middluns would Giddon ask me to marry him?"

His eyes narrowed. "Katsa. You're not serious."

She looked at him blankly, and now he did begin to smile.

"Katsa, don't you know Giddon's in love with you?"

Katsa snorted. "Don't be ridiculous. Giddon lives to criticize me."

Po shook his head, and his laugh began to rumble from his chest. "Katsa, how can you be so blind? He's completely smitten. Don't you see how jealous he is? Don't you remember how he reacted when I scratched your face?"

An unpleasant feeling began to gather in her stomach. "I don't see what that has to do with it. And besides, how would you know? I don't believe Lord Giddon confides in you."

He laughed. "No," he said. "No, he certainly doesn't. Giddon trusts me about as much as he trusts Murgon. I imagine he thinks any man who fights you as I do is no better than an opportunist and no worse than a thug."

"You're deceived," Katsa said. "Giddon feels nothing for me."

"I can't make you see it, Katsa, if you're determined not to see it." Po stretched onto his back and yawned. "All the same, I might think up a response if I were you. Just in case he were to propose." He laughed again. "I'll have to ice my shoulder, as usual. I'd say you won again today, Katsa."

She jumped to her feet. "Are we done here?"

"I suppose so. Are you hungry?"

She waved him off and marched to the door. She left him lying on his back in the light of the windows and ran to find Raffin.

KATSA BURST into Raffin's workrooms. Raffin and Bann sat at a table, huddled together over a book.

"Are you alone?" Katsa asked.

They looked up, surprised. "Yes—"

"Is Giddon in love with me?"

Raffin blinked, and Bann's eyes widened.

"He's never spoken to me about it," Raffin said. "But yes, I think anyone who knows him would say he's in love with you."

Katsa slapped her hand to her forehead. "Of all the fool— how can he—" She paced to the table. She turned and paced back to the door.

"Has he said something to you?" Raffin asked.

"No. Po told me." She spun toward Raffin. "And why did you never tell me?"

"Kat." He sat back from his book. "I thought you knew. I don't see how you could not. He makes himself your escort every time the king's business takes you away from the city. He always sits beside you at dinner."

"Randa decides where we sit at dinner."

"Well, and Randa probably knows Giddon hopes to marry you," Raffin said.

Katsa paced to the table again, clutching her hair. "Oh, this is dreadful. Whatever shall I do?"

"If he asks you to marry him, you'll say no. You'll tell him it's nothing to do with him. You'll tell him you're determined not to marry, that you don't wish children; whatever you need to say so he understands it's nothing to do with him."

"I wouldn't marry Giddon to save my life," Katsa said. "Not even to save yours."

"Well." Raffin's eyes were full of laughter. "I'd leave that part out."

Katsa sighed and walked again to the door.

"You're not the most perceptive person I've ever known, Kat," Raffin said, "if you don't mind my saying so. Your capacity for missing the obvious is astonishing."

She threw her arms into the air. She turned to go. She turned back to him suddenly, at a shocking thought. "*You're* not in love with me, are you?"

He stared at her for a moment, speechless. Then he burst into laughter. Bann laughed, too, though he tried valiantly to hide it behind his hand. Katsa was too relieved to be offended.

"All right, all right," she said, "I suppose I deserve that."

"My dear Katsa," Raffin said, "Giddon is so very handsome, are you sure you won't reconsider?"

Raffin and Bann clutched their stomachs and guffawed. Katsa waved their nonsense away. They were hopeless. She turned to go.

"Council meeting tonight," Raffin said to her back.

She raised her hand to show she'd heard. She closed the door on their laughter.

"THERE'S VERY LITTLE happening in the seven kingdoms," Oll said. "We've called this meeting only because we have some information about Prince Tealiff we can't make any sense of. We're hoping you'll have some ideas."

Bann had joined them for this meeting, because the grandfather was well enough now to be left alone on occasion. Katsa had taken advantage of Bann's broad chest and shoulders, and seated him between herself and Giddon. Giddon could not possibly see her; but just in case, she'd positioned Raffin between them as well. Oll and Po were across from her. Po sat back in his chair, his eyes glimmering in the corner of her vision no matter which way she looked.

"Lord Davit gave us true information," Oll said. "Neither Nander nor Estill knows anything of the kidnapping. Neither was involved. But now we're almost certain that King Birn of Wester is also innocent."

"Could it be Murgon, then?" Giddon asked.

"But with what motive?" Katsa asked.

"He has no motive," Raffin said. "But then, he has no less motive than anyone else. It's what we keep coming up against.

There is no motive for anyone to have done this. Even Po—
Prince Greening—has been able to come up with none."

Po nodded. "My grandfather's only importance is to his
family."

"And if someone had it in mind to provoke the Lienid
royal family," Oll said, "wouldn't they reveal themselves eventually? Otherwise, the power play becomes pointless."

"Has Tealiff said anything more?" Giddon asked.

"He's said they blindfolded him," Po said, "and drugged
him. He's said he was on a boat for a long time, and their land
travel was shorter in comparison, which suggests his captors
took him east by boat from Lienid, possibly to one of the
southern Sunderan ports. And then up through the forests to
Murgon City. He's said that when he heard them speak, he
believed their accents to be southern."

"It does suggest Sunder, and Murgon," Giddon said.

But it didn't make sense. None of the kings had reason,
but Murgon even less. Murgon worked for others, and his sole
motivation was money. Everyone at the table, everyone in the
Council, knew that.

"Po," Katsa said. "Your grandfather had no argument with
your father, or any of your brothers? Your mother?"

"None," Po said. "I'm sure of it."

"I don't see how you can be so sure," Giddon said.

Po's eyes flashed to him. "You'll have to take my word, Lord
Giddon. Neither my father nor my brothers nor my mother nor
anyone else at the Lienid court was involved in the kidnapping."

"Po's word is good enough for the Council," Raffin said. "And if it wasn't Birn, Drowden, Thigpen, Randa, or Ror, that leaves Murgon."

Po raised his eyebrows. "Have none of you considered the King of Monsea?"

"A king with a reputation for kindness to injured animals and lost children," Giddon said, "come out of his isolation to kidnap his wife's aging father? A bit unlikely, don't you think?"

"We've made inquiries and uncovered nothing," Oll said. "King Leck is a peace-loving man. Either it's Murgon, or one of the kings is keeping a secret even from his own spies."

"It may have been Murgon," Katsa said, "or it may not. Either way, Murgon knows who's responsible. If Murgon knows, then the people closest to him know. Couldn't we find one of Murgon's people? I could make him talk."

"Not without revealing your identity, My Lady," Oll said.

"But she could kill him," Giddon said, "after she questioned him."

"Now, hold on." Katsa held up her hand. "I said nothing of killing."

"But it's not worth the information, Katsa," Raffin said, "for you to interrogate someone who'll recognize you and speak of it to Murgon afterward."

"Greening should be the one to do it, anyway," Giddon said, and Po's cool eyes flicked to him again. "Murgon wouldn't question the motivation of a Lienid prince. Murgon would expect it of him. In fact, I don't see why you haven't done it already," Giddon said to Po, "if you wish so much to know who's responsible."

Katsa was too irritated to care about her strategic seating plan. She leaned around Raffin and Bann to address Giddon. "It's because Murgon can't know that Po knows Murgon is involved," she said. "How would Po explain that knowledge, without incriminating us?"

"But that's just why you can't question Murgon's people, Katsa, unless you're willing to kill afterwards." Giddon thumped his hand on the table and glared at her.

"All right," Raffin said, "all right. We're going in circles."

Katsa sat back, seething.

"Katsa," Raffin said, "the information isn't worth the risk to you or to the Council. Nor, I think, is it worth the violence."

She sighed, inwardly. He was right, of course.

"Perhaps it'll be worth it someday in the future," Raffin said. "But for now, Grandfather Tealiff is safe, and we've seen no sign from Murgon or from anyone else that he's being targeted again. Po, if there are steps you wish to take, that's your affair, though I'd ask you to discuss it with us first."

"I must think on it," Po said.

"Then the matter is closed for now," Raffin said, "until we learn something new, or until Po comes to a decision. Oll? Is there anything else on the table?"

Oll began to speak then of a Westeran village that had met a Nanderan raiding party with a pair of catapults, given to them by a Westeran lord who was friend to the Council. The Nanderan raiders had fled, thinking they were being attacked by an army. There was laughter at the table, and Oll began another story, but Katsa's thoughts wandered to Murgon and his dungeons, to the Sunderan forests that likely held the secrets of the kidnapping. She felt Po's gaze, and she glanced at him across the table. His eyes were on her, but he didn't see her. His mind was elsewhere. He got that look sometimes, when they sat together after their fights.

She watched his face. The cut on his forehead was no more than a thin red line now. It would leave a scar. She wondered if that would rankle his Lienid vanity, but then she smiled within herself. He wasn't really vain. He hadn't cared a bit when she'd blackened his eye. He'd done nothing to hide the gash on his forehead. And besides, no vain person would choose to fight her, day after day. No vain person would put his body at the mercy of her hands.

His sleeves were rolled to his elbows again. His manners were so careless. Her eyes rested on the shadows in the hollows of his neck, then rose to his face again. She supposed he would have reason to be vain. He was handsome enough, as handsome as Giddon or Raffin, with his straight nose and the set of his mouth, and his strong shoulders. And even those gleaming eyes. Even they might be considered handsome.

His eyes came back into focus then and looked into hers. And then something mischievous in his eyes, and a grin. Almost as if he knew exactly what she was thinking, exactly what she'd decided about his claims to vanity. Katsa's face closed, and she glowered at him.

The meeting ended, and chairs scraped. Raffin pulled her aside to speak of something. She was grateful for the excuse to turn away. She wouldn't see Po again until their next fight. And the fights always returned her to herself.

Chapter Twelve

The next morning Randa came to their practice for the first time. He stood at the side, so that everyone in the room was compelled to stand as well and watch him instead of the fighters they'd come to see. Katsa was glad to fight, glad for the excuse to ignore him. Except that she couldn't ignore him. He was so tall and broad, and he stood against the white wall in bright blue robes. His lazy laugh carried into every corner of the room. She couldn't shake the sense of him—and there must be something he wanted. He never sought out his lady killer unless there was something he wanted.

She had been running through a drill with Po when Randa had arrived, a drill that was giving her some trouble. It began with Katsa on her knees and Po behind her, pinning her arms behind her back. Her task was to break free of Po's grip and then grapple with him until she had trapped him in the same position. She could always fight her way free of Po's grip. That wasn't the problem. It was the counterpin that frustrated her. Even if she managed to knock him to his knees and trap his arms, she couldn't keep him down. It was a matter of brute strength. If he tried to muscle himself to his feet, she didn't have the force to stop him, not unless she knocked him unconscious or injured him seriously, and that wasn't the point of the exercise. She needed to find a holding position that would make the effort of rising too painful to be worth his while.

They began the drill again. She knelt with Po at her back, and Po's hands tightened around her wrists. Randa's voice rose and fell, and one of the stewards responded. Flattering, fawning. Everyone flattered Randa.

Katsa was ready for Po this time. She twisted out of his grip and was on him like a wildcat. She pummeled his stomach, hooked her foot between his legs, and battered him to his knees. She yanked at his arms. His right shoulder—that was the one he was always icing. She twisted his right arm and leaned all her weight against it, so that any attempt to move would require him to wrench his shoulder and bring more pain to it than she was already causing him to feel.

"I surrender," he gasped. She released him, and he heaved himself to his feet. He massaged his shoulder. "Good work, Katsa."

"Again."

They ran through the drill again, and then once more, and both times she trapped him easily.

"You've got it," Po said. "Good. What next? Shall I try it?"

Her name cut through the air then, and her hackles rose. She'd been right. He hadn't come only to watch; and now, before all these people, she must act pleasant and civil. She fought against the frown that rose to her face, and turned to the king.

"It's so amusing," Randa said, "to see you struggling with an opponent, Katsa."

"I'm glad it gives you amusement, Lord King."

"Prince Greening. How do you find our lady killer?"

"She's the superior fighter by far, Lord King," Po said. "If she didn't hold herself back, I'd be in great trouble."

Randa laughed. "Indeed. I've noticed it's you who comes to dinner with bruises, and not she."

Pride in his possession. Katsa forced herself to unclench her fists. She forced herself to breathe, to hold her uncle's gaze even though she wanted to scratch the leer from his face.

"Katsa," the king said. "Come to me later today. I have a job for you."

"Yes, Lord King," she said. "Thank you, Lord King."

Randa leaned back on his heels and surveyed the room. Then, with his stewards rushing into their places behind him, he exited with a great swish of blue robes, and Katsa stared after him until he and his entourage had vanished; and then she stared at the door the stewards slammed behind him.

Around the room, slowly, lords and soldiers sat down. Katsa was vaguely aware of their movements. Vaguely aware of Po's eyes on her face, watching her, silently.

"What's it to be now, Katsa?"

She knew what she wanted. She felt it shooting down her arms and into her fingers, tingling in her legs and feet. "A straight fight," she said. "Anything fair. Until one of us surrenders."

Po narrowed his eyes. He considered her tight fists and her hard mouth. "We'll have that fight, but we'll have it tomorrow. We're done for today."

"No. We fight."

"Katsa. We're done."

She stalked up to him, close, so that no one else could hear. "What's the matter, Po? Do you fear me?"

"Yes, I fear you, as I should when you're angry. I won't fight you when you're angry. Nor should you fight me when I'm angry. That's not the purpose of these practices."

And when he told her she was angry, she realized it was true. And just as quickly, her anger fizzled into despair. Randa would send her on another strong-arm mission. He would send her to hurt some poor petty criminal, some fool who deserved to keep his fingers even if he was dishonorable. He would send her, and she must go, for the power sat with him.

THEY ATE in her dining room. Katsa stared at her plate. He was talking about his brothers, how his brothers would love to see their practices. She must come to Lienid one day and fight with him for his family. They'd be amazed by her skill, and they'd honor her greatly. And he could show her the most beautiful sights in his father's city.

She wasn't listening. She was picturing the arms she'd broken for her uncle. The arms, bent the wrong way at the elbow, bone splinters sticking through the skin. He said something about his shoulder, and she shook herself, and looked at him.

"What did you say?" she asked. "About your shoulder? I'm sorry."

He dropped his gaze and fiddled with his fork. "Your

uncle has quite an effect on you," he said. "You haven't been yourself since he walked into the practice room."

"Or maybe I have been myself, and the other times I'm not myself."

"What do you mean?"

"My uncle thinks me savage. He thinks me a killer. Well, isn't he right? Didn't I become savage when he entered the room? And what is it we're practicing every day?" She tore apart a piece of bread and threw it onto her plate. She glared at her meal.

"I don't believe you're savage," he said.

She sighed, sharply. "You haven't seen me with Randa's enemies."

He raised his cup to his lips and drank, then lowered it, watching her. "What will he ask you to do this time?"

She pushed the fire down that rose up from her stomach. She wondered what would happen if she slammed her plate on the ground, how many pieces it would break into.

"It'll be some lord who owes him money," she said, "or who refused to agree to some bargain, or who looked at him wrong. I'll be told to hurt the man, enough so that he never dishonors my uncle again."

"And you'll do what he tells you to do?"

"Who are these fools who continue to resist Randa's will? Haven't they heard the stories? Don't they know he'll send me?"

"Isn't it in your power to refuse?" Po asked. "How can anyone force you to do anything?"

The fire burst into her throat and choked her. "He is the king. And you're a fool, too, if you think I have choice in the matter."

"But you do have choice. He's not the one who makes you savage. You make yourself savage, when you bend yourself to his will."

She sprang to her feet and swung at his jaw with the side of her hand. She lessened the force of the blow only at the last instant, when she realized he hadn't raised his arm to block her. Her hand hit his face with a sickening crack. She watched, horrified, as his chair toppled backward and his head slammed against the floor. She'd hit him hard. She knew she'd hit him hard. And he hadn't defended himself.

She ran to him. He lay on his side, both hands over his jaw. A tear trickled from his eye, over his fingers, and onto the floor. He grunted, or sobbed—she didn't know which. She knelt beside him and touched his shoulder. "Did I break your jaw? Can you speak?"

He shifted then, pushed himself up to a sitting position. He felt at the side of his jaw and opened and closed his mouth. He moved his jaw left and right.

"I don't think it's broken." His voice was a whisper.

She put her hand to his face and felt the bones under his skin. She felt the other side of his face to compare. She could tell no difference, and she caught her breath with relief.

"It's not broken," he said, "though it seems it should be."

"I pulled back," she said, "when I realized you weren't fighting me." She reached up to the table and dipped her hands into the water pitcher. She scooped blocks of ice onto a cloth and wrapped them up. She brought the ice to his jaw. "Why didn't you fight back?"

He held the ice to his face and groaned. "This'll hurt for days."

"Po . . ."

He looked at her, and sighed. "I told you before, Katsa. I won't fight when you're angry. I won't solve a disagreement between us with blows." He lifted the ice and fingered his jaw. He moaned, and held the ice to his face again. "What we do in the practice rooms—that's to help each other. We don't use it against each other. We're friends, Katsa."

Shame pricked behind her eyes. It was so elemental, so obvious. It wasn't what one friend did to another, yet she'd done it.

"We're too dangerous to each other, Katsa. And even if we weren't, it's not right."

"I'll never do it again," she said. "I swear to it."

He caught her eyes then, and held them. "I know you won't. Katsa. Wildcat. Don't blame yourself. You expected me to fight back. You wouldn't have struck me otherwise."

But still she should have known better. "It wasn't even you who angered me. It was him."

Po considered her for a moment. "What do you think would happen," he said, "if you refused to do what Randa ordered?"

She didn't know, really. She only imagined him sneering at her, his words crackling with contempt. "If I don't do what he says, he'll become angry. When he becomes angry, I'll become angry. And then I'll want to kill him."

"Hmm." He worked his mouth back and forth. "You're afraid of your own anger."

She stopped then and looked at him, because that seemed right to her. She was afraid of her own anger.

"But Randa isn't even worth your anger," Po said. "He's no more than a bully."

Katsa snorted. "A bully who chops off people's fingers or breaks their arms."

"Not if you stop doing it for him," Po said. "Much of his power comes from you."

She was afraid of her own anger: She repeated it in her mind. She was afraid of what she would do to the king—and with good reason. Look at Po, his jaw red and beginning to swell. She'd learned to control her skill, but she hadn't learned to control her anger. And that meant she still didn't control her Grace.

"Should we move back to the table?" he said, for they were still sitting on the floor.

"You should probably go see Raff," she said, "just to be sure nothing's broken." Her eyes dropped. "Forgive me, Po."

Po heaved himself to his feet. He reached for her hand and pulled her up. "You're forgiven, Lady."

She shook her head, disbelieving his kindness. "You Lienid are so odd; your reactions are never what mine would be. You, so calm, when I've hurt you so badly. Your father's sister, so strange in her grief."

Po narrowed his eyes then. "What do you mean?"

"About what? Isn't the Queen of Monsea your father's sister?"

"What's she done, my father's sister?"

"The word is, she stopped eating when she heard of your grandfather's disappearance. You didn't know? And then she closed herself and her child into her rooms. And wouldn't let anyone enter, not even the king."

"She wouldn't let the king enter," he repeated, puzzlement in his voice.

"Nor anyone else," Katsa said, "except a handmaiden to bring them meals."

"Why did no one tell me about this before?"

"I assumed you knew, Po. I'd no idea it would matter so much to you. Are you close to her?"

Po stared at the table, at the mess of melting ice and their half-eaten meal. His mind was elsewhere, his brow furrowed.

"Po, what is it?"

He shook his head. "It's not how I would've expected Ashen to behave," he said. "But it's no matter. I must find Raffin, or Bann."

She watched his face then. "There's something you're not telling me."

He wouldn't meet her eyes. "How long will you be away on Randa's errand?"

"It's not likely to be more than a few days."

"When you return, I must speak with you."

"Why don't you speak with me now?"

He shook his head. "I need to think. I need to work something out."

Why were his eyes so uneasy? Why was he looking at the table and the floor, but never into her face?

It was concern, for his father's sister. It was worry for the people he cared about. For that was his way, this Lienid. His friendship was true.

He looked at her then. The smallest of smiles flickered across his face, but it didn't reach his eyes. "Don't feel too kindly toward me, Katsa. Neither of us is blameless as a friend."

He left her then, to find Raffin. She stood and stared at the place where he'd just been. And tried to shake off the eerie sense that he had just answered something she'd thought, rather than something she'd said.

CHAPTER THIRTEEN

Not that it was the first time he'd left her with that feeling. Po had a way about him. He knew her opinions, sometimes, before she expressed them. He looked at her from across a table and knew she was angry, and why; or that she'd decided he was handsome.

Raffin had told her she wasn't perceptive. Po was perceptive. And talkative. Perhaps that was why they got along so well. She didn't have to explain herself to Po, and he explained himself to her without her having to ask. She'd never known a person with whom she could communicate so freely—so unused was she to the phenomenon of friendship.

She mused about this as the horses carried them west, until the hills began to even out and give way to great grassy flatlands, and the pleasure of smooth, hard riding distracted her. Giddon was in good humor, for this was his country. They would visit his estate on their way to one just beyond his. They would sleep in his castle, first on their outward journey and then again on their return. Giddon rode eagerly and fast, and though Katsa didn't relish his company, for once she couldn't complain of their pace.

"It's a bit awkward, isn't it?" Oll said, when they stopped

at midday to rest. "For the king to have asked you to punish your neighbor?"

"It is awkward," Giddon said. "Lord Ellis is a good neighbor. I can't imagine what has possessed him to create this trouble with Randa."

"Well, he's protecting his daughters," Oll said. "No man can fault him for that. It's Ellis's bad luck that it puts him at odds with the king."

Randa had made a deal with a Nanderan underlord. The underlord couldn't attract a wife, because his holding was in the south-central region of Nander, directly in the path of Westeran and Estillan raiding parties. It was a dangerous place, especially for a woman. And it was a desolate holding, without even sufficient servants, for the raiders had killed and stolen so many. The underlord was desperate for a wife, so desperate that he was willing to forgo her dowry. King Randa had offered to take the trouble to find him a bride, on the condition that her dowry went to Randa.

Lord Ellis had two daughters of marriageable age. Two daughters, and two very great dowries. Randa had ordered Ellis to choose which daughter he would prefer to send as a bride to Nander. "Choose the daughter who is stronger in spirit," Randa had written, "for it is not a match for the weakhearted."

Lord Ellis had refused to choose either daughter. "Both of my daughters are strong in spirit," he wrote to the king, "but I will send neither to the wastelands of Nander. The king has greater power than any, but I do not think he has the power to force an unsuitable marriage for his own convenience."

Katsa had gasped when Raffin told her what Lord Ellis said in his letter. He was a brave man, as brave as any Randa had come up against. Randa wanted Giddon to talk to Ellis, and if talk didn't work, he wanted Katsa to hurt Ellis—in the presence of his daughters, so that one of them would step forward and offer herself to the marriage to protect her father. Randa expected them to return to his court with one or the other of the daughters, and her dowry.

"This is a gruesome task we're asked to perform," Oll said. "Even without Ellis being your neighbor, it's gruesome."

"It is," Giddon said. "But I see no way around it."

They sat on an outcropping of stone and ate bread and fruit. Katsa watched the long grass moving around them. The wind pushed it, attacked it, struck it in one place and then another. It rose and fell and rose again. It flowed, like water.

"Is this what the sea is like?" Katsa asked, and they both turned to her, surprised. "Does the sea move the way this grass moves?"

"It is like this, My Lady," Oll said, "but different. The sea makes rushing noises, and it's gray and cold. But it does move a bit like this."

"I should like to see the sea," she said.

Giddon's eyes on her were incredulous.

"What? Is it such a strange thing to say?"

"It's a strange thing for you to say." He shook his head. He gathered their bread and fruit, then rose. "The Lienid fighter is filling your mind with romantic notions." He went to his horse.

She ignored him so that she didn't have to think about his own notions of romance or his suit or his jealousy. She rode hard across the flatlands, and imagined she rode across the sea.

IT WAS MORE difficult to ignore the reality of Giddon once they'd reached his castle. The walls were great, gray, and impressive. The servants flowed into the sunny courtyard to greet their lord and bow to him, and he called them by name and asked after the grain in the storehouses, the castle, the bridge that was being repaired. He was king here, and she could see that he was comfortable with this, and that his servants were happy to see him.

Giddon's servants were always attentive to Katsa, whenever she was at his court. They approached her to ask if she needed anything; they lit a fire for her and brought her water so she could wash. When she walked past them in the hallways, they greeted her. She wasn't treated this way anywhere else, not even in her own home. It occurred to her now that of course, Giddon had specifically ordered his servants to treat her like a lady—not to fear her, or if they did fear her, to pretend they didn't. All of this Giddon had done for her. She realized his servants must look upon her as their future mistress, for if all of Randa's court knew Giddon's feelings, then surely Giddon's servants had interpreted them as well.

She didn't know how to be at Giddon's court now, realizing they all expected something of her she would never give.

She thought they'd be relieved to know she wouldn't marry Giddon. They would exhale and smile, and prepare cheerfully for whatever kind, harmless lady was his second choice. But perhaps they only hoped for their lord what he hoped for himself.

Giddon's hope bewildered her. She couldn't fathom his foolishness, to fall in love with her, and she still didn't entirely believe it to be true.

OLL GREW increasingly morose about Lord Ellis.

"It's a cruel task the king has asked us to perform," he said at dinner, in Giddon's private dining room, where the three of them ate with a pair of servants to attend to them. "I can't remember if he's ever asked us to perform a task so cruel."

"He has," Giddon said, "and we've performed it. And you've never spoken like this before."

"It just seems . . ." Oll broke off to stare absently at Giddon's walls, covered with rich tapestries in red and gold. "It just seems that this is a task the Council wouldn't condone. The Council would send someone to protect these daughters. From us."

Giddon pushed potatoes onto his fork and chewed. He considered Oll's words. "We can't do any work for the Council," he said, "if we don't also follow Randa's commands. We're no use to anyone if we're sitting in the dungeons."

"Yes," Oll said. "But still, it doesn't seem right."

By the end of the meal, Giddon was as morose as Oll. Katsa watched Oll's craggy face and his unhappy eyes. She watched Giddon eating, his knife reflecting the gold and red of the walls as he cut his meat. His voice was low, and he sighed—they both sighed, Oll and Giddon, as they talked and ate.

They didn't want to perform this task for Randa. As Katsa watched them and listened, the fingers of her mind began to open and reach around for some means by which they might thwart Randa's instructions.

Po HAD SAID it was in her power to refuse Randa. And maybe it was in her power, as it was not in Oll's or Giddon's, because Randa could punish them in ways he couldn't punish her. Could he punish her? He could use his entire army, perhaps, to force her into his dungeons. He could kill her. Not in a fight, but he could poison her, one night at dinner. If he thought her a danger, or didn't think her useful, he would certainly have her imprisoned or killed.

And what if his anger, when she returned to court without Ellis's daughter, inflamed her own? What would happen at court, if she stood before Randa and felt an anger in her hands and feet she couldn't contain? What would she do?

It didn't matter. When Katsa awoke the next morning in her comfortable bed in Giddon's castle, she knew it didn't matter what Randa might do to her, or what she might do to Randa. If she were forced to injure Lord Ellis today as Randa wished, it would set her into a rage. She sensed the rage building, just at the thought of it. Her rage if she hurt Lord Ellis would be no less catastrophic than her rage if she didn't and

Randa retaliated. She would not do it. She wouldn't torture a man who was only trying to protect his children.

She didn't know what would happen because of this. But she knew that today, she would hurt no one. She threw back her blankets and thought only of today.

GIDDON AND OLL dragged their feet as they prepared their bags and their horses. "Perhaps we'll be able to talk him into an agreement," Giddon said, lamely. "Humph," was Oll's only response.

Ellis's castle was a few short hours' ride distant. When they arrived, a steward showed them into the great library, where Ellis sat writing at a desk. The walls were lined with books, some so high they could only be reached by ladders made of fine dark wood that leaned against the shelves. Lord Ellis stood as they entered, his eyes bold and his chin high. He was a small man, with a thatch of black hair, and small fingers which he spread across the top of his desk.

"I know why you're here, Giddon," he said.

Giddon cleared his throat uncomfortably. "We wish to talk with you, Ellis, and with your daughters."

"I will not bring my daughters into present company," Ellis said, his eyes flicking to Katsa. He didn't flinch under her gaze, and he went up another notch in her estimation.

Now was the time for her to act. She counted three servants standing rigidly against the walls.

"Lord Ellis," she said, "if you care at all for the safety of your servants, you'll send them from this room."

Giddon glanced at her, surprise apparent on his face, for this was not their usual mode of operation. "Katsa—"

"Don't waste my time, Lord Ellis," Katsa said. "I can remove them myself if you will not."

Lord Ellis waved his men to the door. "Go," he said to them. "Go. Allow no one to enter. See to your duties."

Their duties most likely involved removing the lord's daughters from the grounds immediately, if the daughters were even at home; Lord Ellis struck Katsa as the type to have prepared for this. When the door had closed, she held her hand up to silence Giddon. He shot her a look of puzzled irritation, which she ignored.

"Lord Ellis," she said. "The king wishes us to talk you into sending one of your daughters to Nander. I imagine we're unlikely to succeed."

Ellis's face was hard, and still he held her eyes. "Correct."

Katsa nodded. "Very well. That failing, Randa wishes me to torture you until one of your daughters steps forward and offers herself to the marriage."

Ellis's face didn't change. "I suspected as much."

Giddon's voice was low. "Katsa, what are you doing?"

"The king," Katsa said, and then she felt such a rush of blood to her head that she touched the desk to steady herself. "The king is just in some matters. In this matter, he is not. He wishes to bully you. But the king doesn't do his own bullying—he looks to me for that. And I—" Katsa felt strong suddenly. She pushed away from the desk and stood tall. "I won't do what Randa says. I won't compel you or your daughters to follow his command. My Lord, you may do what you will."

The room was silent. Ellis's eyes were big with astonishment, and he leaned heavily on the desk now, as if danger had strengthened him before and its lack now made him weak. Beside Katsa, Giddon didn't seem to be breathing, and when she glanced at him, his mouth hung slightly ajar. Oll stood a little aside, his face kind and worried.

"Well," Lord Ellis said. "This is quite a surprise, My Lady. I thank you, My Lady. Indeed, I can't thank you enough."

Katsa didn't think a person should thank her for not causing pain. Causing joy was worthy of thanks, and causing pain worthy of disgust. Causing neither was neither, it was nothing, and nothing didn't warrant thanks.

"You don't owe me gratitude," she said. "And I fear this won't put an end to your troubles with Randa."

"Katsa." It was Oll. "Are you certain this is what you want?"

"What will Randa do to you?" Giddon asked.

"Whatever he does," Oll said, "we'll support you."

"No," Katsa said. "You won't support me. I must be on my own in this. Randa must believe that you and Giddon tried to force me to follow his order, but couldn't." She wondered if she should injure them, to make it more convincing.

"But we don't want to perform this task any more than you do," Giddon said. "It's our talk that propelled you to make this choice. We can't stand by and let you—"

Katsa spoke deliberately. "If he knows you disobeyed him, he'll imprison you or kill you. He can't hurt me the way he can hurt you. I don't think his entire guard could capture me. And if they did, at least I don't have a holding that depends on me, as you do, Giddon. I don't have a wife, as you do, Oll."

Giddon's face was dark. He opened his mouth to speak, but Katsa cut through his words. "You two are no use if you're in prison. Raffin needs you. Wherever I may be, *I* will need you."

Giddon tried to speak. "I won't—"

She would make him see this. She would cut through his obtuseness and make him see this. She slammed her hand on the desk so hard that papers cascaded onto the floor. "I'll kill the king," she said. "I'll kill the king, unless you both agree not to support me. This is my rebellion, and mine alone, and if you don't agree, I swear to you on my Grace I will murder the king."

She didn't know if she would do it. But she knew she seemed wild enough for them to believe she would. She turned to Oll. "Say you agree."

Oll cleared his throat. "It will be as you say, My Lady."

She faced Giddon. "Giddon?"

"I don't like it," he said.

"Giddon—"

"It will be as you say," he said, his eyes on the floor and his face red and gloomy.

Katsa turned to Ellis. "Lord Ellis, if Randa learns that Captain Oll or Lord Giddon agreed to this willingly, I'll know that you spoke. I'll kill you. I'll kill your daughters. Do you understand?"

"I understand, My Lady," Ellis said. "And again, I thank you."

Something caught in her throat at this second thanks, when she'd threatened him so brutally. When you're a monster, she thought, you are thanked and praised for not behaving like a monster. She would like to restrain from cruelty and receive no admiration for it.

"And now in this room, with only ourselves present," she said, "we'll work out the details of what we'll claim happened here today."

THEY ATE DINNER in Giddon's dining room, in Giddon's castle, just as they had the night before. Giddon had given her permission to cut his neck with her knife, and Oll had allowed her to bruise his cheekbone. She would have done it without their permission, for she knew Randa would expect evidence of a scuffle. But Oll and Giddon had seen the wisdom of it; or perhaps they'd guessed she would do it whether or not they agreed. They'd stood still, and bravely. She hadn't enjoyed the task, but she'd caused them as little pain as her skill allowed.

There was not much conversation at dinner. Katsa broke bread, chewed, and swallowed. She stared at the fork and knife in her hands. She stared at her silver goblet.

"The Estillan lord," she said. The men's eyes jumped up from their plates. "The lord who took more lumber from Randa than he should have. You remember him?"

They nodded.

"I didn't hurt him," she said. "That is, I knocked him unconscious. But I didn't injure him." She put her knife and fork down, and looked from Giddon to Oll. "I couldn't. He more than paid for his crime in gold. I couldn't hurt him."

They watched her for a moment. Giddon's eyes dropped to his plate. Oll cleared his throat. "Perhaps the Council work has put us in touch with our better natures," he said.

Katsa picked up her knife and fork, cut into her mutton, and thought about that. She knew her nature. She would recognize it if she came face-to-face with it. It would be a blue-eyed, green-eyed monster, wolflike and snarling. A vicious beast that struck out at friends in uncontrollable anger, a killer that offered itself as the vessel of the king's fury.

But then, it was a strange monster, for beneath its exterior it was frightened and sickened by its own violence. It chastised itself for its savagery. And sometimes it had no heart for violence and rebelled against it utterly.

A monster that refused, sometimes, to behave like a monster. When a monster stopped behaving like a monster, did it stop being a monster? Did it become something else?

Perhaps she wouldn't recognize her own nature after all.

There were too many questions, and too few answers, at this dinner table in Giddon's castle. She would like to be traveling with Raffin, or Po, rather than Oll and Giddon; they would have answers, of one kind or another.

She must guard against using her Grace in anger. This was where her nature's struggle lay.

———

AFTER DINNER, she went to Giddon's archery range, hoping the thunk of arrows into a target would calm her mind. There, he found her.

She had wanted to be by herself. But when Giddon stepped out of the shadows, tall and quiet, she wished they were in a great hall with hundreds of people. A party even, she in a dress and horrible shoes. A dance. Any place other than alone with Giddon, where no one would stumble upon them and no one would interrupt.

"You're shooting arrows at a target in the dark," Giddon said.

She lowered her bow. She supposed this was one of his criticisms. "Yes," she said, for she could think of no other response.

"Are you as good a shot in the dark as you are in the light?"

"Yes," she said, and he smiled, which made her nervous. If he was going to be pleasant, then she feared where this was heading; she would much prefer him to be arrogant and critical, and unpleasant, if they must be alone together.

"There's nothing you cannot do, Katsa."

"Don't be absurd."

But he seemed determined not to argue. He smiled again and leaned against the wooden railing that separated her lane from the others. "What do you think will happen at Randa's court tomorrow?" he asked.

"Truly, I don't know," Katsa said. "Randa will be very angry."

"I don't like that you're protecting me from his anger, Katsa. I don't like it at all."

"I'm sorry, Giddon, as I'm sorry for the cut on your neck. Shall we return to the castle?" She lifted the strap of the quiver over her head, and set it on the ground. He watched her, quietly, and a small panic began to stir in her chest.

"You should let me protect you," he said.

"You can't protect me from the king. It would be fatal to you, and a waste of your energies. Let's go back to the castle."

"Marry me," he said, "and our marriage will protect you."

Well then, he had said it, as Po had predicted, and it hit her like one of Po's punches to the stomach. She didn't know where to look; she couldn't stand still. She put her hand to her head, she put it to the railing. She willed herself to think.

"Our marriage wouldn't protect me," she said. "Randa wouldn't pardon me simply because I married."

"But he would be more lenient," Giddon said. "Our engagement would offer him an alternative. It would be dangerous for him to try to punish you, and he knows that. If we say we're to be married, then he can send us away from court; he can send us here, and he'll be out of your reach, and you out of his. And there will be some pretense of good feeling between you."

And she would be married, and to Giddon. She would be his wife, the lady of his house. She'd be charged with entertaining his wretched guests. Expected to hire and dismiss his servants, based on their skill with a pastry, or some such nonsense. Expected to bear him children, and stay at home to love them. She would go to his bed at night, Giddon's bed, and lie with a man who considered a scratch to her face an affront to his person. A man who thought himself her protector—her protector when she could outduel him if she used a toothpick to his sword.

She breathed it away, breathed away the fury. He was a friend, and loyal to the Council. She wouldn't speak what she thought. She would speak what Raffin had told her to speak.

"Giddon," she said. "Surely you've heard I don't intend to marry."

"But would you refuse a suitable proposal? And you must admit, it seems a solution to your problem with the king."

"Giddon." He stood before her, his face even, his eyes warm. So confident. He didn't imagine she could refuse him. And perhaps that was forgivable, for perhaps no other woman would. "Giddon. You need a wife who will give you children. I've never wished children. You must marry a woman who wishes babies."

"You're not an unnatural woman, Katsa. You can fight as other women can't, but you're not so different from other women. You'll want babies. I'm certain of it."

She hadn't expected to have such an immediate opportunity to practice containing her temper. For he deserved a thumping, to knock his certainty out of his head and onto the ground where it belonged. "I can't marry you, Giddon. It's nothing to do with you. It's only to do with me. I won't marry, not anyone, and I won't bear any man children."

He stared at her then, and his face changed. She knew that look on Giddon's face, the sarcastic curl of his lip and the glint in his eye. He was beginning to hear her.

"I don't think you've considered what you're saying, Katsa. Do you expect ever to receive a more attractive proposal?"

"It's nothing to do with you, Giddon. It's only to do with me."

"Do you imagine there are others who would form an interest in a lady killer?"

"Giddon—"

"You're hoping the Lienid will ask for your hand." He pointed at her, his face mocking. "You prefer him, for he's a prince, and I'm only a lord."

Katsa threw her arms in the air. "Giddon, of all the preposterous—"

"He won't ask you," Giddon said, "and if he did you'd be a fool to accept. He's about as trustworthy as Murgon."

"Giddon, I assure you—"

"Nor is he honorable," Giddon said. "A man who fights you as he does is no better than an opportunist and no worse than a thug."

She froze. She stared at Giddon and didn't even see his finger jabbing in the air, his puffed-up face. Instead she saw Po, sitting on the floor of the practice room, using the exact words Giddon had just used. Before Giddon had used them.

"Giddon. Have you spoken those words to Po?"

"Katsa, I've never even had a conversation with him when you were not present."

"What about to anyone else? Have you spoken those words to anyone else?"

"Of course not. If you think I waste my time—"

"Are you certain?"

"Yes, I'm certain. What does it matter? If he asked me, I would not be afraid to tell him what I think."

She stared at Giddon, disbelieving, defenseless against the realization that trickled into her mind and clicked into place. She put her hand to her throat. She couldn't catch her breath. She asked the question she felt she had to ask, and cringed against the answer she knew she would receive.

"Have you had those thoughts before? Had you thought those things, while you were in his presence?"

"That I don't trust him? That he's an opportunist and a thug? I think of it every time I look at him."

Giddon was practically spitting, but Katsa didn't see. She bent her knees and set her bow on the ground, slowly, deliberately. She stood, and turned away from him. She walked, one step at a time. She breathed in and breathed out and stared straight ahead.

"You're afraid I'll cause him offense," Giddon yelled after her, "your precious Lienid prince. And perhaps I will tell him my opinion. Perhaps he'll leave more quickly if I encourage him."

She didn't listen, she didn't hear. For there was too much noise inside her head. He had known Giddon's thoughts. And he had known her own, she knew he had. When she'd been angry, when she'd thought highly of him. Other times, too.

There must be other times, though her head screamed too much for her to think of them.

She had thought him a fighter, just a fighter. And in her foolishness, she had thought him perceptive. Had even admired him for his perceptiveness.

She, admire a mind reader.

She had trusted him. She had trusted him, and she should not have. He had misrepresented himself, misrepresented his Grace. And that was the same as if he'd lied.

CHAPTER FOURTEEN

SHE BURST into Raffin's workrooms, and he looked up from his work, startled. "Where is he?" she demanded, and then she stopped in her tracks, because he was there, right there, sitting at the edge of Raffin's table, his jaw purple and his sleeves rolled up.

"There's something I must tell you, Katsa," he said.

"You're a mind reader," she said. "You're a mind reader, and you lied to me."

Raffin swore shortly and jumped up. He ran to the door behind her and pushed it closed.

Po's face flushed, but he held her gaze. "I'm not a mind reader," he said.

"And I'm not a fool," she yelled, "so stop lying to me. Tell me, what have you learned? What thoughts of mine have you stolen?"

"I'm not a mind reader," he said. "I sense people."

"And what's that supposed to mean? It's people's thoughts that you sense."

"No, Katsa. Listen. I sense people. Think of it as my night vision, Katsa, or the eyes in the back of my head you've accused me of having. I sense people when they're near me, thinking and feeling and moving around, their bodies, their physical energy. It is only—" He swallowed. "It is only when they're thinking about me that I also sense their thoughts."

"And that's not mind reading?" She screamed it so loudly that he flinched, but still he held her gaze.

"All right. It does involve some mind reading. But I can't do what you think I can do."

"You lied to me," she said. "I trusted you."

Raffin's soft voice broke through her distress. "Let him explain, Katsa."

She turned to Raffin, incredulous, flabbergasted that he should know the truth and still take Po's side. She whirled back on Po, who still dared to hold her eyes, as if he'd done nothing wrong, nothing completely and absolutely wrong.

"Please, Katsa," Po said. "Please hear me. I can't sit and listen in to whatever thoughts I want. I don't know what you think of Raffin, or what Raffin thinks of Bann, or whether Oll enjoys his dinner. You can be behind the door running in circles and thinking about how much you hate Randa, and all I'll know is that you're running in circles—until your thoughts turn to me. Only then do I know what you're feeling."

This was what it felt like to be betrayed by a friend. No. By a traitor pretending to be a friend. Such a wonderful friend he'd seemed, so sympathetic, so understanding—and no wonder, if he'd always known her thoughts, always known her feelings. The perfect pretense of friendship.

"No," he said. "No. I have lied, Katsa, but my friendship has not been a pretense. I've always been your true friend."

Even now he was reading her mind. "Stop it," she spat out. "Stop it. How dare you, you traitor, imposter, you . . ."

She couldn't find words strong enough. But his eyes dropped from hers now, miserably, and she saw that he felt her full meaning. She was cruelly glad his Grace communicated to him what she couldn't verbalize. He slumped against the table, his face contorted with unhappiness. His voice, when he spoke, toneless.

"Only two people have known this is my Grace: my mother and my grandfather. And now Raffin and you. My father doesn't know, nor my brothers. My mother and my grandfather forbade me to tell anyone, the moment I revealed it to them as a child."

Well. She would take care of that problem. For Giddon was right, though he couldn't have realized why. Po was not to be trusted. People must know, and she would tell everyone.

"If you do," Po said, "you'll take away any freedom I have. You'll ruin my life."

She looked at him then, but his image blurred behind tears that swelled into her eyes. She must leave. She must leave this room, because she wanted to hit him, as she had sworn she never would do. She wanted to cause him pain for taking a place in her heart that she wouldn't have given him if she'd known the truth.

"You lied to me," she said.

She turned and ran from the room.

———

HELDA TOOK her damp eyes, and her silence, in stride.

"I hope no one is ill, My Lady," she said. She sat beside Katsa's bath and worked soap through the knots in Katsa's hair.

"No one is ill."

"Then something has upset you," Helda said. "It'll be one of your young men."

One of her young men. One of her friends. Her list of friends was dwindling, from few to fewer. "I've disobeyed the king," she said. "He'll be very angry with me."

"Yes?" Helda said. "But that doesn't account for the pain in your eyes. That will be the doing of one of your young men."

Katsa said nothing. Everyone in this castle was a mind reader. Everyone could see through her, and she saw nothing.

"If the king is angry with you," Helda said, "and if you're having trouble with one of your young men, then we'll make you especially beautiful for the evening. You'll wear your red dress."

Katsa almost laughed at that bit of Helda logic, but the laugh got caught in her throat. She would leave the court after this night. For she didn't want to be here any longer, with her uncle's fury, Giddon's sarcastic, hurt pride, and, most of all, Po's betrayal.

LATER, WHEN Katsa was dressed and Helda grappled with her wet hair before the fire, there was a knock at her entrance. Katsa's heart flew into her throat, for it would be a steward, summoning her to her uncle; or even worse, Po, come to read her mind and hurt her again with his explanations and his excuses. But when Helda went to the door, she came back with Raffin.

"He's not the one I expected," Helda said. She folded her hands across her stomach and clucked.

Katsa pressed her fingers to her temples. "I must speak to him alone, Helda."

Helda left. Raffin sat on her bed and curled his legs up, as he had done when he was a child. As they both had done so many times, sitting together on her bed, talking and laughing. He didn't laugh now, and he didn't talk. He only sat, all arms and legs, and looked at her in her chair by the fire. His face kind and dear, and open with worry.

"That dress suits you, Kat," he said. "Your eyes are very bright."

"Helda imagines that a dress will solve all my problems," Katsa said.

"Your problems have multiplied since you last left the court. I spoke to Giddon."

"Giddon." His very name made her tired.

"Yes. He told me what happened with Lord Ellis. Honestly, Katsa. It's quite serious, isn't it? What will you do?"

"I don't know. I haven't decided."

"Honestly, Katsa."

"Why do you keep saying that? I suppose you think I should have tortured the fellow, for doing no wrong?"

"Of course not. You did right. Of course you did right."

"And the king won't control me anymore. I won't be his animal anymore."

"Kat." He shifted, and sighed. He looked at her closely. "I can see you've made up your mind. And you know I'll do anything in my power to stop his hand. I'm on your side in anything to do with Randa, always. It's just . . . it's just that . . ."

She knew. It was just that Randa paid little heed to his son the medicine maker. There was very little in Raffin's power to do, while his father lived.

"I'm worried for you, Kat," he said. "That's all. We all are. Giddon was quite desperate."

"Giddon." She sighed. "Giddon proposed marriage to me."

"Great hills. Before or after you saw Ellis?"

"After." She gestured impatiently. "Giddon thinks marriage is the solution to all my problems."

"Hmm. Well, how did it go?"

How did it go? She felt like laughing, though there was no humor in it. "It began badly and progressed to worse," she said, "and ended with my coming to the realization that Po is a mind reader. And a liar."

Raffin considered her for a moment. He started to speak, then stopped. His eyes were very gentle. "Dear Katsa," he finally said. "You've had a rough few days, what with Randa and Giddon and Po."

And Po the roughest, though all the danger might lie with Randa. Po the wound she would remove, if she could choose one to remove. Randa could never hurt her as Po had.

They sat quietly. The fire crackled beside her. The fire was a luxury; there was barely a chill to the air, but Helda had wanted her hair to dry more quickly, so they'd set the great logs burning. Her hair fell now in curls around her shoulders. She pushed it behind her ears and tied it into a knot.

"His Grace has been a secret since he was a child, Kat."

Here they came, then, the explanations and the rationalizations. She looked away from him and braced herself.

"His mother knew he'd only be used as a tool, if the truth came out. Imagine the uses of a child who can sense reactions to the things he says, or who knows what someone's doing on the other side of a wall. Imagine his uses when his father is the king. His mother knew he wouldn't be able to relate with people or form friendships, because no one would trust him. No one would want anything to do with him. Think about it, Katsa. Think about what that would be like."

She looked up at him then, her eyes on fire, and his face softened. "What a thing for me to say. Of course you don't need to imagine it."

No, for it was her reality. She hadn't had the luxury of hiding her Grace.

"We can't blame him for not telling us sooner," Raffin said. "To be honest, I'm touched that he told us at all. He told me just after you left. He has some ideas about the kidnapping, Kat."

Yes, as he must have ideas about a great many things he was in no position to know anything about. A mind reader could never be short on ideas. "What are his ideas?"

"Why don't you let him tell you about it?"

"I don't crave the company of a mind reader."

"He's leaving tomorrow, Kat."

She stared at him. "What do you mean, he's leaving?"

"He's leaving the court," Raffin said, "for good. He's going to Sunder, and then Monsea, possibly. He hasn't worked out the details."

Her eyes swam with tears. She seemed unable to control this strange water that flowed into her eyes. She stared at her hands, and one tear plopped into her palm.

"I think I'll send him," Raffin said, "to tell you about it."

He climbed from the bed and came to her. He bent down and kissed her forehead. "Dear Katsa," he said, and then he left the room.

She stared at the checked pattern of her marble floor and wondered how she could feel so desolate that her eyes filled with tears. She couldn't remember crying, not once in her life. Not until this fool Lienid had come to her court, and lied to her, and then announced that he was leaving.

HE HOVERED just inside the doorway; he seemed unsure whether to come closer or keep his distance. She didn't know what she wanted, either; she only knew she wanted to remain calm and not look at him and not think any thoughts for him to steal. She stood, crossed into her dining room, went to the window, and looked out. The courtyard was empty, and yellow in the light of the lowering sun. She felt him moving into the entrance behind her.

"Forgive me, Katsa," he said. "I beg you to forgive me."

Well, and that was easily answered. She did not forgive him.

The trees in Randa's garden were still green, and some of the flowers still in bloom. But soon the leaves would turn and fall. The gardeners would come with their great rakes, and scrape the leaves from the marble floor, and carry them away in wheelbarrows. She didn't know where they carried them. To the vegetable gardens, she guessed, or to the fields. They were industrious, the gardeners.

She did not forgive him.

She heard him move a step closer. "How . . . how did you know?" he asked. "If you would tell me?"

She rested her forehead on the glass pane. "And why don't you use your Grace to find the answer to that?"

He paused. "I could," he said, "possibly, if you were thinking about it specifically. But you're not, and I can't wander around inside you and retrieve any information I want. Any more than I can stop my Grace from showing me things I don't want."

She didn't answer.

"Katsa, all I know right now is that you're angry, furious, from the top of your head to your toes; and that I've hurt you, and that you don't forgive me. Or trust me. That's all I know at this moment. And my Grace only confirms what I see with my own eyes."

She sighed sharply, and spoke into the windowpane. "Giddon told me he didn't trust you. And when he told me, he used the same words you'd used before, the same words exactly. And"—she waved her hand in the air—"there were other hints. But Giddon's words made it clear."

He was closer now. Leaning against the table, most likely, with his hands in his pockets and his eyes on her back. She focused on the view outside. Two ladies crossed the courtyard below her, on each other's arms. The curls of their hair sat gathered at the tops of their heads and bobbed up and down.

"I haven't been very careful with you," he said. "Careful to hide it. I'd go so far as to say I've been careless at times." He paused, and his voice was quiet, as if he was talking down to his boots. "It's because I've wanted you to know."

And that did not absolve him. He had taken her thoughts without telling her, and he had wanted to tell her, and that did not begin to absolve him.

"I couldn't tell you, Katsa, not possibly," he said, and she swung around to face him.

"Stop it! Stop that! Stop responding to my thoughts!"

"I won't hide it from you, Katsa! I won't hide it anymore!"

He wasn't leaning against the table, hands in pockets. He was standing, clutching his hair. His face—she would not look at his face. She turned away, turned back to the window.

"I'm not going to hide it from you anymore, Katsa," he said again. "Please. Let me explain it. It's not as bad as you think."

"It's easy for you to say," she said. "You're not the one whose thoughts are not your own."

"Almost all of your thoughts are your own," he said. "My Grace only shows me how you stand in relation to *me*. Where you are nearby physically, and what you're doing; and any thoughts or feelings or instincts you have regarding me. I—I suppose it's meant to be a kind of self-preservation," he finished lamely. "Anyway, it's why I can fight you. I sense the movement of your body, without seeing it. And more to the point, I feel the energy of your intentions toward me. I know every move you intend to make against me, before you make it."

She almost couldn't breathe at that extraordinary statement. She wondered vaguely if this was how it felt to her victims, to be kicked in the chest.

"I know when someone wants to hurt me, and how," he said. "I know if a person looks on me kindly, or if he trusts me. I know if a person doesn't like me. I know when someone intends to deceive me."

"As you've deceived me," she said, "about being a mind reader."

He continued doggedly. "Yes, that's true. But all you've told me about your struggles with Randa, Katsa, I needed to hear from your mouth. All you've told me about Raffin, or Giddon. When I met you in Murgon's courtyard," he said. "Do you remember? When I met you, I didn't know why you were there. I couldn't look into your mind and know you were in the process of rescuing my grandfather from Murgon's dungeons. I wasn't even sure my grandfather was in the dungeons, for I hadn't gotten close enough to him to sense his physical presence yet. Nor had I spoken with Murgon; I'd learned nothing yet from Murgon's lies. I didn't know you'd attacked every guard in the castle. All I knew for sure was that you didn't know who I was, and you didn't know whether to trust me, but you didn't want to kill me, because I was Lienid, and possibly because of something to do with some other Lienid, though I couldn't be certain who, or how he factored into it. And also that you—I don't know how to explain it, but you *felt* trustworthy to me. That's all, that's all I knew. It was on the basis of that information that I decided to trust you."

"It must be convenient," she said bitterly, "to know if another person is trustworthy. We wouldn't be here now if I had that capability."

"I'm sorry," he said. "I can't tell you how sorry. I've hated not telling you. It's rankled me every day since we became friends."

"We are not friends." She whispered it into the glass of the window.

"If you're not my friend, then I have no friends."

"Friends don't lie," she said.

"Friends try to understand," he said. "How could I have become your friend without lying? How much have I risked to tell you and Raffin the truth? What would you have done differently, Katsa, if this were your Grace and your secret? Hidden yourself in a hole and dared to burden no one with your grievous friendship? I will have friends, Katsa. I will have a life, even though I carry this burden."

He stopped for a moment, his voice rough and choked, and Katsa fought against his distress, fought to keep it from touching her. She found that she was gripping the window frame very hard.

"You would have me friendless, Katsa," he finished quietly. "You would have my Grace control every aspect of my life and shut me off from every happiness."

She didn't want to hear these words, words that called to her sympathy, to her understanding. She who had hurt so many with her own Grace, and been reviled because of it. She who still struggled to keep her Grace from mastering her, and who, like him, had never asked for the power it gave her.

"Yes," he said, "I didn't ask for this. I would turn it off for you, if I could."

Rage then, rage again, because she couldn't even feel sympathy without him knowing it. This was madness. She could not comprehend the madness of this situation. How did his mother relate to him? Or his grandfather? How could anyone?

She took a breath and tried to consider it, piece by piece.

"Your fighting," she said, her eyes on the darkening court-yard. "You expect me to believe your fighting isn't Graced?"

"I'm an exceptional natural fighter," he said. "All of my brothers are. The royal family is well-known in Lienid for hand fighting. But my Grace—it's an enormous advantage in a fight, to anticipate every move your opponent makes against you. Combine with that my immediate sense of your body, a sense that goes beyond sight—you can understand why no one has ever beaten me, save you."

She thought about that and found she couldn't believe it. "But you're too good. You must have a fighting Grace as well. You couldn't fight me so well if you didn't."

"Katsa," he said, "think about it. You're five times the fighter I am. When we fight, you're holding back—don't tell me you aren't, because I know you are—and I'm not holding back, not a bit. And you can do anything you want to me, and I can't hurt you—"

"It hurts when you strike me—"

"It hurts you for only an instant, and besides, if I hit you it's only because you've let me, because you're too busy wrenching my arm out of its socket to care that I'm hitting you in the stomach. How long do you think it would take you to kill me, or break my bones, if you decided to?"

If she truly decided to?

He was right. If her purpose were to hurt him, to break his arm or his neck, she didn't think it would take her very long.

"When we fight," he said, "you go to great pains to win without hurting me. That you usually can is a mark of your phenomenal skill. I've never hurt you once, and believe me, I've tried."

"It's a front," she said. "The fighting is only a front."

"Yes. My mother seized on it the instant it became clear that I shared the skill of my brothers, and that my Grace magnified that skill."

"Why didn't you know I would strike you," she said, "in Murgon's courtyard?"

"I did know," he said, "but only in the last instant, and I didn't react quickly enough. Until that first strike, I didn't realize your speed. I'd never encountered the like of it before."

The mortar was cracking in the frame of the window. She pulled out a small chunk and rolled it between her fingers. "Does your Grace make mistakes? Or are you always right?"

He breathed; it almost sounded like a laugh. "It's not always exact. And it's always changing. I'm still growing into it. My sense of the physical is pretty reliable, as long as I'm not in an enormous crowd. I know where people are and what they're doing. But what they feel toward me—there's never been a time when I thought someone was lying and they weren't. Or a time when I thought someone intended to hit me and they didn't. But there are times when I'm not sure— when I have a sense of something but I'm not sure. Other people's feelings can be very . . . complicated, and difficult to understand."

She hadn't thought of that, that a person might be difficult to understand, even to a mind reader.

"I'm more sure of things now than I used to be," he said. "When I was a child I was rarely sure. These enormous waves of energy and feeling and thought were always crashing into me, and most of the time I was drowning in them. For one thing, it's taken me a long time to learn to distinguish between thoughts that matter and thoughts that don't. Thoughts that are just thoughts, fleeting, and thoughts that carry some kind of relevant intent. I've gotten much better at that, but my Grace still gives me things I've no idea what to do with."

It sounded ridiculous to her, thoroughly ridiculous. And she had thought her own Grace overwhelming. Alongside his, it seemed quite straightforward.

"It's hard to get a handle on it sometimes," he said, "my Grace."

She turned sideways for a moment. "Did you say that because I thought it?"

"No. I said it because I thought it."

She turned back to the window. "I thought it, too," she said. "Or something like it."

"Well," he said. "I imagine it's a feeling you would understand."

She sighed again. There were things about this she could understand, though she didn't want to. "How close do you have to be to someone, physically, for your Grace to sense them?"

"It differs. And it's changed over time."

"What do you mean?"

"If it's someone I know well," he said, "my range is broad. For strangers, I need to be closer. I knew when you neared the castle today; I knew when you burst into the courtyard and leaped out of your saddle, and I felt your anger strong and clear as you flew up to Raffin's rooms. My range for you is . . . broader than most."

It was darker outside now than it was in her dining room. She saw him, suddenly, in the reflection of the window. He was leaning back against the table, as she had pictured him before. His face, his shoulders, his arms sagged. Everything about him sagged. He was unhappy. He was looking down at his feet, but as she watched him he raised his eyes, and met hers in the glass. She felt the tears again, suddenly, and she grasped at something to say.

"Do you sense the presence of animals and plants? Rocks and dirt?"

"I'm leaving," he said, "tomorrow."

"Do you know when an animal is near?"

"Will you turn around," he said, "so I can see you while we speak?"

"Can you read my mind more easily when I'm facing you?"

"No. I'd just like to see you, Katsa. That's all."

His voice was soft, and sorry. He was sorry about all of this, sorry for his Grace. His Grace that was not his fault and that would have driven her away had he told her of it at the beginning.

She turned to face him.

"I didn't used to sense animals and plants or landscapes," he said, "but lately that's been changing. Sometimes I'll get a fuzzy sense of something that isn't human. If something moves, I might sense it. It's erratic."

Katsa watched his face.

"I'm going to Sunder," he said.

Katsa folded her arms across her stomach and said nothing.

"When Murgon questioned me after your rescue, it became obvious to me the object you'd taken was my grandfather. It became just as obvious Murgon had been keeping him for someone else. But I couldn't tell who, not without asking questions that would've given away what I knew."

She listened vaguely. She was tired, overwhelmed by too

many things in the present to focus on the details of the kidnapping.

"I'm beginning to think it's something to do with Monsea," he said. "We've ruled out the Middluns, Wester, Nander, Estill, Sunder—and you'll remember, I've been to most of those courts. I know I was not lied to, except in Sunder. Lienid is not responsible, I'm sure of it."

She'd lost her fury, somewhere, as they'd talked. She didn't feel it anymore. She wished she did, because she preferred it to the emptiness that had settled in its place. She was sorry for everything that had changed now with Po. Sorry to see it all go.

"Katsa," he said. "I need you to listen to me."

She blinked and worked her mind back to the words he had spoken.

"But King Leck of Monsea is a kind man," she said. "He would have no reason."

"He might," he said, "though I don't know what it is. Something isn't right, Katsa. Some impressions I got from Murgon that I dismissed at the time, perhaps I dismissed them in error. And my father's sister, Queen Ashen, she wouldn't behave as you told me. She's so stoical, she is strong. She wouldn't have hysterics and lock herself and her child away from her husband. I swear to you, if you knew her . . ."

He stopped, his brow furrowed. He kicked the floor. "I've a feeling Monsea has something to do with it. I don't know if it's my Grace, or just instinct. Anyway, I'm going back to

Sunder, to see what I can learn of it. Grandfather's doing better, but for his own sake I want him to stay hidden until I get
to the bottom of this."

That was it, then. He was going to Sunder, to get to the
bottom of it. And it was good that he was going, for she didn't
want him in her head.

But neither did she want him to go. And he must know
that, since she had thought it. And now, did he know that she
knew that he knew, since she had thought that, too?

This was absurd, it was impossible. Being with him was
impossible.

But still she didn't want him to go.

"I hoped you would come with me," he said, and she
stared at him, openmouthed. "We'd make a good team. I don't
even know where I'm going, for sure. But I hoped you would
consider coming. If you're still my friend."

She couldn't think what to say. "Doesn't your Grace tell
you if I'm your friend?"

"Do you know, yourself?"

She tried to think, but there was nothing in her mind. She
knew only that she was numb and sad and completely without any clarity of feeling.

"I can't know your feelings," he said, "if you don't know
them yourself."

He looked to the door suddenly; and then there was a
knock, and a steward burst in without waiting for Katsa's response. At the sight of his pale, tight face, it all came flooding
back to her. Randa. Randa wanted to see her, most likely

wanted to kill her. Before this confusion with Po, she had disobeyed Randa.

"The king orders you to come before him at once, My Lady," the steward said. "Forgive me, My Lady. He says that if you don't, he'll send his entire guard to fetch you."

"Very well," Katsa said. "Tell him I'll go to him immediately."

"Thank you, My Lady." The steward turned and scampered away.

Katsa scowled after him. "His entire guard. What does he think they could do to me? I should've told the steward to send them, just for the amusement of it." She looked around the room. "I wonder if I should take a knife."

Po watched her with narrowed eyes. "What have you done? What's this about?"

"I've disobeyed him. He sent me to torture some poor, innocent lord, and I decided I wouldn't. Do you think I should take a knife?" She walked across to her weapons room.

He followed her. "To do what? What do you think will happen at this meeting?"

"I don't know, I don't know. Oh, Po, if he angers me, I fear I'll want to kill him. And what if he threatens me and gives me no choice?" She threw herself into a chair and dropped her head down on the Council table. How could she go to Randa now, of all times, when there was a whirlwind in her head? She would lose herself at the sound of his voice. She would do something dreadful.

Po slid into the chair next to her and sat sideways, facing

her. "Katsa," he said. "Listen to me. You're the most powerful person I've ever met. You can do whatever you want, whatever you want in the world. No one can make you do anything, and your uncle can't touch you. The instant you walk into his presence, you have all the power. If you wish not to hurt him, Katsa, then you have only to choose not to."

"But what will I do?"

"You'll figure it out," Po said. "You only have to go in knowing what you won't do. You won't hurt him, you won't let him hurt you. You'll figure the rest out as you go along."

She sighed into the table. She didn't think much of his plan.

"It's the only possible plan, Katsa. You have the power to do whatever you want."

She sat up and turned to him. "You keep saying that, but it's not true," she said. "I don't have the power to stop you from sensing my thoughts."

He raised his eyebrows. "You could kill me."

"I couldn't," she said, "for you would know I meant to kill you, and you'd escape me. You'd stay far away from me, always."

"Ah, but I wouldn't."

"You would," she said, "if I wished to kill you."

"I wouldn't."

On that senseless note she threw her arms into the air. "Enough. Enough of this." She stood up from the table, and marched out of her apartments to answer the king's call.

CHAPTER FIFTEEN

HER FIRST THOUGHT when she entered the throne room was to wish she'd brought a knife after all. Her second thought was to wish that Po's sense of bodies had extended to this room, so that he might have warned her of what was waiting for her here, and she might have known not to come.

A long, blue carpet led from the doors to Randa's throne. The throne was raised high on a platform of white marble. Randa sat high on his throne, blue robes and bright blue eyes. His face hard, his smile frozen. An archer to either side of him, an arrow notched in each bow and trained, as she entered the room, on her forehead, on the place just above her blue and green eyes. Two more archers, one in each far corner, also with arrows notched.

The king's guard lined the carpet on either side, three men deep, swords drawn and held at their sides. Randa usually kept a tenth this many guards in his throne room. Impressive; it was an impressive battalion Randa had arranged in preparation for her appearance. But as Katsa took stock of the room, it occurred to her that Birn or Drowden or Thigpen would have done better. It was good he was an unwarring king, for Randa was not so clever when it came to assembling battalions. This one, he'd assembled all wrong. Too few archers, and too many of these clumsy, armored, lumbering men who would trip all over each other if they tried to attack her. Tall, broad men who could shield her easily from an arrow's flight. And armed, all of them armed with swords, and each with a dagger in his opposite belt, swords and daggers she might as well be carrying on her own person, so easily could she snatch them from their owners. And the king himself raised high on a platform, a long blue carpet leading straight to him like a pathway to direct the flight of her blade.

If a fight erupted in this room, it would be a massacre.

Katsa stepped forward, her eyes and ears finely tuned to the archers. Randa's archers were good, but they were not Graced. Katsa spared a moment to drily pity the guards at her back, if this encounter came down to arrow dodging.

And then, when she'd progressed about halfway to the throne, her uncle called out. "Stop there. I've no wish for your closer company, Katsa." Her name sounded like steam hissing down the carpet when Randa spoke it. "You return to court today with no woman. No dowry. My underlord and my captain injured by your hand. What do you have to say for yourself?"

When a battalion of soldiers didn't trouble her, why should one voice rile her so? She forced herself to hold his contemptuous eyes. "I didn't agree with your order, Lord King."

"Can I possibly have heard you correctly? You didn't agree with my order?"

"No, Lord King."

Randa sat back, his smile twisted tighter now. "Charming," he said. "Charming, truly. Tell me, Katsa. What, pre-cisely, possessed you with the notion that you are in a position to consider the king's orders? To think about them? To form opinions regarding them? Have I ever asked you to share your thoughts on anything?"

"No, Lord King."

"Have I ever encouraged you to bestow upon us your sage advice?"

"No, Lord King."

"Do you imagine it is your wit, your stunning intellect, that warrants your position in this court?"

And here was where Randa was clever. This was how he'd kept her a caged animal for so long. He knew the words to make her feel stupid and brutish and turn her into a dog.

Well, and if she must be a dog, at least she would no longer be in this man's cage. She would be her own, she would possess her own viciousness, and she would do what she liked with it. Even now, she felt her arms and legs beginning to thrill with readiness. She narrowed her eyes at the king. She could not keep the challenge out of her voice.

"And what exactly is the purpose of all these men, Uncle?"

Randa smiled blandly. "These men will attack if you make the slightest move. And at the end of this interview they'll ac-company you to my dungeons."

"And do you imagine I'll go willingly to your dungeons?"

"I don't care if you go willingly or not."

"That's because you think these men could force me to go against my will."

"Katsa. Of course we all have the highest regard for your skill. But even you have no chance against two hundred guards and my best archers. The end of this conversation will see you either in my dungeons, or dead."

Katsa saw and heard everything in the room. The king and his archers; the arrows notched and aimed; the guards ready with their swords; her arms in red sleeves, her feet beneath red skirts. The room was still, completely still, excepting the breath of the men around her, and the tingling she felt inside her. She held her hands at her sides, away from her body, so that everyone could see them. She breathed around a thing that she recognized now as hatred. She hated this king. Her body was alive with it.

"Uncle," she said. "Let me explain what will happen the instant one of your men makes a move toward me. Let's say, for instance, one of your archers lets an arrow fly. You've not come to many of my practices, Uncle. You haven't seen me dodge arrows; but your archers have. If one of your archers releases an arrow, I'll drop to the floor. The arrow will doubt-less hit one of your guards. The sword and the dagger of that guard will be in my hands before anyone in the room has time to realize what's happened. A fight will break out with the guards; but only seven or eight of them can surround me at once, Uncle, and seven or eight are nothing to me. As I kill the guards I'll take their daggers and begin throwing them into the hearts of your archers, who of course will have no sight-ing on me once the brawl with the guards has broken out. I'll get out of the room alive, Uncle; but most of the rest of you will be dead. Of course, this is only what will happen if I wait for one of your men to make a move. I could move first. I could attack a guard, steal his dagger, and hurl it into your chest this instant."

Randa's mouth was fixed into a sneer, but under this he had begun to tremble. A threat of death, given and received; and Katsa felt it ringing in her fingertips. And she saw that she could do it now, she could kill him right now. The disdain in his eyes would disappear, and his sneer would slide away. Her fingers itched, for she could do it now with the snatch of a dagger.

And then what? a small voice inside herself whispered; and Katsa caught her breath, stricken. And then what? A bloodbath, one she'd be lucky to escape. Raffin would become king, and his first inheritance would be the task of killing the murderer of his father. A charge he couldn't avoid if he meant to rule justly as the King of the Middluns; and a charge that would break his heart, and make her an enemy, and a stranger.

And Po would hear of it as he was leaving. He'd hear that she'd lost control and killed her uncle, that she'd caused her own exile and broken Raffin's spirit. He would return to Lienid and watch from his balcony as the sun dropped behind the sea; and he'd shake his head in the orange light and wonder why she'd allowed this to happen, when she held so much power in her hands.

Where is your faith in your power? the voice whispered now. *You don't have to shed blood.* And Katsa saw what she was doing, here in this throne room. She saw Randa, pale, gripping the arms of his throne so hard it seemed he might break them. In a moment he would motion to his archers to strike, out of fear, out of the terror of waiting for her to make the first move.

Tears came to her eyes. Mercy was more frightening than murder, because it was harder, and Randa didn't deserve it. And even though she wanted what the voice wanted, she didn't think she had the courage for it.

Po thinks you have the courage, the voice said fiercely. *Pretend that you believe he's right. Believe him, for just a moment.*

Pretend. Her fingers were screaming, but maybe she could pretend long enough to get out of this room.

Katsa raised burning eyes to the king. Her voice shook. "I'm leaving the court," she said. "Don't try to stop me. I promise you'll regret it if you do. Forget about me once I'm gone, for I won't consent to live like a tracked animal. I'm no longer yours to command."

His eyes were wide, and his mouth open. She turned and rushed down the long carpet, her ears tuned to the silence, readying her to spin around at the first hint of a bowstring or a sword. As she passed through her uncle's great doors she felt the weight of hundreds of astonished eyes on her back; and none of them knew she had been only a breath, a twitch, away from changing her mind.

PART TWO

The Twisted King

CHAPTER SIXTEEN

THEY LEFT well before daylight. Raffin and Bann saw them off, the two medicine makers bleary-eyed, Bann yawning endlessly. The morning was cold, and Katsa was wide awake, and quiet. For she was shy of her riding partner; and she felt strange about Raffin, so strange that she wished he wasn't there. If Raffin hadn't been there watching her go, then perhaps she'd have been able to pretend she wasn't leaving him. With Raffin there, there was no pretense, and she was unable to do anything about the strange painful water that rose into her eyes and throat, every time she looked at him.

They were impossible, these two men, for if one did not make her cry, the other did. What Helda would make of it she could only imagine; and she hadn't liked saying good-bye to Helda either, or Oll. No, there was little to be happy of this morning, except that she was not, at least, leaving Po; and he was probably standing there beside his horse registering her every feeling on the matter. She gave him a withering look for good measure, and he raised his eyebrows and smiled and yawned. Well. And he'd better not ride as if he were half asleep, or she'd leave him in the dust. She was not in the mood to dawdle.

Raffin fussed back and forth between their horses, checking saddles, testing the holds of their stirrups. "I suppose I needn't worry about your safety," he said, "with the two of you riding together."

"We'll be safe." Katsa yanked at a strap that held a bag to her saddle. She tossed a bag over her horse's back to Po.

"You have the list of Council contacts in Sunder?" Raffin asked. "And the maps? You have food for the day? You have money?"

Katsa smiled up at him then, for he sounded as she imagined a mother would sound if her child were leaving forever. "Po's a prince of Lienid," she said. "Why do you think he rides such a big horse, if not to carry his bags of gold?"

Raffin's eyes laughed down at her. "Take this." He closed her hands over a small satchel. "It's a bag of medicines, in case you should need them. I've marked them so you'll know what each is for."

Po came forward then and held his hand out to Bann. "Thank you for all you've done." He took Raffin's hand. "You'll take care of my grandfather in my absence?"

"He'll be safe with us," Raffin said.

Po swung onto the back of his horse, and Katsa took Bann's hands and squeezed them. And then she stood before Raffin and looked up into his face.

"Well," Raffin said. "You'll let us know how you're faring, when you're able?"

"Of course," Katsa said.

He looked at his feet and cleared his throat. He rubbed his neck, and sighed. How she wished again that he weren't here. For the tears would spill onto her cheeks, and she couldn't stop them.

"Well," Raffin said. "And I'll see you again someday, my love."

She reached up for him then and wrapped her arms around his neck, and he lifted her up off the ground and hugged her tight. She breathed into the collar of his shirt and held on.

And then her feet were on the ground again. She turned away and climbed into her saddle. "We leave now," she said to Po. As their horses cantered out of the stable yard, she didn't look back.

THEIR ROUTE was rough and changeable, for their only certain plan was to follow whatever path seemed likely to bring them closer to the truth of the kidnapping. Their first destination was an inn, south of Murgon City, three days' ride from Randa City—an inn sitting along the route which they supposed the kidnappers had taken. Murgon's spies frequented the inn, as did merchants and travelers from the port cities of Sunder, often even from Monsea. It was as good a place to start as any, Po thought, and it didn't take them out of their way, if their ultimate destination was Monsea.

They didn't travel anonymously. Katsa's eyes identified her to anyone in the seven kingdoms who had ears to hear the stories. Po was conspicuously a Lienid and enough the subject of idle talk to be recognized by virtue of his own eyes and by the

Graceling company he kept. The story of Katsa's hasty departure from Randa's court with the Lienid prince would spread. Any attempt to disguise themselves would be foolish; Katsa didn't even bother to change from the blue tunic and trousers that marked her as a member of Randa's family. Their purpose would be assumed, for it was well enough agreed that the Graceling Lienid searched for his missing grandfather, and it would now be supposed that the Graceling lady assisted him. Their inquiries, the route they chose, the very dinners they ate would be the stuff of gossip.

But still, they would be safe in their deception. For no one would know that Katsa and Po searched not for the grandfather but for the motive of his kidnapping. No one would know that Katsa and Po knew of Murgon's involvement and suspected Leck of Monsea. And no one could even guess how much Po could learn by asking the most mundane questions.

He rode well, and almost as fast as she would have liked. The trees of the southern forest flew past. The pounding of hooves comforted her and numbed her sense of the distance stretching between her and the people she'd left behind.

She was glad of Po's company. Their riding was companionable. But then when they stopped to stretch their legs and eat something, she was shy of him again, and didn't know how to be with him, or what to say.

"Sit with me, Katsa."

He sat on the trunk of a great fallen tree, and she glared at him from around her horse.

"Katsa," he said. "Dear Katsa, I won't bite. I'm not sensing your thoughts right now, except to know that I make you uncomfortable. Come and talk to me."

And so she came and sat beside him, but she didn't talk, and she didn't exactly look at him either, for she was afraid of becoming trapped in his eyes.

"Katsa," he said finally, when they had sat and chewed in silence for a number of minutes, "you'll get used to me, in time. We'll find the way to relate to each other. How can I help you with this? Should I tell you whenever I sense something with my Grace? So you can come to understand it?"

It didn't sound very appealing to her. She'd prefer to pretend that he sensed nothing. But he was right. They were together now, and the sooner she faced this, the better.

"Yes," she said.

"Very well then, I will. Do you have any questions for me? You have only to ask."

"I think," she said, "if you always know what I feel about you, then you should always tell me what you're feeling about me, as you feel it. Always."

"Hmm." He glanced at her sideways. "I'm not wild about that idea."

"Nor am I wild about you knowing my feelings, but I have no choice."

"Hmmm." He rubbed his head. "I suppose, in theory, it'd be fair."

"It would."

"Very well, let's see. I'm very sympathetic about your having left Raffin. I think you're brave to have defied Randa as you did with that Ellis fellow; I don't know if I could've gone through with it. I think you have more energy than anyone I've ever encountered, though I wonder if you aren't a bit hard on your horse. I find myself wondering why you haven't wanted to marry Giddon, and if it's because you've intended to marry Raffin, and if so, whether you're even more unhappy to have left him than I realized. I'm very pleased you've come with me. I'd like to see you defend yourself for real, fight someone to the death, for it would be a thrilling sight. I think my mother would take to you. My brothers, of course, would worship you. I think you're the most quarrelsome person I've ever met. And I really do worry about your horse."

He stopped then, broke a piece of bread, and chewed and swallowed. She stared at him, her eyes wide.

"That's all, for now," he said.

"You can't possibly have been thinking all those things, in that moment," she said, and then he laughed, and the sound was a comfort to her, and she fought against the gold and silver lights that shone in his eyes, and lost. When he spoke, his voice was soft.

"And now I'm wondering," he said, "how it is you don't realize your eyes ensnare me, just as mine do you. I can't explain it, Katsa, but you shouldn't let it embarrass you. For we're both overtaken by the same—foolishness."

A flush rose into her neck, and she was doubly embarrassed, by his eyes and by his words. But there was relief for her, too. Because if he was also foolish, then her foolishness bothered her less.

"I thought you might be doing it on purpose," she said, "with your eyes. I thought it might be a part of your Grace, to trap me with your eyes and read my mind."

"It's not. It's nothing like that."

"Most people won't look into my eyes," she said. "Most people fear them."

"Yes. Most people don't look into my eyes for very long either. They're too strange."

She looked at his eyes then, leaned in and really studied them, as she hadn't had the courage to do before. "Your eyes are like lights. They don't seem quite natural."

He grinned. "My mother says when I opened my eyes on the day they settled, she almost dropped me, she was so startled."

"What color were they before?"

"Gray, like most Lienid. And yours?"

"I've no idea. No one's ever told me, and I don't think there's anyone left I could ask."

"Your eyes are beautiful," he said, and she felt warm suddenly, warm in the sun that dappled through the treetops and rested on them in patches. And as they climbed back into their saddles and returned to the forest road, she didn't feel exactly comfortable with him; but she felt at least that she could look him in the face now and not fear she was surrendering her entire soul.

THE ROAD LED them around the outskirts of Murgon City and became wider and more traveled. Whenever Katsa and Po were seen, they were stared at. It would soon be known in the inns and houses around the city that the two Graceling fighters traveled south together along Murgon Road.

"Are you sure you don't want to stop in on King Murgon," Katsa said, "and ask him your questions? It would be much faster, wouldn't it?"

"He made it quite clear after the robbery that I was no longer welcome at his court. He suspects I know what was stolen."

"He's afraid of you."

"Yes, and he's the type to do something foolish. If we arrived at his court he'd probably mount an offensive, and we'd have to start hurting people. I'd prefer to avoid that, wouldn't you? If there's going to be an enormous mess, let it be at the court of the guilty king, not the king who's merely complicitous."

"We'll go to the inn."

"Yes," Po said. "We'll go to the inn."

The forest road narrowed again and grew quieter once they left Murgon City behind. They stopped before night fell. They set up camp some distance from the road, in a small clearing with a mossy floor, a cover of thick branches, and a trickle of water that seemed to please the horses.

"This is all a man needs," Po said. "I could live here, quite contented. What do you think, Katsa?"

"Are you hungry for meat? I'll catch us something."

"Even better," he said. "But it'll be dark in a few minutes. I wouldn't want you to get lost, even in the pitch dark."

Katsa smiled then and stepped across the stream. "It'll only take me a few minutes. And I never get lost, even in the pitch dark."

"You won't even take your bow? Are you planning to throttle a moose with your bare hands, then?"

"I've a knife in my boot," she said, and then wondered, for a moment, if she *could* throttle a moose with her bare hands. It seemed possible. But right now she only sought a rabbit or a bird, and her knife would serve as weapon. She slipped between the gnarled trees and into the damp silence of the forest. It was simply a matter of listening, remaining quiet, and making herself invisible.

When she came back minutes later with a great, fat, skinned rabbit, Po had built a fire. The flames cast orange light on the horses and on himself. "It was the least I could do," Po said, drily, "and I see you've already skinned that hare. I'm beginning to think I won't have much responsibility as we travel through the forest together."

"Does it bother you? You're welcome to do the hunting yourself. Perhaps I can stay by the fire and mend your socks, and scream if I hear any strange noises."

He smiled then. "Do you treat Giddon like this, when the two of you travel? I imagine he finds it quite humiliating."

"Poor Po. You may content yourself with reading my mind, if you wish to feel superior."

He laughed. "I know you're teasing me. And you should know I'm not easily humiliated. You may hunt for my food, and pound me every time we fight, and protect me when we're attacked, if you like. I'll thank you for it."

"But I'd never need to protect you, if we were attacked. And I doubt you need me to do your hunting, either."

"True. But you're better than I am, Katsa. And it doesn't humiliate me." He fed a branch to the fire. "It humbles me. But it doesn't humiliate me."

She sat quietly as night closed in and watched the blood drip from the hunk of meat she held on a stick over the fire. She listened to it sizzle as it hit the flames. She tried to separate in her mind the idea of being humbled from the idea of being humiliated, and she understood what Po meant. She wouldn't have thought to make the distinction. He was so clear with his thoughts, while hers were a constant storm that she could never make sense of and never control. She felt suddenly and sharply that Po was smarter than she, worlds smarter, and that she was a brute in comparison. An unthinking and unfeeling brute.

"Katsa."

She looked up. The flames danced in the silver and gold of his eyes and caught the hoops in his ears. His face was all light.

"Tell me," he said. "Whose idea was the Council?"

"It was mine."

"And who has decided what missions the Council carries out?"

"I have, ultimately."

"Who has planned each mission?"

"I have, with Raffin and Oll and the others."

He watched his meat cooking over the fire. He turned it, and shook it absently, so the juice fell spitting into the flames. He raised his eyes to her again.

"I don't see how you can compare us," he said, "and find yourself lacking in intelligence, or unthinking or unfeeling. I've had to spend my entire life hammering out the emotions of others, and myself, in my mind. If my mind is clearer, sometimes, than yours, it's because I've had more practice. That's the only difference between us."

He focused on his meat again. She watched him, listening.

"I wish you would remember the Council," he said. "I wish you would remember that when we met, you were rescuing my grandfather, for no other reason than that you didn't believe he deserved to be kidnapped."

He leaned into the fire then and added another branch to the flames. They sat quietly, huddled in the light, surrounded by darkness.

CHAPTER SEVENTEEN

In the morning, she woke before he did. She followed the dribble of water downstream, until she found a place where it formed something larger than a puddle but smaller than a pool. There she bathed as well as she could. She shivered, but she didn't mind the coldness of air and water; it woke her completely. When she tried to untie her hair and untangle it she met with the usual frustration. She yanked and tugged, but her fingers could not find a way through the knots. She tied it back up. She dried herself as best she could, and dressed. When she walked back into the clearing, he was awake, tying his bags together.

"Would you cut my hair off, if I asked you?"

He looked up, eyebrows raised. "You're not thinking of trying to disguise yourself?"

"No, it's not that. It's just that it drives me mad, and I've never wanted it, and I'd be so much more comfortable if I could have it all off."

"Hmm." He examined the great knot gathered at the nape of her neck. "It is rather wound together, like a bird's nest," he said, and at her glare, he laughed. "If you truly wanted me to, I could cut it off, but I don't imagine you'd be particularly pleased with the result. Why don't you wait until we've reached the inn and have the innkeeper's wife do it, or one of the women in town?"

Katsa sighed. "Very well. I can live with it for one more day."

Po disappeared down the path from which she'd come. She rolled up her blanket and began to carry their belongings to the horses.

THE ROAD grew narrower as they continued south, and the forest grew thicker and darker. Po led, despite Katsa's protests. He insisted that when she set the pace, they always started out reasonably, but without fail, before long they were racing along at breakneck speed. He was taking it upon himself to protect Katsa's horse from its rider.

"You say you're thinking of the horse," Katsa said, when they stopped once to water the horses at a stream that crossed the road. "But I think it's just that you can't keep up with me."

He laughed at that. "You're trying to bait me, and it won't work."

"By the way," Katsa said, "it occurs to me that we haven't practiced our fighting since I uncovered your deception and you agreed to stop lying to me."

"No, nor since you punched me in the jaw because you were angry with Randa."

She couldn't hold back her smile. "Fine," she said. "You'll lead. But what about our practices? Don't you want to continue them?"

"Of course," he said. "Tonight, perhaps, if it's still light when we stop."

They rode quietly. Katsa's mind wandered; and she found that when it wandered to anything to do with Po, she would check herself and proceed carefully. If she must think of him, then it would be nothing significant. He would gain nothing from his intrusions into her mind as they rode along this quiet forest path.

It occurred to her how susceptible he must be to intrusions. What if he were working out some complicated problem in his mind, concentrating very hard, and a great crowd of people approached? Or even a single person, who saw him and thought his eyes strange or admired his rings or wanted to buy his horse. Did he lose his concentration when other people filtered into his mind? How aggravating that would be.

And then she wondered: Could she get his attention, without saying a word? If she needed his help or wanted to stop, could she call to him in his mind? It must be possible; if a person within his range wanted to communicate with him, he must know it.

She looked at him, riding before her, his back straight and his arms steady; his white shirtsleeves rolled to the elbows, as always. She looked at the trees then, and at her horse's ears, and at the ground before her. She cleared her mind of anything to do with Po. I'll hunt down a goose for dinner, she thought. The leaves on these trees are just beginning to change color. The weather is so lovely and cool.

And then, with all her might, she focused her attention

on the back of Po's head and screamed his name, inside her mind. He pulled on his reins so hard that his horse screeched and staggered and almost sat down. Her own horse nearly collided with his. And he looked so startled and flabbergasted— and irritated—that she couldn't help it: She exploded with laughter.

"What in the name of Lienid is wrong with you? Are you trying to scare me out of my wits? Is it not enough to ruin your own horse, but you must ruin mine as well?"

She knew he was angry, but she couldn't stop laughing. "Forgive me, Po. I was only trying to get your attention."

"And I suppose it never occurs to you to start small. If I told you my roof needed rebuilding, you'd start by knocking down the house."

"Oh, Po," she said, "don't be angry." She stifled the laugh that rose into her throat. "Truly, Po, I had no idea it would startle you like that. I didn't think I *could* startle you. I didn't think your Grace allowed it."

She coughed, and forced her face into a mask of penitence, which wouldn't have fooled even the most incompetent of mind readers. But she hadn't meant it, truly she hadn't, and he must know that. And finally his hard mouth softened, and a flicker of a smile played across his face.

"Look at me," he said, unnecessarily, for the smile had already trapped her. "Now, say my name, in your mind, as if you wanted to get my attention—quietly. As quietly as you would if you were speaking it aloud."

She waited a moment, and then she thought it. *Po.*

He nodded. "That's all it takes."

"Well. That was easy."

"And you'll notice it caused no abuse to the horse."

"Very funny. Can we practice, while we're riding?"

And for the rest of the day she called to him on occasion, in her mind. Every time, he raised his hand, to show that he'd heard. Even when she whispered. So then she decided to stop calling to him, for it was clear that it worked, and she didn't want to badger him. He looked back at her then and nodded, and she knew that he had understood her. And she rode behind him with her eyes wide and tried to make some sense of their having had an entire conversation, of sorts, without saying a word.

THEY MADE CAMP beside a pond, surrounded by great Sunderan trees. As they unhooked their bags from the horses, Katsa was sure she saw a goose through the reeds, waddling around on the opposite shore. Po squinted.

"It does appear to be a goose," he said, "and I wouldn't mind a drumstick for dinner."

So Katsa set out, approaching the creature quietly. It didn't notice her. She decided to walk right up to it and break its neck, as the kitchen women did in the chicken houses of the castle. But as she snuck forward, the goose heard her and began to squawk and run for the water. She ran after the bird, and it spread its massive wings and took to the air. She leaped and wrapped her arms around its middle. She brought it down, straight into the pond, surprised by its size. And now she was wrestling in the water with an enormous, flapping, biting, splashing, kicking goose—but only for a moment. For her hands were around its neck, and its neck was snapped, before it could close its sharp beak around any part of her body.

She turned to the shore then, and was surprised to find Po standing there, gaping. She stood in the pond, the water streaming from her hair and clothing, and held the huge bird up by the neck for him to see. "I got it," she said.

He stared at her for a moment, his chest rising and falling, for he had run, apparently, at the sight of the underwater struggle. He rubbed his temples. "Katsa. What in Lienid are you doing?"

"What do you mean? I've caught us a goose."

"Why didn't you use your knife? You're standing in the pond. You're soaked through."

"It's only water," she said. "It was time I washed my clothing anyway."

"Katsa—"

"I wanted to see if I could do it," she said. "What if I'm ever traveling without weapons and I need to eat? It's good to know how to catch a goose without weapons."

"You could've stood at our camp and shot it, across the pond, if you wanted. I've seen your aim."

"But now I know I can do this," she said, simply.

He shook his head and held out a hand. "Come out of there, before you catch a chill. And give me that. I'll pluck it while you change into dry clothing."

"I never catch a chill," she said as she waded to shore.

He laughed then. "Oh, Katsa. I'm sure you don't." He took the goose from her hands. "Do you still have a fight in you? We can practice while your goose is cooking."

FIGHTING HIM was different, now that she knew his true advantages. It was a waste of her energy, she realized, to fake a blow. She could have no mental advantage over him; no amount of cleverness would serve her. Her only advantages were her speed and her ferocity. And now that she knew this, it became easy enough to adjust her strategy. She didn't waste time being creative. She only pummeled him as fast and as hard as she could. He might know where she aimed her next blow, but after a barrage of hits he simply couldn't keep up with her anymore; he couldn't move fast enough to block her. They struggled and wrestled as the light faded and the night moved in. Over and over again he surrendered and heaved himself back up to his feet, laughing and moaning.

"This is good practice for me," he said, "but I can't see what you have to gain from it. Other than the satisfaction of beating me to a pulp."

"We'll have to come up with some new drills," she said. "Something to challenge both of our Graces."

"Keep fighting me once the sky is dark. You'll find us more evenly matched then."

It was true. The night sky closed in around them, a black sky with no moon and no stars. Eventually Katsa could no longer see, could only make out his vaguest outline. Her blows, as she threw them, were approximate. He knew she couldn't see, and moved in ways that would confuse her. His defense became stronger. And his own strikes hit her squarely.

She stopped him. "It's that exact, your sense of my hands and feet?"

"Hands and feet, fingers and toes," he said. "You're so physical, Katsa. You've so much physical energy. I sense it constantly. Even your emotions seem physical sometimes."

She squinted at him and considered. "Could you fight a person blindfolded?"

"I never have—I could never have tried it, of course, without arousing suspicion. But yes, I could, though it would be easier on flat ground. My sense of the forest floor is too inconsistent."

She stared at him, a black shape against a blacker sky. "Wonderful," she said. "It's wonderful. I envy you. We must fight more often at night."

He laughed. "I won't complain. It'd be nice to be on the offensive every once in a while."

They fought just a bit longer, until they both tripped over a fallen branch, and Po landed on his back, half submerged in the pond. He came up spluttering.

"I think we've done enough barreling around in the dark," he said. "Shall we check on your goose?"

THE GOOSE sizzled over the fire. Katsa poked at it with her knife, and the meat fell away from the bone. "It's perfect," she said. "I'll cut you your drumstick." She glanced up at him, and in that moment he pulled his wet shirt over his head. She forced her mind blank. Blank as a new sheet of paper, blank as a starless sky. He came to the fire and crouched before it. He rubbed the water from his bare arms and flicked it into the flames. She stared at the goose and sliced his drumstick carefully and thought of the blankest expression on the blankest face she could possibly imagine. It was a chilly evening; she thought about that. The goose would be delicious, they must eat as much of it as possible, they must not waste it; she thought about that.

"I hope you're hungry," she said to him. "I don't want this goose to go to waste."

"I'm ravenous."

He was going to sit there shirtless, apparently, until the fire dried him. A mark on his arm caught her eye, and she took a breath and imagined a blank book full of page after empty page. But then a similar mark on his other arm drew her attention, and her curiosity got the better of her. She couldn't help herself; she squinted at his arms. And it was all right, this was acceptable. For there was nothing wrong with being curious about the marks that seemed to be painted onto his skin. Dark, thick bands, like a ribbon wrapped around each arm, in the place where the muscles of his shoulder ended and the muscles of his arm began. The bands, one circling each arm, were decorated with intricate designs that she thought might be a number of different colors. It was hard to tell in the firelight.

"It's a Lienid ornamentation," he said, "like the rings in my ears."

"But what is it?" she asked. "Is it paint?"

"It's a kind of dye."

"And it doesn't wash away?"

"Not for many years."

He reached into one of his bags and pulled out a dry shirt. He slipped it down over his head, and Katsa thought of a great blank field of snow and breathed a small sigh of relief. She handed him his drumstick.

"The Lienid people are fond of decoration," he said.

"Do the women wear the markings?"

"No, only the men."

"Do the people?"

"Yes."

"But no one ever sees it," Katsa said. "Lienid clothing doesn't show a man's upper arms, does it?"

"No," Po said. "It doesn't. It's a decoration hardly anyone sees."

She caught a smile in his eyes that flashed at her in the light.

"What? What are you grinning about?"

"It's meant to be attractive to my wife," he said.

Katsa nearly dropped her knife into the fire. "You have a wife?"

"Great seas, no! Honestly, Katsa. Don't you think I would have mentioned her?"

He was laughing now, and she snorted. "I never know what you'll choose to mention about yourself, Po."

"It's meant for the eyes of the wife I'm supposed to have," he said.

"Whom will you marry?"

He shrugged. "I hadn't pictured myself marrying anyone."

She moved to his side of the fire and sliced the other drumstick for herself. She went back and sat down. "Aren't you concerned about your castle and your land? About producing heirs?"

He shrugged again. "Not enough to attach me to a person I don't wish to be attached to. I'm content enough on my own."

Katsa was surprised. "I had thought of you as more of a—social creature, when you're in your own land."

"When I'm in Lienid I do a decent job of folding myself into normal society, when I must. But it's an act, Katsa; it's always an act. It's a strain to hide my Grace, especially from my family. When I'm in my father's city there's a part of me that's simply waiting until I can travel again. Or return to my own castle, where I'm left alone."

This she could understand perfectly. "I suppose if you married, it could only be to a woman trustworthy enough to know the truth of your Grace."

He barked out a short laugh. "Yes. The woman I married would have to meet a number of rather impossible requirements." He threw the bone from his drumstick into the fire and cut another piece of meat from the goose. He blew on the meat, to cool it. "And what of you, Katsa? You've broken Giddon's heart with your departure, haven't you?"

His very name filled her with impatience. "Giddon. And can you really not see why I wouldn't wish to marry him?"

"I can see a thousand reasons why you wouldn't wish to marry him. But I don't know which is your reason."

"Even if I wished to marry, I wouldn't marry Giddon," Katsa said. "But I won't marry, not anyone. I'm surprised you hadn't heard that rumor. You were at Randa's court long enough."

"Oh, I heard it. But I also heard you were some kind of feckless thug and that Randa had you under his thumb. Neither of which turned out to be true."

She smiled then and threw her own bone into the fire. One of the horses whickered. Some small creature slipped into the pond, the water closing around it with a gulp. She suddenly felt warm and content, and full of good food.

"Raffin and I talked once about marrying," she said. "For he's not wild about the idea of marrying some noblewoman who thinks only of being rich or being queen. And of course, he must marry someone, he has no choice in the matter. And to marry me would be an easy solution. We get along, I wouldn't try to keep him from his experiments. He wouldn't expect me to entertain his guests, he wouldn't keep me from the Council." She thought of Raffin bending over his books and his flasks. He was probably working on some experiment right now, with Bann at his side. By the time she returned to court, perhaps he would be married to some lady or another. He married, and she not there for him to come to and talk of it; she not there to tell him her thoughts, if he wished to hear them, as he always did.

"In the end," she said, "it was out of the question. We laughed about it, for I couldn't even begin to consider it seriously. I wouldn't ever consent to be queen. And Raffin will require children, which I'd also never consent to. And I won't be so tied to another person. Not even Raffin." She squinted into the fire, and sighed over her cousin whose responsibilities were so heavy. "I hope he'll fall in love with some woman who'll make a happy queen and mother. That would be the best thing for him. Some woman who wants a whole roost of children."

Po tilted his head at her. "Do you dislike children?"

"I've never disliked the children I've met. I've just never wanted them. I haven't wanted to mother them. I can't explain it."

She remembered Giddon then, who had assured her that this would change. As if he knew her heart, as if he had the slightest understanding of her heart. She threw another bone into the fire and hacked another piece of meat from the goose. She felt Po's eyes, and looked up at him, scowling.

"Why are you glaring at me," he asked, "when for all I can tell, you're not angry with me?"

She smiled. "I was only thinking Giddon would have found me a very vexing wife. I wonder if he would've understood when I planted a patch of seabane in the gardens. Or perhaps he would've thought me charmingly domestic."

Po looked puzzled. "What's seabane?"

"I don't know if you have another name for it in Lienid.

It's a small purple flower. A woman who eats its leaves will not bear a child."

THEY WRAPPED themselves in their blankets and lay before the dying fire. Po yawned a great, deep yawn, but Katsa wasn't tired. A question occurred to her. But she didn't want to wake him, if he was falling asleep.

"What is it, Katsa? I'm awake."

She didn't know if she would ever get used to that.

"I was wondering whether I could wake you," she said, "by calling to you inside your mind when you're sleeping."

"I don't know," he said. "I don't sense things while I'm sleeping, but if I'm in danger or if someone approaches, I always wake. You may try it"—he yawned again—"if you must."

"I'll try it another night," she said, "when you're less tired."

"Aren't you ever tired, Katsa?"

"I'm sure I am," she said, though she couldn't bring a specific example to mind.

"Do you know the story of King Leck of Monsea?"

"I didn't know there was a story."

"There is," Po said, "a story from ages ago, and you should know it if we're to travel to his kingdom. I'll tell it to you, and perhaps you'll feel more tired."

He rolled onto his back. She lay on her side and watched the line of his profile in the light of the dying fire.

"The last King and Queen of Monsea were kind people. Not particularly great state minds," he said, "but they had good advisers, and they were kinder to their people than most today could even imagine, for a king and queen. But they were childless. It wasn't a good thing, Katsa, as it would be for you. They wanted a child desperately, so that they might have an heir—but also just because they wanted one, as I suppose most people do. And then one day, a boy came to their court. A handsome boy of about thirteen years, clever-looking, with a patch over one eye, for he'd lost an eye when he was younger. He didn't say where he came from, or who his parents were, or what had happened to his eye. He only came to court begging and telling stories in return for food and money.

"The servants took him in, for he told such wonderful stories—wild stories about a place beyond the seven kingdoms, where monsters come out of the sea and air, and armies burst out of holes in the mountains, and the people are different from anyone we've ever known. Eventually the king and queen learned of him and he was brought before them to tell his stories. The boy charmed them completely—charmed them from the first day. They pitied him, for his poverty and loneliness and his missing eye. They began to bring him into their presence for meals, or ask for him when they'd returned from long journeys, or call him to their rooms in the evenings. They treated him like a noble boy; he was educated, and taught to fight and ride. They treated him almost as if he were their own son. And when the boy was sixteen and the king and queen still didn't have a child of their own, the king did something extraordinary. He named the boy his heir."

"Even though they knew nothing of his past?"

"Even though they knew nothing of his past. And this is where the story truly becomes interesting, Katsa. For not a week after the king had named the boy his heir, the king and queen died of a sudden sickness. And their two closest advisers fell into despair and threw themselves into the river. Or so the story goes. I don't know that there were any witnesses."

Katsa propped herself on her elbow and stared at him.

"Do you think that strange?" he asked. "I've always thought it strange. But the Monsean people never questioned it, and all in my family who've met Leck tell me I'm foolish to wonder. They say Leck is utterly charming, even his eyepatch is charming. They say he grieved for the king and queen terribly and couldn't possibly have had anything to do with their deaths."

"I've never known this story," Katsa said. "I didn't even know Leck was missing an eye. Have you met him?"

"I haven't," Po said. "But I've always had a feeling I wouldn't take to him as others have. Despite his great reputation for kindness to the small and the powerless." He yawned and turned onto his side. "Well, and I suppose we'll both learn soon enough whether we take to him, if things go as I expect. Good night to you, Katsa. We may reach the inn tomorrow."

Katsa closed her eyes and listened to his breath grow steady and even. She considered the tale he'd told. It was hard to reconcile King Leck's pleasant reputation with this story. Still, perhaps he was innocent. Perhaps there was some logical explanation.

She wondered what reception they would receive at the inn, and whether they'd be lucky enough to cross paths with someone who held the information they sought. She listened to the sounds of the pond and the breeze in the grasses.

When she thought Po had fallen asleep, she said his name aloud once, quietly. He didn't stir. She thought his name once, quietly, like a whisper in her mind. Again, he didn't stir, and his breathing didn't change.

He was asleep.

Katsa exhaled, slowly.

She was the greatest fool in all the seven kingdoms.

Why, when she fought with him almost every day, when she knew every part of his body; why, when she'd sat on his stomach, and wrestled with him on the ground and could probably identify his arm hold faster than any wife would recognize the embrace of her own husband, had the sight of his arms and his shoulders so embarrassed her? She had seen a thousand shirtless men before, in the practice rooms or when traveling with Giddon and Oll. Raffin practically undressed in front of her, they were so used to each other. It was like his eyes. Unless they were fighting, Po's body had the same effect on her as his eyes.

His breathing changed, and she froze her thoughts. She listened as his breathing settled back into a rhythm.

It was not going to be simple with Po. Nothing with Po was going to be simple. But he was her friend, and so she would travel with him. She would help him uncover the kid-napper of his grandfather. And by all means, she would take care not to tumble him into any more ponds.

And now she must sleep. She turned her back to him and willed her mind to darkness.

CHAPTER EIGHTEEN

THE INN was a great, tall building made of solid lumber. The farther south one rode into Sunder, the heavier and thicker the wood of the trees, and the stronger and more imposing the houses and inns. Katsa had not spent much time in central Sunder; her uncle had sent her there two or three times, perhaps. But the wild forests and simple, sturdy little towns, too far from the borders to be involved in the nonsense of the kings, had always pleased Katsa. The walls of the inn felt like castle walls, but darker, and warmer.

They sat at a table, in a roomful of men sitting at tables— heavy, dark tables built from the same wood as the walls. It was the time of day when men of the town and travelers alike poured into the inn's great eating room and sat down, to talk and laugh over a cup of something strong to drink. The room had recovered from the hush that afflicted it when Po and Katsa first walked through the door. The men were noisy now, and jovial, and if they did peek at the Graceling royalty over their cups and around their chairs, well, at least they didn't stare outright.

Po sat back in his chair. His eyes flicked lazily around the room. He drank from his cup of cider, and his finger traced the wet ring it left on the table. He leaned his elbow on the table and propped his head in his hand. He yawned. He looked, Katsa thought, as if he only needed a lullaby and he would nod off to sleep. It was a good act.

His eyes flashed at her then, and with them a glimmer of a smile. "I don't think we'll stay long at this inn," he said, his voice low. "There are men in this room who've already taken an interest in us."

Po had informed the innkeeper that they would offer money for any information about the kidnapping of Grandfather Tealiff. Men—particularly Sunderan men, if men are like their king—would do a great deal for money. They would change allegiances. They would tell truths they had promised not to reveal. They would also make up stories, but it didn't matter, for Po could tell as much from a lie as he could from the truth.

Katsa sipped from her cup and looked out into the sea of men. The finery of the merchants stood out among the muted browns and oranges of the people of the town. Katsa was the only woman in the room, save a harried serving girl, the innkeeper's daughter, who ran among the tables with a tray full of cups and pitchers. She was small in stature, dark, and pretty, and a bit younger than Katsa. She caught no one's eye as she worked, and didn't smile, except to the occasional townsman old enough to be her father. She had brought Katsa and Po their drinks silently, with only a quick, shy glance at Po. Most of the men in the room showed her the proper respect; but Katsa didn't much like the smiles on the faces of the merchants whose table she served at the moment.

"How old is that girl, do you think?" Katsa asked. "Do you think she's married?"

Po watched the table of merchants and sipped from his drink. "Sixteen or seventeen, I'd guess. She's not married."

"How do you know?"

He paused. "I don't. It was a guess."

"It didn't sound like a guess."

He drank from his cup. His face was impassive. It hadn't been a guess, this she knew; and it occurred to her suddenly how he could know such a thing with such certainty. She took a moment to nurse her irritation on behalf of every girl who'd ever admired Po and thought her feelings private. "You're impossible," she said. "You're no better than those merchants. And besides, just because she has her eyes on you doesn't mean—"

"And that's not fair," Po protested. "I can't help what I know. My error was in revealing it to you. I'm not used to traveling with someone who knows my Grace; I spoke before thinking how unfair it would be, to the girl."

She rolled her eyes. "Spare me your confessions. If she's unmarried, I don't understand why her father sends her out to serve these men. I'm not certain she's safe among them."

"Her father stands at the bar, most of the time. No one would dare harm her."

"But he's not there always—he's not there now. And just because they don't assault her doesn't mean they respect her." Or that they would not seek her out later.

The girl circled the table of merchants, pouring cider into each cup. When one of the men reached for her arm, she recoiled. The merchants burst into laughter. The man reached out to her then and drew back, reached out and drew back, taunting her. His friends laughed harder. And then the man at the girl's other side grabbed her wrist and held on, and there was a great whoop from the men. She tried to pull away, but the laughing man wouldn't let go. Red with shame, she looked into none of their faces, only pulled at her arm. She was too much like a dumb, confused rabbit caught in a trap, and suddenly Katsa was standing. And Po was standing, too, and he had Katsa by the arm.

For an instant Katsa appreciated the strange symmetry; except that unlike the serving girl, she could break from Po's grip, and unlike the merchant, Po had good reason to hold her arm. And Katsa wouldn't break from the grip of his fingers, for she didn't need to. Her rise to her feet had been enough. The room froze into stillness. The man dropped the girl's arm. He stared at Katsa with a white face and an open mouth—fear, as familiar to Katsa as the feel of her own body. The girl stared, too, and caught her breath and pressed her hand to her chest.

"Sit down, Katsa." Po's voice was low. "It's over now. Sit down."

She did sit down. The room let out its breath. After a few moments, voices murmured, and then talked and laughed again. But Katsa wasn't sure that it was over. Perhaps it was over with this girl, and these merchants. But there would be a new group of merchants tomorrow. And these merchants would move on, and find themselves another girl.

LATER THAT EVENING, as Katsa prepared for bed, two girls came to her room to cut her hair. "Is it too late, My Lady?" asked the elder, who carried scissors and a brush.

"No. The sooner I have it off, the better. Please, come in."

They were young, younger than the serving girl. The younger, a child of ten or eleven years, carried a broom and a dustpan. They sat Katsa down and moved around her shyly. They spoke little. Breathless around her, not quite frightened but near to it. The older girl untied Katsa's hair and began to work her fingers through the tangle. "Forgive me if I hurt you, My Lady."

"It won't hurt me," Katsa said. "And you needn't unravel the knots. I want you to cut it all off, as short as you can. As short as a man's."

The eyes of both girls widened. "I've cut the hair of many men," the older girl said.

"You may cut mine just as you've cut theirs," Katsa said. "The shorter you cut it, the happier I'll be."

The scissors snipped around Katsa's ears, and her head grew lighter and lighter. How odd to turn her neck and not feel the pull of hair, the heavy snarl swinging around behind her. The younger girl held the broom and swept the hair clippings away the instant they fell to the floor.

"Is it your sister I saw serving drinks in the eating room?" Katsa asked.

"Yes, My Lady."

"How old is she?"

"Sixteen, My Lady."

"And you?"

"I'm fourteen, and my sister eleven, My Lady."

Katsa watched the younger girl collecting hair with a broom taller than she was.

"Does anyone teach the girls of the inn to protect themselves?" she asked. "Do you carry a knife?"

"Our father protects us, and our brother," the girl said, simply.

The girls clipped and swept, and Katsa's hair fell away. She thrilled at the unfamiliar chill of air on her neck. And wondered if other girls in Sunder, and across the seven kingdoms, carried knives; or if they all looked to their fathers and brothers for every protection.

A KNOCK woke her. She sat up. It came from the door that adjoined her room to Po's. She hadn't been asleep long, and it was midnight; and enough moonlight spilled through her window so that if it wasn't Po who knocked, and if it was an enemy, she could see well enough to beat the person senseless. All these thoughts swept through her mind in the instant she sat up.

"Katsa, it's only I," his voice called, through the keyhole. "It's a double lock. You must unlock it from your side."

She rolled out of bed. And where was the key?

"My key was hanging beside the door," he called, and she took a moment to glare in his general direction.

"I only guessed you were looking for the key. It wasn't my Grace, so you needn't get all huffy about it."

Katsa felt along the wall. Her fingers touched a key. "Doesn't it make you nervous to holler like that? Anyone could hear you. You could be revealing your precious Grace to a whole legion of my lovers."

His laughter came muffled through the door. "I would know if anyone heard my voice. And I'd also know if you were in there with a legion of lovers. Katsa—have you cut your hair?"

She snorted. "Wonderful. That's just wonderful. I've no privacy, and you sense even my hair." She turned the key in the lock and swung the door open. Po straightened, a candle in his hand.

"Great seas," he said.

"What do you want?"

He held his candle up to her face.

"Po, what do you want?"

"She did a far better job than I would have done."

"I'm going back to bed," Katsa said, and she reached for the door.

"All right, all right. The men, the merchants. The Sunderan men who were bothering that girl. I think they intend to come to us this night and speak to us."

"How do you know?"

"Their rooms are below us."

She shook her head, disbelieving. "No one in this inn has privacy."

"My sense of them is faint, Katsa. I cannot sense everyone down to the ends of their hair, as I do you."

She sighed. "What an honor, then, to be me. They're coming in the middle of the night?"

"Yes."

"Do they have information?"

"I believe they do."

"Do you trust them?"

"Not particularly. I think they'll come soon, Katsa. When they do I'll knock on your outer door."

Katsa nodded. "Very well. I'll be ready."

She stepped back into her room and pulled the door behind her. She lit a candle, splashed water on her face, and prepared herself for the arrival of the late-night merchants.

SIX MERCHANTS had sat around the table in the eating room and laughed at the serving girl. When Po's knock brought her to the door, she found him standing in the hallway with all six, each carrying a candle that cast a dark light over a bearded face. They were tall, and broad-backed, all six of them, enormous next to her, and even the smallest taller and broader than Po. Quite a band of bullies. She followed them back to Po's room.

"You're awake and dressed, My Lord Prince, My Lady," the biggest of the merchants said as they filed into Po's chamber. It was the man who'd first tried to grab the girl's arm, the one who'd first teased her. Katsa registered the mockery as he spoke their titles. He had no more respect for them than they had for him. The one who'd taken the girl's wrist stood beside him, and those two seemed to be the leaders of the group. They stood together, in the middle of the room, facing Po, while the other four faded into the background.

They were well spread out, these merchants. Katsa moved to the side door, the door that led to her room, and leaned against it with her arms crossed. She was steps from Po and the two leaders, and she could see the other four. It was more precaution than was necessary. But it didn't hurt for any of them to know she was watching.

"We've been receiving visitors throughout the night," Po said, an easy lie. "You're not the only travelers at the inn who have information about my grandfather."

"Be careful of the others, Lord Prince," said the biggest merchant. "Men will lie for money."

Po raised an eyebrow. "Thank you for your warning." He slouched against the table behind him and put his hands in his pockets. Katsa swallowed her smile. She rather enjoyed Po's cocky laziness.

"What information do you have for us?" Po asked.

"How much will you pay?" the man said.

"I'll pay whatever the information warrants."

"There are six of us," the man said.

"I'll give it to you in coins divisible by six," Po said, "if that's what you wish."

"I meant, Lord Prince, that it's not worth our time to

divulge information if you'll not compensate us enough for six men."

Po chose that moment to yawn. When he spoke, his voice was calm, even friendly. "I won't haggle over a price when I don't know the breadth of your information. You'll be fairly compensated. If that doesn't satisfy you, you're free to leave."

The man rocked on his feet for a moment. He glanced sideways at his partner. His partner nodded, and the man cleared his throat.

"Very well," he said. "We have information that links the kidnapping to King Birn of Wester."

"How interesting," Po said, and the farce had begun. Po asked all the questions one would ask if one were conducting this interrogation seriously. What was the source of their information? Was the man trustworthy who had spoken of Birn? What was the motivation for the kidnapping? Had Birn the assistance of any other kingdoms? Was Grandfather Tealiff in Birn's dungeons? How were Birn's dungeons guarded?

"Well, Lady," Po said, with a glance in her direction, "we'll have to send word quickly, so that my brothers know to investigate the dungeons of Birn of Wester."

"You won't travel there yourselves?" The man was surprised. And disappointed, most likely, that he hadn't managed to send Po and Katsa on a futile mission.

"We go south, and east," Po said. "To Monsea, and King Leck."

"Leck was not responsible for the kidnapping," the man said.

"I never said he was."

"Leck is blameless. You waste your energies searching Monsea, when your grandfather is in Wester."

Po yawned again. He shifted his weight against the table and crossed his arms. He looked back at the man blandly. "We don't go to Monsea in search of my grandfather," he said. "It is a social visit. My father's sister is the Queen of Monsea. She's been most distressed by the kidnapping. We mean to call on her. Perhaps we can bring the comfort of your news to the Monsean court."

One of the merchants in the background cleared his throat. "A lot of sickness there," he said from his corner. "At the Monsean court."

Po's eyes moved to the man calmly. "Is that so?"

The man grunted. "I've family in Leck's service, distant family. Two little girls who worked in his shelter, cousins of some kind—well, they died a few months back."

"What do you mean, in his shelter?"

"Leck's animal shelter. He rescues animals, Lord Prince, you'll know that."

"Yes, of course," Po said. "But I didn't know about the shelter."

The man seemed to enjoy being the center of Po's attention. He glanced at his companions and lifted his chin. "Well, Lord Prince, he's got hundreds of them, dogs, squirrels, rabbits, bleeding from slashes on their backs and bellies."

Po narrowed his eyes. "Slashes on their backs and bellies," he repeated carefully.

"You know. As if they'd run into something sharp," the man said.

Po stared at him for a moment. "Of course. And any broken bones? Any sickness?"

The man considered. "I've never heard tell of any of that, Lord Prince. Just lots of cuts and slashes that take a wondrous long time to heal. He's got a staff of children who help him nurse the little creatures to recovery. They say he's very dedicated to his animals."

Po pursed his lips. He glanced at Katsa. "I see," he said. "And do you know what sickness the girls died of?"

The man shrugged. "Children are not very strong."

"We've moved to a different topic now," the biggest merchant said, interrupting. "We agreed to give you information about the kidnapping, not about this. We'll be wanting more money to compensate."

"And anyway, I'm suddenly dying of a sickness called boredom," his partner said.

"Oh," said the first, "perhaps you have a more amusing diversion in mind?"

"With different company," said the man in the corner.

They were laughing now, the six of them chuckling over a private joke Katsa had a feeling she understood. "Alas for protective fathers and locked bedroom doors," the partner said, very low to his friends, but not too low for Katsa's sensitive ears. She surged toward the men before the burst of laughter had even begun.

Po blocked her so fast that she knew he must have started

imperceptibly first. "Stop," he said to her softly. "Think. Breathe."

The wave of impulsive anger swept over her, and she allowed his body to block her path to the merchant, to the two of them, to all six of them, for these men were all the same to her.

"You're the only man in seven kingdoms who can keep that wildcat on a leash," said one of the two men. She wasn't sure which one, for she was distracted by the effect the words had on Po's face.

"It's fortunate for us she has such a sensible keeper," the man continued. "And you're a lucky fellow yourself. The wild ones are the most fun, if you can control them."

Po looked at her, but he didn't see her. His eyes snapped, silver ice and gold fire. The arm that blocked her stiffened, and his hand tightened into a fist. He inhaled, endlessly it seemed. He was furious; she saw this, and she thought he was going to strike the man who had spoken; and for a panicky moment she didn't know whether to stop him or help him.

Stop him. She would stop him, for he wasn't thinking. She took his forearms, and gripped them tightly. She thought his name into his head. *Po. Stop. Think,* she thought into his mind, just as he had said to her. *Think.* He began to breathe out, as slowly as he'd breathed in. His eyes refocused and he saw her.

He turned around and stood beside her. He faced the two men; it didn't even matter which of them had spoken.

"Get out." His voice was very quiet.

"We would have our payment—"

Po took a step toward the men, and they stepped back. He held his arms at his sides with a casual calmness that didn't fool anyone in the room. "Have you the slightest notion to whom you're speaking?" he asked. "Do you imagine you'll receive a coin of my money, when you've spoken this way? You're lucky I let you go without knocking your teeth from your mouths."

"Are you sure we shouldn't?" Katsa said, looking into the eyes of each man, one after the other. "I'd like to do something to discourage them from touching the innkeeper's daughter."

"We won't," one of them gasped. "We won't touch anyone, I swear it."

"You'll be sorry if you do," she said. "Sorry for the rest of your short, wretched lives."

"We won't, My Lady. We won't." They backed to the door, their faces white, their smirks vanished now. "It was only a joke, My Lady, I swear it."

"Get out," Po said. "Your payment is that we won't kill you for your insults."

The men scrambled from the room. Po slammed the door behind them. Then he leaned his back against the door and slid down until he sat on the floor. He rubbed his face with his hands and heaved a deep sigh.

Katsa took a candle from the table and came to crouch

before him. She tried to measure his tiredness and his anger, in the bend of his head and the hardness of his shoulders. He dropped his hands from his face and rested his head against the door. He watched her face for a moment.

"I truly thought I might hurt that man," he said, "very badly."

"I didn't know you were capable of such temper."

"Apparently I am."

"Po," Katsa said, as a thought occurred to her. "How did you know I intended to attack them? My intentions were toward them, not you."

"Yes, but my sense of your energy heightened suddenly, and I know you well enough to guess when you're likely to take a swing at someone." He half-smiled, tiredly. "No one could ever accuse you of being inconsistent."

She snorted. She sat on the floor before him and crossed her legs. "And now will you tell me what you learned from them?"

"Yes." He closed his eyes. "What I learned. To start with, other than that fellow in the corner, they barely spoke a true word. It was a game. They wanted to trick us into paying them for false information. To get back at us, for the incident in the eating room."

"They're small-minded," Katsa said.

"Very small-minded, but they've helped us, nonetheless. It's Leck, Katsa, I'm sure of it. The man lied when he said Leck was not responsible. And yet—and yet there was something else very strange that I could make no sense of." He shook his head and stared into his hands, thinking. "It's so odd, Katsa. I felt this strange . . . defensiveness rise in them."

"What do you mean, defensiveness?"

"As if they all truly believed Leck's innocence and wished to defend him to me."

"But you just said Leck is guilty."

"He is guilty, and these men know it. But they also believe him innocent."

"That makes utterly no sense."

He shook his head again. "I know. But I'm sure of what I sensed. I tell you, Katsa, when the man said that Leck was not responsible for the kidnapping, he was lying. But when he said, a moment later, 'Leck is blameless,' he meant it. He believed himself to be telling the truth." Po gazed up at the dark ceiling. "Are we supposed to conclude that Leck kidnapped my grandfather, but for some innocent reason? It simply cannot be."

Katsa couldn't comprehend the things Po had learned, any more than she could comprehend the manner in which he'd learned them. "None of this makes sense," she said, weakly.

He came down out of his thoughts for a moment and focused on her. "Katsa. I'm sorry. This must be overwhelming to you. I'm capable of sensing quite a lot, you see, from people who want to fool me but don't know to guard their thoughts and feelings."

She couldn't understand it. She gave up trying to make sense of the king who was both guilty and innocent. She watched Po as he became distracted by his thoughts again and stared again into his hands. The merchants hadn't known to guard their thoughts and feelings. If it was a thing that could be done, then she, at least, wanted to learn how to do it.

She felt his eyes and realized he was watching her. "You do keep some things from me," he said.

She started, then focused on blankness for a moment.

"Or you have," he continued, "since you've learned of my Grace. I mean, I've felt you keeping things from me—you're doing it now—and I can tell you it works, because my Grace shows me nothing. I'm always a bit relieved when it works, Katsa. Truly, I don't wish to take your secrets from you." He sat up straight, his face lit with an idea. "You know, you could always knock me unconscious. I wouldn't stop you."

Katsa laughed then. "I wouldn't. I've promised you I won't hit you, except in our practices."

"But it's self-defense, in this case."

"It is not."

"It is," he insisted, and she laughed again at his earnestness.

"I'd rather strengthen my mind against you," she said, "than knock you out every time I have a thought I don't want you to know."

"Yes, well, and I'd prefer that also, believe me. But I grant you permission to knock me out, if ever you need to."

"I wish you wouldn't. You know how impulsive I am."

"I don't care."

"If you grant me permission, I'll probably do it, Po. I'll probably—"

He held up his hand. "It's an equalizer. When we fight,

you hold your Grace back. I can't hold my Grace back. So you must have the right to defend yourself."

She didn't like it. But she could not miss his point. And she could not miss his willingness, his dear willingness, to give over his Grace for her. "You will always have a headache," she warned.

"Perhaps Raffin included his salve for headaches among the medicines. I should like to change my hair, now that you've changed yours. Blue would suit me, don't you think?"

She was laughing again, and she swore to herself that she wouldn't hit him; she wouldn't, unless she were entirely desperate. And then the candle on the floor beside them dimmed and died. Their conversation had gotten entirely off track. They were leaving for Monsea early in the morning, most likely, and it was the middle of the night and everyone in the inn and the town slept. Yet here they were, sitting on the floor, laughing in the dark.

"We leave for Monsea tomorrow, then?" she said. "We'll fall asleep on our horses."

"I'll fall asleep on my horse. You'll ride as if you've slept for days—as if it's a race between us to see who reaches Monsea first."

"And what will we find when we get there? A king who's innocent of the things of which he's guilty?"

He rubbed his head. "I've always thought it strange that my mother and father have no suspicions about Leck, even knowing his story. And now these men seem to think him blameless in the kidnapping, even knowing he's not."

"Can he be so kind in the rest of his life that everyone forgives his crimes, or fails to see them?"

He sat for a moment, quietly. "I've wondered . . . it occurs to me recently . . . that he could be Graced. That he could have a Grace that changes the way people think of him. Are there such Graces? I don't even know."

It had never occurred to her. But he could be Graced. With one eye missing, he could be Graced and no one would ever know. No one would even suspect, for who could suspect a Grace that controlled suspicions?

"He could have the Grace of fooling people," Po said. "The Grace of confusing people with lies, lies that spread from kingdom to kingdom. Imagine it, Katsa—people carrying his lies in their own mouths, and spreading them to believing ears; absurd lies, erasing logic and truth, all the way to Lienid. Can you imagine the power of a person who had such a Grace? He could create whatever reputation for himself he wished. He could take whatever he wanted and no one would ever hold him responsible."

Katsa thought of the boy who was named heir, and the king and queen who died shortly thereafter. The advisers who supposedly jumped into the river together. And a whole kingdom of mourners who never thought to question the boy who had no family, no past, no Monsean blood flowing through his veins—but who had become king. "But his kindness," Katsa said urgently. "The animals. That man spoke of the animals he restores to health."

"And that's the other thing," Po said. "That man truly believed in Leck's philanthropy. But am I the only person who finds it a bit odd that there should be so many slashed-up dogs and squirrels in Monsea that need rescuing? Are the trees and the rocks made of broken glass?"

"But he's a kind man if he cares for them."

Po peered at Katsa strangely. "You're defending him, too, in the face of logic that tells you not to, just like my parents and just like those merchants. He's got hundreds of animals with bizarre cuts that don't heal, Katsa, and children in his employ dying of mysterious illnesses, and you're not the slightest bit suspicious."

He was right. Katsa saw it; and the truth in all its gruesomeness trickled into her mind. She began to have a conception of a power that spread like a bad feeling, like a sickness itself, seizing all minds that it touched.

Could there be a Grace more dangerous than one that replaced sight with a fog of falseness?

Katsa shuddered. For she would be in the presence of this king soon enough. She wasn't certain what defense even she could raise against a man who could fool her into believing his innocent reputation.

Her eyes traced Po's silhouette, dark against the black door. His white shirt was the only part of him truly visible, a luminous gray in the darkness. She wished, suddenly, that she could see him better. He stood and pulled her to her feet. He pulled her to the window and looked down into her face. The moonlight caught a glimmer in his silver eye, and a gleam in the gold of his ear. She didn't know why she had felt so anxious or why the lines of his nose and his mouth, or the concern in his eyes, should comfort her.

"What is it?" he asked. "What's bothering you?"

"If Leck has this Grace, as you suspect . . ." she began.

"Yes?"

". . . how will I protect myself from him?"

He considered her seriously. "Well. And that's easy," he said. "My Grace will protect me from him. And I'll protect you. You'll be safe with me, Katsa."

IN HER BED, thoughts swirled like a windstorm in her mind; but she ordered herself to sleep. In an instant, the storm quieted. She slept under a blanket of calm.

CHAPTER NINETEEN

THERE WERE two ways to get to Leck City from the inn or from any point in Sunder. One was to travel south to one of the Sunderan ports and sail southeast to Monport, the westernmost port city of the Monsean peninsula, where a road led north to Leck City, across flat land just east of Monsea's highest peaks. This route was traveled by merchants who carried goods, and most parties containing women, children, or the elderly.

The other way was shorter but more difficult. It led southeast through a Sunderan forest that grew thicker and wilder and rose to meet the mountains that formed Monsea's border with Sunder and Estill. The path became too rocky and uneven for horses. Those who crossed the mountain pass did so on foot. An inn on either side of the pass bought or kept the horses of those who approached the mountains and sold or returned them to those who came from the mountains. This was the route Katsa and Po would take.

Leck City was the walk of a day or so beyond the mountain pass, less if they purchased new horses. The walk to the city wound through valleys grown lush with the water that flowed down from the mountaintops. It was a landscape of rivers and streams, similar to that of inland Lienid, Po told

Katsa—or so the Monsean queen had written—which made it a landscape unlike anything Katsa had ever seen.

As they rode, Katsa couldn't content herself with imagining the strange landscapes ahead. For when she'd awakened to morning in the Sunderan inn, the windstorm of the night before had returned to her mind.

Po's Grace would protect Po from Leck. And Po would protect her.

With Po, Katsa would be safe.

He'd said it simply, as if it were nothing. But it wasn't nothing for Katsa to rely on someone else's protection. She'd never done such a thing in her life.

And besides, wouldn't it be easier for her to kill Leck immediately, before he said a word or raised a finger? Or gag him, immobilize him, find some way to disempower him completely? Maintain control and ensure her own defense? Katsa didn't need protection. There would be a solution; there would be a way for her to protect herself from Leck, if indeed he had the power they suspected. She only needed to think of it.

LATE IN THE morning the skies began to drip. By afternoon the drizzle had turned to rain, a cold, relentless rain that beat down and hid the forest road from their sight. Finally they stopped, soaked to the skin, to see what they could do about shelter before night fell. The tangle of trees on either side of the road provided some cover. They tethered the horses under an enormous pine that smelled of the sap dripping from its branches with the rainwater. "It's as dry a place as we're likely to find," Po said. "A fire will be impossible, but at least we won't sleep in the rain."

"A fire is never impossible," Katsa said. "I'll build it, and you find us something to cook on it."

So Po set out into the trees with his bow, somewhat skeptically, and Katsa set to work building a fire. It wasn't easy, with the world around her soaked right through. But the pine tree had protected some of the needles nestled closely to its trunk, and she uncovered some leaves and a stick or two that were not quite waterlogged. With the strike of her knife, a number of gentle breaths, and whatever protection her own open arms could give, a flame began to lick its way through the damp little tower of kindling. It warmed her face as she leaned into it. It pleased her. She'd always had a way with fires. With Oll and Giddon the fire had always been her responsibility.

Further evidence, of course, that she didn't need to rely on anyone for her survival.

She left the flicker of light, and scrambled to find it more food. When Po came back, dripping, to their camp, she was grateful for the fat rabbit in his hand.

"My Grace is definitely still growing," he said, wiping water from his face. "Since we entered this forest I've noticed a greater sensitivity to animals. This rabbit was hiding in the hollow of a tree, and it seems to me I shouldn't have known he was there—" He stopped at the sight of her small, smoky fire. He watched as she breathed into it and fed it with her collection of twigs and branches. "Katsa, how did you manage it? You're a wonder."

She laughed at that. He crouched beside her. "It's good to hear you laugh," he said. "You've been so quiet today. You know, I'm quite cold, though I didn't realize it until I felt the heat of these flames."

Po warmed himself, saw to their dinner, and chatted. Katsa began to open their bags and hang blankets and clothing from the lowest branches of the pine, to dry them as best they could. When the meat of the rabbit was propped sizzling above the flames, Po joined her. He unrolled their maps and held a soggy corner near the fire. He opened Raffin's packet of medicines and inspected them, setting the labeled envelopes onto rocks to dry.

It was comfortable, their camp, with the drops plopping down from above and the warmth of the fire, and the smell of burning wood and cooking meat. Po's patter of conversation was comfortable. Katsa kept the fire alive and smiled at his talk. She fell asleep that night, in a blanket partly dried, secure in the certainty that she could survive anywhere, on her own.

SHE WOKE in the middle of the night in a panic, certain that Po had gone and that she was alone. But it must have been the tail end of a dream, snagging into her consciousness as it departed, for she could hear his breath through the even fall of rain. When she turned over and sat up, she could make out his form on the ground beside her. She reached out and touched his shoulder. Just to make sure. He had not left her; he was here, and they were traveling together through the Sunderan forest, to the Monsean border. She lay down again, and watched the outline of his sleeping body in the darkness.

She would accept his protection after all, if truly she needed it. She was not too proud to be helped by this friend. He'd helped her in a thousand ways already.

And she would protect him as fiercely, if it were ever his need—if a fight ever became too much for him or if he needed shelter, or food, or a fire in the rain. Or anything she could provide. She would protect him from everything.

That was settled then. She closed her eyes and slipped into sleep.

KATSA DIDN'T KNOW what was wrong with her when she woke the next morning. She couldn't explain the fury she felt toward him. There was no explanation; and perhaps he knew that, because he asked for none. He only commented that the rain had stopped, watched her as she rolled her blanket, deliberately not looking at him, and carried his things to the horses. As they rode, still she did not look at him. And though he couldn't have missed the force of her fury, he made no comment.

She wasn't angry that there was a person who could provide her with help and protection. That would be arrogance, and she saw that arrogance was foolishness; she should strive for humility—and there was another way he'd helped her. He'd gotten her thinking about humility. But it wasn't that. It was that she hadn't *asked* for a person whom she trusted, whom she would do so much for, whom she would give herself over to. She hadn't *asked* for a person whose absence, if she woke in the middle of the night, would distress her—not because of the protection he would then fail to give, but simply because she wished his company. She hadn't asked for a person whose company she wished.

Katsa couldn't bear her own inanity. She drew herself into a shell of sullenness and chased away every thought that entered her mind.

WHEN THEY STOPPED to rest the horses beside a pond swollen with rainwater, he leaned against a tree and ate a piece of bread. He watched her, calmly, silently. She didn't look at him, but she was aware of his eyes on her, always on her. Nothing was more infuriating than the way he leaned against the tree, and ate bread, and watched her with those gleaming eyes.

"What are you staring at?" she finally demanded.

"This pond is full of fish," he said, "and frogs. Catfish, hundreds of them. Don't you think it's funny I should know that with such clarity?"

She would hit him, for his calmness, and his latest ability to count frogs and catfish he couldn't see. She clenched her fists and turned, forced herself to walk away. Off the road, into the trees, past the trees, and then she was running through the forest, startling birds into flight. She ran past streams and patches of fern, and hills covered with moss. She shot into a clearing with a waterfall that fell over rocks and plummeted into a pool. She yanked off her boots, pulled off her clothing, and leaped into the water. She screamed at the cold that surrounded her body all at once, and her nose and mouth filled with water. She surfaced, coughed and snorted, teeth chattering. She laughed at the coldness and scrambled to shore.

And now, standing in the dirt, the cold raising every hair of her body on end, she was calm.

IT WAS WHEN she returned to him, chilled and clearheaded, that it happened. He sat against the tree, his knees bent and his head in his hands. His shoulders slumped. Tired, unhappy. Something tender caught in her breath at the sight of him. And then he raised his eyes and looked at her, and she saw what she had not seen before. She gasped.

His eyes were beautiful. His face was beautiful to her in every way, and his shoulders and hands. And his arms that hung over his knees, and his chest that was not moving, because he held his breath as he watched her. And the heart in his chest. This friend. How had she not seen this before? How had she not seen him? She was blind. And then tears choked her eyes, for she had not asked for this. She had not asked for this beautiful man before her, with something hopeful in his eyes that she did not want.

He stood, and her legs shook. She put her hand out to her horse to steady herself.

"I don't want this," she said.

"Katsa. I hadn't planned for it either."

She gripped the edges of her saddle to keep herself from sitting down on the ground between the feet of her horse.

"You . . . you have a way of upending my plans," he said, and she cried out and sank to her knees, then heaved herself up furiously before he could come to her, and help her, and touch her.

"Get on your horse," she said, "right now. We're riding."

She mounted and took off, without even waiting to be sure he followed. They rode, and she allowed only one thought to enter her mind, over and over. *I don't want a husband. I don't want a husband.* She matched it to the rhythm of her horse's hooves. And if he knew her thought, all the better.

WHEN THEY STOPPED for the night she did not speak to him, but she couldn't pretend he wasn't there. She felt every move he made, without seeing it. She felt his eyes watching her across the fire he built. It was like this every night, and this was how it would continue to be. He would sit there gleaming in the light of the fire, and she unable to look at him, because he glowed, and he was beautiful, and she couldn't stand it.

"Please, Katsa," he finally said. "At least talk to me."

She swung around to face him. "What is there to talk about? You know how I feel, and what I think about it."

"And what I feel? Doesn't that matter?"

His voice was small, so unexpectedly small, in the face of her bitterness that it shamed her. She sat down across from him. "Po. Forgive me. Of course it matters. You may tell me anything you feel."

He seemed suddenly not to know what to say. He looked

into his lap and played with his rings; he took a breath and rubbed his head; and when he raised his face to her again she felt that his eyes were naked, that she could see right through them into the lights of his soul. She knew what he was going to say.

"I know you don't want this, Katsa. But I can't help myself. The moment you came barreling into my life I was lost. I'm afraid to tell you what I wish for, for fear you'll . . . oh, I don't know, throw me into the fire. Or more likely, refuse me. Or worst of all, despise me," he said, his voice breaking and his eyes dropping from her face. His face dropping into his hands. "I love you," he said. "You're more dear to my heart than I ever knew anyone could be. And I've made you cry; and there I'll stop."

She was crying, but not because of his words. It was because of a certainty she refused to consider while she sat before him. She stood. "I need to go."

He jumped up. "No, Katsa, please."

"I won't go far, Po. I just need to think, without you in my head."

"I'm afraid if you leave you won't come back."

"Po." This assurance, at least, she could give him. "I'll come back."

He looked at her for a moment. "I know you mean that now. But I'm afraid once you've gone off to think, you'll decide the solution is to leave me."

"I won't."

"I can't know that."

"No," Katsa said, "you can't. But I need to think on my own, and I refuse to knock you out, so you have to let me go. And once I'm gone you'll just have to trust me, as any person without your Grace would have to do. And as I have to do always, with you."

He looked at her with those naked, unhappy eyes again. Then he took a breath and sat down. "Put a good ten minutes between us," he said, "if you want privacy."

Ten minutes was a far greater range than she'd understood his Grace to encompass; but that was an argument for another time. She felt his eyes on her back as she passed through the trees. She groped forward, hands and feet, in search of darkness, distance, and solitude.

ALONE IN the forest, Katsa sat on a stump and cried. She cried like a person whose heart is broken and wondered how, when two people loved each other, there could be such a broken heart.

She couldn't have him, and there was no mistaking it. She could never be his wife. She could not steal herself back from Randa only to give herself away again—belong to another person, be answerable to another person, build her very being around another person. No matter how she loved him.

Katsa sat in the darkness of the Sunderan forest and understood three truths. She loved Po. She wanted Po. And she could never be anyone's but her own.

After a while, she began to thread her way back to the fire.

Nothing had changed in her feeling, and she wasn't tired. But Po would suffer if he didn't sleep; and she knew he wouldn't sleep until she had returned.

HE WAS LYING on his back, wide awake, staring up at a half-moon. She went to him and sat before him. He watched her with soft eyes and didn't say anything. She looked back at him, and opened up her feelings to him, so that he would understand what she felt, what she wanted, and what she couldn't do. He sat up. He watched her face for a long time.

"You know I'd never expect you to change who you are, if you were my wife," he finally said.

"It would change me to be your wife," she said.

He watched her eyes. "Yes. I understand you."

A log fell into the fire. They sat quietly. His voice, when he spoke, was hesitant.

"It strikes me that heartbreak isn't the only alternative to marriage," he said.

"What do you mean?"

He ducked his head for a moment. He raised his eyes to her again. "I'll give myself to you however you'll take me," he said, so simply that Katsa found she wasn't embarrassed. She watched his face.

"And where would that lead?"

"I don't know. But I trust you."

She watched his eyes.

He offered himself to her. He trusted her. As she trusted him.

She hadn't considered this possibility, when she'd sat alone in the forest crying. She hadn't even thought of it. And his offer hung suspended before her now, for her to reach out and claim; and that which had seemed clear and simple and heart-breaking was confused and complicated again. But also touched with hope.

Could she be his lover and still belong to herself?

That was the question; and she didn't know the answer.

"I need to think," she said.

"Think here," he said, "please. I'm so tired, Katsa. I'll fall right asleep."

She nodded. "All right. I'll stay."

He reached up, and wiped away a tear that sat on her cheek. She felt the touch of his fingertip in the base of her spine, and fought against it, against allowing him to know of it. He lay down. She stood and moved to a tree outside the light of their fire. She sat against it and watched Po's silhouette, waiting for him to fall asleep.

Chapter Twenty

The notion of having a lover was to Katsa something like discovering a limb she'd never noticed before. An extra arm or toe. It was unfamiliar, and she poked and prodded it, as she would have prodded an alien toe unexpectedly her own.

That the lover would be Po reduced her confusion somewhat. It was by thinking of Po, and not of the notion of a lover, that Katsa became comfortable enough to consider what it would mean to lie in his bed but not be his wife.

It took more than the thinking of one night. They moved through the Sunderan forest, and they talked and rested and made camp as before. But their silences were perhaps a bit less easy than they had been; and Katsa broke off occasionally, to keep her own company and think in solitude. They did not practice fighting, for Katsa was shy of his touch. And he didn't press it upon her. He pressed nothing upon her, even conversation, even his gaze.

They moved as quickly as the road allowed. But the farther they traveled, the more the road resembled a trail at best, winding through overgrown gullies and around trees the size of which Katsa had never seen. Trees with trunks as wide as the horses were long, and branches that groaned far above them. They had to duck sometimes to avoid curtains of vines hanging from the branches. The land rose as they moved east, and streams crisscrossed the forest floor.

Their route at least provided some distraction for Po. He couldn't stop looking around, his eyes wide. "It's wild, this forest. Have you ever seen anything like this? It's gorgeous."

Gorgeous, and full of animals fattening themselves for winter. Easy hunting, and easy finding shelter. But Katsa felt palpably that the horses were moving as slowly as her mind.

"I think we would move faster on our feet," she said.

"You'll miss the horses when we have to give them up."

"And when will that be?"

"It looks possibly ten days away on the map."

"I'll prefer traveling by foot."

"You never tire," Po said, "do you?"

"I do, if I haven't slept for a long time. Or if I'm carrying something very heavy. I felt tired when I carried your grandfather up a flight of stairs."

He glanced at her, eyebrows high. "You carried my grandfather up a flight of stairs?"

"Yes, at Randa's castle."

"After a day and a night of hard riding?"

"Yes."

His laugh burst out, but she didn't see the joke. "I had to do it, Po. If I hadn't, the mission would've failed."

"He weighs as much as you, and half as much again."

"Well, and I was tired by the time I got to the top. You wouldn't have been so tired."

"I'm bigger than he is, Katsa. I'm stronger. And I would have been tired, had I spent the night on my horse."

"I had to do it. I had no choice."

"Your Grace is more than fighting," he said.

She didn't respond to that, and after a moment's puzzlement, she forgot it. Her mind returned to the matter at hand. As it couldn't help but do, with Po always before her.

WHAT WAS the difference between a husband and a lover?

If she took Po as her husband, she would be making promises about a future she couldn't yet see. For once she became his wife, she would be his wife forever. And, no matter how much freedom Po gave her, she would always know that it was a gift. Her freedom would not be her own; it would be Po's to give or to withhold. That he never would withhold it made no difference. If it did not come from her, it was not really hers.

If Po were her lover, would she feel captured, cornered into a sense of forever? Or would she still have the freedom that sprang from herself?

They were lying on opposite sides of a dying fire one night when a new worry occurred to her. What if she took more from Po than she could give to him?

"Po?"

She heard him turn onto his side. "Yes?"

"How will you feel if I'm forever leaving? If one day I give myself to you and the next I take myself away—with no promises to return?"

"Katsa, a man would be a fool to try to keep you in a cage."

"But that doesn't tell me how you'll feel, always to be subject to my whim."

"It isn't your whim. It's the need of your heart. You forget that I'm in a unique position to understand you, Katsa. Whenever you pull away from me I'll know it's not for lack of love. Or if it is, I'll know that, too; and I'll know it's right for you to go."

"But you're not answering my question. How will you feel?"

There was a pause. "I don't know. I'll probably feel a lot of things. But only one of the things will be unhappiness; and unhappiness I'm willing to risk."

Katsa stared up into the treetops. "Are you sure of that?"

He sighed. "I'm certain."

He was willing to risk unhappiness. And there was the crux of the matter. She couldn't know where this would lead, and to proceed was to risk all kinds of unhappiness.

The fire gasped and died. She was frightened. For as their camp turned to darkness, she also found herself choosing risk.

THE NEXT DAY Katsa would have given anything for a clear, straight path, for hard riding and thundering hooves to drown out all feeling. Instead the road wound back and forth, up rises and into gullies, and she didn't know how she kept herself from screaming. Nightfall led them into a hollow where water trickled into a low, still pool. Moss covered the trees and the ground. Moss hung from the vines that hung from the trees, and dripped into the pool that shone green like the floor of Randa's courtyard.

"You seem a bit edgy," Po said. "Why don't you hunt? I'll build a fire."

She allowed the first few animals she stumbled across to escape. She thought that if she plunged deeper into the forest and took more time, she might wear down some of her jitters. But when she returned to camp much later with a fox in hand, nothing had changed. He sat calmly before the fire, and she thought she might burst apart. She threw their meat onto the ground beside the flames. She sat on a rock and dropped her head into her hands.

She knew what it was rattling around inside her. It was fear, plain and cold.

She turned to him. "I understand why we shouldn't fight each other when one of us is angry. But is there harm in fighting when one of us is frightened?"

He looked into the fire and considered her question evenly. He looked into her face. "I think it depends on what you hope to gain by fighting."

"I think it'll calm me. I think it'll make me comfortable with—with you being near." She rubbed her forehead, sighing. "It'll return me to myself."

He watched her. "It does seem to have that effect on you."

"Will you fight me now, Po?"

He watched her for a moment longer and then moved away from the fire and motioned for her to follow. She walked after him, dazed, her mind buzzing so crazily it was numb, and when they faced each other she found herself staring at him dumbly. She shook her head to clear it, but it did no good.

"Hit me," she said.

He paused for a fraction of a second. Then he swung at her face with one fist and she flashed her arm upward to block him. The explosion of arm on arm woke her from her stupor. She would fight him, and she would beat him. He hadn't beaten her yet, and he wouldn't beat her tonight. No matter the darkness, and no matter the whirlwind in her mind, for now that they fought, the whirlwind had vanished. Katsa's mind was clear.

She hit hard and fast, with hand, elbow, knee, foot. He hit hard, too, but it was as if every blow focused some energy inside her. Every tree they slammed into, every root they tripped over, centered her. She fell into the comfort of fighting with Po, and the fight was ferocious.

When she wrestled him to the ground and he pushed her face away, she called out. "Wait. Blood. I taste blood."

He stopped struggling. "Where? Not your mouth?"

"I think it's your hand," she said.

He sat up and she crouched beside him. She took his hand and squinted into his palm. "Is it bleeding? Can you tell?"

"It's nothing. It was the edge of your boot."

"We shouldn't be fighting in boots."

"We can't fight barefoot in the forest, Katsa. Truly, it's nothing."

"Nonetheless—"

"There's blood on your mouth," he said, in a funny, distracted sort of voice that made plain how little he cared about his injured hand. He raised a finger and almost touched her lip; and then dropped his finger, as if he realized suddenly that he was doing something he shouldn't. He cleared his throat and looked away from her.

And she felt it then, how near he was. She felt his hand and his wrist, warm under her fingers. He was here, right here, breathing before her; she was touching him; and she felt the risk, as if it were water splashing cold on her skin. She knew that this was the moment to choose. She knew her choice.

He turned his eyes back to her, and in them she saw that he understood. She climbed into his arms. They clung to each other, and she was crying, as much from relief to be holding him as from the fear of what she did. He rocked her in his lap and hugged her, and whispered her name over and over, until finally her tears stopped.

She wiped her face on his shirt. She wrapped her arms around his neck. She felt warm in his arms, and calm, and safe and brave. And then she was laughing, laughing at how nice it felt, how good his body felt against hers. He grinned at her, a wicked, gleaming grin that made her warm everywhere. And then his lips touched her throat and nuzzled her neck. She gasped. His mouth found hers. She turned to fire.

Some time later, as she lay with him in the moss, clinging to him, hypnotized by something his lips did to her throat, she remembered his bleeding hand. "Later," he growled, and then she remembered the blood on her mouth, but that only brought his mouth to hers again, tasting, seeking, and his hands fumbling at her clothing, and her hands fumbling at his. And the warmth of his skin, as their bodies explored each other. And after all, they knew each other's bodies as well as any lovers; but this touch was so different, straining toward instead of against.

"Po," she said once, when one clear thought pierced her mind.

"It's in the medicines," he whispered. "There is seabane in the medicines," and his hands, and his mouth, and his body returned her to mindlessness. He made her drunk, this man made her drunk; and every time his eyes flashed into hers she could not breathe.

She expected the pain, when it came. But she gasped at its sharpness; it was not like any pain she had felt before. He kissed her and slowed and would have stopped. But she laughed, and said that this one time she would consent to hurt, and bleed, at his touch. He smiled into her neck and kissed her again and she moved with him through the pain. The pain became a warmth that grew. Grew, and stopped her breath. And took her breath and her pain and her mind away from her body, so that there was nothing but her body and his body and the light and fire they made together.

THEY LAY afterward, warmed by each other and by the heat of the fire. She touched his nose and his mouth. She played with the hoops in his ears. He held her and kissed her, and his eyes flickered into hers.

"Are you all right?" he asked.

She laughed. "I have not lost myself. And you?"

He smiled. "I'm very happy."

She traced the line of his jaw to his ear and down to his shoulder. She touched the markings that ringed his arms. "And Raffin thought we'd end this way, too," she said. "Apparently, I'm the only one who didn't see it coming."

"Raffin will make a very good king," Po said, and she laughed again, and rested her head in the crook of his arm.

"Let's pick up the pace tomorrow," she said, thinking of men who were not good kings.

"Yes, all right. Are you in pain still?"

"No."

"Why do you suppose it happens that way? Why does a woman feel that pain?"

She had no answer to that. Women felt it, that was all she knew. "Let me clean your hand," she said.

"I'll clean you first."

She shivered as he left her to go to the fire, and find water and cloths. He leaned into the light, and brightness and shadows moved across his body. He was beautiful. She admired him, and he flashed a grin at her. *Almost as beautiful as you are conceited,* she thought at him, and he laughed out loud.

It struck her that this should feel strange, to be lying here, watching him, teasing him. To have done what they'd done, and be what they'd become. But instead it felt natural and comfortable. Inevitable. And only the smallest bit terrifying.

CHAPTER TWENTY-ONE

THEY HAD entire conversations in which she didn't say a word. For Po could sense when Katsa desired to talk to him, and if there was a thing she wanted him to know, his Grace could capture that thing. It seemed a useful ability for them to practice. And Katsa found that the more comfortable she grew with opening her mind to him, the more practiced she became with closing it as well. It was never entirely satisfying, closing her mind, because whenever she closed her feelings from him she must also close them from herself. But it was something.

They found it was easier for him to pick up her thoughts than it was for her to formulate them. She thought things to him word by word at first, as if she were speaking, but silently. *Do you want to stop and rest? Shall I catch us some dinner? I've run out of water.* "Of course I understand you when you're that precise," he said. "But you don't need to try so hard. I can understand images, too, or feelings, or thoughts in unformed sentences."

This was also hard for her at first. She was afraid of being misunderstood, and she formulated her images as carefully as she'd formulated her words. Fish roasting over their fire. A stream. The herbs, the seabane, that she must eat with dinner.

"If you only open a thought to me, Katsa, I'll see it—no matter how you think it. If you intend me to know it, I will."

But what did it mean to open a thought to him? To intend for him to know it? She tried simply reaching out to his mind whenever she wanted him to know something. *Po.* And then leaving it to him to collect the essence of the thought.

It seemed to work. She practiced constantly, both communicating with him and closing him out. Slowly, the tightness of her mind loosened.

Beside the fire one night, protected from the rain by a shelter of branches she'd built, she asked to see his rings. He placed his hands into hers. She counted. Six plain gold rings, of varying widths, on his right hand. On his left, one plain gold; one thin with an inlaid gray stone running through the middle; one wide and heavy with a sharp, glittery white stone—this the one that must have scratched her that night beside the archery range; and one plain and gold like the first, but engraved all around with a design she recognized, from the markings on his arms. It was this ring that made her wonder if the rings had meaning.

"Yes," he said. "Every ring worn by a Lienid means something. This with the engraving is the ring of the king's seventh son. It's the ring of my castle and my princehood. My inheritance."

Do your brothers have a different ring, and markings on their arms that are different from yours?

"They do."

She fingered the great, heavy ring with the jagged white stone. *This is the ring of a king.*

"Yes, this ring is for my father. And this," he said, fingering the small one with the gray line running through the middle, "for my mother. This plain one for my grandfather."

Was he never king?

"His older brother was king. When his brother died, he would've been king, had he wished it. But his son, my father, was young and strong and ambitious. My grandfather was old and unwell and content to pass the kingship to his son."

And what of your father's mother, and your mother's father and mother? Do you wear rings for them?

"No. They're dead. I never knew them."

She took his right hand. *And these? You don't have enough fingers for the rings on this hand.*

"These are for my brothers," he said. "One for each. The thickest for the oldest and the thinnest for the youngest."

Does this mean that your brothers all wear an even thinner ring, for you?

"That's right, and my mother and grandfather, too, and my father."

Why should yours be the smallest, just because you're the youngest?

"That's the way it is, Katsa. But the ring they wear for me is different from the others. It has a tiny inlaid gold stone, and a silver."

For your eyes.

"Yes."

It's a special ring, for your Grace?

"The Lienid honor the Graced."

Well, and that was a novel idea. She hadn't known that anyone honored the Graced. *You don't wear rings for your brothers' wives, or their children?*

He smiled. "No, thankfully. But I would wear one for my own wife, and if I had children, I'd wear a ring for each. My mother has four brothers, four sisters, seven sons, two parents, and a husband. She wears nineteen rings."

And that is absurd. How can she use her fingers?

He shrugged. "I've no difficulty using mine." He raised her hands to his mouth then and kissed her knuckles.

You wouldn't catch me wearing that many rings.

He laughed, turned her hands over, and kissed her palms and her wrists. "I wouldn't catch you doing anything you didn't want to do."

And here was what was rapidly becoming her favorite aspect of Po's Grace: He knew, without her telling him, the things she *did* want to do. He dropped to his knees before her now, with a smile that looked like mischief. His hand grazed her side and then pulled her closer. His lips brushed her neck. She caught her breath, forgot whatever retort she'd been about to form, and enjoyed the gold chill of his rings on her face and her body and every place that he touched.

"YOU BELIEVE Leck cuts those animals up himself," she said to him one day while they were riding. "Don't you?"

He glanced back at her. "I realize it's a disgusting accusation.

But yes, that's what I believe. And I also wonder about the sickness that man spoke of."

"You think he's killing people off."

Po shrugged and didn't answer.

Katsa said, "Do you think Queen Ashen closed herself away from him because she figured out that he's Graced?"

"I've wondered about that, too."

"But how could she have figured it out? Shouldn't she be completely under his spell?"

"I've no idea. Perhaps he went too far with his abuses and she had a moment of mental clarity." He raised a branch that hung in their path, and ducked under it. "Perhaps his Grace only works to a point."

Or perhaps there was no Grace. Perhaps it was no more than a ridiculous notion they'd come up with in a desperate attempt to explain unexplainable circumstances.

But a king and queen had died, and no one had called foul. A king had kidnapped a grandfather, and no one suspected him.

A one-eyed king.

It was a Grace. Or if it was not, it was something unnatural.

THE PATH grew thinner and more overgrown, and they walked with the horses more than they rode. And now all the trees seemed to change color at once, the leaves orange and yellow and crimson, and purple and brown. Only a day or two to go before they reached the inn that would take their horses. And then the steep climb into the mountains, with their belongings on their backs. There would be snow in the mountains, Po said, and there would not be many travelers. They would need to move cautiously and watch for storms.

"But you're not worried, are you, Katsa?"

"Not particularly."

"Because you never get cold, and you can bring down a bear with your hands and build us a fire in a blizzard, using icicles for kindling."

She would not humor him by laughing, but she couldn't suppress a smile. They had encamped for the evening. She was fishing, and when she fished he always teased her, for she didn't fish with a line, as he would have. She fished by removing her boots, rolling up the legs of her trousers, and wading into the water. She'd then snatch up any fish that came within range of her grasp and throw it to Po, who sat on shore laughing at her, scaling and gutting their dinner, and keeping her company.

"It's not many people whose hands are faster than a fish," he said.

Katsa snatched at a silver pink glimmer that flashed past her ankles, then tossed the fish to Po. "It's not many people who know that a horse has a stone caught in its hoof even when the horse shows no signs of it, either. I may be able to kill my dinner as easily as I kill men, but at least I'm not conversing with the horses."

"I don't converse with the horses. I've only started to know if they want us to stop. And once we've stopped, it's usually easy enough to find what's wrong."

"Well, regardless, it seems to me that you're not in a position to marvel at the strangeness of my Grace."

Po leaned back on his elbows and grinned. "I don't think your Grace is strange. But I think it's not what you think it is."

She grabbed at a dark flash in the water and threw a fish to him. "What is it, then?"

"Now, that I don't know. But a killing Grace can't account for all the things you can do. The way you never tire. Or suffer from the cold, or from hunger."

"I tire."

"Other things, too. The knack you have with fire in a rainstorm."

"I'm just more patient than other people."

Po snorted. "Yes. Patience has always struck me as one of your defining characteristics."

He dodged the fish that flew at his head, and sat back again, laughing. "Your eyes are bright as you stand in that water, with the sun setting before you," he said. "You're beautiful."

Stop it. "And you're a fool."

"Come out of there, wildcat. We've enough fish."

She waded to shore. Meeting her at the edge of the water, he pulled her up onto the moss. Together they gathered up the fish and walked to the fire.

"I tire," Katsa said. "And I feel cold and hunger."

"All right, if you say so. But just compare yourself to other people."

Compare herself to other people.

She sat down and dried her feet.

"Shall we fight tonight?" he asked.

She nodded, absently.

He set the fish above the flames and hummed and washed his hands, and flashed his light at her from across the fire. She sat—and thought to herself about what she found when she compared herself to other people.

She did feel cold, sometimes. But she didn't suffer from it as other people did. And she felt hunger sometimes; but she could go long with little food, and hunger did not make her weak. She couldn't remember ever feeling weak, exactly, for any reason. Nor could she remember ever having been ill. She thought back and was certain. She'd never even had a cough.

She stared into the fire. They were a bit unusual, these things. She could see that. And she knew there was more.

She fought and rode and ran and tumbled, but her skin rarely bruised or broke. She'd never broken a bone. And she didn't suffer from pain the way other people did. Even when Po hit her very hard, the pain was easily manageable. If she was being honest, she'd have to admit that she didn't quite understand what other people meant when they complained of pain.

She didn't tire as other people did. She didn't need much sleep. Most nights she made herself sleep, only because she knew she should.

"Po?"

He looked up from the fire.

"Can you tell yourself to go to sleep?"

"What do you mean?"

"I mean, can you lie down and make yourself fall asleep? Whenever you want, instantly?"

He squinted at her. "No. I've never heard of such a thing."

"Hmm."

He studied her for a moment longer, and then seemed to decide to let her be. She barely noticed him. It had never occurred to her before that the control she had over her sleep might be unusual. And it wasn't just that she could command herself to sleep. She could command herself to sleep for a specific amount of time. And whenever she woke, she always knew exactly what time it was. At every moment of the day, in fact, she always knew the time.

Just as she always knew exactly where she was and what direction she was facing.

"Which way is north?" she asked Po.

He looked up again and considered the light. He pointed in a direction that was loosely north, but not exactly. How did she know that with such certainty?

She never got lost. She never had trouble building a fire, or shelter. She hunted so easily. Her vision and her hearing were better than those of anyone she'd ever known.

She stood abruptly. She strode the few steps back to the pond and stared into it without seeing it.

The physical needs that limited other people did not limit her. The things from which other people suffered did not touch her. She knew instinctively how to live and thrive in the wilderness.

And she could kill anyone. At the slightest threat to her survival.

Katsa sat on the ground suddenly.

Could her Grace be survival?

The instant she asked it, she denied it. She was just a killer, had always been just a killer. She'd killed a cousin, in plain view of Randa's court—a man who wouldn't have hurt her, not really. She'd murdered him, without a thought, without hesitation—just as she'd very nearly murdered her uncle.

But she *hadn't* murdered her uncle. She'd found a way to avoid it and stay alive.

And she hadn't meant for that cousin to die. She'd been a child, her Grace unformed. She hadn't lashed out to kill him; she'd only lashed out to protect herself, to protect herself from his touch. She'd forgotten this, somewhere along the line, when the people of the court had begun to shy away from her and Randa had begun to use her skill for his own purposes, and call her his child killer.

Her Grace was not killing. Her Grace was survival.

She laughed then. For it was almost like saying her Grace was life; and of course, that was ridiculous.

She stood again and turned back to the fire. Po watched her approach. He didn't ask what she was thinking, he didn't intrude; he would wait until she wanted to tell him. She looked at him measuring her from across the flames. He was plainly curious.

"I've been comparing myself to other people," she said.

"I see," he said, cautiously.

She peeled back the skin of one of the roasting fish and sliced off a piece. She chewed on it and thought.

"Po."

He looked up at her.

"If you learned that my Grace wasn't killing," she said, "but survival . . ."

He raised his eyebrows.

"Would it surprise you?"

He pursed his lips. "No. It makes much more sense to me."

"But—it's like saying my Grace is life."

"Yes."

"It's absurd."

"Is it? I don't think so. And it's not just your own life," he said. "You've saved many lives with your Grace."

She shook her head. "Not as many as I've hurt."

"Possibly. But you have the rest of your life to tip the balance. You'll live long."

The rest of her life to tip the balance.

Katsa peeled the flesh of another fish away from its bones. She broke the flaky meat apart and ate it, and thought about that, smiling.

CHAPTER TWENTY-TWO

THE TREES gave way suddenly, and the mountains came upon them all at once; and with the mountains, the town that would take their horses. The buildings were made of stone or of heavy Sunderan wood, but it was the town's backdrop that stopped Katsa's breath. She'd seen the hills of Estill, but she'd never seen mountains. She'd never seen silver trees that climbed straight up into the sky, and rock and snow that climbed even higher, to peaks impossibly high that shone gold in the sun.

"It reminds me of home," Po said.

"Lienid is like this?"

"Parts of Lienid. My father's city stands near mountains like these."

"Well," Katsa said. "It reminds me of nothing, for I've never seen anything like it. I almost can't believe I'm seeing it now."

There was no camping and no hunting for them that night. Their meal was cooked for them and served by the rough, friendly wife of the innkeeper, who seemed unconcerned with their Graceling eyes and wanted to know everything they'd seen on their journey, and everyone they'd passed. They ate in a room warm from the fire in a great stone fireplace. Hot stew, hot vegetables, hot bread, and the entire eating room to themselves. Chairs to sit on, and a table, and plates and spoons. Their baths afterwards warm; their bed warm, and softer than Katsa had remembered a bed could be. It was luxury, and they enjoyed it, for they knew it was the last such comfort they were likely to experience for some time.

THEY LEFT before sunlight broke over the peaks, with provisions wrapped by the innkeeper's wife, and cold water from the inn's well. They carried most of their belongings, all that they had not left behind with the horses. One bow and one quiver, on Katsa's back, as she was the better shot. Neither of their swords, though both carried dagger and knife. Their bedrolls, little clothing, coins, the medicines, the maps, the list of Council contacts.

The sky they climbed toward turned purple, then orange and pink. The mountain path bore the signs of the crossings of others—fires gone cold, boot impressions in the dirt. In some places huts had been built for the use of travelers, empty of furniture but with crude, functional fireplaces. Built by the combined efforts of Sunder, Estill, and Monsea, in a time long ago when the kingdoms worked together for the safe passage of travelers across their borders.

"A roof and four walls can save you, in a blizzard in the mountains," Po said.

"Were you ever caught in the mountains during a blizzard?"

"I was once, with my brother Silvern. We were out climbing, and a storm surprised us. We found the hut of a woodsman—if we hadn't, we'd likely be dead. We were trapped for four days. For four days we ate nothing but the bread and apples we'd brought along, and the snow. Our mother almost gave us up for lost."

"Which brother is Silvern?"

"My father's fifth son."

"It's a shame you hadn't the animal sense then that you have now. You could've gone out and unearthed a mole, or a squirrel."

"And lost myself on the way back to the hut," he said. "Either that, or returned to a brother who'd think it was awfully suspicious that I'd managed to hunt in a blizzard."

They climbed over dirt and grass that gave way at times to rock, climbed always with the mountain peaks rising before them. It felt good to be out of the forest, to climb, to move fast. The vast, empty sky glinted its sun onto her face and filled her lungs with air. She was content.

"Why have you never trusted your brothers with your Grace?"

"My mother forbade me when I was a child, absolutely forbade me to tell them. I hated to keep it from them— particularly Silvern, and Skye, who's closest in age to me. But now I know my brothers as men, and I see my mother was right."

"Why? Aren't they to be trusted?"

"They are, with most things. But they're all made of ambition, Katsa, every one of them, constantly playing off each other to gain favor with my father. As things stand now, I'm no threat to them—because I'm the youngest and have no ambition. And they respect me, for they know it would take all six of them together to beat me in a fight. But if they knew the truth of my Grace they'd try to use me. They wouldn't be able to help themselves."

"But you wouldn't let them."

"No, but then they'd resent me, and I'm not sure one of them wouldn't give in to the temptation to tell his wife or his advisers. And my father would learn . . . It would all fall apart."

They stopped at a trickle of water. Katsa drank some and washed her face. "Your mother had foresight."

"Above all, she feared my father learning of it." He lowered his flask into the water. "He's not an unkind father. But it's hard to be king. Men will trick power away from a king, however they can. I would've been too useful to him. He couldn't have resisted using me—he simply couldn't. And that was the greatest thing my mother feared."

"Did he never want to use you as a fighter?"

"Certainly, and I've helped him. Not as you've helped Randa—my father isn't the bully Randa is. But it was my mind that my mother feared him using. She wanted my mind to be my own, and not his."

It didn't seem right to Katsa that a mother should have to protect her child from its father. But she didn't know much of mothers and fathers. She hadn't had a mother or a father to protect her from Randa's use. Perhaps rather than fathers, it was kings that were the danger.

"Your grandfather agreed that no one should know the truth of your Grace?"

"My grandfather agreed."

"Would your father be very angry, if he learned the truth now?"

"He'd be furious, with me, my mother, and my grandfather. They'd all be furious. And rightfully so; it's a huge deception we've pulled off, Katsa."

"You had to."

"Nonetheless. It would not be easily forgiven."

Katsa pulled herself onto a jumble of stones and stopped to look around. They seemed no closer to the tops of the peaks that rose before them. It was only by looking back, to the forest far below, that she knew they'd climbed; that, and the drop in temperature. She shifted her bags and stepped back onto the trail.

And then the thought of queens protecting children from kings registered more deeply in her mind.

Po. Leck has a daughter.

"Yes, Bitterblue. She's ten."

Bitterblue could have a role in this strange affair. If Leck was trying to hurt her, it would explain Queen Ashen hiding away with her.

Po stopped in his tracks and turned to look at her anxiously. "If he cuts up animals for pleasure, I hate to think what he would want with his own daughter."

The question hung in the air between them, eerie and horrible. Katsa thought suddenly of the two dead little girls.

"Let's hope you're wrong," Po said, his hand to his stomach as if he felt ill.

"Let's move faster," Katsa said, "just in case I'm right."

They set off almost at a run. They followed the path up-ward, through the mountains that separated them from Mon-sea and whatever truth it contained.

THEY WOKE the next morning on the floor of a dusty hut to a dead fire and a winter cold that seeped through the crack under the door. The frozen stars melted as Katsa and Po climbed, and light spread across the horizon. The path grew steeper and more rocky. The pace of their climb pushed away the chill and the stiffness that Katsa didn't feel but that Po complained of.

"I've been thinking about how we should approach Leck's court," Po said. He climbed from one rock to another and jumped to a third.

"What were you thinking?"

"Well, I'd like to be more certain of our suspicions before meeting him."

"Should we find an inn outside the court, and stay there our first night?"

"That's my thought."

"But we shouldn't waste any time."

"No. If we can't learn anything helpful in one night, then perhaps we should go ahead and present ourselves to the court."

They climbed, and Katsa wondered what that would be like—whether they would pose as friends to the court and in-filtrate it gradually, or whether they would enter on the of-fensive and instigate an enormous fight. She pictured Leck as a smirking, insincere man standing at the end of a velvet carpet, his single eye narrowed and clever. She imagined herself shooting an arrow into his heart, so that he crumpled to his knees, bled all over his carpet, and died at the feet of his stewards. At Po's command, her strike. It would have to be at Po's command, for until they knew the truth of his Grace, she couldn't trust her own judgment. *Po? That's true, isn't it?*

He took a moment to gather her thoughts. "I've some ideas about that as well," he said. "Once we're in Monsea, would you consent to do what I say, and only what I say? Just until I have a sense of Leck's power? Would you ever consent to that?"

"Of course I would, Po, in this case."

"And you must expect me to behave strangely. I'll have to pretend I'm Graced with fighting, no more, and that I believe every word he says."

"And I'll practice my archery, and my knife throwing," Katsa said. "For I've a feeling that when all is asked and revealed, King Leck will find himself on the end of my blade."

Po shook his head and did not smile. "I've a feeling it's not going to be that easy."

THE THIRD DAY of their crossing was the windiest, and the coldest. The mountain pass led them between two peaks that were hidden, sometimes, behind cyclones of snow. Their boots crunched through patches of snow; and flakes drifted onto their shoulders from the thin blue sky and melted into Katsa's hair.

"I like winter in the mountains," she said, but Po laughed.

"This isn't winter in the mountains. This is autumn in the mountains, and a mild autumn at that. Winter is ferocious."

"I think I should like that, too," she said, and Po laughed again.

"I wouldn't be a bit surprised. You'd thrive on the challenge of it."

The weather held, so that Katsa's declaration could not be put to the test. They moved as fast as the terrain would permit. For all his marveling at Katsa's energy, Po was strong and quick. He teased her for the pace she set, but he didn't complain; and if he stopped sometimes for food and water, Katsa was grateful, for it reminded her to eat and drink as well. And it gave her an excuse to turn around and stare behind them, at the mountains that stretched from east to west, at the whole world she could see—for she was so high that she felt she could see the whole world.

And then suddenly, they reached the top of the pass. Before them the mountains plunged into a forest of pines. Green valleys stretched beyond, broken by streams and farmhouses and tiny dots that Katsa guessed were cows. And a line, a river, that thinned into the distance and led to a miniature white city at the edge of their sight. Leck City.

"I can barely see it," Po said, "but I trust your vision."

"I see buildings," Katsa said, "and a dark wall around a white castle. And look, see the farmhouses in the valley? Surely you can make those out. And the cows, do you see the cows?"

"Yes, I can see them, now that you mention it. It's gorgeous, Katsa. Have you ever seen a sight so gorgeous?"

She laughed at his happiness. For a moment, as they looked down on Monsea, the world was beautiful and without worry.

THE DOWNHILL scramble was more treacherous than the uphill climb. Po complained that his toes were liable to burst through the front of his boots; and then he complained that he wished they would, for they ached from the constant downhill beat of his feet. And then Katsa noticed that he stopped complaining altogether and sank into a preoccupation.

"Po. We're moving fast."

"Yes." He shaded his eyes with his hand and squinted down at the fields of Monsea. "I only hope it's fast enough."

They camped that night beside a stream that ran with melting snow. She sat on a rock and watched his eyes that glimmered with worry. He glanced at her and smiled suddenly. "Would you like something sweet to eat with this rabbit?"

"Of course," she said, "but it makes little difference what I want, if all we have is rabbit."

He stood then and turned away into the scrub.

Where are you going?

He didn't answer. His boots scraped on rock as he disappeared into blackness.

She stood. "Po!"

"Don't worry your heart, Katsa." His voice came from a distance. "I'm only finding what you want."

"If you think I'm just going to sit here—"

"Sit down. You'll ruin my surprise."

She sat, but she let him know what she thought of him and his surprise, rattling around in the dark and breaking his ankles on the rocks most likely, so she'd have to carry him the rest of the way down the mountain. A few minutes passed, and she heard him returning. He stepped into the light and came to her, his hand cupped before him. When he knelt before her, she saw a little mound of berries in his palm. She looked into the shadows of his face.

"Winterberries?" she asked. "Winterberries." She took one from his hand and bit into it. It popped with a cold sweetness. She swallowed the soft flesh and watched his face, confused. "Your Grace showed them to you, these winterberries."

"Yes."

"Po. This is new, isn't it? That you should sense a plant with such clarity. It's not as if it were moving or thinking or about to crash down on top of you."

He sat back on his heels. He tilted his head. "The world is filling in around me," he said, "piece by piece. The fuzziness is clearing. To be honest, it's a bit disorienting. I'm ever so slightly dizzy."

Katsa stared at him. There was nothing to say in response to this; his Grace was showing him winterberries, and he was ever so slightly dizzy. Tomorrow he would be able to tell her about a landslide on the other side of the world, and they would both faint.

She sighed and touched the gold in his ear. "If you put your feet into the stream, the snow water will soothe your toes, and I'll rub the warmth back into them when you're done."

"And if I'm cold in places other than my toes? Will you warm me there, too?"

His voice was a grin, and she laughed into his face. But then he took her chin in his hand and looked into her eyes, seriously. "Katsa. When we get closer to Leck, you must do whatever I tell you to. Do you promise?"

"I promise."

"You must, Katsa. You must swear it."

"Po. I've promised it before, and I'll promise it again, and swear it, too. I'll do what you say."

He watched her eyes, and then he nodded. He emptied the last few berries into her hand and bent down to his boots.

"My toes are such a misery, I'm not sure it's wise to release them. They may revolt and run off into the mountains and refuse to return."

She ate another winterberry. "I expect I'm more than a match for your toes."

THE NEXT DAY there were no more jokes from Po, about his toes or anything else. He hardly spoke, and the farther they moved down the path that led to King Leck, the more anxious he seemed to become. His mood was contagious. Katsa was uneasy.

"You'll do what I say, when the time comes?" he asked her once.

She opened her mouth to give voice to a surge of irritation at the question she'd already answered and must now answer again. But at the sight of him trudging down the path beside her, tense and worried, she lost hold of her anger.

"I'll do what you say, Po."

Chapter Twenty-three

"K<small>ATSA</small>."

His voice woke her. She opened her eyes and knew it to be about three hours before dawn. "What is it?"

"I can't sleep."

She sat up. "Too worried?"

"Yes."

"Well, I assume you didn't wake me just for my company."

"You don't need the sleep; and if I'm going to be awake we may as well be moving."

And she was up, and her blanket rolled, and her quiver and bow and bags on her back in an instant. A path, sloping downhill, ran through the trees. The forest was black. Po took her arm and led her as best he could, stumbling over stones and resting his hand on trees she couldn't see to steady their passage.

When a cold, gritty light finally brought shadow and shape to their path, they moved faster, practically ran. Snow began to fall, and the trail, wider and flatter, glowed a pale blue. The inn that would sell them horses was beyond the forest, hours away by foot. As they hurried on, Katsa found herself looking forward to the rest for her feet and her lungs that the horses would bring. She opened the thought to Po.

"It takes this," he said, "to tire you. Running, in the dark, on no sleep, and no food, after days of climbing in the mountains." He didn't smile, and he wasn't teasing. "I'm glad. Whatever it is we're running toward, we're likely to need your energy, and your stamina."

That reminded her. She reached into a bag on her back. "Eat," she said. "We must both eat, or we'll be good for nothing."

IT WAS MIDMORNING, and the snow still drifted down, when they neared the place where the forest stopped abruptly and the fields began. Po turned to her suddenly, alarm screaming in every feature of his face. He began to run headlong down the path through the trees, toward the edge of the forest. And then Katsa heard it—men's voices raised, yelling, and the thunder of hooves, coming closer. She ran after Po and broke through the trees several paces behind him. A woman staggered across the fields toward them, a small woman with arms raised, her face a mask of terror. Dark hair and gold hoops in her ears. A black dress, and gold on the fingers she stretched out to Po. And behind her an army of men on galloping horses, led by one man with streaming robes and an eyepatch, and a raised bow, and a notched arrow that flew from the bow and struck the woman square in the back. The woman jerked and stumbled. She fell on her face in the snow.

Po stopped cold. He ran back to Katsa, yelling, "Shoot him! Shoot him!" but she had already swung the bow from her back and reached for an arrow. She pulled the string and took aim. And then the horses stopped. The man with the eyepatch screamed out, and Katsa froze.

"Oh, what an accident!" he cried.

His voice was a choke, a sob. So full of desperate pain that Katsa gasped, and tears rose to her eyes.

"What a terrible, terrible accident!" the man screamed. "My wife! My beloved wife!"

Katsa stared at the crumpled body of the woman, black dress and flung arms, white snow stained red. The man's sobs carried to her across the fields. It was an accident. A terrible, tragic accident. Katsa lowered her bow.

"No! Shoot him!"

Katsa gaped at Po, shocked at his words, at the wildness in his eyes. "But, it was an accident," she said.

"You promised to do what I said."

"Yes, but I'm not going to shoot a grieving man whose wife has had such an accident—"

His voice was angry now, as she'd never heard it. "Give me the bow," he hissed, so strange and rough, so unlike himself.

"No."

"Give it to me."

"No! You're not yourself!"

He clutched his hair then and looked behind him desperately, at the man who watched them, his one eye cocked toward them, his gaze cool, measuring. Po and the man stared at each other for just a moment. Some flicker of recognition stirred inside Katsa, but then it was gone. Po turned back to her, calm now. Desperately, urgently calm.

"Will you do something else, then?" he said. "Something much smaller, that will hurt no one?"

"Yes, if it will hurt no one."

"Will you run with me now, back into the forest? And if he starts to speak, will you cover your ears?"

What an odd request, but she felt that same strange flicker of recognition; and she agreed, without knowing why. "Yes."

"Quickly, Katsa."

In an instant they turned and ran, and when she heard voices she clapped her hands to her ears. But she could still hear words barked here and there, and what she heard confused her. And then Po's voice, yelling at her to keep running; yelling at her, she thought vaguely, to drown out the other voices. She half heard a muffled clatter of hooves growing behind them. The clatter turned into a thunder. And then she saw the arrows striking the trees around them.

The arrows made her angry. *We could kill these men, all of them,* she thought to Po. *We should fight.* But he kept yelling at her to run, and his hand tightened on her shoulder and pushed her forward, and she had that sense again that all was not right, that none of this was normal, and that in this madness, she should trust Po.

They raced around trees and clambered up slopes, rushing in whatever direction Po chose. The arrows dropped off as they moved deeper into the forest, for the woods slowed the horses and confused the men. Still they kept running. They came to a part of the forest so thickly wooded that the snow had caught in the branches of the trees and never reached the ground. Our footprints, Katsa thought. He's taken us here so they can't trace our footprints. She clung to that thought, because it was the only piece of this senselessness she understood.

Finally, Po pulled her hands from her ears. They ran more, until they came to a great, wide tree with brown needles, the ground littered with dead branches that had fallen from its trunk. "There's a hollow place, up high," Po said. "There's an opening in the trunk. Can you climb it? If I go first, can you follow?"

"Of course. Here," she said, making a cup with her hands. He put one foot into her palms and jumped, and she lifted him up as high as she could into the tree. She made handholds and footholds of the rough places in the trunk and hustled up after him. "Avoid that branch," he called down to her. "And this one: A breeze would knock it down." She used the limbs he used; he climbed and she followed. He disappeared, and a moment later his arms reached out of a great hole above her. He pulled her inside the tree, into the hollowed-out space he'd sensed from the ground. They sat in the dark, breathing heavily, their legs entwined in their tree cave.

"We'll be safe here, for now," Po said. "As long as they don't come after us with dogs."

But why were they hiding? Now that they sat still, the strangeness of all that had happened began to pierce Katsa's mind, like the arrows the horsemen had shot at their backs. Why were they hiding, why weren't they fighting? Why were they afraid? That woman had been afraid, too. That woman who looked like a Lienid. Ashen. The wife of Leck was a

Lienid, and her name was Ashen—and yes, that made sense, because that grief-stricken man had called her his wife. That man with the eyepatch and the bow in his hands was Leck.

But wasn't it Leck's arrow that had struck Ashen? Katsa couldn't quite recall; and when she tried to watch that moment again in her mind, a fog and falling snow blocked her sight.

Po might remember. But Po had been so strange, too, telling her to shoot Leck as he grieved over his wife. And then telling her to cover her ears. Why cover her ears?

That thing that she couldn't quite grasp flickered again in her mind. She reached for it and it disappeared. And then she was angry, at her thickheadedness, her stupidity. She couldn't make sense of all this, because she was too unintelligent.

She looked at Po, who leaned against the wall of the tree and stared straight ahead at nothing. The sight of him upset her even more, for his face seemed thin, his mouth tight. He was tired, worn out, most likely hungry. He'd said something about dogs, and she knew his eyes well enough to recognize the shadows of worry that sat within them.

Po. Please tell me what's wrong.

"Katsa." He sighed her name. He rubbed his forehead and then looked into her face. "Do you remember our conversations about King Leck, Katsa? What we said about him, before we saw him today?"

She stared at him and remembered they'd said something; but she couldn't remember what it was.

"About his eyes, Katsa. Something he's hiding."

"He's . . ." It came to her suddenly. "He's Graced."

"Yes. Do you remember what his Grace is?"

And then it began to trickle back to her, piece by piece, from some part of her mind she hadn't been able to reach before. She saw it again clearly. Ashen, terrified, fleeing from her husband and his army; Leck shooting Ashen in the back; Leck crying out in pretended grief, his words fogging Katsa's mind, transforming the murder her eyes had seen into a tragic accident she couldn't remember. Po screaming at her to shoot Leck; and she refusing.

She couldn't look him in the face, for shame overwhelmed her.

"It's not your fault," he said.

"I swore to you I'd do what you said. I swore it, Po."

"Katsa. No one could've kept that promise. If I'd known how powerful Leck was, if I'd had the slightest idea—I never should have brought you here."

"You didn't bring me here. We came together."

"Well, and now we're both in great danger." He stiffened. "Wait," he whispered. He seemed to be listening to something, but Katsa could hear nothing. "They're searching the forest," he said after a minute. "That one turned away. I don't think they have dogs."

"But why are we hiding from them?"

"Katsa—"

"What do you mean, we're in great danger? Why aren't we fighting these butchers, why . . ." She dropped her face into her hands. "I'm so confused. I'm hopelessly stupid."

"You're not stupid. It's Leck's Grace that takes away your own thought, and it's my Grace that sees so much more than a person should. You're confused because Leck confused you deliberately with his words, and because I haven't told you yet what I know."

"Then tell me. Tell me what you know."

"Well, Ashen is dead—that, I don't have to tell you. She's dead because she tried to escape Leck with Bitterblue. Here we see her punishment for protecting her child." She heard his bitterness and remembered that Ashen was not a stranger to him, that he had seen a member of his family murdered today. "I believe you were right about Bitterblue," he said. "I'm almost sure, from what Ashen wanted as she ran toward me."

"What did she want?"

"She wanted me to find Bitterblue, and protect her. I . . . I don't know what it is Leck wants with her, exactly. But I think Bitterblue's in the forest, hiding, like us."

"We must find her before they do."

"Yes, but there's more you need to know, Katsa. We're in particular danger, you and I. Leck saw us, he recognized us. Leck saw us . . ."

He broke off, but it didn't matter. She understood, suddenly, what Leck had seen. He'd seen them run away when they shouldn't have had the slightest idea of their danger. He'd seen her put her hands over her ears when they shouldn't have known the power of his words.

"He doesn't—he doesn't know how much of the truth

I know," Po said. "But he knows his Grace doesn't work on me. I'm a threat to him and he wants me dead. And you he wants alive."

Katsa's eyes snapped to his face. "But they were shooting at us—"

"I heard the command, Katsa. The arrows were meant for me."

"We should have fought," Katsa said. "We could've taken those soldiers. We must find him now and kill him."

"No, Katsa. You know you can't be in his presence."

"I can cover my ears somehow."

"You can't block out all sound, and he'll only talk louder. He'll yell and you'll hear him—your hearing is too good—and his words are no less dangerous if they're muffled. Even the words of his soldiers are dangerous. Katsa, you'll end up confused again and we'll have to run—"

"I won't let him do that to me again, Po—"

"Katsa." There was a tired certainty in his voice, and she didn't want to hear what he was going to say. "It only took him a few words," he said, "and he had you. A few words erased everything you'd seen. He wants you, Katsa, he wants your Grace. And I can't protect you."

She hated the truth of his words, for he was right. Leck could do what he wanted with her. He could make a monster of her, if that was his wish. "Where is he now?"

"I don't know; not nearby. But he's probably in the forest, looking for us or for Bitterblue."

"Will it be difficult to avoid him?"

"I don't think so. My Grace will tell me if he's near, and we can run and hide."

A sick feeling stopped her breath. What if he tried to turn her against Po?

She took her dagger from her belt and held it out to him. He looked back at her with quiet eyes, understanding. "It won't come to that," he said.

"Good," she said. "Take it anyway."

He set his mouth but didn't argue. He took the dagger and slid it into his own belt. She pulled the knife from her boot and passed it to him. She handed him the bow and helped him fasten the quiver of arrows onto his back.

"There's not much we can do about my hands and feet," she said, "but at least I'm unarmed. You'd stand a chance against me, Po, if you had a blade in each hand and I had none."

"It won't come to that."

No, it probably wouldn't. But if it did, there was no harm in being prepared. She watched his face, his eyes, which dimly glowed. His tired eyes, his dear eyes. He'd be better able to defend himself if her hands were bound. She wondered, should they bind her hands?

"And now you've crossed into the realm of the absurd," he said.

She grinned. "We should try it, though, in our fights."

A smile twitched in the corner of his mouth. "I could agree to that, sometime, when all of this is behind us."

"Now," she said, "let's find your cousin."

CHAPTER TWENTY-FOUR

IT WAS NOT easy for her to walk helplessly through the forest, Po deciding where to go and knowing when and where to hide, freezing in his tracks at the sense of things she couldn't see or hear. His Grace was invaluable, she knew that. But Katsa had never felt so much like a child.

"She became hopeful when she saw me," Po said, speaking quickly as they rushed through the trees. "Ashen did. At the sight of me her heart filled with hope, for Bitterblue."

This hope was what directed their steps now. Ashen had hoped so hard for Po to find Bitterblue that she'd left him with a sense of a place she believed Bitterblue to be, a particular spot both she and the child knew from the rides they took together. It was south of the mountain-pass road, in a hollow with a stream.

"I know a bit of how it looks," Po said. "But I don't know exactly where it is, and I don't know if she would've stayed there once she realized the entire army was searching for her."

"At least we know where to start," Katsa said. "She can't have gone too far."

They raced through the forest. The snow had stopped, and water dripped from pine needles and rushed through the streams. They passed patches of mud trampled with the feet of the soldiers who sought them.

"If she's left great footprints like these, they'll have found her by now," Katsa said.

"Let's hope she inherited some of her father's cunning."

More than once a soldier came uncomfortably near, and Po altered their path in order to skirt around him. One time while avoiding one soldier they nearly ran into another. They scrambled up a tree, and Po readied an arrow, but the fellow never took his eyes from the ground. "Princess Bitterblue," the man called. "Come now, Princess. Your father is very worried for you."

The soldier wandered away, but it was a number of minutes before Katsa was able to climb down. She'd heard the man's words, even with her hands over her ears. She'd fought against them, but still they'd clouded her mind. She sat in the tree, shuddering, while Po grasped her chin, looked into her eyes, and talked her through her confusion.

"All right," she said finally. "My mind is clear."

They clambered down. They moved quickly and left as little trace as possible of their own passage.

NEAR THE ENTRANCE to the forest, things became tricky. The soldiers were everywhere, gathered in groups, moving in every direction. She and Po ran for short bursts when Po decided it was safe, and then hid.

Once, Po grabbed her arm and jerked her backward, and they raced back the way they'd come. They found a great mossy rock and hunched behind it, Po's hands clapped over her ears, his eyes glowing with a fierce concentration. Wedged between the rock and Po, his heart beating fast against her body, she knew this time they hid from more than mere soldiers. They waited, it seemed interminably. Then Po took her wrist and motioned for her to follow. They crept away by a different route, one that widened the distance between them and the Monsean king.

WHEN THEY were as close to the entrance to the forest as Po deemed safe, they turned south, as they hoped Bitterblue had done. When a stream bubbled across their path Po stopped. He crouched down and clutched his head. Katsa stood beside him and watched and listened, waiting for him to sense something from the forest or from the memory of Ashen's hope.

"There's nothing," he said finally. "I can't tell if this is the right stream."

Katsa crouched beside him. "If the soldiers haven't found her yet," she said, "then she left no obvious trace, even in all this snow and mud. She must have had the presence of mind to walk through a stream, Po. Every stream in this forest flows from mountain to valley. She would've known to go west, away from the valleys. Is there any harm in following this stream west? If we don't stumble upon her, we can continue south and search the next stream."

"This seems a bit hopeless," Po said, but he stood, turned with her, and followed the water west. When Katsa found a tangle of long, dark hair snagged on a branch that snapped against her stomach, she called Po's name in his mind. She held the tangle of hair up for him to see. She tucked it into her sleeve and enjoyed the slightly more hopeful expression on his face.

When the stream curved sharply and entered a little hollow of grasses and ferns, Po stopped and held up his hand. "I recognize this place. This is it."

"Is she here?"

He stood for a moment. "No. But let's continue up the stream. Quickly. I fear there may be soldiers on our tail."

Only minutes later he turned to her, relief in the lines of his tired face. "I feel her now." He stepped out of the stream and Katsa followed. He wove his way through the trees until he came to a fallen tree trunk stretched across the forest floor. He measured the trunk with his eyes. He walked to one end, crouched down, and looked inside.

"Bitterblue," he said into the trunk. "I'm your cousin Po, the son of Ror. We've come to protect you."

There was no response. Po spoke quietly, and gently. "We're not going to hurt you, cousin. We're here to help you. Are you hungry? We have food."

Still there was no response from the fallen tree. Po stood and turned to Katsa. He spoke in a low voice. "She's afraid of me. You must try."

Katsa snorted. "You think she'll be less afraid of me?"

"She's afraid of me because I'm a man. Take care. She has a knife, and she's willing to use it."

"Good for her." Katsa knelt before the hollow end of the trunk and looked inside. She could just make out the girl, huddled tight, her breath short, panicked. Her hands clutching a knife.

"Princess Bitterblue," she said. "I'm the Lady Katsa, from the Middluns. I've come with Po to help you. You must trust us, Bitterblue. We're both Graced fighters. We can keep you safe."

"Tell her we know about Leck's Grace," Po whispered.

"We know your father is after you," Katsa said into the darkness. "We know he's Graced. We can keep you safe, Bitterbluc."

Katsa waited for some sign from the girl, but there was nothing. She looked up at Po and shrugged her shoulders. "Do you think we could break the tree apart?" she asked. But then from inside the trunk came a small, shaky voice.

"Where is my mother?"

Katsa's eyes snapped up to Po's. They searched each other's faces, uncertain; and then Po sighed, and nodded. Katsa turned back to the trunk. "Your mother is dead, Bitterblue."

She waited for sobbing, screams. But instead there was a pause, and then the voice came again. Even smaller now.

"The king killed her?"

"Yes," Katsa said.

There was another silence inside the tree. Katsa waited. "Soldiers are coming," Po muttered above her. "They're minutes away."

She didn't want to fight these soldiers who carried Leck's poison in their mouths; and they might not have to, if they could only get this child to come out.

"I can see that knife, Princess Bitterblue," she said. "Do you know how to use it? Even a small girl can do a lot of damage with a knife. I could teach you."

Po crouched down and touched her shoulder. "Thank you, Katsa," he breathed, and then he was up again, stalking a few paces into the trees, looking around and listening for anything his Grace could tell him. And she understood why he thanked her, for the child was crawling her way out of the trunk. Her face appeared from the dimness, then her hands and shoulders. Her eyes gray and her hair dark, like her mother's. Her eyes big, her face wet with tears, and her teeth chattering. Her fingers gripped tightly around a knife that was longer than her forearm.

She spilled out of the tree trunk and Katsa caught her and felt her cheeks and forehead. The child was shaking with cold. Her skirts were wet and clung to her legs; her boots were soaked through. She wore no coat or muffler, no gloves.

"Great hills, you're frozen stiff," Katsa said. She yanked off her own coat and pulled it down over the child's head. She tried to pull Bitterblue's arms through the sleeves, but the girl wouldn't loosen her grip on the knife. "Let it go for a minute, child. Just a second. Hurry, there are soldiers coming." She pried the knife from the girl's fingers and fastened the coat into place. She handed the knife back. "Can you walk, Bitterblue?" The girl didn't answer, but swayed, her eyes unfocused.

"We can carry her," Po said, suddenly at Katsa's side. "We must go."

"Wait," Katsa said. "She's too cold."

"Now. This instant, Katsa."

"Give me your coat."

Po tore off his bags, his quiver and bow. He tore off his coat and threw it to Katsa. She tugged the coat over Bitterblue's head, wrestled with the fingers around the knife again. She pulled the hood over the girl's ears and fastened it tight. Bitterblue looked like a potato sack, a small, shivering potato sack with empty eyes and a knife. Po tipped the girl over his shoulder and they gathered their things. "All right," Katsa said. "Let's go."

They ran south, stepping on pine needles and rock whenever they could, leaving as little sign of their passage as possible. But the ground was too wet, and the soldiers were quick on their mounts. Their trail was too easy to follow, and before long Katsa heard branches breaking and the thud of horses' hooves.

Po? How many of them?

"Fifteen," he said, "at least."

She breathed through her panic. *What if their words confuse me?*

His voice was low. "I wish I could fight them alone, Katsa, and out of your hearing. But it would mean us separating, and right now there are soldiers on every side of us. I won't risk your being found when I'm not there."

Katsa snorted. *Nor will I allow you to fight fifteen men alone.*

"We must kill as many of them as possible," Po said, "before they're close enough for conversation. And hope that once they're under attack they're not very talkative. Let's find a place to hide the girl. If they don't see her they're less likely to speak of her."

They tucked the child behind rocks and weeds, inside a niche at the base of a tree. "Don't make a sound, Princess," Katsa said. "And lend me your knife. I'll kill one of your father's men with it." She took the knife from the girl's uncomprehending fingers.

Po, Katsa thought, her mind racing. *Give me the knives and the daggers. I'll kill on first sight.*

Po pulled two daggers from his belt and a knife from each boot and tossed them to her, one by one. She collected the blades together; he readied the bow and cocked an arrow. They crouched behind a rock and waited, but there wasn't long to wait. The men came through the trees, moving quickly on their horses, their eyes skimming the ground for tracks. Katsa counted seventeen men. *I'll go right,* she thought grimly to Po. *You go left.* And with that she stood and hurled a knife, and another and another; Po's arrow flew, and he reached for another. Katsa's knives and daggers were embedded in the chests of five men, and Po had killed two, before the soldiers even comprehended the ambush.

The bodies of the dead slumped from their horses to the ground, and the bodies of the living jumped after them, pulling swords from sheaths, yelling, screaming unintelligibly, a mindful one or two drawing arrows. Katsa ran toward the men; Po continued shooting. The first came at her with wild eyes and a screeching mouth, swinging his sword so erratically that it was no trouble for Katsa to dodge the blade, kick another rushing man in the head, pull the first man's dagger from his belt, and stab them both in the neck. She kept the dagger, grabbed a sword, and came out swinging. She knocked another man's sword from his hands and ran hers through his stomach. She whirled on two men who came from behind and killed them both with her dagger while she fought off a third with her sword. She hurled the dagger into the chest of a soldier on a horse who aimed an arrow at Po.

And suddenly only one man was left, his breath ragged and his eyes wide with fear. That man backed away and began to run. In a flash Katsa pulled a knife from another man's chest and ran after him; but then she heard the smooth release of an arrow, and the man cried out and fell, and lay still.

Katsa looked down at her bloodstained tunic and trousers. She wiped her face, and blood came off onto her sleeve. All around her lay murdered men, men who hadn't known any better, whose minds were no weaker than her own. Katsa was sick and discouraged, and furious with the king who'd made this bloodbath necessary.

"Let's make sure they're dead," she said, "and get them on the horses. We must send them back, to put Leck off our trail."

They were dead, every one of them. Katsa pulled arrows and blades from chests and backs and tried not to look at their faces. She cleaned the knives and daggers and handed them back to Po. She carried Bitterblue's knife back to her and found the girl standing, arms crossed against the cold, eyes alert now, lucid. Katsa glanced down at her bloody clothing. She found herself hoping the child hadn't witnessed the massacre of men.

"I feel warmer," Bitterblue said.

"Good. How much of that fight did you see?"

"They didn't have much of a chance, did they?" It was her only answer. "Where are we going now?"

"I'm not sure. We need to find a safe place to hide, where we can eat and sleep. We need to talk about what happens next."

"You'll have to kill the king," she said, "if you ever want him to stop chasing us."

Katsa looked at this child, who barely came up to her chest. Po's sleeves hanging almost to the girl's knees; her eyes and her nose big under her hood, too big for her little face. Her voice a squeak. But a calmness in her manner of speaking, a certainty as she recommended her father's murder.

CHAPTER TWENTY-FIVE

THEY KEPT two horses for themselves. Bitterblue rode with Katsa. They wound their way back to the stream to clean themselves of the blood of the soldiers. Then they turned west. They walked the horses through the stream, moving toward the mountains, until the land around them grew rocky enough to hide hoofprints. There, they struck out south along the base of the mountains and began their search for a suitable place to hide for the night. A place they could defend; a place far enough from Leck for safety, but not so far that they couldn't reach Leck, to kill him.

For of course, Bitterblue was right. Leck had to die. Katsa knew it, but she didn't like to think of it. For she was a killer, and the murder should be hers; but it was plain that Po would have to be the one to do it. Po kill a king guarded by an army of soldiers. By himself, and without her help.

You mustn't go near his castle, she thought to Po as they rode. *You'd never be able to get close enough to him. You're far too conspicuous. They would ambush you.*

The horses picked their way through the rocks. Po didn't acknowledge her thoughts, didn't even look at her, but she knew he'd heard.

You'd do best to sneak up on him in the forest while he's searching for the child, and shoot him. From as far away as possible.

Po rode before them, his back straight. His arms steady, despite his tiredness and the cold and his lack of a coat.

And then run away as fast as you can.

He slowed then and came beside them. He looked into her face, and something strong in his silver and gold eyes comforted and reassured her. Po was neither weak nor defenseless. He had his Grace and his strength. He reached for her hand. When she gave it to him, he kissed it. He rode ahead, and they continued on.

Bitterblue sat quietly before her. She had stiffened when Po came near; but if she thought their silent exchange odd, she said nothing.

THEY CAME to a place where the land dropped away to the left and formed a deep gully with a lake that shone far below them. To the right the path rose to a cliff that overhung the lake.

"If we cross over to the far side of that cliff and hide there," Katsa said, "anyone coming after us will either have to cross the cliff as we did or climb up from the gully. They'll be easily seen."

"I had the same thought," Po said. "Let's see what's there."

And so they climbed. The cliff path sloped rather unnervingly toward the drop, but it was a wide path, and the horses clung to its top edge. Pebbles slid from under their hooves and rolled down the slope, clattering over the edge and plummeting down into the lake, but the travelers were safe.

On the far side they found little more than rock and scrub and a few scraggly trees growing from crevices. A shallow, hard cave with its back to the gully and the cliff path seemed the best choice for their camp. "It won't make for a soft bed," Po said, "but it'll hide our fire. Are you hungry, cousin?"

The girl sat on a rock, quietly, her hands gripping her knife. She hadn't complained of hunger, or of anything else, for that matter. But now she watched with big eyes as Po unwrapped what little food they had, some meat from the night before, and one small apple carried all the way from the inn at the Sunderan foot of the mountains. Bitterblue's eyes watched the food, and she barely seemed to be breathing. She was ravenous, anyone could see that.

"When did you last eat?" Po asked, as he set the food before her.

"Some berries, this morning."

"And before that?"

"Yesterday. Yesterday morning."

"Slowly," Po said, as Bitterblue took the meat in her hands and tore a great piece off with her teeth. "Slowly, or you'll be sick."

"I'll climb down to the gully and find us some meat," Katsa said. "The sun will set soon. I'll take a knife, Po, if you'll keep a lookout for me."

Po slid a knife from his boot and tossed it to her. "If you hear the sound of an owl hooting, run. Two hoots, run south. Three hoots, run back up here to the camp."

She nodded. "Agreed."

"Try the rushes to the south of the lake," he said. "And pick up a few pebbles on your way down. I think I may have seen some quail."

Katsa snorted but said nothing. She glanced at the girl, who saw only the food in her hands. Then she turned, worked her way around boulders, and began to forge a path down into the gully.

WHEN KATSA returned to camp with a stringful of quail, plucked and gutted, the sun was sinking behind the mountains. Po was piling branches near the back of the cave. Bitterblue lay nearby, wrapped in a blanket.

"I gather she hasn't slept much in the last few days," Po said.

"She'll be all right now that her clothes are dry. We'll keep her warm and fed."

"She's a calm little thing, isn't she? Small for ten years old. She helped me gather wood, until she was practically collapsing from exhaustion. I told her to sleep until we had more food. She's got her fingers wrapped around that knife. And she's still scared of me—I get the feeling she's not used to men showing her kindness."

"Po, I'm beginning to think I don't want to know what

this is all about. I can make no sense of it. I can't factor your grandfather into it at all."

Po shook his head and looked at the girl, who was huddled on the ground in her blankets and coats. "I'm not sure how much any of this has to do with sanity or sense. But we'll keep her safe, and we'll kill Leck. And eventually we'll learn whatever truth there is to know of it."

"She'll make for an awfully young queen."

"Yes, I've thought of that, too. But there's no helping it."

They sat quietly and waited for the darkness that would mask the smoke of their fire. Po pulled another shirt over the one he already wore. She watched his face, his familiar features, his eyes, which caught the pink light of the day's end. She bit her lip against her worry, for she knew it would not be helpful to him.

"How will you do it?" she asked.

"As you said, most likely. We'll talk about it when Bitterblue wakes. I expect she'll be able to help."

Help to plot the murder of her father. Yes, she probably would help, if she could. For such was the madness that rode the air of this kingdom as they sat in their rocky camp at the edge of the Monsean mountains.

THE LIGHT of the fire, or its crackle, or the smell of the meat sizzling above it woke Bitterblue. She came to sit with them by the flames, her blanket around her shoulders and her knife in hand.

"I'll teach you how to use that knife," Katsa told her,

"when you're feeling better. How to defend yourself, how to maim a man. We can use Po as a model."

The child's eyes flicked to Katsa's shyly, and then she looked into her lap.

"Wonderful," Po said. "It's quite boring really, the way you beat me to death with your hands and feet, Katsa. It'll be refreshing to have you coming at me with a knife."

Bitterblue glanced at Katsa again. "Are you the better fighter?"

"Yes," Katsa said.

"Far better," Po said. "There's no comparison."

"But Po has other advantages," Katsa said. "He's stronger. He sees better in the dark."

"But in a fight," Po said, "always bet on the lady, Bitterblue. Even in the dark."

They sat quietly, waiting for the quail to roast. Bitterblue shivered and pulled her blanket more tightly around her shoulders.

"I would like to have a Grace," she said, "that allowed me to protect myself."

Katsa held her breath and forced herself to wait patiently and not ask questions.

After a moment, Bitterblue said, "The king wants me."

"What for?" Katsa asked, because she could not prevent herself.

Bitterblue didn't answer this. She bent her chin to her chest and brought her arms in close to her sides, making herself very small. "He has a Grace," she said. "My mother told me so. She told me he can manipulate people's minds with his words, so that they believe whatever he says. Even if they hear it from someone else's mouth; even if it's a rumor he started that's spread far beyond him. His power weakens as it spreads, but it does not disappear." She stared unhappily at the knife in her hands. "She told me he's the wrong kind of man to have been born with a Grace like this. He makes toys of small and weak people. He likes to cause pain."

Po dropped his hand to Katsa's thigh, which was the only thing that kept her from shooting to her feet with rage.

"My mother has suspected all of this," Bitterblue continued, "from time to time, ever since she first knew him. But he's always been able to confuse her into forgetting about it. Until a few months back, when he began to take a particular interest in me."

She stopped speaking and took a few small breaths. Her eyes settled on Katsa's, flickering with something uncomfortable. "I can't say what he wants me for, exactly. He's always been . . . fond of the company of girls. And he has some strange habits my mother and I came to understand. He cuts animals, with knives. He tortures them and keeps them alive for a long time, then he kills them." She cleared her throat. "I don't think it's only animals he does this to."

Kindness to children and helpless creatures, Katsa thought, fighting back tears of fury. Her whole life she'd believed Leck's reputation for beneficence. Did he convince his victims, too, that he was doing them a kindness, even while he cut them with his knives?

"He told my mother he wanted to start spending time with me alone," Bitterblue said. "He said it was time he got to know his daughter better. He was so angry when she refused. He hit her. He tried to use his Grace on me, tried to get me to go to his cages with him, but whenever I saw the bruises on my mother's face I remembered the truth. It cleared my mind, just barely—enough that I knew to refuse."

Then Po had been right. The deaths at Leck's court began to make even more sense to Katsa. Leck probably arranged for many people to die—people whose use had become more trouble than it was worth, because he'd hurt them so grievously that they'd begun to comprehend the truth.

"So then he kidnapped Grandfather," Bitterblue said, "because he knew there was no one my mother loved more. He told my mother he was going to torture Grandfather, unless she agreed to hand me over. He told her he was going to bring him to Monsea and kill him in our sight. We hoped it was all just his usual lies. But then we got letters from Lienid and knew Grandfather was really missing."

"Grandfather was neither tortured nor killed," Po said. "He's safe now."

"He could have just taken me," Bitterblue said, her voice breaking with sudden shrillness. "He has an entire army that would never defy him. But he didn't. He has this . . . sick patience. It didn't interest him to force us. He wanted to hear us say yes."

Because it was more satisfying to him that way, Katsa thought.

"My mother barricaded us inside her rooms," Bitterblue said. "The king ignored us for a while. He had food and drink brought to us, and water and fresh linen. But he would talk to us through the door sometimes. He would try to persuade my mother to send me out. He would confuse me sometimes. Sometimes he would confuse her. He would come up with the most convincing reasons why I should come out, and we had to keep reminding ourselves of the truth. It was very frightening."

A tear ran down her face now, and she kept talking, quickly, as if she could no longer contain her story. "He began to send animals in to us, mice all cut up, dogs and cats, still alive, crying and bleeding. It was horrible. And then one day the girl who brought our food had cuts on her face, three lines on each cheek, bleeding freely. And other injuries, too, that we couldn't see. She wasn't walking well. When we asked her what happened, she said she couldn't remember. She was a girl my age."

She stopped for a moment, choked with tears. She wiped her face on her shoulder. "That's when my mother decided we had to escape. We tied sheets and blankets together and dropped out through the windows. I thought I wouldn't be able to do it, for fear. But my mother talked me through it, all the way down." She stared into the flames. "My mother killed a guard, with a knife. We ran for the mountains. We hoped the king would assume we'd taken the Port Road to the sea. But on the second morning we saw them coming after us, across the fields. My mother twisted her ankle in some foxhole. She couldn't run. She sent me ahead, to hide in the forest."

The girl breathed furiously, wiped her face again, clenched her hands into fists. Through some massive force of will, she stopped the fall of her tears. She grasped the knife that lay in her lap and spoke bitterly. "If I were trained in archery. Or if I could use a knife. Perhaps I could have killed my father when this whole thing started."

"By some accounts, it's too late," Po said. "But I'll kill him tomorrow, before he does anything more."

Bitterblue's eyes darted to his. "Why you? Why not her, if she's the better fighter?"

"Leck's Grace doesn't work on me," Po said. "It works on Katsa. This we learned today, when we met him in the fields. I must be the one to kill him, for he can't manipulate me or confuse me as he can Katsa."

He offered Bitterblue one of the quail, skewered on a stick. She took it and watched him closely. "It's true that his Grace lost some of its power over me," she said, "when he hurt my mother. And it lost some of its power over my mother when he threatened me. But why does it not work on you?"

"I can't say," Po said. "He's hurt a lot of people. There may be many for whom his Grace is weak—but none likely to admit it, for fear of his vengeance."

Bitterblue narrowed her eyes. "How did he hurt you?"

"He kidnapped my grandfather," Po said. "He murdered my aunt before my eyes. He threatens my cousin."

Bitterblue seemed satisfied by this; or, at least, she turned to her food and ate ravenously for a number of minutes. She glanced at him occasionally, at his hands as he tended the fire.

"My mother wore a lot of rings, like you," she said. "You look like my mother, excepting your eyes. And you sound like her, when you talk." She took a deep breath and stared at the food in her hands. "He'll be camping in the forest tonight, and he'll be looking for me again tomorrow. I don't know how you'll find him."

"We found you," Po said, "didn't we?"

Her eyes flashed up into his and then back to her food. "He'll have his personal guard with him. They are all Graced. I'll tell you what you'll be facing."

IT WAS a simple enough plan. Po would set out early, before first light, with food, a horse, the bow, the quiver, one dagger, and two knives. He would work his way back into the forest and hide his horse. He would find the king—however long that took. He would come no closer to the king than the distance of the flight of an arrow. He would aim, and he would fire. He would ensure that the king was dead. And then he would run, as fast as he could, back to his horse and to the camp.

A simple plan, and Katsa grew more and more uneasy as they talked it through, for both she and Po knew that it would never play out so simply. The king had an inner guard, made up of five Graced sword fighters. These men were little threat to Po; they always stood beside the king, and Po expected never to step within their range. It was the king's outer guard that Po must be prepared to encounter. These were ten men who would be positioned in a broad circle around Leck, some distance from him and from each other, but surrounding the king as he moved through the forest. They were all Graced, some fighters, a couple crack shots with a bow. One Graced with speed on foot; one enormously strong; one who climbed trees and jumped from branch to branch like a squirrel. One with extraordinary sight and hearing.

"You will know that one by his red beard," Bitterblue said. "But if you're close enough to see him, then he's most certainly spotted you already. Once you're spotted they'll raise the alarm."

"Po," Katsa said. "Let me come with you as far as the outer circle. There are too many of them, and you may need help."

"No," Po said.

"I would only fight them and then leave."

"No, Katsa."

"You'll never—"

"Katsa." His voice was sharp. She crossed her arms and glared into the fire. She took a breath and swallowed hard.

"Very well," she said. "Go to sleep now, Po, and I'll keep watch."

Po nodded. "Wake me in a couple of hours and I'll take over."

"No," she said. "You need your sleep if you're to do this thing. I'll keep watch tonight. I'm not tired, Po," she said as he started to protest. "You know I'm not. Let me do this."

And so Po dropped off to sleep, huddled in a blanket beside Bitterblue. Katsa sat in the dark and went over the plan in her mind.

If Po didn't return to their camp above the gully by sunset, then Katsa and Bitterblue must flee without him. For if he didn't return, it might mean the king was not dead. If the king was not dead, then nothing would protect Bitterblue from him, except distance.

Leave Po behind, in this forest of soldiers. It was unimaginable to Katsa, and as she sat on a rock in the cold and the dark, she wouldn't let herself think it. She watched for the slightest movement, listened for the smallest sound. And refused to think about all that could happen tomorrow in the forest.

CHAPTER TWENTY-SIX

PO WOKE in the early morning cold and gathered his things together quietly. He pulled Katsa close and held her against him. "I'll come back," he said; and then he was gone. She sat guard, as she had done all night, and watched the path he had taken. She held her thoughts in check.

She wore a ring on a string around her neck, a ring that Po had given her before he'd climbed onto the back of his horse and clattered across the cliff path. It was cold against the skin of her breast, and she fingered it as she waited for the sun to rise. It was the ring with the engravings that matched the markings on his arms. The ring of Po's castle, and his prince-hood. If Po didn't return today, then Katsa must take Bitter-blue south to the sea. She must arrange passage somehow on a ship to Lienid's western coast, and Po's castle. No Lienid would detain her or question her, if she wore Po's ring. They would know that she acted on Po's instructions; they would welcome and assist her. And Bitterblue might be kept safe in Po's castle while Katsa thought and planned and waited to hear something of Po.

When light came and Bitterblue awoke, she and Katsa led the horse down to the lake to drink and graze. They collected wood, in case they stayed in this camp again that night. They ate winterberries from a clump of bushes beside the water. Katsa caught and gutted fish for their dinner. When they climbed back up to the rock camp, the sun had not even topped the sky.

Katsa thought of doing some exercises, or of teaching Bitterblue to use her knife. But she didn't want to attract attention with the noise it would make. Nor did she want to miss the slightest glimpse or sound of an approaching enemy, or of Po. There was nothing to do but sit still and wait. Katsa's muscles screamed their impatience.

By early afternoon she was pacing back and forth across the camp, utterly stir-crazy. She paced, fists clenched; and Bitterblue sat against the boulders in the sun, knife in hand, watching her.

"Aren't you tired?" Bitterblue asked. "When did you last sleep?"

"I don't need as much sleep as other people," Katsa said.

Bitterblue's eyes followed her as she marched back and forth. "I'm tired," Bitterblue said.

Katsa stopped and crouched before the girl. She felt Bitterblue's hands and forehead. "Are you cold, or hot? Are you hungry?"

Bitterblue shook her head. "I'm only tired."

And of course she was tired, her eyes big and her face tight. Any person in this situation would be tired. "Sleep," Katsa said. "It's safe for you to sleep, and it's best for you to keep up your strength."

Not that the child would need her strength for flight that

night, for doubtless at any moment, Po would come scrambling over the cliff path on his horse.

THE SUN crawled behind the western mountaintops and turned their rocky camp orange, and still Po did not come. Katsa's mind was frozen into place. Surely he would materialize in the next few minutes; but just in case he did not, she woke Bitterblue. She pulled their belongings together and removed all trace of their fire. She scattered their firewood. She saddled the horse and strapped their bags to the fine Monsean saddle.

Then she sat and stared at the cliff path that shone yellow and orange in the falling light.

The sun was setting, and he hadn't come.

She couldn't help the thought, then, that shouldered its way into her mind—that wouldn't be held back any longer, no matter how hard she pushed at it. Po could be in the forest, injured, the king could be murdered and all could be safe, and Po could be somewhere, needing her help, and she not able to give it because of the chance the king was alive. He could even be near, just beyond the cliff path, limping, stumbling toward them. Needing them, needing her; and she, in a matter of minutes, mounting her horse and galloping it in the opposite direction.

They would go then, because they must. But they would backtrack just a bit, on the chance that he was near. Katsa glanced quickly around the rock camp to be sure they'd left no sign of their presence. "Well then, Princess," she said, "we'd better be going." She avoided Bitterblue's eyes and lifted her into the saddle. She untied the horse's reins and handed them to the child. And that's when she heard the pebbles bouncing along the cliff path.

She raced back to the path. The horse was coming across the ledge along the top of the cliff, stumbling across, its head hanging. Too close, just a little too close to the drop. And Po lying on the horse's back, unmoving; and an arrow, an arrow in his shoulder. His shirt soaked with blood. And how many arrows in the horse's neck and side she didn't try to count, for suddenly pebbles were spraying over the cliff edge. The horse was slipping, and the whole path was sliding under its panicked hooves. She screamed Po's name inside her mind, and ran. He raised his head, and his eyes flashed into hers. The horse shrieked and struggled madly for ground to stand on, but she couldn't reach him in time. Over the edge the horse tumbled, over the edge, and she screamed again, aloud this time; and he was gone below her, falling through the yellow light.

The horse twisted and turned in the air. Po smashed face-first into the water and the horse crashed in after him, and stones flew up helter-skelter from Katsa's feet as she tore down the trail to the gully, feeling nothing as her shins bashed against rocks and branches whipped across her face. She knew only that Po was in that water and that she must get him out.

There was the barest ripple on the surface of the water to direct her dive. She threw her boots into the rushes and plunged. In the shock of the lake's icy water, she saw the place where mud and bubbles rose and where a great brown form sank and another, smaller form struggled. He struggled, which meant he was alive. She kicked closer and saw what he struggled with. His boot was caught in a stirrup. The stirrup buckled to the saddle, and the horse sinking fast. His struggles were clumsy, and the water around his shoulder and his head flowed red with his blood. Katsa grabbed his belt and felt around until she found a knife. She whipped the blade out and sawed at the stirrup. The leather broke, and the stirrup sank with the horse. Katsa wrapped her arm around Po and kicked fiercely upward. They burst to the surface.

She lugged his dead weight to shore, for now he was unconscious; but as she pushed him into the rushes at the edge of the lake he became suddenly, violently conscious. He gasped and coughed and vomited lake water, over and over again. He wasn't going to drown, then; but that didn't mean he wouldn't bleed to death. "The other horse," Katsa shouted to Bitterblue, who hovered anxiously nearby. "The horse has the medicines," she shouted, and the girl slipped and scrambled back up to the camp.

Katsa dragged Po up to dry ground and sat him there. The cold and the wet—that could also kill him. He must stop bleeding, and he must be warm and dry. Oh, how she wished for Raffin at this moment. "Po," she said. "Po, what happened?" No response. *Po. Po.* His eyes flashed open, but they were vague, unfocused. He didn't see her. He vomited.

"All right. You sit still. This is going to hurt," she said, but when she pulled the arrow from his shoulder he didn't even seem to notice. His arms flopped lifelessly as she peeled his shirts from his back, and he vomited again.

Bitterblue came clattering down the trail with the horse. "I need your help," Katsa said, and for a good while Bitterblue was Katsa's assistant, tearing open bags to find clothing that could be used to dry him or stanch his bleeding, rifling through the medicines for the ointment that cleaned wounds, soaking bloody cloths in the lake.

"Can you hear me, Po?" Katsa asked as she tore a shirt to make a bandage. "Can you hear me? What happened with the king?" He looked up at her dimly as she bandaged his shoulder. "Po," she said, over and over. "The king. You must tell me if the king is alive." But he was useless, and senseless—no better than unconscious. She peeled off his boots and his trousers and dried him as best she could. She dressed him in new trousers and rubbed his arms and legs to warm them. She took his coat back from Bitterblue, pulled it over his head, and pushed his rubbery arms through the sleeves. He vomited again.

It was the force of his head hitting the water. This Katsa knew: that a man vomited if struck hard enough in the head, that he became forgetful and confused. His head would clear, in time. But they didn't have time, not if the king was alive. And so she knelt before him and grasped his chin. She ignored his wincing, pained eyes. She thought into his mind. *Po. I need to know if the king is alive. I am not going to stop bothering you until you tell me if the king is alive.*

He looked at her then, rubbed his eyes, and squinted at her, hard. "The king," he said thickly. "The king. My arrow. The king is alive."

Katsa's heart sank. For now they must flee, all three of them, with Po in this state and with only one horse. In the dark and the cold, with little food, and without Po's Grace to warn them of their pursuers.

Her Grace would have to serve.

She handed Po her flask. "Drink this," she said, "all of it. Bitterblue," she said, "help me pull these wet things together. It's a good thing you slept today, for I need you to be strong tonight."

Po seemed to understand when it was time for him to mount the horse. He didn't contribute to the effort, but he didn't fight it, either. Both Katsa and Bitterblue pushed him up into the saddle with all their might, and though he almost pitched headlong over the animal and fell to the ground on the other side, some unfocused understanding caused him to grasp Katsa's arm and steady himself. "You behind him," Katsa said to Bitterblue, "so that you can see him. Pinch him if he starts to fall off, and call me if you need help. The horse will be moving quickly, as quickly as I can run."

CHAPTER TWENTY-SEVEN

IN THE DARK on the side of a mountain, no one can move
quickly who doesn't have some particular Grace to do so. They
moved, and Katsa did not break her ankles stepping blindly
before the horse, as others would have, but they didn't move
quickly. Katsa barely breathed, so hard was she listening behind them. Their pursuers would be on horseback, and there
would be many of them, and they would carry torches. If Leck
had sent a party in the right direction, then there would be
little to stop them from succeeding in their search.

Katsa was doubtful that even on flat land they could have
moved much faster, so unwell was Po. He clung to the horse's
mane, eyes closed, concentrating fiercely on not falling off.
He winced at every movement. And he was still bleeding.

"Let me tie you to the horse," Katsa said to him once
when she'd stopped at a stream to fill the flasks. "Then you'd
be able to rest."

He took a moment to process her words. He hunched forward and sighed into the horse's mane. "I don't want to rest,"
he said. "I want to be able to tell you if he's coming."

So they weren't completely without his Grace; but he
was completely without his reason, to make such a comment
while Bitterblue sat directly behind him, quiet, intent, and

missing nothing of what was said. *Careful,* she thought to him. *Bitterblue.*

"I'll tie you both to the horse," she said aloud, "and then each of you can choose whether or not to rest."

Rest, she thought to him, as she wound a rope around his legs. *You're no good to us if you bleed to death.*

"I'll not bleed to death," he said aloud, and Katsa avoided Bitterblue's eyes, determining not to talk to Po inside her mind again until his reason had returned.

THEY CONTINUED south slowly. Katsa tripped and stumbled over rocks, and over the roots of stubborn mountain trees that clung to cracks in the earth. As the night wore on, her stumbling increased, and it occurred to her that she was tired. She sent her mind back along the past few nights, and counted. It was her second night without sleep, and the night before that they'd slept only a few hours. She would have to sleep, then, sometime soon; but for now she wouldn't think of it. There was no use considering the impossible.

Several hours before dawn she began to think of the fish she had caught earlier, the fish scaled and gutted, and wrapped and bound with the bags to the horse. Once light came they wouldn't be able to risk even the smallest fire. They'd eaten very little that day, and they had very little food for the next. If they stopped now for just a few minutes, she could cook the fish. She wouldn't have to think of food again, until the next nightfall.

But even this was risky, for the light of a fire could attract attention in this darkness.

Po whispered her name then, and she stopped the horse and walked back to him.

"There's a cave," he whispered, "a few steps to the southeast." His hand swayed in the air and then rested on her shoulder. "Stay here beside me. I'll lead us there."

He directed her footsteps over stones and around boulders. If she'd been less tired, Katsa would have taken a moment to appreciate the clarity with which his Grace showed him the landscape. But now they were at the entrance to Po's cave, and there was too much else to consume her mind. She must wake Bitterblue, untie her, and help her down. She must get Po from the horse and onto the ground. She must find wood to build a fire, then get the fish cooking. She must dress Po's shoulder again, because it still bled freely no matter how tightly she bound it.

"Sleep while the fish cooks," he said, as she wound clean strips of cloth around his arm and chest to stanch the flow of blood. "Katsa. Get some sleep. I'll wake you if we need you."

"You're the one who needs sleep," she said.

He caught her arm then as she knelt before him. "Katsa. Sleep for a quarter of an hour. No one is near. You won't get another chance to sleep tonight."

She sat on her heels and looked at him. Shirtless, colorless, squinting from pain. Bruises darkening his face. He dropped her arm and sighed. "I'm dizzy," he said. "I'm sure I look like death, Katsa, but I'm not going to bleed to death and I'm not going to die of dizziness. Sleep, for a few minutes."

Bitterblue came forward. "He's right," she said. "You should sleep. I'll take care of him." She picked up his coat and helped him into it, moving his bandaged shoulder gently, carefully. Surely, Katsa thought, they could manage without her, for a few minutes. Surely they would all do better if she got some small sleep.

So she lay down before the fire and instructed herself to sleep for only a quarter of an hour. When she woke, Po and Bitterblue had barely moved. She felt better.

They ate quietly and fast. Po leaned back against the cave wall, eyes closed. He claimed to have little appetite, but Katsa had no sympathy. She sat before him and fed him pieces of fish until she was satisfied that he'd eaten enough.

Katsa was suffocating the fire with her boots, and Bitterblue was binding together the remaining fish, when he spoke.

"It's good you weren't there, Katsa," he said. "For today I listened to Leck prattle on for hours about his love for his kidnapped daughter. About how his heart would be broken until he found her."

Katsa went to sit before him. Bitterblue shuffled closer so that she could hear his whispered words.

"I got through the outer guard easily," Po said. "I came within sight of him, finally, in the early afternoon. His inner guard surrounded him so closely that I couldn't get a shot at him. I waited forever. I followed them. They never once heard me; but they never once moved away from the king."

"He was expecting you," Katsa said. "They were there for you."

He nodded, then winced.

"Tell us later, Po," Katsa said. "Rest for now."

"It's a short story," he said. "I finally decided my only option was to take out one of his guards. So I shot one. But the instant he fell, of course, the king jumped for cover. I shot again, and my arrow grazed Leck's neck, but only barely. It was a job meant for you, Katsa. You'd have hit him squarely. I couldn't do it."

"Well," Katsa said. *I would never have found him in the first place. And even if I had, I would never have killed him. You know that. It was a job meant for neither of us.*

"After that, of course, his inner guard was after me," Po said, "and then his outer guard, and his soldiers, too, once they'd heard the alarm. It—it was a bloodbath. I must have killed a dozen men. It was all I could do to get away, and then I rode north, to throw them off the track." He stopped for a moment and closed his eyes, then opened them again. He squinted at Katsa. "Leck has a bowman who's nearly as good as you, Katsa. You saw what he did to the horse."

And he would have done the same to you, she thought to him. *If it weren't for your newfound ability to sense arrows as they fly toward you.*

He smiled, ever so slightly. Then he squinted at Bitterblue. "You've begun to trust me," he said.

"You tried to kill the king," Bitterblue said, simply.

"All right," Katsa said, "enough talking."

She returned to the fire, and smothered it. They pushed Po up into the saddle again, and again she tied her charges to the horse. And in her mind, over and over, she warned Po, implored Po, to stop announcing aloud every little thing his Grace revealed to him.

IN THE LIGHT of day they moved faster, but the movement was hard on Po. He didn't complain once about the bouncing of the horse. But his breath was short and his eyes flashed with a kind of wildness, and Katsa could recognize pain as easily as she recognized fear. She saw the pain in his face, and in the tightness of the muscles of his arms and his neck whenever she dressed his shoulder.

"Which hurts more?" she asked him in the early morning. "Your shoulder or your head?"

"My head."

A person with an aching head shouldn't be riding an animal whose every step reverberated like an axe to his skull; but walking was out of the question. He had no balance. He was forever dizzy and nauseated. He was forever rubbing his eyes; they bothered him. At least the bleeding of his shoulder had slowed to a dribble. And talking no longer confused him; he seemed to remember, finally, to hide his Grace from his cousin.

"We're not moving fast enough," he said several times that day. Katsa, too, chafed at their pace. But until his head improved, she wasn't going to run the horse over the rocky hills.

Bitterblue was more of a help than Katsa could have hoped. She seemed to consider Po her special charge. Whenever they stopped, she helped him settle onto a rock. She brought him food and water. If Katsa stepped away for a minute to chase a rabbit, when she returned Bitterblue was cleaning Po's shoulder and wrapping it in clean bandages. Katsa became accustomed to the sight of Po swaying above his little cousin, his hand resting on her shoulder.

By the time the sun began to set, Katsa felt the fatigue of the last few days and the last few sleepless nights. Po and Bitterblue were asleep on the horse's back. Perhaps if Po rested now, he would be able to stand some sort of watch later and give her some few hours' sleep. The horse, too, needed rest. They couldn't stop for the whole night, not when they traveled at this pace. But a few hours. A few hours' rest might be possible.

When he woke again in the moon's pale light, he called her back to him. He helped her find a hollow in a ring of rocks that would hide the light of a fire. "We're not moving fast enough," he said again, and she shrugged, for there was little to be done about it. She woke Bitterblue, untied her, and slid her down from the horse. Po slid himself down, carefully.

"Katsa," he said. "Come here, my Katsa."

He reached for her, and she came to him. He wrapped his arms around her. His hurt shoulder slow and stiff, but his unhurt arm strong and warm. He held her tight, and she held him steady. She rested her face in the hollow of his neck, and a great sigh rose within her. She was so tired, and he was so unwell. They weren't moving fast enough. But at least they could stand with their arms around each other, and she could feel his warmth against her face.

"There's something we need to do," he said, "and you're not going to like it."

"What is it?" she murmured into his neck.

"We—" He took a breath and stopped. "You need to leave me behind."

"What?" She pulled away from him. He swayed, but grabbed at the horse to steady himself. She glared at him, and then stormed after Bitterblue, who was collecting branches for the fire. Let him cope for himself. Let him make his own way to the campfire if he was going to make such absurd statements.

But he didn't move. He just stood beside the horse, his arm clutching the animal's back, waiting for someone to help him; and tears rose to her eyes at the sight of Po's helplessness. She went back to him. *Forgive me, Po.* She gave him her shoulder and led him across the rocky ground to the place where they would make their fire. She sat him down and crouched before him. She felt his face; his forehead burned. She listened to his breath and heard pain in its shortness.

"Katsa," he said. "Look at me. I can't even walk. The most important thing right now is speed, and I'm holding you back. I'm no more than a burden."

"That's not true. We need your Grace."

"I can tell you they're seeking you," he said, "and I can promise you they'll continue to seek you, as long as you're in Monsea. I can tell you they're likely to find your trail, and I can tell you that once they do, the king will be on your heels. You don't need me with you, to repeat that over and over."

"I need you to keep my mind straight."

"I can't keep your mind straight. The only way for you to keep your mind straight is to run from those who would confuse you. Running is the only hope for the child."

Bitterblue came beside them then, with an armload of sticks and branches. "Thank you, Princess," Katsa said to her. "Here, bring the rabbit I caught. I'll build the fire." She would think about the fire, and she would pay Po no attention.

"If you left me behind," Po said, "you could ride fast. Faster than an army of soldiers."

Katsa ignored him. She piled twigs together and focused on the flame growing between her hands.

"He will catch up with us, Katsa, if we continue at this pace. And you won't be able to defend either of us from him."

Katsa added more twigs to her fire and blew on the flames, gently. She piled sticks on top of the twigs.

"You have to leave me behind," Po said. "You're risking Bitterblue's safety otherwise."

Katsa shot up to her feet, her fists angry and hard, suddenly beyond any pretense of calmness. "And I'm risking yours if I leave you. I'm not going to leave you on this mountain, to find your own food and build your own shelter and defend yourself when Leck comes along, when you . . . you can't even walk, Po. What are you going to do, crawl away from his soldiers? Your head will feel better soon. You'll get your balance back and we'll move faster."

He squinted up at her then and sighed. He looked into his hands. He turned his rings around on his fingers.

"I won't get my balance back for some time, I think," he said, and something strange in his voice stopped her.

"What do you mean?"

"It doesn't matter, Katsa. Even if I woke up tomorrow completely healed, you'd have to leave me behind. We've only one horse. Unless you and Bitterblue ride the horse fast, you'll be overtaken."

"I'll not leave you behind."

"Katsa. This isn't about you or me. This is about Bitterblue."

She sat down suddenly, the strength knocked out of her legs. For it *was* about Bitterblue. They'd come all this way for Bitterblue, and she was Bitterblue's only hope. She swallowed. She made her face expressionless, for the child must not know how much it hurt her to rank Bitterblue's safety above Po's.

And then she knew suddenly that she was going to cry. She held her breath steady and didn't look at him. "I'd thought to get a few hours of sleep," she said.

"Yes," he said. "Sleep for a bit, love."

She wished that his voice was not so soft and kind. She wrapped herself in a blanket and lay beside the fire with her back to him. She commanded herself to sleep. A tear trickled over the bridge of her nose and down into her ear, but she commanded herself again.

She slept.

WHEN SHE WOKE, Bitterblue slept on the ground beside her. Po sat on a rock before the crackling fire and looked into his hands. Katsa sat with him. The meat was cooked, and she ate it gratefully, for if she ate she did not have to talk, and if she talked she knew she would cry.

"We could get another horse," she finally managed to say. She stared at the fire, and tried not to look at the lights that glowed in his face.

"Here, at the base of the mountains, Katsa?"

All right then. There was no other horse.

"Even if we could," he said, "it would be ages before I could ride fast enough. My head won't heal while I'm rattling around on a horse. It's best for me, too, Katsa, if you leave me behind. I'll recover faster."

"And how will you defend yourself? How will you eat?"

"I'll hide. We'll find a place, early tomorrow, for me to hide. Come, Katsa, you know I hide better than anyone you've ever known, or heard of." She heard a smile in his voice. "Come, my wildcat. Come here."

There was no helping her tears. For they would leave Po behind, to fend for himself and keep himself alive by hiding, though he couldn't even walk unassisted. She knelt before him, and he took her into the crook of his uninjured arm. She cried into his shoulder like a child. Ashamed of herself, for it was only a parting, and Bitterblue had not wept like this even over a death. "Don't be ashamed," Po whispered. "Your sadness is dear to me. Don't be frightened. I won't die, Katsa. I won't die, and we'll meet again."

———

WHEN BITTERBLUE WOKE, Katsa was packing their belongings. Bitterblue watched Katsa's face for a moment. Then she watched Po, who stared into the fire.

"We're leaving you, then," she said to Po.

He looked up at the child and nodded.

"Here?"

"No, cousin. When morning comes we'll search for a hiding place."

Bitterblue kicked at the ground. She crossed her arms and considered Po. "What will you do in your hiding place?"

"I'll hide," Po said, "and recover my strength."

"And when you're strong again?"

"I'll join you in Lienid, or wherever you are, and we'll plan the death of King Leck."

The girl considered Po for a moment longer. She nodded. "We'll look for you, cousin."

Katsa glanced up to see the slightest smile on Po's face, at the child's words. Then Bitterblue turned away to help Katsa with the medicines.

The child's teeth chattered as she knelt beside Katsa. She had no coat, and the blanket she wore as they traveled was threadbare. The girl carried their packages to the horse, brought water to Po, and shivered.

Why had Katsa not saved the hides of the rabbits she'd killed?

She would have to do something. She would have to find Bitterblue something warmer to wear. For this child's protection was her charge, and she must think of everything. Her care of Bitterblue must be worthy of Po's sacrifice.

CHAPTER TWENTY-EIGHT

IN THE PINK of dawn they stumbled upon a small cabin with little to offer except its shell; an abandoned cabin, perhaps once the lair of some Monsean hermit. It stood in a hollow more grassy than rocky, with a tree or two and a patch of weeds that looked as if it might once have served as a garden. Broken shutters and a cold fireplace. A blanket of dust on the rough wooden floor, on the table and the bed, on the cabinet that leaned on three lopsided legs with its door hanging open crookedly.

"This is where I'll hide," Po said.

"This is a place to live, Po," Katsa said. "It's not a place to hide. It's far too obvious; no one will pass it without going inside."

"But I could stay here, Katsa, and hide someplace nearby if I hear them coming."

And what hiding place had he sensed nearby? "Po—"

"I wonder if there's a pond anywhere near?" he said. "Come with me, ladies. I'm sure I hear water running."

There was no sound of water that Katsa could hear, which meant that Po could hear none, either. She sighed. "Yes," she said. "I think I hear it, too."

They moved across the grasses behind the cabin. Po leaned

against Katsa, and Bitterblue led the horse. Soon Katsa actually did hear water, and when they topped a brownish rise and the grass gave way to boulders, she saw it. Three great streams clambered down from the rocks above, joined together, and poured over a ledge into a deep pool. Here and there at its edges the pool overflowed, and a number of streams trickled downward and eastward toward the Monsean forest.

Very well, Katsa thought to him. *And where's the hiding place?*

"There's a waterfall like this in the mountains near my brother Skye's castle," Po said. "We were swimming one day, and we found a tunnel underwater that led to a cave."

Katsa knew where this was going, and Bitterblue's puzzled look—no, it would be more accurate to call it her suspicious look—suggested that Po had already said more than enough. Katsa sat Po down. She pulled off one of her boots. "If there's a hiding place in this pool, Po, I'll find it for you." She pulled off her other boot. "But just because a hiding place exists doesn't mean it'll do you any good. You can't get from the cabin to this pool on your own."

"I can," he said, "to save my life."

"What will you do? Crawl?"

"There's no shame in crawling when one can't walk. And swimming requires less balance."

She glared at him, and he looked calmly back, the slightest hint of amusement on his face. And why shouldn't he be amused? For she was about to plunge into near-freezing water to search for a tunnel that he already knew existed, and explore a cave of which he already knew the exact size, shape, and location.

"I'm taking my clothes off," she said, "so look away, Lord Prince." For she could at least spare her clothing; and if this entire episode was a performance for Bitterblue, then they might as well also pretend Po was in no position to see her with her clothes off. Though Katsa didn't suppose Bitterblue was any more fooled by that pretense than by the others. She stood beside the horse and kept her own counsel; and her eyes were big and childlike, but they were not unseeing.

Katsa sighed. She pulled off her coat. *Point me in the right direction, Po.*

She followed his gaze to the base of the waterfall. She threw her trousers onto the rocks beside her coat and boots. She clenched her teeth against the cold and stepped into the pool. Its bottom sloped steeply, and with a yelp she was submerged. She dived.

The rocks of the pool floor shone green far below her, and silver fish flashed in the light. She was surprised by the depth of this water hole. She kicked toward the waterfall. Her vision was all but useless in the cascade of bubbles at its base, but she felt along the rocks with her hands and found, in the dark below the pouring water, a cavity that must be Po's tunnel. She smiled, despite herself. She would never have found this secret place on her own; likely not a single person had ever done what she was about to do. She shot to the surface for a breath of air, then dived back down and pulled herself through the opening.

It was dark in this tunnel, black, and the water was even colder than the water in the pool. She could see nothing. She kicked forward through the tunnel and counted steadily. Rocks scratched her arms, and she felt in front of her with her hands to avoid cracking her head against anything unexpected. It was narrow, but not dangerously so. Po would have no trouble, if he were well enough to swim.

As her count neared the number thirty, the passageway widened, and then the tunnel walls disappeared all around. She shot upward, hoping to break through the surface, for she didn't know where to find the air of this black cave if it wasn't straight above. She was conscious now of her sense of direction, at which Po had always marveled. If she lost the tunnel in this darkness, and if she couldn't find an opening to the surface, it was over for Katsa. But Katsa knew exactly where the tunnel was, behind her and below her. She knew how far she'd gone, and in what direction; she knew up and down, east and west. The darkness wouldn't claim her.

And of course, Po would never have sent her into this cave if it were a place she could not endure. Her shoulder hit rock, and she heard a muffled slap that sounded like surface water on shore. She kicked forward toward the sound, and then her head burst above water, and she was breathing. She felt around and found the rock whose underside she'd struck. It jutted above the surface and felt flat and mossy on top. She pulled herself onto it, teeth chattering.

It was blacker in this cave than any night she had ever

known. There was not a flash on the water, not even a thinner blackness to give shape to the space around her. She stretched her arms but touched nothing. She had no sense of the height of the ceiling or the depth of these walls. She thought she heard water slapping against rock for some distance, but she couldn't be sure without exploring. And she wouldn't explore, because they hadn't the time.

So this was Po's cave. He would be safe enough here, if he could get himself here, for no one who didn't share his Grace could ever find him in this cold, black hole under the mountain.

Katsa slipped back into the icy water and dived for the tunnel.

SHE CAME ASHORE with a pair of wriggling fish in her hands. "I found your cave," she said. "It'll be easy enough for you to manage, if by some wonder of medicine and healing you're able to swim. The tunnel is just below the fall of water. And here's your dinner." She threw the fish onto the rocks and dried herself with a cloth Bitterblue brought to her. She dressed. She held out her hand for Po's knife, and he tossed it to her. She beheaded the fish and cut them open. She threw the entrails back into the pond.

"You must go now," Po said. "There's no point in delay."

"There's some point in delay," Katsa said. "What'll you eat after these fish are gone?"

"I'll manage."

Katsa snorted. "You'll manage? You don't even have a bow, and even if you did I'd like to see your aim right now. We'll not leave until you've plenty of food and firewood."

"Katsa, honestly. You must go, you simply must—"

"The horse needs the rest of a morning," Katsa said. "From now on it will ride hard. And—and—" She refused, simply refused, to give in to the panic that rattled around inside her. *And winter's coming, and you can make me leave you here, but you can't make me leave you here to starve to death.*

Po rubbed his eyes. He sighed.

"You'll need a lot of firewood. I'll get started," Bitterblue said, and Po laughed outright.

"I'm outnumbered," he said. "Very well, Katsa. Do what you must. But before morning passes, you'll be on your way."

THE MORNING was a whirlwind. The faster Katsa moved, the less she could think, and so she moved as fast as her feet and her fingers were capable of. She caught him two rabbits, which he could cook with the fish that night and store safely for a number of days. She cursed the weather. It was cold enough for Po to be uncomfortable during the day, when he couldn't risk a fire. But it wasn't cold enough for freezing meat; nor did they have salt to treat it. She couldn't kill him meat now to last the winter, or even to last him a number of weeks. And in a number of weeks the hunting would become difficult for even those hunters who walked steadily on their feet and carried a bow.

"Have you ever made a bow?" she asked him.

"Never."

"I'll find you the wood," she said, "before we leave. And you'll have the hides of these rabbits to reinforce the stave, and for the string. I'll explain to you how it's done."

She cursed herself for the feathers she'd discarded from all of the birds she'd killed. But when her rushed passage over the rocks disturbed a roost of quail, she swept stones up from the ground and managed to knock the majority of them down. They would be Bitterblue's dinner and her own, and Po would have the feathers for arrows.

When she found a young tree with strong, flexible limbs, she chose a curved piece for the bow and some long, straight branches for arrows. And then she had a thought. She cut more branches and split them apart. She began to weave a sort of basket, square, with sides, top, and bottom about the length of her arm. She wove it tightly, with small openings between the slats. When she came back to the pool where Po still sat and Bitterblue still scrambled for firewood, she carried the basket on one shoulder, and the quail and the branches under her other arm. She cut a couple of lengths of rope and tied them to the edges of her basket. She lowered the basket into the pool, just deep enough that it couldn't be seen, and tied the ropes to the base of a bush on shore. Then she pulled off her boots, her coat, and her trousers, and prepared herself once more for the icy shock of the water.

She dived. She hung suspended under the water, and waited, and waited. When a fish flashed nearby, she grabbed.

She swam to the basket and slid back the slats. She squeezed the wriggling fish inside and fastened the slats again. She dived back down, snatched another fish, swam to shore, and deposited the squirming body into the basket. She caught fish for Po; so many fish that by the time she was done, the basket swarmed with their crowded bodies.

"You may have to feed them," she said, once she'd returned to shore and dressed. "But they should last you some time."

"And now you must go," Po said.

"I want to make you crutches first."

"No," Po said. "You'll go now."

"I want—"

"Katsa, do you think I want you to go? If I'm telling you to go it's because you must."

She looked into his face, and then looked away. "We need to divide our belongings," she said.

"Bitterblue and I have done that."

"I must dress your shoulder one last time."

"The child has already done so."

"Your water flask—"

"It's full."

Bitterblue came over the top of the rise then and joined them. "The cabin is bursting with firewood," she said.

"It's time for you to go," Po said, and he leaned forward, balanced himself, and stood. Katsa bit back her protests and gave him her shoulder. Bitterblue untied the horse, and they made their way back to the cabin.

Your balance is better, Katsa thought to him. *Come with us.*

"Cousin," Po said, "don't let her run the horse ragged. And be sure she sleeps and eats every once in a while. She'll try to give all the food to you."

"As you have done," Bitterblue said, and Po smiled.

"I've tried to give you most of the food," he said. "Katsa will try to give you all of it."

They stopped at the entrance to the cabin, and Po leaned back against the door frame. *Come with us,* Katsa thought as she stood before him.

"They'll be on your tail," Po said. "You must not let them get close enough to talk to you. Think about disguising yourself. You're dirty and bedraggled, but any fool would recognize either of you. Katsa, I don't know what you can do about your eyes, but you must do something."

Come with us.

"Bitterblue, you must help Katsa if she's confused by any words she hears. You must help each other. Don't trust any Monsean, do you understand? You mustn't trust anyone who may have been touched by Leck's Grace. And don't for a moment think you can defeat him, Katsa. Your only safety is in escaping him. Do you understand?"

Come with us.

"Katsa." His voice was rough, yet gentle. "Do you understand what I'm saying?"

"I understand," she said, and when a tear trickled down her cheek, he reached out and wiped it away with one finger.

He studied her face for a moment, and then he turned to Bitterblue. He bent down on one knee and took her hands. "Farewell, cousin," he said.

"Farewell," the child said gravely.

He stood again, gingerly, and leaned back against the door frame. He closed his eyes and sighed. He opened his eyes and looked into Katsa's face. His mouth twitched into the slightest grin. "You've always intended to leave me, Katsa."

She choked on a sob. "How can you joke? You know this isn't what I meant."

"Oh, Katsa. Wildcat." He touched her face. He smiled, so that it hurt her to look at him, and she was sure she couldn't leave him alone. He pulled her close and kissed her, and he whispered something into her ear. She held on to him so hard that his shoulder must have ached, but he did not complain.

Katsa didn't look back as they rode away. But she gripped Bitterblue tightly; and she called out to him, his name bursting inside her so painfully that for a long while, she could feel nothing else.

Chapter Twenty-nine

THEY FOLLOWED the edges of the Monsean mountains and pushed the poor horse south. They ran occasionally over open land, but more often than not their progress was slowed by cliffs, crevices, and waterfalls—places where there was no footing whatsoever for the horse. There, Katsa needed to dismount, backtrack, and lead the beast to lower ground. And then the hair would stand on the back of her neck and every sound would stop her breath; she couldn't breathe freely until they'd climbed again. For the lower land gave way to the forest, and Katsa knew the forest must be swarming with Leck's army.

The army would comb the forest, the Port Road, and the land between. They would comb the mountain pass at the border of Sunder and Estill. They would make camp in Monport and watch the ships that came and went, searching any ship likely to be hiding the kidnapped daughter of the king.

No. As the day turned to evening, Katsa knew she was fooling herself. They would search every ship, suspicious or not. They would search every building in the port city. They would comb the coastline east of Monport, and west to the mountains, and search every ship that chanced to approach the Monsean shore. They would tear the Lienid ships apart.

And within a day or two, Katsa and Bitterblue would be sharing the base of the Monsean peaks with hordes of Leck's soldiers. For there were only two paths out of Monsea: the sea, and the mountain pass on the Sunderan-Estillan border. If the fugitives weren't found on the Port Road or in the forest, if the fugitives had not appeared on the mountain pass, in Monport, or aboard a ship, then Leck would know they were in the mountains, trapped by forest and sea, with the peaks that formed the border of Monsea and Sunder at their back.

When night fell, Katsa built a small fire against a wall of rock. "Are you tired?" she asked Bitterblue.

"Yes, but not terribly," the child said. "I'm learning to sleep on the horse."

"You'll have to sleep on the horse again tonight," Katsa said, "for we must keep moving. Tell me, Princess. What do you know of this mountain range?"

"The range that divides us from Sunder? Very little. I don't think anyone knows much about these mountains. Not many people have gone into them, except up north, of course, at the pass."

"Hmm." Katsa dug through her bags and unearthed the roll of maps. She flattened them in her lap and flipped through them. Clearly, Raffin had taken Po at his word when Po said he wasn't sure where they were going. She thumbed past maps of Nander and Wester, maps of Drowden City and Birn City. A map of Sunder, and another of Murgon City. Numerous maps of various parts of Monsea. She pulled a curling page out of the pile, laid it on the ground beside the fire, and dropped stones onto its edges to hold it flat. Then she sat back on her heels and studied the princess, who stood guard over the roasting quail.

There were people in all seven kingdoms with gray eyes and dark hair; Bitterblue's coloring was not unusual. But even in the dim glow of the fire, she stood out. Her straight nose, and the quiet line of her mouth. Or was it the thickness of her hair, or the way the hair swept itself back from her forehead? Katsa couldn't quite decide what it was, but she knew that even without hoops in her ears or rings on her fingers, the child had something of the Lienid in her appearance. Something that went beyond her dark hair and light eyes.

In a kingdom searching desperately for the ten-year-old child of a Lienid mother, Bitterblue would be very difficult to disguise. Even once they did the obvious: Cut her hair, change her clothes, and turn her into a boy.

And the child's companion was no less of a problem. Katsa didn't make as convincing a boy in daylight as she did in the dark. And she would have to cover her green eye somehow. A feminine boy with one very bright blue eye, an eyepatch, and a Lienidish child charge would attract more attention in daylight than they could possibly weather. And they couldn't afford to travel only at night. And even if they made it as far as Monport without being seen, once they were seen they would be recognized instantly. They would be apprehended, and she would have to kill people. She would have to commandeer a boat, or steal one, she who didn't know the first thing about boats. Leck would hear of it and know exactly where to find them.

Her eyes dropped from the princess to the map on the ground before her. It was a map of the Sunderan-Monsean border, the impassable Monsean peaks. If Po were here he would suspect what she was thinking. She could imagine the monstrous argument they would be having.

She imagined the argument, because it helped her to come to her decision.

When they'd eaten their dinner she rolled up the maps and fastened their belongings to the saddle. "Up you go, Bitterblue. We can't waste this night. We must move on."

"Po warned you not to run the horse ragged," Bitterblue said.

"The horse is about to enjoy a very thorough rest. We're heading into the mountains, and once we get a bit higher we'll be setting him free."

"Into the mountains," Bitterblue said. "What do you mean, into the mountains?"

Katsa scattered the remains of their fire. She dug a hole with her dagger to hide the bones of their dinner. "There's no safety for us in Monsea. We're going to cross the mountains into Sunder."

Bitterblue stood still beside the horse and stared at her. "Cross the mountains? These mountains, here?"

"Yes. The mountain pass at the northern border will be guarded. We must find our own passageway, here."

"Even in summer, no one crosses these mountains," the girl said. "It's almost winter. We have no warmer clothes. We have no tools, only your dagger and my knife. It's not possible. We'll never survive."

Katsa had a response to that, though she knew none of the particulars. She lifted the girl into the saddle and swung onto the horse behind her. She turned the animal west.

She said, "I will keep you alive."

THEY DIDN'T really have only one dagger and one knife to bring them over the Monsean peaks into Sunder. They had the dagger and the knife; a length of rope; a needle and some cord; the maps; a fraction of the medicines; most of the gold; a small amount of extra clothing; the ratty blanket Bitterblue wore; two saddlebags; one saddle; and one bridle. And they had anything that Katsa could capture, kill, or construct with her own two hands as they climbed. This, first and foremost, should include the fur of some beast, to protect the child from the nagging cold they encountered here and the dangerous cold that awaited them—and that Katsa wouldn't dwell on, because when she dwelled she began to doubt herself.

She would make a bow, and possibly snowshoes—like the ones she'd worn once or twice in the winter forests outside Randa City. She thought she remembered how the snowshoes looked, and how they worked.

When the sky behind them began to lighten and color, Katsa pulled the child down from the horse. They slept for an hour or so, huddled together in a mossy crevice of rock. The sun rose around them. Katsa woke to the sound of the girl's teeth chattering. She must wake Bitterblue, and they must get moving; and before the day was out, she must have a solution to the cold that gave this girl no rest.

BITTERBLUE BLINKED at the light.

"We're higher," she said. "We've climbed in the night."

Katsa handed the child what was left of yesterday's dinner. "Yes."

"You still have it in your head for us to cross the mountains."

"It's the only place in Monsea Leck won't search for us."

"Because he knows we'd be mad to try it."

There was something petulant in the child's tone, the first hint of complaint from the girl since Katsa and Po had found her in the forest. Well, she had a right. She was tired and cold; her mother was dead. Katsa spread the map of the Monsean peaks across her lap and said nothing.

"There are bears in the mountains," Bitterblue said.

"The bears are asleep until spring," Katsa said.

"There are other animals. Wolves. Mountain lions. Animals you've not seen in the Middluns. And snow you've not seen. You don't know what these mountains are like."

Between two mountain peaks on Katsa's map was a path that seemed likely to be the least complicated route into Sunder. *Grella's Pass,* according to the scrawled words, and presumably the only route through the peaks that had been traveled by another.

Katsa rolled up her maps and slipped them into a saddlebag. She hoisted the girl back up into the saddle. "Who is Grella?" she asked.

Bitterblue snorted and said nothing. Katsa swung onto the horse behind the child. They rode for a number of minutes before Bitterblue spoke.

"Grella was a famous Monsean mountain explorer," she said. "He died in the pass that bears his name."

"Was he Graced?"

"No. He wasn't Graced like you. But he was mad like you."

The sting of the remark didn't touch Katsa. There was no reason for Bitterblue to believe that a Graceling who'd only recently seen her first mountain could guide them through Grella's Pass. Katsa herself wasn't sure of it. She knew only that when she weighed the danger of the King of Monsea against the danger of bears, wolves, blizzards, and ice, she found with utter certainty her Grace to be better equipped to face the mountains.

So Katsa said nothing, and she didn't change her mind. When the wind picked up and Katsa felt Bitterblue shivering, she drew the child close, and covered her hands with her own. The horse stumbled its way upward, and Katsa thought about their saddle. If she took it apart and soaked it and beat it, its leather would soften. It would make a rough coat for Bitterblue, or perhaps trousers. There was no reason to waste it, if it could be made to provide warmth; and very soon the horse would need it no longer.

———

They climbed blindly, even during the day, never knowing what they might encounter next, for the hills and trees rose before them and hid the higher terrain from their view. Katsa caught squirrels and fish and mice for their meals, and rabbits, if they were lucky. Beside their fire every night, she stretched and dried the pelts of their dinners. She rubbed fish oils and fat into the hides. She pieced together the pelts, experimenting with them and persisting until she'd made the child a rough fur hood, with ends that wrapped around her neck like a scarf. "It looks a bit odd," Katsa said when it was done and the child tried it on. "But vanity doesn't strike me as one of your qualities, Princess."

"It smells funny," Bitterblue said, "but it's warm."

That was all Katsa needed to hear.

The terrain grew rougher, and the brush wilder and more desperate looking. At night as the fire burned and Bitterblue slept, Katsa heard rustles around their camp that she hadn't heard before. Rustles that made the horse nervous; and howls sometimes, not so far away, that woke the child and brought her, shivering, to Katsa's side, admitting to nightmares. About strange howling monsters and sometimes her mother, she said, not seeming to want to elaborate. Katsa didn't prod.

It was on one of these nights when the sound of the wolves drove the child to Katsa that Katsa set down the stick she was whittling into an arrow and put her arm around the girl. She rubbed warmth into Bitterblue's chapped hands. And then she told the child, because it was on her own mind, about Katsa's cousin Raffin, who loved the art of medicine and would be ten times the king his father was; and about Helda, who had befriended Katsa when no one else would and thought of nothing but marrying her off to some lord; and about the Council, and the night Katsa and Oll and Giddon had rescued Bitterblue's grandfather and Katsa had scuffled with a stranger in Murgon's gardens and left him lying unconscious on the ground—a stranger who'd turned out to be Po.

Bitterblue laughed at that, and Katsa told her how she and Po had become friends, and how Raffin had nursed Bitterblue's grandfather back to health; and how Katsa and Po had gone to Sunder to unravel the truth behind the kidnapping and followed the clues into Monsea and to the mountains, the forest, and the girl.

"You aren't really like the person in the stories," Bitterblue said. "The stories I heard before I met you."

Katsa braced herself against the flood of memories that never seemed to lose their freshness and always made her ashamed. "The stories are true," she said. "I am that person."

"But how can you be? You wouldn't break an innocent man's arm, or cut off his fingers."

"I did those things for my uncle," Katsa said, "at a time when he had power over me."

And Katsa felt certain again that they were doing the right thing, to climb toward Grella's Pass, to the only place Leck wouldn't follow. Because Katsa couldn't protect Bitterblue unless her power remained her own. Her arm tightened around the girl. "You should know that my Grace isn't just fighting, child. My Grace is survival. I'll bring you through these mountains."

The child didn't answer, but she put her head on Katsa's lap, curled her arm onto Katsa's leg, and burrowed against her. She fell asleep like that, to the howl of the wolves, and Katsa decided not to pick up her whittling again. They dozed together before the fire; and then Katsa woke and lifted the girl onto the horse. She took the reins and led the beast upward through the Monsean night.

THE DAY came when the terrain grew impossible for the horse. Katsa didn't want to kill the animal, but she forced herself to consider it. There was leather to be gotten from him. And if he were left alive, he would wander the hills and give the soldiers who found him a clue to the fugitives' location. On the other hand, if Katsa killed the horse, she couldn't possibly dispose of his entire body. They would have to leave the carcass on the mountainside for the scavengers; and if soldiers found it, its bones picked clean, it would serve as a much more definite marker of their location and direction than a horse wandering free. Katsa decided with some relief that the horse must live. They removed his bags, his saddle, and his bridle. They wished him well and sent him on his way.

They climbed with their own hands and feet, Katsa helping Bitterblue up the steepest slopes, and lifting her onto rocks too big for her to climb. Thankfully, on the day she'd slid down the walls of her castle clinging to knotted sheets, Bitterblue had worn good boots. But she tripped now over her ratty dress. Finally, Katsa cut the skirts away and fashioned them into a crude pair of trousers. The girl's passage after that was faster and less frustrating.

The saddle leather was stiffer than Katsa had anticipated. She fought with it at night while Bitterblue slept, and finally decided to cut the girl four makeshift leggings, one for each lower leg and one for each upper leg, with straps to tie them in place over the trousers. They looked rather comical, but they gave her some protection from the cold and the damp. For more and more often now, as they trudged upward, snow drifted from the sky.

FOOD BECAME SCARCE. Katsa let no animal go to waste; if something moved, she brought it down. She ate little and gave most of their food to Bitterblue, who gobbled down whatever she was given.

In the light of each morning, Katsa removed the girl's boots and checked her feet for blisters. She inspected the girl's hands to make sure that her fingers weren't frostbitten. She rubbed ointment into Bitterblue's cracked skin. She handed Bitterblue the water flask every time they stopped to rest. And Katsa stopped them often for these rests, for she began to suspect that this child would collapse before admitting she was tired.

Katsa was not tired. She felt the strength of her arms and legs and the quickness of her blade. She felt most acutely the slowness of their pace. At times she wanted to hoist the child over her shoulder and run up the mountainside at full tilt. But

Katsa suspected that eventually on this mountain she would need every bit of her Graceling strength; and so she must not exhaust herself now. She curbed her impatience as best she could, and focused her energies on providing for the child.

The mountain lion was a gift, really, coming as it did at the beginning of the first true snowstorm they encountered.

The storm had been building all afternoon. The clouds knitted together. The snowflakes swelled and sharpened. Katsa made camp at the first possible place, a deep crevice in the mountain sheltered by a rocky overhang. Bitterblue went off to collect kindling, and Katsa set out, her dagger in her belt, to find them some dinner.

She struck a path upward, over the sheet of rock that formed the roof of their shelter. She headed into one of the clumps of trees that grew skyward on this mountain, roots clinging more to rock than to soil. Her senses were alert for any movement.

What she saw first was the slightest flicker, in the corner of her eye. A brown flicker up high in a tree, a flicker that curled and lifted, different somehow from the way a tree branch moved; and the limb of a tree that swung in an odd way—bounced, really, not as a wind would move it, but as if something heavy weighed it down.

Her body moved faster than her mind, recognizing predator and comprehending itself as prey. Instantly her dagger was in her hand. The great cat plunged, screeching, and she hurled the blade into its stomach. As she dropped and rolled away, its claws tore into her shoulder. Then the cat was upon her, great heavy paws slamming her shoulders against the ground and pinning her to her back. It came snarling at her, claws swiping and teeth bared, so fast that it was all she could do to keep her chest and neck from being ripped apart. She wrestled with its hopelessly strong forearms and swung her head away as its teeth came crashing together right where her face had just been. It slashed her breast savagely. When its teeth lunged for her throat Katsa grabbed its neck and screamed, pushed its snapping jaws away from her face. The animal reared above her and raked her arms with its claws. She saw a flash of something in its stomach, and remembered the dagger. Its teeth descended again and Katsa swung out, smashing its nose with her fist. It recoiled for the merest second, stunned, and in that second she reached desperately for the dagger. The cat lunged again, and Katsa thrust the dagger into its throat.

The cat made one horrible hissing, bubbling noise. Then it collapsed onto Katsa's chest, and its claws slid away from her skin. The mountain was quiet, and the lion was dead.

Katsa heaved the cat away. She propped herself onto her right elbow and wiped the animal's hot blood out of her eyes. She tested her left shoulder and winced at the pain. She choked back an enormous surge of irritation that she should now have an injury that might slow them down; and she tore open her coat and sighed, disgusted, at the gashes in her breast that stung almost as badly as those in her shoulder. And other rips and tears, she realized now, as each movement uncovered a new sting. Smaller cuts, on her neck and across her stomach and arms; deeper cuts in her thighs, where the cat had pinned her with its hind feet.

Well, there was no reason to lie around feeling sorry for herself. The snow was falling harder now. This fight had brought her injury and inconvenience, but it had also brought food that would last them a good long time, and fur for a coat that Bitterblue very much needed.

Katsa heaved herself to her feet. She considered the great lion that lay dead and bloody before her. Its tail—that's what she'd seen lifting and curling in that tree. The first clue that had saved her life. From head to tail the cat was longer than her height, and she guessed it weighed a good deal more than she did. Its neck was thick and powerful, its shoulders and back heavily muscled. Its teeth were as long as her fingers, and its claws longer. It occurred to her that she had not done so badly in this fight, despite what Bitterblue would think when she saw her. This was not an animal she would have chosen to fight in hand-to-hand combat. This animal could have killed her.

She realized then how long she had left Bitterblue alone, and a gust of wind blew thickening snow into her face. She pulled the dagger from the cat's throat, wiped it on the ground, and slipped it into her belt. She rolled the cat onto its back and grasped one of its forelegs in each hand. She gritted her teeth against the ache in her shoulder, and dragged the cat down to their cave.

———

BITTERBLUE RAN up from the camp when she saw Katsa coming. Her eyes widened. She made an unintelligible noise that sounded like choking.

"I'm all right, child," Katsa said. "It only scratched me."

"You're covered in blood."

"Mostly the cat's blood."

The girl shook her head and pulled at the rips in Katsa's coat. "Great seas," she said, when she saw the gashes in Katsa's breast. "Great seas," she whispered again, at the sight of Katsa's shoulder, arms, and stomach. "We'll have to sew some of these cuts closed. Let's clean you up. I'll get the medicines."

THAT NIGHT their camp was crowded, but the fire warmed their small space, and cooked their cat steaks, and dried the tawny pelt that would soon become Bitterblue's coat. Bitterblue supervised the cooking of the meat; they would carry the extra frozen as they climbed.

The snow fell harder now. The wind gusted snowflakes into their fire, where they hissed and died. If this storm lasted, they'd be comfortable enough here. Food, water, a roof, and warmth; they had all they needed. Katsa shifted so that the fire's heat would touch her and dry the tattered clothing she'd put on again after washing because she had nothing else to wear.

She was working on the great bow she'd been making for the past few days. She bent the stave, and tested its strength. She cut a length of cord for the string. She bound the string tightly to one end of the stave and pulled on it, hard, to stretch it to the other end. She groaned at the ache in her shoulder, and the soreness of her leg where the bow pressed into one of her cuts. "If this is what it's like to be injured, I'll never understand why Po loves so much to fight me. Not if this is how he feels afterwards."

"I don't understand much of what either of you do," the girl said.

Katsa stood and pulled experimentally at the string. She reached for one of the arrows she'd whittled. She notched the arrow and fired a test shot through the falling snow into a tree outside their cave. The arrow hit the tree with a thud and embedded itself deeply. "Not bad," Katsa said. "It will serve." She marched out into the snow and yanked the arrow from the tree. She came back, sat down, and set herself to whittling more arrows. "I must say I'd trade a cat steak for a single carrot. Or a potato. Can you imagine what a luxury it's going to be to eat a meal in an inn, once we're in Sunder, Princess?"

Bitterblue only watched her, and chewed on the cat meat. She didn't respond. The wind moaned, and the carpet of snow that formed outside their cave grew thicker. Katsa fired another test arrow into the tree and tramped out into the storm to retrieve it. When she stamped back again and knocked her boots against the walls to shake off the snow, she noticed that Bitterblue's eyes still watched her.

"What is it, child?"

Bitterblue shook her head. She chewed a piece of meat and swallowed. She pulled a steak out of the fire and passed it to Katsa. "You're not acting particularly injured."

Katsa shrugged. She bit into the cat meat and wrinkled her nose.

"I've been fantasizing about bread, myself," Bitterblue said.

Katsa laughed. They sat together companionably, the child and the lion killer, listening to the wind that drove the snow outside their mountain cave.

CHAPTER THIRTY

THE GIRL was exhausted. Warmer now in the hide of the cat, but exhausted. It was the never-ending upward trudge, and the stones that slid under her feet, pulling her back when she tried to go forward. It was the steep slope of rock that she couldn't climb unless Katsa pushed her from behind; and it was the hopeless knowledge that at the top of this slope was another just as steep, or another river of stones that would slide down while she tried to climb up. It was the snow that soaked her boots and the wind that worked its way under the edges of her clothing. And it was the wolves and cats that always appeared so suddenly, spitting and roaring, tearing toward them across rock. Katsa was quick with her bow. The creatures were always dead before they were within range, sometimes before Bitterblue was even aware of their presence. But Katsa saw how long it took Bitterblue's breath to calm and grow even again after each yowling attack, and she knew that the girl's tiredness stemmed not only from physical exertion, but from fear.

Katsa almost couldn't bear to slow their pace even more. But she did it, because she had to. "It's no use if our rescue kills him," Oll had said the night they'd rescued Grandfather

Tealiff. If Bitterblue collapsed in these mountains, the responsibility would be Katsa's.

It snowed hard now, almost constantly, and so now when it snowed, they kept moving. Katsa wrapped Bitterblue's hands in furs, and her face, so that only her eyes were exposed. She knew from the map that there were no trees in Grella's Pass. Before they reached that high, windy pathway between the peaks, the trees would end. And so she began to construct snowshoes, so that she wouldn't find herself needing them in a place with no wood to make them. She planned to make only one pair. She didn't know what terrain they would find in the pass. But she had an idea of the wind and the cold. It wouldn't be the place to move slowly, unless they wanted to freeze to death. She guessed she would be carrying the child.

At night Bitterblue sank immediately into an exhausted sleep, whimpering sometimes, as if she were having bad dreams. Katsa watched over her, and kept the fire alive. She pieced together slats of wood, and tried not to think of Po. Tried and usually failed.

Her wounds were healing well. The smallest ones barely showed anymore, and even the largest had stopped losing blood after a few hours. They were no more than an irritation, though the bags she carried pulled on the cuts and the half-constructed snowshoes banged against them. Her shoulder and her breast protested a bit every time her hand flew to the quiver on her back, the quiver she'd fashioned with a bit of saddle leather. She would have scars on her shoulder and her breast, possibly on her thighs. But they would be the only marks the cat left on her body.

She would make some sort of halter next, when she was done with the snowshoes. In anticipation of carrying the child. Some arrangement of straps and ties, made from the horse's gear, so that if she must carry Bitterblue, her arms would be free to use the bow. And perhaps a coat for herself, now that Bitterblue was warmer. A coat, from the next wolf or mountain lion they encountered.

And every night, with the fire stoked and her work done, and thoughts of Po so close she couldn't escape them, she curled up against Bitterblue and gave herself a few hours' sleep.

WHEN KATSA FOUND that she was shivering herself to sleep at night, wrapping her own head and neck with furs, and stamping the numbness out of her feet, she thought they must be nearing Grella's Pass. It couldn't be much farther. Because Grella's Pass would be even colder than this; and Katsa didn't believe the world could get much colder.

She became frightened for the child's fingers and toes, and the skin of her face. She stopped often to massage Bitterblue's fingers and her feet. The child wasn't talking, and climbed numbly, wearily; but her mind was present. She nodded and shook her head in response to Katsa's questions. She wrapped her arms around Katsa whenever Katsa lifted her or carried her. She cried, with relief, when their nightly fire warmed her. She cried from pain when Katsa woke her to the cold mornings.

They had to be close to Grella's Pass. They had to, because Katsa wasn't sure how much more of this the child could endure.

An ice storm erupted one morning as they trudged upward through trees and scrub. For the better part of the morning they were blind, heads bent into the wind, bodies battered by snow and ice. Katsa kept her arm around the child, as she always did during the storms, and followed her strong sense of direction upward and westward. And noticed, after some time, that the path grew less steep, and that she was no longer tripping over tree roots or mountain scrub. Her feet felt heavy, as if the snow had deepened and she must push her way through it.

When the storm lifted, as abruptly as it had begun, the landscape had changed. They stood at the base of a long, even, snow-covered slope, clear of vegetation, the wind catching ice crystals on its surface and dancing them up into the sky. Some distance ahead, two black crags towered to the left and right. The slope rose to pass between them.

The whiteness was blinding, the sky so close and so searingly blue that Bitterblue held her hand up to block her eyes. Grella's Pass: No animals to fend off, no boulders or scrub to navigate. Only a simple rising length of clean snow for them to walk across, right over the mountain range and down into Sunder.

It almost looked peaceful.

A warning began to buzz, and then clamor, in Katsa's mind. She watched the swirls of snow that whipped along the pass's surface. For one thing, it would be a greater distance than it looked. For another, there would be no shelter from the wind. Nor would it be as smooth as it seemed from here, with the sun shining on it directly. And if it stormed, or rather, when it stormed, it would be weather befitting these mountaintops, where no living thing survived, and all that had any hope of lasting was rock or ice.

Katsa wiped away the snow that clung to the girl's furs. She broke pieces of ice from the wrapping around Bitterblue's face. She unslung the snowshoes from her back and stepped into them, wrapped the straps around her feet and ankles, and bound them tightly. She untangled the halter she'd constructed, and helped the child into it, one weary leg at a time. Bitterblue didn't protest or ask for an explanation. She moved sluggishly. Katsa bent down, grabbed her chin, and looked into her eyes.

"Bitterblue," she said. "Bitterblue. You must stay alert. I'll carry you, but only because we have to move fast. You've got to stay awake. If I think you're falling asleep, I'll put you down and make you walk. Do you understand? I'll make you walk, Princess, no matter how hard it is for you."

"I'm tired," the child whispered, and Katsa grabbed her shoulders and shook them.

"I don't care if you're tired. You'll do what I tell you. You'll put every ounce of strength into staying awake. Do you understand?"

"I don't want to die," Bitterblue said, and a tear seeped from her eye and froze on her eyelash. Katsa knelt and held the cold little bundle of girl close.

"You won't die," Katsa said. "I won't let you die." But it would take more than her own will to keep Bitterblue alive, and so she reached into her cloak and pulled out the water flask. "Drink this," she said, "all of it."

"It's cold," Bitterblue said.

"It will help to keep you alive. Quickly, before it freezes."

The child drank, and Katsa made a split-second decision. She threw the bow onto the ground. She pulled the bags and the quiver over her head and dropped them beside the bow. Then she took off the wolf furs she wore over her shoulders, the furs she'd allowed herself to keep and wear only after the child was covered in several layers of fur from head to toe. The wind found the rips in Katsa's bloodstained coat, and the cold knifed at her stomach, at the remaining wounds in her breast and her shoulder; but soon she would be running, she told herself, and the movement would warm her. The furs that covered her neck and head would be enough. She wrapped the great wolf hides around the child, like a blanket.

"You've lost your mind," Bitterblue said, and Katsa almost smiled, because if the girl could form insulting opinions, then at least she was somewhat lucid.

"I'm about to engage in some very serious exercise," Katsa said. "I wouldn't want to overheat. Now, give me that flask, child." Katsa bent down and filled the flask with snow. Then she fastened it closed, and buried it inside Bitterblue's coats. "You'll have to carry it," she said, "if it's not to freeze."

The wind came from all directions, but Katsa thought it blew most fiercely from the west and into their faces. So she would carry the child on her back. She hung everything else across her front and pulled the straps of the girl's halter over her shoulders. She stood under the weight of the child, and straightened. She took a few cautious steps in the snowshoes. "Ball up your fists," she said to the girl, "and put them in my armpits. Put your face against the fur around my neck. Pay attention to your feet. If you start to think you can't feel them, tell me. Do you understand, Bitterblue?"

"I understand," the girl said.

"All right then," Katsa said. "We're off."

She ran.

SHE ADJUSTED quickly to the snowshoes and to the precariously balanced loads on her back and her front. The girl weighed practically nothing, and the snowshoes worked well enough once she mastered the knack of running with legs slightly splayed. She couldn't believe the coldness of this passageway over the mountains. She couldn't believe wind could blow so hard and so insistently, without ever easing. Every breath of this air was a blade gouging into her lungs. Her arms, her legs, her torso, especially her hands—every part of her that was not covered with fur burned with cold, as if she had thrown herself into a fire.

She ran, and at first she thought the pounding of her feet and legs created some warmth; and then the incessant thud, thud, thud became a biting ache, and then a dull one; and finally, she could no longer feel the pounding at all, but forced it to continue, forward, upward, closer to the peaks that always seemed the same distance away.

The clouds gathered again and pummeled her with snow. The wind shrieked, and she ran blindly. Over and over, she yelled to Bitterblue. She asked the girl questions, meaningless questions about Monsea, about Leck City, about her mother. And always the same questions about whether she could feel her hands, whether she could move her toes, whether she felt dizzy or numb. She didn't know if Bitterblue understood her questions. She didn't know what it was Bitterblue yelled back. But Bitterblue did yell; and if Bitterblue was yelling, then Bitterblue was awake. Katsa squeezed her arms over the child's hands. She reached back and grasped the child's boots every once in a while, doing what she could to rub her toes. And she ran, and kept running, even when it felt like the wind was pushing her backward. Even when her own questions began to make less and less sense, and her fingers couldn't rub and her arms couldn't squeeze anymore.

Eventually, she was conscious of only two things: the girl's voice, which continued in her ear, and the slope before them that she had to keep running up.

WHEN THE GREAT red sun sank from the sky and began to dip behind the horizon, Katsa registered it dully. If she saw the sunset, it must mean the snow no longer fell. Yes, now that she considered the question, she could see that it had stopped snowing, though she couldn't remember when. But sunset meant the day was ending. Night was coming; and night was always colder than day.

Katsa kept running, because soon it would be even colder. Her legs moved; the child spoke now and again; she could not feel anything except the coldness stabbing her lungs with each breath. And then something else began to register in the fog of her mind.

She could see a horizon that lay far below her.

She was watching the sun sink behind a horizon that lay far below her.

She didn't know when the view had changed. She didn't know at what point she had passed over the top and begun to descend. But she had done it. She couldn't see the black peaks anymore, and so they must be behind her. What she could see was the other side of the mountain; and forests, endless forests; and the sun bringing the day to a close as she ran, the child living and breathing on her back, down into Sunder. And not too far ahead of her, the end of this snowy slope, and the beginning of trees and scrub, and a downhill climb that would be so much easier for the child than the uphill climb had been.

She noticed the shivering then, the violent shivering, and panic consumed her, racked her dull mind awake. The child must not sicken now, not now that they were so close to safety. She reached back and grabbed Bitterblue's boots. She screamed her name. But then she heard Bitterblue's voice, crying something in her ear; and she felt the girl's arms snake around her front and hold her tight. The line below her breasts where Bitterblue's arms encircled her felt different suddenly. Warm, oddly warm. Katsa heard her own teeth chattering. She realized that it was not the girl who shivered. It was herself.

She found herself laughing, though nothing was funny. If she couldn't even keep herself alive, there was no hope for the child. She shouldn't have let this happen; she'd been mad to bring them into Sunder this way. She thought of her hands and held them up to her face. She opened her fingers, forced them to open, and cursed herself when she saw her white fingertips. She shoved her fists into her armpits. She willed her mind to think clearly, lucidly. She was cold, too cold. She must get them to the place where the trees started, so that they could have firewood, and protection from the wind. She must start a fire. Get to that place, and start a fire. And keep the child alive. Those were her needs, those were her ends, and she would keep those thoughts in her head as she ran.

BY THE TIME they reached the trees, Bitterblue was whimpering from numbness and cold. But when Katsa collapsed to her knees, the girl unwound herself from the halter. She fumbled to remove the wolf furs from her own back and wrapped them around Katsa's body. Then she knelt before Katsa and tugged at the straps of the snowshoes with her chapped, bleeding fingers. Katsa roused herself and helped with the straps. She crawled out of the snowshoes and flung off the bags, the quiver, the halter, and the bow.

"Firewood," Katsa said. "Firewood."

The girl sniffled and nodded and stumbled around under the trees, collecting what she could find. The wood she brought back to Katsa was damp with snow. Katsa's fingers were slow and clumsy with her dagger, unsteady with the shivering that racked her body. She had never in her life had difficulty starting a fire before, never once in her life. She concentrated fiercely, and on her tenth or eleventh try, a flame sparked and caught a dry corner of wood. Katsa fed pine needles to the flame and nursed it, directed it, and willed it not to die, until it licked at the edges of the branches she'd assembled. It grew and smoked and crackled. They had fire.

Katsa crouched, shivering, and watched the flames, ignoring fiercely the stabbings of pain they brought to her fingers and the throbbing in her feet. "No," she whispered, when Bitterblue stood and moved away to find more firewood. "Warm yourself first. Stay here and warm yourself first."

Katsa built up the fire, slowly, and as she leaned over it, and as it grew, her shivering quieted. She looked at the girl, who sat on the ground, her arms wrapped around her legs. Her eyes closed, her face resting on her knees. Her cheeks streaked with tears. Alive.

"What a fool I am," Katsa whispered. "What a fool I am." She forced herself to her feet and pushed herself from tree to tree to collect more wood. Her bones ached, her hands and feet screamed with pain. Maybe it was for the best that she'd been so foolish, for if she'd known how hard this would be, perhaps she wouldn't have done it.

She returned to their campsite and built the fire up more. Tonight the fire would be enormous; tonight they would have a fire all of Sunder could see. She shuffled over to the child and took her hands. She inspected the girl's fingers. "You can feel them?" she asked. "You can move them?"

Bitterblue nodded. Katsa yanked at the bags, and groped inside them until she found the medicines. She massaged Raffin's healing ointment into the girl's cracked, bleeding hands. "Let me see your feet now, Princess." She rubbed warmth into the girl's toes and buttoned her back into her boots.

"You've made it across Grella's Pass," she said to Bitterblue, "all in one piece. You're a strong girl."

Bitterblue wrapped her arms around Katsa. She kissed Katsa's cheek and held on to her tightly. If Katsa had had enough energy for astonishment, she would have been astonished. Instead, she hugged the girl back numbly.

Katsa and Bitterblue held on to each other, and their bodies crawled their ways back to warmth. When Katsa lay down that night before the roaring fire, the child curled in her arms, not even the pain in her hands and feet could have kept her awake.

PART THREE

The Shifting World

CHAPTER THIRTY-ONE

THE INN SAT in what passed for a clearing here in the south of Sunder, but would have been called a forest anywhere else. There was space between oaks and maples for the inn, a stable, a barn, and a patch of garden; and enough open sky to allow sunlight to flicker down and reflect the surrounding trees in the windows of the buildings.

The inn wasn't busy, though neither was it empty. Traffic through Sunder was always steady, even at winter's outset, even at the edge of the mountains. Cart horses labored northward pulling barrels of Monsean cider, or the wood of Sunder's fine forests, or the ice of Sunder's eastern mountains. Merchants bore Lienid tomatoes, grapes, apricots; Lienid jewelry and ornaments; and fish found only in Lienid's seas, north from the Sunderan port cities, up into the Middluns, to Wester, Nander, and Estill. And southward from those same kingdoms came freshwater fish, grains and hay, corn, potatoes, carrots— all the things a people who live in the forests want—and herbs and apples and pears, and horses, to be loaded onto ships and transported to Lienid and Monsea.

A merchant stood now in the yard of the inn, beside a cart stacked high with barrels. He stamped his feet and blew into his hands. The barrels were unmarked and the merchant nondescript, his coat and boots plain, none of his six horses bearing a brand or ornamentation indicating from which kingdom they came. The innkeeper burst into the yard with his sons, gesturing to them and to the horses. He yelled something to the merchant and his breath froze in the air. The merchant called back, but not loudly enough to carry to the thick stand of trees outside the clearing, where Katsa and Bitterblue crouched, watching.

"He's likely to be Monsean," Bitterblue whispered, "come up from the ports and making his way through Sunder. His cart is very full. If he'd come from one of the other kingdoms, wouldn't he have sold more of whatever he's carrying by now? Excepting Lienid, of course—but he doesn't have the look of a Lienid, does he?"

Katsa rifled through her maps. "It hardly matters. Even if we determine he's from Nander or Wester, we don't know who else is at the inn, or who else is likely to arrive. We can't risk it, not until we know whether one of your father's stories has spread into Sunder. We were weeks in the mountains, child. We've no idea what these people have heard."

"The story may not have reached this far. We're some distance from the ports and the mountain pass, and this place is isolated."

"True," Katsa said, "but we don't want to provide them with a story, either, to spread up to the mountain pass or down to the ports. The less Leck knows about where we've been, the better."

"But in that case, no inn will be safe. We'll have to get ourselves from here to Lienid without anyone seeing us."

Katsa examined her maps and didn't answer.

"Unless you're planning to kill everyone we see," Bitterblue grumbled. "Oh, Katsa, look—that girl is carrying eggs. Oh, I would kill for an egg."

Katsa glanced up to see the girl, bareheaded and shivering, scuttling from barn to inn with a basket of eggs hung over one arm. The innkeeper gestured to her and called out. The girl set the basket at the base of an enormous tree and hurried over to him. He and the merchant handed her bag after bag, and she slung them over her back and shoulders, until Katsa could barely see her anymore for the bags that covered her. She staggered into the inn. She came out again, and they loaded her down again.

Katsa counted the scattered trees that stood between their hiding place and the basket of eggs. She glanced at the frozen remains of the vegetable garden. Then she shuffled through the maps again and grabbed hold of the list of Council contacts in Sunder. She flattened the page onto her lap.

"I know where we are," Katsa said. "There's a town not far from here, perhaps two days' walk. According to Raffin, a storekeeper there is friendly to the Council. I think we might go there safely."

"Just because he's friendly to the Council doesn't mean he'll be able to see through whatever story Leck's spreading."

"True," Katsa said. "But we need clothing and information. And you need a hot bath. If we could get to Lienid without encountering anyone, we would; but it's impossible. If we must trust someone, I'd prefer it to be a Council sympathizer."

Bitterblue scowled. "You need a hot bath as much as I do."

Katsa grinned. "I need a *bath* as much as you do. Mine doesn't have to be hot. I'm not going to stick you into some half-frozen pond, to sicken and die, after all you've survived. Now, child," Katsa said, as the merchant and the innkeeper shouldered bags of their own and headed for the inn's entrance, "don't move until I get back."

"Where . . ." Bitterblue began, but Katsa was already flying from tree to tree, hiding behind one massive trunk and then another, peeking out to watch the windows and doors of the inn. When moments later Katsa and Bitterblue resumed their trek through the Sunderan forest, Katsa had four eggs inside her sleeve and a frozen pumpkin on her shoulder. Their dinner that night had the air of a celebration.

THERE WASN'T MUCH Katsa could do about her appearance or Bitterblue's when it came time to knock on the storekeeper's door, other than clean the dirt and grime as best she could from their faces, manhandle Bitterblue's tangle of hair into some semblance of a braid, and wait until darkness fell. It was too cold to expect Bitterblue to remove her patchwork of furs, and Katsa's wolf hides, no matter how alarming, were less appalling than the stained, tattered coat they hid.

The storekeeper was easily identified, his building the largest and busiest in the town save the inn. He was a man of average height and average build, had a sturdy, no-nonsense wife and an inordinate number of children who seemed to run the gamut from infancy to Katsa's age and older. Or so Katsa gathered, as she and Bitterblue passed their time among the trees at the edge of the town waiting for night to fall. His store was sizable, and the brown house that rose above and behind it enormous. As it would have to be, Katsa thought, to contain so many children. Katsa wished, as the day progressed and more and more children issued from the building to feed the chickens, to help the merchants unload their goods, to play and fight, and squabble in the yard, that this Council contact had not taken his duty to procreate quite so seriously. They would have to wait not only until the town quieted, but until most of these children slept, if Katsa wished their appearance on the doorstep to cause less than an uproar.

When most of the houses were dark, and when light shone from only one of the windows in the storekeeper's home, Katsa and Bitterblue crept from the trees. They passed through the yard and snuck to the back door. Katsa wrapped her fist in her sleeve and thumped on the solid Sunderan wood as quietly as she could and still hope to be heard. After a moment the light in the window shifted. After another moment the door was pushed open a crack, and the storekeeper peered out at them, a candle in his hand. He looked them up and down, two slight, furry figures on his doorstep, and kept a firm grip on the door handle.

"If it's food you want, or beds," he said gruffly, "you'll find the inn at the head of the road."

Katsa's first question was the most risky, and she steeled herself against the answer. "It's information we seek. Have you heard any news of Monsea?"

"Nothing for months. We hear little of Monsea in this corner of the woods."

Katsa released her breath. "Hold your light to my face, storekeeper."

The man grunted. He extended his arm through the crack in the door and held the candle to Katsa's face. His eyes narrowed, then widened, and his entire manner changed. In an instant he'd opened the door, shuffled them through, and thrown the latch behind them.

"Forgive me, My Lady." He gestured to a table and began to pull out chairs. "Please, please sit down. Marta!" he called into an adjacent room. "Food," he said to the confused woman who appeared in the doorway, "and more light. And wake the—"

"No," Katsa said sharply. "No. Please, wake no one. No one must know we're here."

"Of course, My Lady," the man said. "You must forgive my . . . my . . ."

"You weren't expecting us," Katsa said. "We understand."

"Indeed," the man said. "We'd heard what happened at King Randa's court, My Lady, and we knew you'd passed through Sunder with the Lienid prince. But somewhere along the way the rumors lost track of you."

The woman came bustling back into the room and set a

platter of bread and cheese on the table. A girl about Katsa's age followed with mugs and a pitcher. A boy, a young man taller even than Raffin, brought up the rear, and lit the torches in the walls around the table. Katsa heard a soft sigh and glanced at Bitterblue. The child stared, wide-eyed and mouth watering, at the bread and cheese on the table before her. She caught Katsa's eye. "Bread," she whispered, and Katsa couldn't help smiling.

"Eat, child," Katsa said.

"By all means, young miss," the woman said. "Eat as much as you like."

Katsa waited until everyone was seated, and until Bitterblue was contentedly stuffing her mouth with bread. Then she spoke.

"We need information," she said. "We need counsel. We need baths and any clothing—preferably boy's clothing—you might be able to spare. Above all, we need utter secrecy regarding our presence in this town."

"We're at your service, My Lady," the storekeeper said.

"We've enough clothing in this house to dress an army," his wife said. "And any supplies you'll need in the store. And a horse, I warrant, if you're wanting one. You can be sure we'll keep quiet, My Lady. We know what you've done with your Council and we'll do for you whatever we can."

"We thank you."

"What information do you seek, My Lady?" the storekeeper asked. "We've heard very little from any of the kingdoms."

Katsa's eyes rested on Bitterblue, who tore into the bread and cheese like a wild thing. "Slowly, child," she said, absently. She rubbed her head and considered how much to tell this Sunderan family. Some things they needed to know, and certainly the one thing most likely to combat the influence of whatever deception Leck spread next was the truth.

"We come from Monsea," Katsa said. "We crossed the mountains through Grella's Pass."

This was met with silence, and a widening of eyes. Katsa sighed.

"If that's hard for you to believe," she said, "you'll find the rest of our story no less than incredible. Truly, I'm unsure where to start."

"Start with Leck's Grace," Bitterblue said around her mouthful of bread.

Katsa watched the child lick crumbs from her fingers. Bitterblue looked as if she were approaching a state of rapture that even the story of her father's treachery couldn't disturb. "Very well," Katsa said. "We'll start with Leck's Grace."

KATSA TOOK not one bath that night, but two. The first to loosen the dirt and peel off the top layer of grime, the second to become truly clean. Bitterblue did the same. The storekeeper, his wife, and his two eldest children moved quietly and efficiently, drawing water, heating water, emptying the tub, and burning their old, tattered garments. Producing new clothing, boy's clothing, and fitting it to their guests. Gathering hats, coats, scarves, and gloves from their own cabinets and from the store. Cutting Bitterblue's hair to the length of a boy's, and trimming Katsa's so it lay close to her scalp again.

The sensation of cleanliness was astonishing. Katsa couldn't count the number of times she heard Bitterblue's quiet sigh. A sigh at being warm and clean, at washing oneself with soap; and at the taste of bread in one's mouth, and the feeling of bread in one's stomach.

"I'm afraid we won't get much sleep tonight, child," Katsa said. "We must leave this house before the rest of the family wakes in the morning."

"And you think that bothers me? This evening has been bliss. The lack of sleep will be nothing."

Nonetheless, when Katsa and Bitterblue lay down in a bed for the first time in a very long time—the bed of the storekeeper and his wife, though Katsa had protested their sacrifice—Bitterblue dropped into an exhausted sleep. Katsa lay on her back and tried not to let the calm breath of her bed companion, the softness of mattress and pillow delude her into believing they were safe. She thought of the gaps she'd left in the story she'd told that night.

The family of the storekeeper now understood the horror that was King Leck's Grace. They understood Ashen's murder and the events surrounding the kidnapping of Grandfather Tealiff. They'd surmised, though Katsa had never told them explicitly, that the child eating bread and cheese as if she'd never seen it before was the Monsean princess who fled her father. They even understood that if Leck chose to spread a false story through Sunder, their minds might lose the truth of everything she'd told them. All of this the family marveled at, accepted, and understood.

Katsa had omitted one truth, and she had told one lie. The truth omitted was their destination. Leck might be able to confuse this family into admitting the lady and the princess had knocked on their door and slept under their roof. But he'd never be able to talk them into revealing a destination they didn't know.

The lie told was that the Lienid prince was dead, killed by Leck's guards when he'd tried to murder the Monsean king. Katsa supposed this lie was a waste of her breath. The opportunity for the family to speak of it would never arise. But when she could, she would make Po out to be dead. The more people who thought him dead, the fewer people would think to seek him out and do him harm.

To the Sunderan port cities they must now go. Ride south to sail west. But her thoughts as she lay beside the sleeping princess tended east, to a cabin beside a waterfall; and north, to a workroom in a castle and a figure bent over a book, a beaker, or a fire.

How she wished she could take Bitterblue north to Randa City and hide her there as they'd hidden her grandfather. North to Raffin's comfort, Raffin's patience and care. But even ignoring the complications of her own status at Randa's court, it was impossible. Unthinkable to hide the child in such an obvious place, and so close to Leck's dominion; unthinkable to take this crisis to those Katsa held most dear. She would not entangle Raffin with a man who took away all reason, and warped intention. She would not lead Leck to her friends. She would not involve her friends at all.

She and the child would start tomorrow. They would ride the horse into the ground. They would find passage to Lienid, and she would hide the child; and then she would think.

She closed her eyes and ordered herself to sleep.

CHAPTER THIRTY-TWO

KATSA'S FIRST VIEW of the sea was like her first view of the mountains, though mountains and sea were nothing like each other. The mountains were silent, and the sea was rushing noise, calm, and rushing noise again. The mountains were high, and the sea was flatness reaching so far into the distance she was surprised she couldn't see the lights of some faraway land twinkling back at her. They were nothing alike. But she couldn't stop staring at the sea, or breathing in the sea air, and thus had the mountains affected her.

The cloth tied over her green eye limited her view. Katsa itched to tear it off, but she dared not, when they'd made it this far, first through the outskirts of this city and finally through the city streets themselves. They'd moved only at night, and no one had recognized them. Which was the same as saying she hadn't had to kill anyone. A scuffle here and there, when thugs on a dark street had grown a little too curious about the two boys slipping southward toward the water at midnight. But never recognition, and never more trouble than Katsa could handle without arousing suspicion.

This was Suncliff, the largest of the Sunderan port cities and the one with the heaviest traffic in trade. A city that by night struck Katsa as run-down and grim, crowded with narrow, seedy streets that seemed as if they should lead to a prison or a slum, and not to this astonishing expanse of water. Water stretching out, filling her, erasing any consciousness of the drunkards and thieves, the broken buildings and streets at her back.

"How will we find a Lienid ship?" Bitterblue asked.

"Not just a Lienid ship," Katsa said. "A Lienid ship that hasn't recently been to Monsea."

"I could check around," Bitterblue said, "while you hide."

"Absolutely not. Even if you weren't who you are, this place would be unsafe. Even if it weren't night. Even if you weren't so small."

Bitterblue wrapped her arms tightly around herself and turned her back to the wind. "I envy you your Grace."

"Let's go," Katsa said. "We must find a ship tonight, or we spend tomorrow hiding under the noses of thousands of people."

Katsa pulled the girl into the protection of her arm. They worked their way across the rocks to the streets and stairways that led down to the docks.

THE DOCKS were eerie at night. The ships were black bodies as big as castles rising out of the sea, skeleton masts and flapping sails, with voices of invisible men echoing down from the riggings.

Each ship was its own little kingdom, with its own guards who stood, swords drawn, before the gangplank, and its own sailors who came and went from deck to dock or gathered around small fires on shore. Two boys moving among the ships, bundled against the cold and carrying a couple of worn bags, were far from noteworthy in this setting. They were runaways, or paupers, looking for work or passage.

A familiar lilt in the conversation of one group of guards caught Katsa's ear. Bitterblue turned to her, eyebrows raised. "I hear it," Katsa said. "We'll keep walking, but remember that ship."

"Why not speak to them?"

"There are four of them, and there are too many others nearby. If there's trouble I'll never be able to keep it quiet."

Katsa wished suddenly for Po, for his Grace, so they might know if they were recognized, and if it mattered. If Po were here, he would know with a single question whether those Lienid guards were safe.

Of course, if Po were here their difficulty of disguise would be multiplied manyfold; between his eyes and the rings in his ears, and his accent, and even his manner of carrying himself, he would need to wear a sack over his head to avoid drawing attention. But perhaps the Lienid sailors would do anything their prince wished, despite what they'd heard? She felt his ring lying cold against the skin of her breast, the ring with the engravings that matched his arms. This ring was their ticket if any Lienid ship was to serve them willingly, and not in response to the threat of her Grace or the weight of her purse. Though she would capitulate to her Grace or her purse if necessary.

They slipped past a group of smaller ships whose guards seemed to be involved in some kind of boasting match between them. One group Westeran and another—

"Monsean," Bitterblue whispered, and though Katsa didn't change her gait, her senses sharpened and her whole body tingled with readiness until they'd left those ships behind and several more beyond them. They continued on, blending into the darkness.

THE SAILOR sat alone at the edge of a wooden walkway, his feet dangling over the water. The dock on which he sat led to a ship in an unusual state of activity, the deck swarming with men and boys. Lienid men and boys, for in ears and on fingers, in the light of their lanterns, Katsa caught flashes of gold. She knew nothing of ships, but she thought this one must either have just arrived or just be departing.

"Do ships set out in the dead of night?" she asked.

"I have no idea," Bitterblue said.

"Quickly. If it's on its way out, all the better." And if that lone sailor gave them trouble, she could drop him into the water and trust the men rushing across the deck of the ship above not to notice his absence.

Katsa slipped up onto the walkway, Bitterblue close behind. The man perceived them immediately. His hand went to his belt.

"Easy, sailor," Katsa said, her voice low. "We've only a few questions."

The man said nothing, and kept his hand at his belt, but he allowed the two figures to approach. As Katsa sat beside him, he shifted and leaned away—for better leverage, she knew, in case he decided to use his knife. Bitterblue sat next to Katsa, hidden from the man by Katsa's body. Katsa thanked the Middluns for the darkness and their heavy coats, which hid her face and her form from this fellow.

"Where does your ship come from last, sailor?" Katsa asked.

"From Ror City," he answered in a voice little deeper than hers, and Katsa knew him to be not a man but a boy—broad and solid, but younger than she.

"You depart tonight?"

"Yes."

"And where do you go?"

"To Sunport and South Bay, Westport, and Ror City again."

"Not to Monport?"

"We have no trade with Monsea this time around."

"Have you any news of Monsea?"

"It's clear enough we're a Lienid ship, isn't it? Find a Monsean ship if it's Monsean news you're wanting."

"What kind of man is your captain," Katsa asked, "and what do you carry?"

"This is a good many questions," the boy said. "You want news of Monsea and news of our captain. You want where we've been and what we're carrying. Is Murgon employing children to be his spies, then?"

"I've no idea who Murgon employs to be his spies. We seek passage," Katsa said, "west."

"You're out of luck," the boy said. "We don't need extra hands, and you don't look the type to pay."

"Oh? Graced with night vision, are you?"

"I can see you well enough to know you for a pair of raga-muffins," the boy said, "who've been fighting, by the looks of that bandage on your eye."

"We can pay."

The boy hesitated. "Either you're lying, or you're thieves. I'd wager both are true."

"We're neither." Katsa reached for the purse in the pocket of her coat. The boy unsheathed his knife and jumped to his feet.

"Hold, sailor. I only reach for my purse," Katsa said. "You may take it from my pocket yourself, if you wish. Go on," she said, as he hesitated. "I'll keep my hands in the air and my friend will stand away."

Bitterblue stood and backed up a few steps, obligingly. Katsa stood, her arms raised away from her body. The boy paused, and then reached toward her pocket. As one hand fiddled to uncover the purse, the other held the knife just below Katsa's throat. She thought she ought to appear nervous. Yet another reason to be grateful for the darkness that made her face unreadable.

Her purse finally in hand, the boy backed up a step or two. He opened it and shook a few gold pieces into his palm. He inspected the coins in the moonlight, and then in the firelight glimmering dimly from shore.

"This is Lienid gold," he said. "Not only are you thieves, but you're thieves who've stolen from Lienid men."

"Take us to your captain and let him decide whether to accept our gold. If you do so, a piece of it's yours—regardless of what he chooses."

The boy considered the offer, and Katsa waited. Truly, it didn't matter if he agreed to their terms or not, for they wouldn't find a ship better suited to their purposes than this one. Katsa would get them aboard one way or another, even if she had to clunk this boy on the head and drag him up the gangplank, waving Po's ring before the noses of the guards.

"All right," the boy said. He chose a coin from the pile in his palm and tucked it inside his coat. "I'll take you to Captain Faun for a piece of gold. But I warrant you'll find yourself thrown into the brig for thievery. She won't believe you came upon this honestly, and we don't have time to report you to the authorities in the city."

The word had not escaped Katsa's attention. "She? Your captain is a woman?"

"A woman," the boy said, "and Graced."

A woman and Graced. Katsa didn't know which should surprise her more. "Is this a ship of the king, then?"

"It's her ship."

"How—"

"The Graced in Lienid are free. The king doesn't own them."

Yes, she remembered that Po had explained this.

"Are you coming," the boy said, "or are we going to stand here conversing?"

"What's her Grace?"

The boy stepped aside and waved them forward with his knife. "Go on," he said. And so Katsa and Bitterblue moved up the dock, but Katsa listened for his answer. If this captain was a mind reader, or even a very competent fighter, she wanted to know before they reached the guards so she could decide whether to continue forward or shove this boy into the water and run.

Ahead of them, the guards spoke to each other and laughed at some joke. One of them held a torch. The flame strained against the wind and flashed across their rough faces, their broad chests, their unsheathed swords. Bitterblue gasped, ever so slightly, and Katsa shifted her attention to the child. Bitterblue was frightened. Katsa laid her hand on the girl's shoulder and squeezed.

"It'll be a swimming Grace," she said idly to the boy behind them, "or some navigational ability. Am I right?"

"Her Grace is the reason we leave in the middle of the night," the boy said. "She sees storms before they hit. We set out now to beat a blizzard coming up from the east."

A weather seer. The prescient Graces were better than the mind-reading Graces, better by far, but still they gave Katsa a crawling feeling along her skin. Well, this captain's profession was well suited to her Grace, anyway, and it wasn't adverse to their purposes—might even be advantageous. Katsa would meet this Captain Faun and measure her, then decide how much to tell her.

The guards stared at them as they approached. One held the torch to their faces. Katsa ducked her chin into the neck of her coat and stared back at him with her single visible eye. "What's this you're bringing aboard, Jem?" the man asked.

"They go to the captain," the boy said.

"Prisoners?"

"Prisoners or passengers. The captain will decide."

The guard gestured to one of his companions. "Go with them, Bear," he said, "and make sure no danger befalls our young Jem."

"I can handle myself," Jem said.

"Of course you can. But Bear can handle yourself, too, and himself, and your two prisoners, and carry a sword, and hold a light—all at the same time. And keep our captain safe."

Jem might have been about to protest, but at the mention of the captain he nodded. He took the lead as Katsa and Bitterblue climbed up the gangplank. Bear fell in behind them, his sword swinging in one hand and a lantern raised in the other. He was one of the largest men Katsa had ever seen. As they stepped onto the deck of the ship, sailors moved aside, partly to stare at the two small and bedraggled strangers and partly to get out of Bear's way. "What's this, Jem?" voices asked. "We go to the captain," Jem responded, over and over, and the men fell away and went back to their duties.

The deck was long, and it was crowded with jostling men and with unfamiliar shapes that loomed to all sides of them

and cast strange shadows against the light of Bear's lantern. A
sail billowed down suddenly, released from its confinement in
the riggings. It flapped over Katsa's head, glowing a luminous
gray, looking very much like an enormous bird trying to break
its leash and take off into the sky; and then it rose again just
as suddenly, folded and strapped back into place. Katsa had no
idea what it all meant, all this activity, but felt a kind of excitement at the strangeness and the rush, the voices shouting
commands she didn't recognize, the gusting wind, the pitch-
ing floor.

It took her about two steps to adjust to the tilt and roll of
the deck. Bitterblue was not so comfortable, and her balance
wasn't helped by her constant alarm at the happenings around
her. Katsa finally took hold of the girl and held her close
against her side. Bitterblue leaned into her, relieved, and re-
linquished to Katsa the job of keeping her upright.

Jem stopped at an opening in the deck floor. "Follow me,"
he said. He clamped his knife between his teeth, stepped into
the blackness of the opening, and disappeared. Katsa followed,
trusting the ladder she couldn't see to materialize beneath her
hands and feet, pausing to help the child onto the rungs just
above her. Bear climbed down last, his light casting their shadows against the walls of the narrow corridor in which they finally stood.

They followed Jem's dark form down a hallway. Bitterblue
leaned against Katsa and turned her face against Katsa's
breast. Yes, the air was stuffy down here, and stale and unpleasant. Katsa had heard that people got used to ships. Until

Bitterblue got used to it, Katsa would keep her standing and breathing.

Jem led them past black doorways, toward a rectangle of orange light that Katsa guessed opened to the quarters of the Graced captain. The woman captain. Voices emanated from the lighted opening, and one of them was strong, commanding, and female.

When they reached the doorway the conversation stopped. From her place in the shadows behind the boy, Katsa heard the woman's voice.

"What is it, Jem?"

"Begging your pardon, Captain," Jem said. "These two Sunderan boys wish to buy passage west, but I don't trust their gold."

"And what's wrong with their gold?" the voice asked.

"It's Lienid gold, Captain, and more of it than it seems to me they should have."

"Bring them in," the voice said, "and let me see this gold."

They followed Jem into a well-lit room that reminded Katsa of one of Raffin's workrooms, always cluttered with open books, bottles of oddly colored liquids, herbs drying from hooks, and strange experiments Katsa didn't understand. Except here, the books were replaced by maps and charts, the bottles by instruments of copper and gold Katsa didn't recognize, the herbs by ropes, cords, hooks, nets—items Katsa knew belonged on ships but didn't know the purpose of any more than she knew the purpose of Raffin's experiments. A narrow bed stood in one corner, a chest at its foot. This, too, was like Raffin's workrooms, for sometimes he slept there, in a bed he'd installed for those nights when his mind was more on his work than his comfort.

The captain stood before a table, a sailor almost as big as Bear at her side, a map spread out before them. She was a woman past childbearing years, her hair steel gray and pulled tightly into a knot at the nape of her neck. Her clothing like that of the other sailors: brown trousers, brown coat, heavy boots, and a knife at her belt. Her left eye pale gray, and her right a blue as brilliant as Katsa's blue eye. Her face stern, and her gaze, as she turned to the two strangers, quick and piercing. Katsa felt for the first time, in this bright room with this woman's bright eyes flashing over them, that their disguises had come to the end of their usefulness.

Jem dropped Katsa's coins into the captain's outstretched hand. "There's plenty more of it, too, Captain, in this purse."

The captain considered the gold in her hand. She raised narrowed eyes to Katsa and Bitterblue. "Where did you get this?"

"We're friends of Prince Greening of Lienid," Katsa said. "It's his gold."

The big sailor beside the captain snorted. "Friends of Prince Po," he said. "Of course they are."

"If you've stolen from our prince—" Jem began, but Captain Faun held up a hand. She looked at Katsa so hard that Katsa felt as if the woman's gaze were scraping at the back of her skull. She looked at Katsa's coat, at her belt, at her trousers, her boots, and Katsa felt naked before the intelligence of those uneven eyes.

"You expect me to believe that Prince Po gave a purse of gold to two raggedy Sunderan boys?" the captain finally asked.

"I think you know we're not Sunderan boys," Katsa said, reaching into the neck of her coat. "He gave me his ring so you may know to trust us." She pulled the cord over her head. She held the ring out for the captain to see. She registered the woman's shocked expression, and then the outraged cries of Jem and Bear alerted her to the room's sudden descent into bedlam. They were lunging toward her, both of them, Jem brandishing his knife, Bear swinging his sword; and the sailor beside the captain had also pulled a blade.

Po could have mentioned that at the sight of his ring his people devolved into madness; but she would act now and contemplate her annoyance later. She swirled Bitterblue into the corner so that her own body was between the child and everyone else in the room. She turned back and blocked Jem's knife arm so hard that he cried out and dropped the blade to the floor. She knocked his feet out from under him, dodged the swing of Bear's sword, and swung her boot up to clock Bear on the head. By the time Bear's body had crumpled to the ground, Katsa held Jem's own knife to Jem's throat. Hooking her foot under Bear's sword and kicking it up into the air, she caught it with her free hand and held it out toward the re-maining sailor, who stood just out of her range, knife drawn, ready to spring. The ring still dangled from its cord, gripped in the same hand that gripped the sword, and it was the ring that held the gaze of the captain.

"Stop," Katsa said to the remaining sailor. "I don't wish to harm you, and we're not thieves."

"Prince Po would never give that ring to a Sunderan urchin," Jem gasped.

"And you do your Graceling prince little honor," Katsa said, digging her knee into his back, "if you think a Sunderan urchin could've robbed him."

"All right," the captain said. "That's more than enough. Drop those blades, Lady, and release my man."

"If this other fellow comes toward me," Katsa said, pointing the sword at the remaining sailor, "he'll end up sleeping beside Bear."

"Come back, Patch," the captain said to her man, "and lower that knife. Do it," she said sharply, when Patch hesitated. The expression he shot at Katsa was ugly, but he obeyed.

Katsa dropped her blades to the floor. Jem stood, rubbed his neck, and focused a scowl in her direction. Katsa thought of a few choice words she would like to say to Po. She looped his ring back around her neck.

"What exactly have you done to Bear?" the captain asked.

"He'll wake soon enough."

"He'd better."

"He will."

"And now you'll explain yourself," the captain said. "The last we heard of our prince, he was in the Middluns, at the court of King Randa. Training with you, if I'm not mistaken."

A noise came from the corner. They turned to see Bitterblue on her knees, huddled against the wall, vomiting onto the floor. Katsa went to the girl and helped her to her feet. Bitterblue clung to her clumsily. "The floor is moving."

"Yes," Katsa said. "You'll get used to it."

"When? When will I get used to it?"

"Come, child."

Katsa practically carried Bitterblue back to the captain. "Captain Faun," she said, "this is Princess Bitterblue of Monsea. Po's cousin. As you've guessed, I'm Katsa of the Middluns."

"I would also guess there's nothing wrong with that eye," the captain said.

Katsa pulled the cloth away from her green eye. She looked into the face of the captain, who met her gaze coolly. She turned to Patch and Jem, who looked back at her, understanding now, eyebrows high. So familiar, in the features of their faces, their dark hair, the gold in their ears. The evenness with which they looked into her eyes.

Katsa turned back to the captain. "The princess is in great danger," she said. "I'm taking her to Lienid to hide her from . . . from those who wish to harm her. Po said you would help us when I showed you his ring. But if you won't, I'll do everything in the power of my Grace to force your assistance."

The captain stared at her, eyes narrowed and face hard to read. "Let me see that ring more closely."

Katsa stepped forward. She wouldn't remove the ring from its place around her neck again, not when the sight of it inspired such madness. But the captain didn't fear her, and she reached out to Katsa's throat to take the gold circle in her fingers. She turned it this way and that in the light. She dropped the ring and narrowed her eyes at Bitterblue. She turned back to Katsa.

"Where is our prince?" she asked.

Katsa deliberated and decided that she must give this woman pieces, at least, of the truth. "Some distance from here, recovering from injury."

"Is he dying?"

"No," Katsa said, startled. "Of course not."

The captain peered at her, and frowned. "Then why did he give you his ring?"

"I told you. He gave it to me so that a Lienid ship would help us."

"Nonsense. If that's all he wanted, then why didn't he give you the king's ring, or the queen's?"

"I don't know," Katsa said. "I don't know the meanings of the rings, aside from which people they represent. This is the one he chose to give me."

The captain *humph*ed. Katsa clenched her teeth and prepared herself to say something very caustic, but Bitterblue's voice stopped her.

"Po did give the ring to Katsa," she said miserably. Her voice was thick, her body hunched over itself. "Po meant for her to have it. And as he didn't explain what it meant, you should explain for him. Right now."

The captain considered Bitterblue. Bitterblue raised her chin, grim and stubborn. The captain sighed. "It's very rare for a Lienid to give away one of his rings, and almost unheard of for him to give away the ring of his own identity. To give that ring is to forsake his own identity. Princess Bitterblue, your lady has around her neck the ring of the Seventh Prince of Lienid. If Prince Po had truly given her that ring, it would mean that he'd abdicated his princehood. He'd no longer be a prince of Lienid. He'd make her a princess and give her his castle and his inheritance."

Katsa stared. She pulled at a chair and sat down hard. "That can't be."

"Not one in a thousand Lienid gives that ring away," the captain said. "Most wear it to their graves in the sea. But occasionally—if a woman is dying and wants a sister to take her place as the mother of her children, or if a dying shopkeeper wants his shop to go to a friend, or if a prince is dying and wants to change the line of succession—a Lienid will make a gift of that ring." The captain turned to glare at Katsa. "The Lienid love their princes, most especially the youngest prince, the Graceling prince. To steal Prince Po's ring would be considered a terrible crime."

But Katsa was shaking her head, from confusion that Po should have done such a thing, and from fear of the word the captain kept saying over and over. Dying. Po wasn't dying. "I don't want it," she said. "That he should give me this, and not explain—"

Bitterblue leaned against the table, her face gray, and moaned. "Katsa, don't worry. You can be sure he had some reason."

"But what reason would he have? His injuries weren't so bad—"

"Katsa." The child's voice was patient but tired. "Think. He gave you the ring before he was injured. It wasn't such a strange thing for him to do, knowing he might die in the fight."

Katsa saw then what it meant; and her hand went to her throat. It was just like him. And now she was fighting back tears because it was just the sort of mad thing he would get it into his mind to do—mad and foolish, far too kind, and unnecessary, because he wasn't going to die. "Why in the Middluns didn't he tell me?"

"If he had," Bitterblue said, "you wouldn't have taken it."

"You're right, I wouldn't have taken it. Can you see me taking such a thing from Po? Can you see me agreeing to such a thing? And he's right to have given it, because he is going to die, because I'm going to kill him when next I see him, for doing such a thing and frightening me and not telling me what it meant."

"Of course you will," Bitterblue said soothingly.

"It's not permanent, is it?" Katsa asked, turning to the captain. She then noticed for the first time that the captain was looking at her differently. So were Patch and Jem. Their faces white, and something shocked and quiet in their eyes. They believed her now, that she hadn't stolen the ring, and they believed that their prince had given it to her. And Katsa was relieved that at least that part of this ordeal was behind them. "I can give it back to him," she asked the captain, "can't I?"

The captain cleared her throat. She nodded. "Yes, Lady Princess."

"Great hills," Katsa said, distressed. "Don't call me that."

"You may give it back to him at any time, Lady Princess," the captain said, "or give it to someone else. And he may reclaim it. In the meantime, your position entitles you to every power and authority held by a prince of Lienid. It's ours to do your bidding."

"I'll be content if you'll take us quickly to Po's castle on the western shore," Katsa said, "and stop calling me Princess."

"It's your castle now, Lady Princess."

Katsa's temper was beginning to throw out sparks, for she wanted none of this treatment; but before she could argue, a man knocked on the door frame. "We're ready, Captain."

Katsa pulled Bitterblue to the side as the room erupted with commotion. The captain began to bark instructions. "Patch, get back to your post and get us out of here. Jem, see to Bear. And clean up that mess in the corner. I'm needed on deck, Lady Princess. Come above, if you wish. Princess Bitterblue's seasickness will be less there."

"I've told you not to call me that," Katsa said.

The captain ignored her and marched to the doorway. Katsa swept Bitterblue under her arm and followed her, glaring at the woman's back as they passed through the corridor.

And then in the blackness at the foot of the ladder, the captain stopped. She turned back to Katsa. "Lady Princess," she said. "What you're doing here—and why you're disguised, and why the child princess is in danger—is your affair. I won't ask for an explanation. But if there's any assistance I can give, you need only to voice it. I'm at your service, completely."

Katsa reached to her breast and touched the circle of gold. She was thankful, after all, for the power it gave her, if that power would help her to serve Bitterblue. And that might be an explanation for Po's gift as well; perhaps he'd only wanted her to have full authority, so that she might protect the child better. But she didn't want everyone on deck to see the ring, if it inspired such adoration. She didn't want everyone talking about it and pointing it out and treating her this way. She loosened the neck of her coat and tucked the ring inside.

"Prince Po is recovering from his injuries?" Captain Faun asked; and Katsa heard the worry, the authentic worry, as if the captain were inquiring after a member of her own family. And Katsa also heard the royal title, less easily dropped from Po's name than added to her own.

"He's recovering," she said.

And it occurred to her to wonder then if the Lienid would love their prince so much if they knew the truth of his Grace.

It was all too confusing, all that had happened since she'd come aboard this vessel, and too many parts of it hurt her heart.

On deck, she led Bitterblue to the side of the ship. Together they breathed the sea air and watched the dark sparkle of the water.

CHAPTER THIRTY-THREE

Wʜᴀᴛ sʜᴇ really loved was to hang over the edge and watch the bow of the ship slice through the waves. She loved it especially when the waves were high and the ship rose and fell, or when it was snowing and the flakes stung her face. The men laughed and told each other that Princess Katsa was a born sailor. To which Bitterblue added, once Bitterblue was well enough to come above deck and join in their banter, that Katsa was born to do anything normal people might consider terrifying.

What she really wanted was to climb into the highest riggings of the highest mast and hang down from the sky; and one clear day when Patch, who happened to be the first mate, sent a fellow named Red up to unravel a tangle of ropes, he told her to go along.

"You shouldn't encourage her," Bitterblue said to Patch, her hands on her hips and her face turned up to glare into his. Her countenance fierce, for all that she was a fifth Patch's size.

"Lady Princess, I reckon she'll go up there eventually with or without my say-so, and I'd rather it be now while I'm watching, than at night, or during a squall."

"If you think sending her up there now will keep her from—"

"Watch yourself," Patch said as the deck lurched and Bitterblue pitched forward. He caught her and lifted her into his arms. They watched Katsa climb hand and foot up the mast behind Red; and when Katsa finally looked down at them from her place in the sky, swinging so wildly back and forth that she marveled at Red's ability to untangle anything, she thought of how Bitterblue had trusted no man when first they'd met. And now the girl allowed this enormous sailor to pick her up and hold her, like a father, and the girl's arm was around Patch's neck, and she and Patch laughed up at Katsa together.

THE CAPTAIN predicted the journey would last four or five weeks, give or take. The ship moved fast, and most of the time they were alone on the ocean. Katsa never climbed up into the riggings without straining her eyes behind them for some sign of pursuit, but no one was after them. It was a relief not to feel hunted, and not to feel as if one must hide. It was safe on the open sea, isolated with Captain Faun and her crew, for not one sailor seemed to look upon them with suspicion, and she came gradually to trust that none had been touched by any rumors of Leck's.

"We weren't even a day in Suncliff," the captain told her. "You're lucky, Lady Princess. You have my Grace to thank for it."

"And for our speed," Katsa said. For it was a stormy winter at sea, and though they changed course so often their path must look like some odd dance across the water, they managed to avoid the worst of it. Their progress west was steady.

Katsa had told the captain of Leck's Grace and the reasons they fled, in the first few days when Bitterblue had been very sick and Katsa had had nothing to do but care for the girl and think. She'd told the captain because it had occurred to her, with a sinking feeling, that the forty-some men aboard this ship knew exactly who she and Bitterblue were and exactly where they were going. That made forty-some informants, once Katsa and Bitterblue were delivered to their destination and the ship returned to its trade route.

"I can vouch for the confidence of most of my men, Lady Princess," Captain Faun said. "Most, if not all."

"You don't understand," Katsa said. "Where King Leck is involved I can't even vouch for my own confidence. It's not good enough for them to swear to say nothing to no one. If one of Leck's stories touches their ears, they'll forget their vows."

"What would you have me do then, Lady Princess?"

Katsa hated to ask it, and so she stared at the charts on the table before them, pursed her lips, and waited for the captain to understand her. It didn't take long.

"You want us to remain at sea, once we've left you in Lienid," the captain said, her voice sharp and growing sharper as she spoke. "You want us to hold at sea, out of the way, all winter—longer, perhaps indefinitely—until you and Prince Po, who aren't even in communication, have found some way to immobilize the King of Monsea. At which point I suppose we must wait for someone to come in search of us and invite us back ashore? What's left of us, because we'll run out of supplies, Lady Princess—we're a trade vessel, you know, designed to sail from port to port and replenish our food and water at each stop. It's strain enough that we go now straight back to Lienid—"

"Your cargo hold is full of the fruits and vegetables of your trade," Katsa said, "and your men know how to fish."

"We'll run out of water."

"Then ride your ship into a storm," Katsa said.

The captain's face was incredulous. Katsa supposed it was an absurd suggestion—all of it absurd, for her to expect this ship to turn circles in some frozen corner of the sea, waiting for the approach of news that might never come. All for the safety of one young life. The captain made a noise part disbelief and part laughter, and Katsa prepared for an argument.

But the woman stared into her hands, thinking; and when she finally spoke, she surprised Katsa.

"You ask a great deal," she said, "but I can't pretend I don't understand why you ask it. Leck must be stopped, and not just for the sake of Princess Bitterblue. His Grace is limitless, and a king with his proclivities is a danger to all seven kingdoms. If my crew avoids any contact with gossip and rumors, that's forty-three men and one woman whose minds are clear to the task at hand.

"And," she continued, "I've promised to help you in any way I can."

It was Katsa's turn now to disbelieve. "You'll really do this thing?"

"Lady Princess," the captain said. "It's not in my power to refuse anything you ask. But this thing I'll do willingly, for as long as I can without endangering my men and my ship. And on the condition that I'll be reimbursed for my lost trade."

"That goes without saying."

"Nothing in business goes without saying, Lady Princess."

And so they made an agreement. The captain would hold at sea in a place near to Lienid, a specific place just west of an uninhabited island she could describe and another vessel could find, until such time as the other vessel came for her, or circumstances aboard her ship rendered it impossible for her isolation to continue.

"I've no idea what I'll tell my crew," the captain said.

"When the time comes for explanations," Katsa said, "tell them the truth."

THE CAPTAIN asked Katsa and Bitterblue one day, as they sat in the galley over a meal, how they'd gotten to Suncliff without being seen.

"We crossed the Monsean peaks into Sunder," Katsa said, "and traveled through the forests. When we reached the outskirts of Suncliff, we traveled only by night."

"How did you cross the mountain pass, Lady Princess? Wasn't it guarded?"

"We didn't cross at the mountain pass. We took Grella's Pass."

The captain peered at Katsa over the cup she'd raised to her face. She set the cup down. "I don't believe you."

"It's true."

"You crossed Grella's Pass and kept your fingers and toes,

let alone your lives? I might believe it of you, Lady Princess, but I can't believe it of the child."

"Katsa carried me," Bitterblue said.

"And we had good weather," Katsa added.

The captain's laugh rang out. "It's no use lying to me about the weather, Lady Princess. It's snowed in Grella's Pass every day since summer, and there are few places in the seven kingdoms colder."

"Nonetheless, it could have been worse the day we crossed."

The captain was still laughing. "If I ever need a protector, Lady Princess, I hope to find you nearby."

A day or two later, after Katsa had come up from one of the frigid ocean baths she liked to take—the baths that Bitterblue considered further proof she was mad—she sat on Bitterblue's bunk and peeled away her soaking clothing. Their quarters were barely big enough for the two bunks they slept in and badly lit by a lantern that swung from the ceiling. Bitterblue brought Katsa a cloth to dry her wet skin and frozen hair. She reached out to touch Katsa's shoulder. Katsa looked down and saw, in the wavering light, the lines of white skin that had caught the girl's attention. The scars, where the claws of the mountain lion had torn her flesh. Lines on her breast, too.

"You've healed well," Bitterblue said. "There's no question who won that fight."

"For all that," Katsa said, "we weren't evenly matched, and the cat had the advantage. On a different day it would've killed me."

"I wish I had your skill," Bitterblue said. "I'd like to be able to defend myself against anything."

It wasn't the first time Bitterblue had said something like that. And it was only one of countless times Katsa had remembered, with a stab of panic, that Bitterblue was wrong; that in her one and only encounter with Leck, Katsa had been defenseless.

STILL, BITTERBLUE didn't have to be as defenseless as she was. When Patch teased her one day about the knife she wore sheathed at her belt—the same knife, big as her forearm, she'd carried since the day Katsa and Po had found her in Leck's forest—Katsa decided the time had come to make a threat of Bitterblue. Or as much of a threat as the child could be. How absurd it was that in all seven kingdoms, the weakest and most vulnerable of people—girls, women—went unarmed and were taught nothing of fighting, while the strong were trained to the highest reaches of their skill.

And so Katsa began to teach the girl. First to feel comfortable with a knife in her hand. To hold it properly, so that it wouldn't slip from her fingers; to carry it easily, as if it were a natural extension of her arm. This first lesson gave the child more trouble than Katsa had anticipated. The knife was heavy. It was also sharp. It made Bitterblue nervous to carry an open blade across a floor that lurched and dipped. She held the hilt much too tightly, so tightly her arm ached and blisters formed on her palm.

"You fear your own knife," Katsa said.

"I'm afraid of falling on it," Bitterblue said, "or hurting someone with it by accident."

"That's natural enough. But you're just as likely to lose control of it if you're holding it too tightly as too loosely. Loosen your grip, child. It won't fall from your fingers if you hold it as I've taught you."

And so the child would relax the hand that held the knife, until the floor tipped again or one of the sailors came near; and then she would forget what Katsa had said and grip the blade again with all her strength.

Katsa changed tactics. She put an end to official lessons, and instead had Bitterblue walk around the ship with the knife in her hand all afternoon for several days. Knife in hand, the child visited the sailors who were her friends, climbed the ladder between decks, ate meals in the galley, and craned her neck to watch Katsa scrambling around in the riggings. At first she sighed often and passed the knife heavily from one hand to the other. But then, after a day or two, it seemed not to bother her so much. A few days more and the knife swung loosely at her side. Not forgotten, for Katsa could see the care she took with the blade when the floor rocked, or when a friend was near. But comfortable in her hand. Familiar. And now, finally, it was time for the girl to learn how to use the weapon she held.

The next few lessons progressed slowly. Bitterblue was persistent and ferociously determined; but her muscles were untrained, unused to the motions Katsa now expected of her.

Katsa was hard-pressed sometimes to know what to teach her. There was some use in teaching the child to block or deliver blows in the traditional sense—some, but not much. She would never last long in a battle if she tried to fight by the usual rules. "What you must do," Katsa told her, "is inflict as much pain as possible and watch for an opening."

"And ignore your own pain," Jem said, "as best you can." Jem helped with the lessons, as did Bear, and any other of the sailors who could find the time. Some days the lessons served as mealtime distractions for the men in the galley, or on fine days as diversions in the corner of the deck. The sailors didn't all understand why a young girl should be learning to fight. But none of them laughed at her efforts, even when the methods Katsa encouraged her to use were as undignified as biting, scratching, and hair pulling.

"You don't need to be strong to drive your thumbs into a man's eyeballs," Katsa said, "but it does a lot of damage."

"That's disgusting," Bitterblue said.

"Someone your size doesn't have the luxury of fighting cleanly, Bitterblue."

"I'm not saying I won't do it. I'm only saying it's disgusting."

Katsa tried to hide her smile. "Yes, well. I suppose it is disgusting."

She showed Bitterblue all of the soft places to stab a man if she wanted to kill him—throat, neck, stomach, eyes—the easy places that required less force. She taught Bitterblue to hide a small knife in her boot and how to whip it out quickly.

How to drive a knife with both hands and how to hold one in either hand. How to keep from dropping a knife in the bedlam of an attack, when everything was happening so fast your mind couldn't keep up.

"That's the way to do it," Red called out one day when Bitterblue had elbowed Bear successfully in the groin and bent him over double, groaning.

"And now that he's distracted," Katsa said, "what will you do?"

"Stab him in the neck with my knife," Bitterblue said.

"Good girl."

"She's a plucky little thing," Red said, approvingly.

She *was* a plucky little thing. So little, so completely little, that Katsa knew, as every one of these sailors must know, how much luck she would need if she were to defend herself from an attacker. But what she was learning would give her a fighting chance. The confidence she was gaining would also help. These men, these sailors who stood on the side shouting their encouragement—they helped, too, more than they could know.

"Of course, she'll never need these skills," Red added. "A princess of Monsea will always have bodyguards."

Katsa didn't say the first words that came to her mind. "It seems better to me for a child to have these skills and never use them, than not have them and one day need them," she said.

"I can't deny that, Lady Princess. No one would know that

better than you, or Prince Po. I imagine the two of you could whip a whole troop of children into a decent army."

A vision of Po, dizzy and unsteady on his feet, flashed into Katsa's mind. She pushed it away. She went to check on Bear and focused her thoughts on Bitterblue's next drill.

CHAPTER THIRTY-FOUR

Katsa was in the riggings with Red when she first saw Lienid. It was just how Po had described it; and it was unreal, like something out of a tapestry, or a song. Dark cliffs rose from the sea, snow-covered fields atop them. Rising from the fields a pillar of rock, and atop the rock, a city. Gleaming so bright that at first Katsa was sure it was made of gold.

As the ship drew closer she saw that she wasn't so wrong. The buildings of the city were brown sandstone, yellow marble, and white quartz that sparkled with the light from sky and water. And the domes and turrets of the structure that rose above the others and sprawled across the skyline were, in fact, gold: Ror's castle and Po's childhood home. So big and so bright that Katsa hung from the riggings with her mouth hanging open. Red laughed at her and yelled down to Patch that one thing, at least, stilled the Lady Princess's climbing and scrambling.

"Land ho!" he called then, and men up and down the deck cheered. Red slithered down, but Katsa stayed in the riggings and watched Ror City grow larger before her. She could make out the road that spiraled from the base of the pillar up to the city, and the platforms, too, rising from fields to city on ropes too thin for her eyes to discern. When the ship skirted the southeast edge of Lienid and headed north, she swung around and kept the city in her sight until it disappeared. It hurt her eyes, almost, Ror City; and it didn't surprise her that Po should come from a place that shone.

Or a land so dramatically beautiful. The ship wound around the island kingdom, north and then west, and Katsa barely blinked. She saw beaches white with sand, and sometimes with snow. Mountains disappearing into storm clouds. Towns of stone built into stone and hanging, camouflaged, above the sea. Trees on a cliff, stark and leafless, black against a winter sky.

"Po trees," Patch said to her when she pointed them out. "Did our prince tell you? The leaves turn silver and gold in the fall. They were beautiful two months ago."

"They're beautiful now."

"I suppose. But Lienid is gray in the winter. The other seasons are an explosion of color. You'll see, Lady Princess."

Katsa glanced at him in surprise, and then wondered why she should be surprised. She would see, if she stayed here long enough, and likely she'd be here some time. Her plans once they reached Po's castle were vague. She would explore the building, learn its hiding places, and fortify it. She would set a guard, with whatever staff she found there. She would think and plan and wait to hear something of Po or Leck. And just as she fortified the castle, she would fortify her mind, against any news she heard that might carry the poison of Leck's lies.

"I know what you've asked us to do, Lady Princess," Patch said beside her.

This time she looked at him with true surprise. He watched the passing trees, his face grave.

"Captain Faun told me," he said. "She's told a few of us— a very few. She wants a number of us on her side when the time comes to tell the rest."

"And are you on her side, then?" Katsa asked.

"She brought me to her side, eventually."

"I'm glad," Katsa said. "And I'm sorry."

"It isn't your doing, Lady Princess. It's the doing of the monster who's the King of Monsea."

A light snow began to fall. Katsa reached her hands out to meet it.

"What do you think is wrong with him, Lady Princess?" Patch asked.

Katsa caught a snowflake in the middle of her palm. "What do you mean, wrong with him?"

"Well, why does it pleasure him to hurt people?"

Katsa shrugged. "His Grace makes it so easy."

"But everyone has some kind of power to hurt people," Patch said. "It doesn't mean they do."

"I don't know," Katsa said, thinking of Randa and Murgon and the other kings and their senseless acts. "It seems to me that a fair number of people are happy to be as cruel as their power allows, and no one's more powerful than Leck. I don't know why he does it, I only know we need to stop him."

"Do you think Leck knows where you are, Lady Princess?"

Katsa watched flakes melting into the sea. She sighed.

"We crossed paths with very few people," she said, "once

we left Monsea. And we told no one our destination, until we boarded this ship. But—he saw both of us, Patch, both me and Po, and of course he recognized us. There are only a few places we could hide the child. He'll look for her here eventually. I must find a place to hide, in the castle or on the lands. Or even someplace in the Lienid wilderness."

"The weather will be harsh, Lady Princess, until spring."

"Yes. Well, I may not be able to keep her comfortable. But I'll keep her safe."

Po HAD SAID his castle was small, more akin to a large house than a castle. But after seeing the way Ror's castle filled the sky, Katsa wondered if Po's scale of measure might differ from other people's. Randa's castle was large. Ror's was gargantuan. Where Po's fit in was yet to be seen.

When she finally did see Po's castle, she was pleased. It was small, or at least it seemed it from her position in the riggings of the ship far below. It was simply built of whitewashed stone, the balconies and the window frames painted a blue to match the sky, and only a single square tower, rising somewhere from the back, to suggest it was more than a house.

Its position, of course, was far from simple, and its position pleased Katsa even more than its simplicity. A cliff reached up and out from the water, and the castle balanced at the cliff's very edge. It looked as if it might tumble forward at any moment, as if the wind might find purchase in some crack in the foundations, and tip the castle, creaking and screaming, over the drop and into the sea. She could understand why the balconies were dangerous in winter. Some of them hung over empty space.

Below the castle, the sea threw itself against the base of the cliff. But there was one nook in the rock, one small inlet where water broke and foamed onto sand. A tiny beach. And a stairway leading up from the beach, rising against the side of the cliff, turning back on itself, disappearing occasionally, and climbing finally up the side of the castle and onto one of those dizzying balconies.

"Where will we dock?" she asked the captain when she'd scrambled down to the deck.

"There's a bay on the other side of this rise of rock, some distance beyond the beach. We'll dock there. A path leads up from the bay and away from the castle—you'll think you're going the wrong way, Lady Princess—but then it loops back, and takes you up a great hill to the castle's front. There may be snow, but the path is kept clear in case the prince returns."

"You speak as if you know it well."

"I captained a smaller ship a few years back, Lady Princess, a supply ship. The castles of Lienid are all beautifully situated, but believe me when I tell you they're none of them easy to supply. It's a steep path to the door."

"How large a staff does he keep?"

"I'd expect very few people, Lady Princess. And I'll remind you that it's your castle at the moment, and your servants, though you continue to refer to them as his."

Yes, this she knew; and it was one of the reasons she wasn't looking forward to her first encounter with the inhabitants of the castle. The appearance of Lady Katsa of the Middluns, renowned Graceling thug, in possession of Po's ring; the absurd, tragic story she had to tell about Leck and Ashen; and her subsequent intentions to turn the castle into a fortress and cut off contact with the outside world. Katsa had a feeling it wouldn't go smoothly.

THE PATH was just as Captain Faun had described, and the hill steep and ridged with drifts of snow. But the greater problem was Bitterblue's sea legs. She walked on land almost as clumsily as she'd walked at first at sea, and Katsa held her up as they climbed toward Po's front door. The wind gusted from behind, so that it felt as if they were being blown up the hill.

The castle wasn't much more castlelike from this angle. It seemed a tall white house at the top of a slope, with a number of massive trees overshadowing a courtyard that would be pleasant in better weather; a great tower rising behind the trees; tall windows, high roofs, at least one widow's walk; stables to one side and a frozen garden to the other; and no indication, as long as one's ears didn't catch the crash of waves, that behind it all was a drop to the sea.

They reached the top of the hill. A gust of wind pushed them onto the colorful tiled surface of the courtyard. Bitterblue sighed, relieved to encounter flat land. They approached the house, and Katsa raised her fist to Po's great wooden door. Before she could knock, the door swung open and a rush of warmth hit their faces. A Lienid man stood before her, oldish, dressed like a servant in a long brown coat.

"Greetings," he said. "Please come into the receiving room. Quickly," the man said, as Katsa stood unmoving, startled by his hasty reception. "We're letting the heat escape."

The man ushered them into a dark hall. At first glance, Katsa saw high ceilings, a stairway leading to banistered passageways above, and at least three burning fireplaces. Bitterblue steadied herself on Katsa's arm.

"I'm Lady Katsa of the Middluns," Katsa began, but the man waved them forward toward a set of double doors.

"This way," he said. "My master is expecting you."

Katsa's jaw went slack with surprise. She stared at the man, incredulous. "Your master! Do you mean he's here? How is that possible? Where is he?"

"Please, My Lady," the servant said. "Come this way. The whole family is in the receiving room."

"The whole family!"

The man swept his hand toward the doors straight ahead. Katsa looked at Bitterblue and knew that the girl's astonished face must mirror her own. Certainly there had been time for Po to make his way home; Katsa and Bitterblue had been ages in the mountains. But how could he, in such health? And how leave his hiding place, without being seen? Why, how—

The man shooed them forward to the doors, and Katsa tried to formulate a question, any question.

"How long has the prince been here?" she asked.

"The princes have only just arrived," the man said, and before she could ask what he meant he opened the doors.

"How wonderful," a voice inside said. "Welcome, my

friends! Come in and take your honored place among our happy circle!"

It was a familiar voice, and she caught Bitterblue and held the girl to her side when the child gasped and fell. Katsa looked up to see strangers sitting around the walls of a long room; and at the room's end, smiling and appraising them through a single eye, King Leck of Monsea.

CHAPTER THIRTY-FIVE

WELCOME. FRIENDS. Honored place. Happy circle.

Katsa felt immediately that there was something she didn't trust about this man who said such nice things, and in such a nice, warm voice. There was something about him, some quality that kept her senses strung out to a high readiness. She did not like him.

Still, his words were kind and welcoming, and this room of strangers smiled at him, and smiled at her, and there was no reason for her discomfort. No reason to dislike the man so instantly. She hesitated in the doorway, and stepped forward. She would proceed carefully.

The child was sick. Giving in finally, Katsa thought, to the dizzying steadiness under her feet. Bitterblue cried and clung to Katsa, and kept telling her to come away. "He's lying," she kept saying. "He's lying." Katsa looked at her blankly. Clearly the child didn't like this man, either. Katsa would take that into consideration.

"My daughter is ill. It pains me to see my daughter suffer," Leck said; and Katsa remembered and understood that this man was Bitterblue's father. "Help your niece," Leck said to a woman on his left. The woman jumped up and came toward them with outstretched arms.

"Poor child," the woman said. She tried to pull the girl away from Katsa, embracing her and murmuring to her comfortingly; but Bitterblue began to scream and slapped at the woman, and clung to Katsa like a crazed, frightened thing. Katsa took the child in her arms and shushed her, absently. She looked over Bitterblue's head at the woman who was somehow Bitterblue's aunt. The woman's face jarred into her mind. Her forehead, her nose were familiar. Not the color of her eyes, but the shape of them. Katsa glanced at the woman's hands and understood. This was Po's mother.

"She's hysterical," Po's mother said to Katsa.

"Yes," Katsa said. She held the child close. "I'll take care of her."

"Where's my son?" the woman asked, her eyes going wide with worry. "Do you know where my son is?"

"Indeed," Leck said in his booming voice. He tilted his head, and his single eye watched Katsa. "You're missing one of your party. I hope he's alive?"

"Yes," Katsa said—and then wondered, vaguely, if she'd meant to pretend he was dead. Hadn't she pretended once before that Po was dead? But why would she have done that?

Leck's eye snapped. "Is he really? Such wonderful news. Perhaps we can help him. Where is he?"

Bitterblue cried out. "Don't tell him, Katsa. Don't tell him where Po is, don't tell him, don't tell him—"

Katsa shushed the girl. "It's all right, child."

"Please don't tell him."

GRACELING — 413

"I won't," Katsa said. "I won't." She bent her face into Bitterblue's hat and decided it was right not to tell this man where Po was, not when it upset the child so.

"Very well," Leck said. "I see how things are."

He was silent for a moment. He seemed to be thinking. His fingers fiddled at the hilt of a knife in his belt. His eyes slid to Bitterblue and lingered; and Katsa found herself pulling the child closer to her own body, and covering the child with her arms.

"My daughter isn't herself," Leck said. "She's confused, she's ill, her mind is disturbed; and she thinks that I would hurt her. I've been telling Prince Po's family about my daughter's illness." He swept his hand around the room. "I've been telling them about how she ran away from home after her mother's accident. About how you and Prince Po found her, Lady Katsa, and how you've been keeping her safe for me."

Katsa followed his gesture around the room. More familiar faces, one of them a man older than Leck, a king. Po's father. His features strong and proud, but a vagueness to his eyes. A vagueness to the eyes of everyone in this room, to these younger men who must be Po's brothers, and these women who must be their wives. Or was it a vagueness in her own mind that stopped her from seeing their faces clearly? "Yes," she said, to whatever comment Leck had just made. Something about Bitterblue's safety. "Yes. I've kept her safe."

"Tell me," Leck's voice boomed. "How did you leave Monsea? Did you cross the mountains?"

"Yes," Katsa said.

Leck threw back his head and laughed. "I thought you must have, when we lost track of you. I very nearly decided to sit back and wait. I knew you'd surface somewhere, eventually. But when I made inquiries, I learned that you weren't welcome at your own court, Lady Katsa. And it made me crazy, absolutely crazy, to sit around doing nothing while my dear child was—" His eye rested again on Bitterblue and he rubbed his hand over his mouth. "While my girl was apart from me. I decided to take a chance. I ordered my people to continue the search, of course, across the other kingdoms; but I decided to try Lienid myself."

Katsa shook her head, but the fog in her mind wouldn't clear. "You needn't have worried," she said. "I've kept her safe."

"Yes," he said. "And now you've brought her to me, straight to my doorstep, to my castle here on Lienid's western shore."

"Your castle," Katsa said dully. She had thought this was Po's castle. Or had she thought it was her own castle? No, that was absurd; she was a lady of the Middluns, and she had no castle. She must have misunderstood something someone said, somewhere.

"Now it's time for you to give my child back to me," Leck said.

"Yes," Katsa said, but it worried her to relinquish care of the girl, who had stopped struggling but was collapsed now against Katsa muttering nonsense to herself and whimpering. Repeating the words Leck said over and over, in whispered bewilderment, as if she were testing how they sounded in her own voice.

"Yes," Katsa said again. "I will—but not until she's feeling better."

"No," Leck said. "Bring her to me now. I know how to make her feel better."

Katsa truly did not like this man. The way he ordered her around—and the way he looked at Bitterblue, with something in his gaze Katsa had seen before but couldn't quite place. Bitterblue was Katsa's responsibility. Katsa raised her chin. "No. She'll stay with me until she's feeling better."

Leck laughed. He looked around the room. "The Lady Katsa is nothing if not contrary," he said. "But I don't suppose any of us should blame her for being protective. Well, no matter. I'll enjoy my daughter's company"—his eye flicked to the girl again—"later."

"And now will you tell me of my son?" the woman beside Katsa asked. "Why isn't he here? He isn't injured, is he?"

"Yes," Leck said. "Comfort an anxious mother, Lady Katsa. Tell us all about Prince Po. Is he nearby?"

Katsa turned to the woman, flustered, trying to work out too many puzzles at once. Certainly there were some things it was safe to say about Po; but weren't some topics meant to be kept quiet? The categories were blurring. Perhaps it was best to say nothing at all. "I don't wish to talk of Po," she said.

"Don't you?" Leck asked. "That's unfortunate. For I do wish to talk of Po."

He tapped the arm of his chair for a moment, thoughtfully.

"He's a strong young man, our Po," he continued. "Strong and brave. A credit to his family. But he's not without his secrets, is he?"

Katsa felt, suddenly, her nerves jangling to the tips of her fingers.

Leck watched her. "Yes," he said. "Po's a bit of a problem, isn't he?" He lowered his eyebrows and pursed his lips; and then he seemed to come to a decision. He looked around the room, at the various members of Po's family, and beamed. He spoke pleasantly.

"I had thought to keep something to myself," he said. "But it occurs to me now that Po is indeed very strong; and he may appear someday on our doorstep. And perhaps, in anticipation of that event, it would be best for me to tell you all something that may"—he smiled shortly—"have some bearing on how you receive him. For you see, my Lady Katsa," he said, his eye locking into hers, "I've been thinking quite a lot about our dear Po, and I've developed a theory. A theory that you'll all find fascinating, if a bit upsetting. Yes," he said, smiling into the puzzled faces that watched him. "It's always a bit upsetting to learn that one has been double-crossed, and by a member of the family. And you're the very person to test my theory on, Lady Katsa, because I think you may be in possession of Prince Po's truth."

Po's father and his brothers shifted in their chairs and furrowed their eyebrows; and Katsa's mind was numb with panic and confusion.

"It's a theory about Prince Po's Grace," Leck said.

Katsa heard a small breath beside her, from the woman who was Po's mother. The woman took one step toward Leck, and put her hand to her throat. "Wait," she said. "I don't know—" She stopped. She turned her eyes to Katsa, puzzled, afraid. And Katsa was on fire with bewilderment and with desperate alarm. She felt—she understood—she could almost just barely remember—

"I believe your Po has been hiding a secret from you," Leck said. "Tell me if I'm right, Lady Katsa, that Prince Po is actually—"

It was then, at last, that a bolt of certainty struck Katsa. In that moment she moved. She dropped the child, snatched the dagger from her belt, and threw. Not because she remembered Leck must die. Not because she remembered the truth of Po's Grace. But because she remembered that Po did have a secret, a terrible secret, the revelation of which would hurt him in some horrible way she felt deeply but couldn't remember— and here this man sat, the secret on the tip of his tongue. And she must stop him, somehow stop him; she must silence this man, before the ruinous words were said.

In the end, Leck should have stuck to his lies. For it was the truth he almost told that killed him.

THE DAGGER flew straight and true. It embedded itself in Leck's open mouth and nailed him to the back of his chair. He sat there, arms and legs sagging, his single eye wide and lifeless. Blood spilling around the hilt of the blade and down the front of his robes. And now women were screaming, and men were shouting in outrage, running toward her with swords drawn, and Katsa knew instantly she must be careful in this fight. She must not hurt Po's brothers and his father. And suddenly they stopped, because with one long look at Leck, Bitterblue staggered to her feet.

She placed herself before Katsa, pulled her own knife from its sheath, and held it shakily against them.

"You will not hurt her," Bitterblue said. "She did right."

"Child," King Ror said. "Move aside, for we don't wish to hurt you. You aren't well. Princess Bitterblue, you're protecting the murderer of your own father."

"I'm perfectly well now that he's dead," Bitterblue said, her voice growing stronger and her hand steadying. "And I'm not a princess. I'm the Queen of Monsea. Katsa's punishment is my responsibility, and I say she did right, and you will not hurt her."

She did seem well—competent with the knife in her hand, composed, and very determined. Po's brothers and his father stood in a semicircle, swords raised. Rings on their fingers and hoops in their ears. Like seven variations on Po, Katsa thought vaguely—but with no lights in their eyes. She rubbed her own eyes. She was tired, she couldn't quite think. Several women in the background were crying.

"She murdered your father," King Ror said again now, but weakly. He raised his hand to his forehead. He peered at Bitterblue, puzzled.

"My father was evil," Bitterblue said. "My father had the

Grace of deceiving people with his words. He's been deceiving you—about my mother's death, my illness, his intentions toward me. Katsa has been protecting me from him. Today she saved me altogether."

All their hands were to their heads. All their eyebrows were drawn, all their faces masks of bewilderment.

"Did he say—did Leck say that he owned this castle? Did he—" Ror's voice trailed away. His eyes stared into the rings on his hands.

Po's mother drew a shaky breath. She turned to her husband. "It seems possible to me that what Lady Katsa has done wasn't entirely unwarranted," she said. "He was clearly about to make some absurd accusation regarding our Po. I, for one, am willing to consider the possibility that he's been lying all along." She pressed her hand to her chest. "We should sit down and try to sort this out."

Her husband and her sons scratched their heads, nodded their heads vaguely. "Let's all sit," Ror said, waving his arms to the chairs. He glanced at Leck's body and started, as if he'd forgotten it sat there, slumped and bleeding. "Bring the chairs here, to the middle of the room, away from that—spectacle. Sons, help the ladies. There, there, they are crying. Princess— Queen—Bitterblue, will you repeat again the things you've just said? I confess my head is muddled. Sons, keep your swords drawn—there's no point in being careless."

"I'll disarm her," Bitterblue said, "if it will make you more comfortable. Please, Katsa," she said apologetically, holding out her hand.

Katsa reached into her boot and handed the child her knife, numbly. She sat in the chair that was brought to her and numbly registered the bustle of people forming a circle, the clanking of swords, the women wiping their faces and gasping, clinging to their husbands' arms. She dropped her head into her hands. For her mind was returning, and she understood now what she had done.

IT WAS LIKE a spell that fizzled away slowly, popping one bubble at a time, and leaving their minds empty. Truly empty; they spoke stupidly, slowly, straining to reconstruct a conversation they couldn't remember, even though every one of them had been present for it.

Ror couldn't even give straight answers to Bitterblue's questions, about when Leck had arrived in Lienid, what he'd said; what he'd done to convince them that Po's castle was his. To convince Ror to leave his city and his court and come to a remote corner of his kingdom, with his wife and his sons, and amuse Leck and subjugate himself to Leck, while Leck waited for a daughter who might never arrive. What things Leck had said during that waiting time came slowly, incredulously from Ror's lips. "I believe . . . I believe he told me that he would like to establish himself in my city. Beside my throne!"

"I believe he said something about my serving girls, something I won't repeat," Ror's queen said.

"He spoke of altering our trade agreements! I'm sure of it!" Ror exclaimed. "In favor of Monsea!"

Ror stood and began to stride around the room. Katsa rose woodenly, in respect for a rising king, but the queen pulled her back down. "If we stood every time he marched around we'd always be standing," she said. Her hand rested on Katsa's arm a bit longer than was necessary, and her gaze on Katsa's face. Her voice was gentle. The further the assembly moved toward unraveling Leck's manipulations, the more kindly the Queen of Lienid seemed to look upon the lady Graceling at her side.

Ror's fury escalated, and the fury of his sons, each shaking off his stupor and rising one by one. Shouting their outrage, arguing with each other about what had been said. "Is Po really all right?" one of them asked Katsa, one of the younger ones who paused before her chair and looked into her face. A tear dropped onto her cheek, and she left it to Bitterblue to tell their story, to tell truths about Leck that struck the assembly like arrows. That Leck had desired to hurt the child in some eerie, horrible way; that Leck had kidnapped Grandfather Tealiff; that Leck had murdered Ashen. That his men had nearly murdered Po. And now Ror's grief matched his fury, and he knelt on the floor sobbing, for his father and his son and especially his sister; and his sons' shouts grew even louder and more incredulous. Katsa thought dumbly that it was no wonder Po was so voluble. In Licnid everyone was, and everyone spoke at once. She wiped the tears from her face and fought against her own confusion.

When the young brother crouched before Katsa again and offered her his handkerchief, she took it and stared stupidly into his face. "Do you think Po's all right?" he asked. "Will you go back for him now? I'd like to go with you."

She wiped her face with the handkerchief. "Which one are you?"

The brother smiled. "I'm Skye. I've never seen anyone throw a dagger so fast. You're exactly as I imagined you."

He rose to his feet again and went to his father. Katsa held her stomach and tried to calm the sourness surging inside her. The fog of Leck's Grace was slower to leave her than to leave the others, and she was sick with what she'd done. Yes, Leck was dead, and that was a good thing. But it was because she'd used a dagger—a *dagger*—to stop someone talking. It was as violent as anything she'd ever done for Randa. And she hadn't even known what she was doing.

SHE MUST go to Po. She must leave them all to piece the truth together by themselves. It didn't matter, these details they picked apart and discussed and argued over, on and on, as the day turned to night. Bitterblue was saved, and that mattered; Po was alone and hurt, and struggling through a Monsean winter, and that mattered.

"Will you tell them about the ring?" Bitterblue asked her that night as Katsa sat in their bedroom forcing her sluggish mind to take stock of their supply situation.

"No," she said. "There's no need. It'll only worry them. The first thing I'll do when I reach Po is give it back to him."

"Will we leave very early?"

Katsa's eyes snapped to the child who stood before her, her face serious, one hand resting on the knife at her belt. The Queen of Monsea, in trousers and short hair, looking for all the world like a miniature pirate.

"You needn't come," Katsa said. "It'll be a difficult journey. Once we reach Monport we'll be traveling very fast, and I won't lessen my pace for your comfort."

"Of course I'm coming."

"You're the Queen of Monsea now. You can commission a great ship and travel in luxury. You can wait until the season turns."

"And fret, here in Lienid, until you send word that Po's all right? Of course I'll come with you."

Katsa looked into her lap and swallowed a lump in her throat. She didn't like to admit how it comforted her, to know Bitterblue would be with her for this. "We leave at first light," she said, "on a boat Ror's furnished from the village nearby. We go first to collect Captain Faun and resupply her ship. Then she'll take us to Monport."

Bitterblue nodded. "Then I'm going to take a bath and go to sleep. Where do you suppose I must go to find someone who'll bring hot water?"

Katsa smiled, mildly. "Ring the bell, Lady Queen. Po's servants are a bit overtaxed at the moment, I do believe; but for the ruler of Monsea, someone will come."

It was, in fact, Po's mother who came. She appraised the situation and produced a servant girl who swept Bitterblue off to another room, murmuring reassurances about the temperature of the water and curtsying as best she could with her arms full of towels.

Po's mother stayed behind and sat beside Katsa on the bed. She clasped her hands in her lap. The rings on her fingers caught the light from the fireplace and drew Katsa's eyes.

"Po told me you wear nineteen rings," she heard herself saying, senselessly. She took a breath. She gripped her forehead and tried, for the hundredth time, to drive from her mind the image of Leck nailed to his chair by her dagger.

The queen opened her hands and considered her rings. She closed them again, and looked sideways at Katsa. "The others think you remembered the truth, suddenly, about Leck," she said. "They think you remembered it suddenly and silenced him right away, before his lies caused you to forget again. And perhaps that is what happened. But I believe I understand why you found the strength to act at that moment."

Katsa looked back at the woman, at her calm face and quiet, intelligent eyes. She answered the question she saw in those eyes. "Po has told me the truth of his Grace."

"He must love you very much," the queen said, so simply that Katsa started. Katsa ducked her head.

"I was very angry," she said, "when first he told me. But I have . . . recovered from my anger."

It was a woefully inadequate description of her feelings, this Katsa knew. But the queen watched her, and Katsa thought the woman understood some of what she didn't say.

"Will you marry him?" the queen asked, so plainly that Katsa started again; but this she could answer as plainly. She looked into the queen's eyes.

"I won't ever marry," she said.

The queen's forehead creased in puzzlement, but she didn't say anything. She hesitated, and then spoke. "You saved my son's life in Monsea," she said, "and you saved it again today. I'll never forget it."

She stood, bent forward, and kissed Katsa's forehead, and for the third time since this woman's arrival, Katsa started with surprise. The queen turned and left the room, her skirts sweeping through the doorway. As the door closed behind her, and Katsa stared at the blankness where Po's mother had been, the image of Leck rose again into her mind.

CHAPTER THIRTY-SIX

KATSA KEPT to a far corner of the deck as Bear and Red and a number of other men hauled the ropes that swung Leck's coffin on board. She wished to have nothing to do with it, wished even that the ropes would snap and pitch Leck's body into the sea, to be torn apart by sea creatures. She climbed up the mast and sat alone in the riggings.

It was a grand procession of royalty that charted a course now to Monsea. For not only was Bitterblue a queen, but Prince Skye and King Ror attended her. His sister's child, Ror had pointed out, was a child. And even if she weren't, she returned to an impossible situation. A kingdom deeply under a spell; a kingdom that believed its king to be virtuous and its princess to be ill, weak, possibly even mad. The child queen could not be sent off trippingly to Monsea to announce that she was now in charge, and denounce the dead king an entire kingdom adored. Bitterblue would need authority, and she would need guidance. Both of these Ror could provide.

Ror would send Skye to Po. Silvern, Ror had sent on a different ship to the Middluns, to collect Grandfather Tealiff and bring him home. His remaining sons Ror had sent home to their families and their duties, turning a deaf ear to each son's insistence that his proper place was in Ror City, managing

Ror's affairs. Ror left his affairs instead to his queen, as he always did when circumstances took him away from his throne. The queen was more than capable.

Katsa watched Ror, day after day, from her place in the riggings. She became familiar with the sound of his laughter, and his good-natured conversation that set the sailors at ease. There was nothing humble or compromising about Ror. He was handsome, like Po, and confident, like Po, and so much more authoritative in his bearing than Po could ever be. But—and this Katsa came gradually to understand—he was not drunk on his power. He might never dream of helping a sailor to haul a rope, but he would stand with the sailor interestedly while the sailor hauled the rope, and ask him questions about the rope, about his work, his home, his mother and father, his cousin who spent a year once fishing in the lakes of Nander. It struck Katsa that here was a thing she'd never encountered: a king who looked at his people, instead of over their heads, a king who saw outside himself.

Katsa took easily to Skye. He climbed occasionally into the riggings, gasping, his gray eyes flying wide with laughter every time the ship plunged into the trough of a wave. He sat near her, never quite as relaxed in his perch as she was in hers, but quiet, content, and good company.

"I thought, after meeting your family, that Po was the only male among you capable of silence," Katsa said to him once, when they'd sat for some time without speaking.

A smile warmed his face. "I'd jump into an argument quick enough if you wanted one," he said. "And I have a thousand questions I'd like to ask you. But I figure if you felt like talking—well, you'd be talking, wouldn't you? Instead of climbing up here nearly to be hurled to your death every time we crest a wave."

His company, and the friendly rumble of Ror's voice below. The small kindnesses of the sailors toward Bitterblue when the girl came onto the cold deck for exercise. Captain Faun, who was so competent and so steady, and who always met Katsa's eyes with respect. All these things comforted Katsa, and a tough little skin began to stretch across the wound that had opened in her when her dagger had hit Leck.

She found herself thinking of her uncle. How small Randa seemed now, how baseless in his power. How silly that such a person had ever been able to control her.

Control. This was Katsa's wound: Leck had taken away her control. It had nothing to do with self-condemnation; she couldn't blame herself for what had happened. How could it not have happened? Leck had been too strong. She could respect a strong opponent, as she'd respected the wildcat and the mountain. But no amount of humility or respect made it any less horrifying to have lost control.

"Forgive me, Katsa," Skye said once, as they hung together above the sea. "But there's one question I must ask you."

She had seen the puzzlement in his eyes at times before. She knew what he was going to ask.

"You're not my brother's wife, are you?"

She smiled grimly. "No."

"Then why do the Lienid on this ship call you Princess?"

She took a breath, to ease the jarring of his question against her wound. She reached into the neck of her coat and pulled the ring out for him to see.

"When he gave it to me," she said, "he didn't tell me what it meant. Nor did he tell me why he gave it."

Skye stared at the ring. His face registered astonishment, then dismay, then a stubborn, self-willed sort of denial. "He'll have some rational reason for it," he said.

"Yes," Katsa said. "I intend to beat it out of him."

Skye laughed a short laugh, and lapsed into silence. A crease of worry lingered low on his forehead. And Katsa knew that the tough scar that formed over the ache within her had as much to do with her future lack of control as her past. She could not *make* Po be well, any more than she had been able to make herself think clearly in Leck's presence. Some things were beyond her power, and she had to prepare herself for whatever she found when she reached Po's cabin at the base of the Monsean mountains.

THE DELAY, once the ship had docked in Monport and the party had disembarked, was unbearable. The captain of the Monport guard and the nobles of Leck's court stationed in Monport had to be summoned and made to understand the incredible truths Ror presented to them. The search for Bitterblue, still under way, had to be called off, as did the instructions to take Katsa alive and Po dead. Ror's tone on this last point froze into something very cold.

"Has he been found?" Katsa interrupted.

"Has . . . has who?" the captain of the Monport guard asked, stupidly, his hand to his head, his manner afflicted with a vagueness the Lienid party recognized.

"Have your men found the Lienid prince?" Ror snapped; and then more gently, as the eyes of the captain and the nobles moved confusedly to Skye, "the younger prince. He's a Graceling, with silver and gold eyes. Has anyone seen him?"

"I don't believe he's been seen, Lord King. Yes, I'm quite sure that's correct. We've not found him. Forgive me, Lord King. This story you've told . . . my memory . . ."

"Yes," Ror said. "I understand. We must go slowly."

Katsa could have torn the city down stone by stone, so wild did it make her to go slowly. She began to stalk back and forth behind the Lienid king. She crouched to the floor and grasped her hair. The conversation droned on. It would take hours—hours—for these men to disengage themselves from Leck's spell, and Katsa couldn't bear it.

"Perhaps we could see to some horses, Father," Skye murmured, "and be on our way?"

Katsa shot to her feet. "Yes," she said. "Yes, in the name of the Middluns, please."

Ror glanced from Skye to Katsa, and then to Bitterblue. "Queen Bitterblue," he said, "if you'll trust me to manage this situation in your absence, I see no reason to delay you."

"Of course I trust you," the child said, "and my men will defer to your judgment in all things while I'm gone."

The captain and the nobles stared openmouthed at their new queen, half Ror's height, dressed like a boy, and utterly dignified. They furrowed their eyebrows and scratched their heads, and Katsa was ready to scratch her own eyes out. Ror turned to her.

"The sooner you reach Po, the better," he said. "I'll not keep you."

"We need two horses," Katsa said, "the fastest in the city."

"And you need a Monsean guard," Ror said, "for no one you pass will realize what has happened. Any Monsean soldiers who sight you will try to capture you."

Katsa flicked her hand impatiently. "Very well, a guard. But if they can't keep up with me, I'll leave them behind." She swung toward Skye. "I hope you ride as well as your brother."

"Or you'll leave him behind as well?" Ror said. "And the Monsean queen—if she's weighing down your horse, will you leave her behind? And the horse itself, I suppose, once it collapses from exhaustion and disuse?" He had drawn himself up very tall, and his voice was sharp. "Be rational, Katsa. You will take a guard, and it will ride before you and behind you. For the entire journey, is that clear? You carry the Queen of Monsea, and you travel with my son."

Katsa practically spit back at him. "Do you imagine that I need a guard to protect them from the soldiers of Monsea?"

"No," Ror snapped. "I have no doubt that you are more than capable of bringing the Monsean queen and my son and the rest of my sons and a hundred Nanderan kittens through an onslaught of howling raiders if you chose to." He drew himself up even taller. "You will listen to sense. It does none of us any good at this juncture for you to barrel through

Monsea with the queen of the kingdom on your horse, killing her soldiers left and right. What exactly would that accomplish? You will travel with a guard, and the guard will make your explanations and ensure that you're not attacked. Am I clear?"

He didn't wait to know if he was clear. He turned abruptly to the captain, who flinched at the entire exchange as if it hurt his head. "Captain, the four fastest horsemen in your guard," he said, "and your six fastest horses, immediately." He swung back on Katsa and glared down at her. "Have you regained your reason?" he roared.

It was her temper she had lost, not her reason—or if it was her reason, it returned to her now, with the promise of four fast horsemen, six fast horses, and a thundering ride to Po.

THEY RODE FAST and passed few people. The Port Road was wide, its surface a mixture of dirt and snow tramped down under the hooves of innumerable horses. Banks of snow rose on either side of the road, and fields of snow beyond them. Far to the west, they could just make out the dark line of the forest, and the mountains beyond. The air was icy, but the child on the horse before her was warm enough, and content to be pushed harder than was comfortable. The queen on the horse before her, Katsa thought, correcting herself. And Queen Bitterblue was very changed from the skittish creature she and Po had cajoled from the inside of a hollow log months ago.

Bitterblue would make a good ruler someday. And Raffin a good king; and Ror was strong and capable and would live a long time. That was three of the seven kingdoms in good hands. Three of seven, however inadequate it seemed, would be a vast improvement.

THERE WERE TOWNS along the Port Road, towns with inns. The party stopped occasionally for a hasty meal, or to seek shelter from the bitter late-winter nights. Their guard was the only thing that made this possible, for every soldier in every room they entered jumped up at the sight of them, hand to weapon, and remained in that guise until the explanations of the guard, and some words from Bitterblue, relaxed his vigilance. At one inn, the guard's explanations came too slowly. A marksman across an empty room fired an arrow that would have hit Skye, had Katsa not jumped on the prince and knocked him to the floor. She was up again before Skye had even registered his fall, her body blocking the queen's and her own arrow drawn; but the guards had intervened, and by then it was over. Katsa had hauled Skye up. She'd looked into his eyes and understood what had happened.

"He thought you were Po," she said to Skye. "That archer. He saw the hoops in your ears, the rings, and the dark hair, and he fired before he saw your eyes. You should wait until the guards have spoken, from now on, before entering a room."

Skye kissed her forehead. "You saved my life."

Katsa smiled. "You Lienid are very outward in your affection."

"I'm going to name my firstborn child after you."

Katsa laughed at that. "For the child's sake, wait for a girl.

Or even better, wait until all your children are older and give my name to whichever is the most troublesome and obstinate."

Skye burst into laughter and hugged her, and Katsa returned his embrace. And realized that quite without her intending it, her guarded heart had made another friend.

The party was swept upstairs to the briefest of sleeps. The archer was taken away, most likely to be punished soundly for loosing an arrow so close to a small gray-eyed girl who happened to be Bitterblue. And if the people living in the towns and traveling the roads did not yet know the details of Leck's death, or suspect his treachery, at least it began to be understood in Monsea that Bitterblue was safe, Bitterblue was well, and Bitterblue was queen.

THE ROAD was clear and swift, but the road didn't lead straight to Po. The party turned west eventually into fields piled high with ice and snow, and Katsa felt the slackening of their pace severely. The horses labored to break a path through snow that reached sometimes to their shoulders.

Days later the party burst under the cover of the forest, and this was easier going. And then the land began to rise, and the trees to peter out. Soon they were climbing. They swung down from their mounts, all except for the queen, and picked their way uphill on foot.

They were nearly there, nearly there; and Katsa drove her companions fiercely, dragging the horses, emptying her mind of everything but their ferocious progress forward.

"I believe we've lamed one of the horses," Skye called up to her, early one morning when they were so close she could feel her body humming with it. She stopped and turned to look back. Skye gestured to the horse he was leading. "See? I'm sure the poor beast is limping."

The animal's head drooped, and it sighed deeply through its nostrils. Katsa grasped for her patience. "It's not limping," she said. "It's only tired, and we're nearly there."

"How can you say that when you haven't even seen it take one step?"

"Well, step, then."

"I can't until you've moved."

Katsa glared at him, murderously. She clenched her teeth. "Hold on tight, Lady Queen," she said to Bitterblue, who sat on her horse. She gripped the animal's halter and yanked the beast forward.

"Still doing your best to ruin the horses, I see."

Katsa froze. The voice came from above rather than behind, and it didn't quite sound like Skye. She turned.

"I thought it was supposed to be impossible to sneak up on you. Eyes of a hawk and ears of a wolf and all that," he said—and there, he was there, standing straight, eyes glimmering, mouth twitching, and the path he'd plowed through the snow stretching behind him. Katsa cried out and ran, tackling Po so hard that he fell back into the snow and she on top of him. And he laughed, and held her tight, and she was crying; and then Bitterblue came and threw herself squealing on top of them; and Skye came and helped them all up. Po embraced his cousin properly. He embraced his brother, and they messed up each other's hair and laughed at each other and embraced again. And then Katsa was in his arms again, crying hot tears into his neck, and holding him so tightly he complained he could not breathe.

Po shook the hands of the smiling, exhausted guards and led the party, lame horse and all, up to his cabin.

CHAPTER THIRTY-SEVEN

THE CABIN was clean, and in better repair than it had been when they'd found it. A stack of wood stood outside the door; a fire burned brightly in the fireplace; the cabinet still stood crookedly on three legs, but the dust was gone: a handsome bow hung on the wall. Katsa absorbed all this in a glance. And that was enough of that, for it was Po she wanted to fill her eyes with.

He walked smoothly, with his old ease. He seemed strong. Too thin, but when she commented on it, he said, "Fish aren't particularly fattening, Katsa, and I've eaten little but fish since you left. I can't tell you how sick to the skies I am of fish." They brought out bread for him then, and apples, and dried apricots and cheese, and spread it across the table. He ate, and laughed, and declared himself to be in raptures.

"The apricots come from Lienid," Katsa said, "by way of Suncliff, and Lienid again, and a place in the middle of the Lienid seas, and finally Monport."

He grinned at her, and his eyes caught the light of the fire in the fireplace, and Katsa was very happy. "You have a story to tell me," he said, "and I can see it has a happy ending. But will you start at the beginning?"

And so they started at the beginning. Katsa supplied the major points, and Bitterblue the details. "Katsa made me a hat of animal furs," Bitterblue said. "Katsa fought a mountain lion." Katsa made snowshoes. Katsa stole a pumpkin. Bitterblue listed Katsa's achievements one by one, as if she were bragging about her older sister; and Katsa didn't mind. The amusing parts of the tale made it easier to relate the grim.

It was during the story of what had happened at Po's castle that Katsa's mind caught on something that had nagged at her. Po was distracted. He watched the table instead of the people speaking; his face was absent, he wasn't listening. At the very moment she recognized his inattention he raised his eyes to her. For an instant he seemed to see her and focus on her, but then he stared emptily into his hands again. She could have sworn a kind of sadness settled into the lines of his mouth.

Katsa paused in her story, suddenly—strangely—frightened. She studied his face, but she wasn't quite sure what she was looking for. "The long and the short of it is that Leck had us under his spell," she said, "until I had one flash of clarity and killed him." *I'll tell you the truth of what really happened later,* she thought to him.

He winced, perceptibly, and she was alarmed; but an instant later he was smiling as if nothing was wrong, and she wondered if she'd imagined it. "And then you came back," he said cheerily.

"As fast as we could," Katsa said, biting her lip, confused. "And now I've a ring to return to you. Your castle is a gorgeous place, just as you said."

The pain that broke across his face, the misery, was so acute that she gasped. It vanished as quickly as it had come but she'd seen it this time, she knew she'd seen it, and she could no longer mask her alarm. She shot up from her seat and reached out to him, not certain what she was going to do or say.

Po rose, too—did he check his balance? She wasn't sure, but she thought he might have. He took her hand and smiled. "Come out hunting with me, Katsa," he said. "You can try the bow I made."

His voice was light, and Skye and Bitterblue were smiling. Katsa felt that she was the only person in the world with any idea that something was wrong. She forced a smile. "Of course," she said. "I'd love to."

"What's wrong?" she asked, the instant they'd left the cabin behind.

He smiled slightly. "Nothing's wrong."

Katsa climbed hard and bit back her feeling. They tromped through a path in the snow she supposed Po had broken. They passed the pool. The waterfall was a mass of ice, with only the slightest living trickle in its middle.

"Did my fish trap work for you?"

"It worked beautifully. I still use it."

"Did his soldiers search the cabin?"

"They did."

"You made it to the cave all right, despite your injury?"

"I was feeling much better by then. I made it easily."

"But you would have been cold and wet."

"They didn't stay long, Katsa. I returned to the cabin soon after and built up the fire."

Katsa climbed a rocky rise. She grasped a thin tree trunk and pulled herself onto a hillock. A long, flat rock jutted up from the untouched snow. She plowed over to it and sat down. He followed and sat beside her. She considered him. He didn't look at her.

"I want to know what's wrong," she said.

He pursed his lips, and still he didn't look at her. His voice was carefully matter-of-fact. "I wouldn't force your feelings from you, if you didn't want to share them."

She stared at him, eyes wide. "True. But I wouldn't lie to you, as you're lying now when you say nothing's wrong."

A strange expression came over his face. Open, vulnerable, as if he were a child of ten years, trying to keep from crying. Her throat ached to see that look in his face. *Po—*

He winced, and the expression vanished. "Don't, please," he said. "It makes me dizzy, when you talk to me in my mind. It hurts my head."

She swallowed, and tried to think of what to say. "Your head still hurts, from your fall?"

"Occasionally."

"Is that what's wrong?"

"I've told you, nothing's wrong."

She touched his arm. "Po, please—"

"It's nothing worth your worry," he said, and he brushed her hand away.

And now she was shocked and hurt, and tears stung her

eyes. The Po she remembered didn't flick away her concern, he didn't flinch from her touch. This wasn't Po; this was a stranger; and there was something missing here that had been there before. She reached into the neck of her coat and pulled the cord over her head. She held the ring out to him.

"This is yours," she said.

He didn't even look at it; his eyes were glued to his hands. "I don't want it."

"What in the Middluns are you talking about? It's your ring."

"You should keep it."

She stared at him, disbelieving. "Po, what makes you think I would ever keep your ring? I don't know why you gave it to me in the first place. I wish you hadn't."

His mouth was tight with unhappiness, and still he stared into his hands. "At the time I gave it to you, I did so because I knew I might die. I knew Leck's men might kill me and that you didn't have a home. If I died I wanted you to have my home. My home suits you," he said, with a bitterness that stung her, and that she couldn't understand.

She found that she was crying. She wiped tears from her face, furiously, and turned away from him, because she couldn't stand the sight of him staring stone-faced into his hands. "Po, I beg you to tell me what's the matter."

"Is it so wrong that you should keep the ring? My castle is isolated, in a wild corner of the world. You'd be happy there. My family would respect your privacy."

"Have you gone raving mad? What are you going to do,

once I've taken your home and your possessions? Where are you going to live?"

His voice was very quiet. "I don't want to go back to my home. I've been thinking of staying here, where it's peaceful, and far away from everyone. I—I want to be alone."

She gaped at him, her mouth open.

"You should go on with your life, Katsa. Keep the ring. I've said I don't want it."

She couldn't speak. She shook her head, woodenly, then reached out and dropped the ring into his hands.

He stared at it, then sighed. "I'll give it to Skye," he said, "to take back to my father. He can decide what to do with it."

He stood, and this time she was certain he checked his balance. He trudged away from her, his bow in hand. He caught hold of the root of a shrubbery and pulled himself onto a ledge of rock. She watched as he climbed into the mountains, and away from her.

DURING THE NIGHT, the sound of breathing all around her, Katsa tried to work it out. She sat against the wall and watched Po lying in a blanket on the floor beside his brother and the Monsean guards. He slept, and his face was peaceful. His beautiful face.

When he'd come back to the cabin after their conversation, with his bow in one hand and an armload of rabbits in the other, he'd unloaded his quarry contentedly on his brother and shrugged himself out of his coat. Then he'd come to her, where she sat brooding against the wall. He'd crouched before her, taken her hands in his and kissed them, and rubbed his cold face against them. "I'm sorry," he'd said; and she'd felt suddenly that everything was normal, and Po was himself, and they'd start again, fresh and new. Then over dinner, as the others bantered and Bitterblue teased her guards, Katsa watched Po withdraw. He ate little. He sank into silence, unhappiness in the lines of his face. And her heart ached so much to look at him that she walked out of the cabin and stumped around for ages alone in the dark.

At moments he seemed happy. But something was clearly wrong. If he would just . . . if he would only just look at her. If he would only look into her face.

And of course, if alone was what he needed, alone was what she would give. But—and she thought this might be unfair, but still she decided it—she was going to require proof. He was going to have to convince her, convince her utterly, that solitude was his need. Only then would she leave him to his strange anguish.

IN THE MORNING Po seemed cheerful enough; but Katsa, who was beginning to feel like a henpecking mother, registered his lack of interest in the food, even the Lienid food, spread across the table. He ate practically nothing, and then made some vague, unlikely remark about checking on the lame horse. He wandered outside.

"What's wrong with him?" Bitterblue asked.

Katsa's eyes slid to the child's face, and held her steady gray gaze. There was no point pretending she didn't know what Bitterblue meant. Bitterblue had never been stupid.

"I don't know," Katsa said. "He won't tell me."

"Sometimes he seems himself," Skye said, "and other times he sinks into a mood." He cleared his throat. "But I thought it might be a lovers' quarrel."

Katsa looked at him levelly. She ate a piece of bread. "It's possible, but I don't think so."

Skye raised an eyebrow and grinned. "Seems to me you'd know if it were."

"If only things were that simple," Katsa said, drily.

"There's something strange about his eyes," Bitterblue said.

"Yes," Katsa said, "well, it's likely he has the strangest eyes in all seven kingdoms. But I'd have expected you to notice that before now."

"No," Bitterblue said. "I mean there's something *different* about his eyes."

Something different about his eyes.

Yes, there was a difference. The difference was that he wouldn't look at her, or at any of them. Almost as if it pained his heart to raise his eyes and focus on another person. Almost as if—

An image flashed into her mind then, out of nowhere. Po falling through the light, a horse's enormous body falling above him. Po, slamming into the water face-first, the horse crashing in after him.

And more images. Po, sick and gray before the fire, the skin of his face bruised black. Po squinting at her and rubbing his eyes.

Katsa choked on her bread. She shot to her feet and knocked over her chair.

Skye thumped her back. "Great seas, Katsa. Are you all right?"

Katsa coughed, and gasped something about checking on the lame horse. She ran out of the cabin.

Po wasn't with the horses, but when Katsa asked after him, one of the guards pointed in the direction of the pool. Katsa ran behind the cabin and over the hill.

He was standing, his back to her, staring into the frozen pond. His shoulders slumped and his hands in his pockets.

"I know you're invincible, Katsa," he said without turning around. "But even you should put on a coat when you come outside."

"Po," she said. "Turn around and look at me."

He dropped his head. His shoulders rose and fell with one deep breath. He didn't turn around.

"Po," she said. "Look at me."

He turned then, slowly. He looked into her face. His eyes seemed to focus on hers, for just an instant; and then his eyes dropped. They emptied. She saw it happen; she saw his eyes empty.

She whispered. "Po. Are you blind?"

At that, something in him seemed to break. He fell to his

knees. A tear made an icy track down his face. When Katsa went to him and dropped down before him, he let her come; the fight had gone out of him and he let her in. Katsa's arms came around him. He pulled Katsa against him, practically smothered her with his grip, and cried into her neck. She held him, simply held him, and touched him, and kissed his cold face.

"Oh, Katsa," he cried. "Katsa."

They knelt like that for a very long time.

CHAPTER THIRTY-EIGHT

THAT MORNING a squall kicked up. By afternoon the squall had turned into a gentle but soggy storm. "I can't bear the thought of more winter-weather travel," Bitterblue said, half asleep before the fire. "Now that we're here with Po, can't we stay here, Katsa, until it stops snowing?"

But on the heels of that storm came another, and after that storm another, as if winter had torn up the schedule and decided it wasn't going to end after all. Bitterblue sent two guards with a letter for Ror. Ror wrote back from Bitterblue's court that the weather was just as well; the more time Bitterblue gave him to sort out the stories Leck had left behind, the smoother and the safer her transition to the throne would be. He would plan the coronation for true spring, and she could wait out the storms for as long as she wished.

Katsa knew the cabin's close quarters were trying to Po, burdened as he was with his unhappy secret. But if everyone was staying, then at least he didn't have to justify quite yet his own intention not to leave. He kept his discomfort to himself and helped the guards lead the horses to a nearby rock shelter he claimed to have found during his recovery.

His story came out slowly, whenever he and Katsa were able to contrive ways to be alone.

The day of Katsa and Bitterblue's departure had not been easy for Po. He'd still had his sight, but it hadn't felt quite right to him; it had changed in some way his head was too muddled to quantify, some way that gave him a deep sense of misgiving.

"You didn't tell me," Katsa said. "You let me leave you like that."

"If I'd told you, you never would have gone. You had to go."

Po had stumbled his way to the cabin's bed. He'd spent most of that day lying on his unhurt side with his eyes closed, waiting for Leck's soldiers and for his dizziness to pass. He'd tried to convince himself that when his head cleared, his sight would, too. But waking the next morning, he'd opened his eyes to blackness.

"I was angry," he told her. "And unsteady on my feet. And I was out of food, which meant that I had to find my way to the fish trap. I couldn't be bothered. I didn't eat, that day or the next."

What had driven him finally to the pool was not his hunger. It was Leck's soldiers. He'd sensed them climbing the rocks toward the cabin. "I was up and stumbling," he told her, "before I even realized what I was doing. I was barreling around the cabin collecting my things; and then I was outside, finding a crack in a rock to hide them. I wasn't at my most lucid. I'm sure I must have fallen down, over and over. But I knew where the pool was, and I got myself to it. The water was awful, so cold, but it woke me, and it was less dizzying, somehow, to be swimming, rather than walking. I made it to the cave somehow, and somehow I pulled myself onto the rocks.

And then, in the cave, with the soldiers shouting outside and my body so cold I thought I would bite off my own tongue with my chattering teeth—I found it, Katsa."

He stopped talking, and he was quiet for so long that she wondered if he'd forgotten what he'd been saying.

"What did you find?"

He turned his head to her, surprised. "Clarity," he said. "My thoughts cleared. There was no light in the cave; there was nothing to see. And yet I sensed the cave with my Grace, so vividly. And I realized what I was doing. Sitting in the cabin, feeling sorry for myself, when Leck was out there somewhere and people were in danger. In the cave it struck me how despicable that was."

The thought of Leck had brought Po back into the water, out of the cave and to the fish trap. Back to the cabin to fumble, numb from cold, with the lighting of the fire. The next few days were grim. "I was weak and dizzy and sick. I walked, at first, never farther than the fish trap. Then with Leck in my mind I pushed a bit farther. My balance was passable, if I was sitting still. I made the bow. With Leck in my mind, I began to practice shooting it."

His head dropped. Silence settled over him. And Katsa thought she understood the rest. Po had held the notion of Leck close to himself; Leck had given him a reason to reach for his strength. He'd driven himself toward health and balance. And then they'd returned to him with the happy news that Leck was dead. Po was left without a reason. Unhappiness had choked him once again.

The very fact of his unhappiness made him unhappy.

"I've no right to feel sorry for myself," he said to her one day, when they'd gone out into a quiet snowfall to fetch water. "I see everything. I see things I shouldn't see. I'm wallowing in self-pity, when I've lost nothing."

Katsa crouched with him before the pool. "That's the first truly idiotic thing you've ever said to me."

His mouth tightened. He picked up one of the rocks they used to bash through the ice. He lifted the rock above his head and drove it, hard, into the frozen surface of the pool; and finally she was rewarded with a low rumble of something that almost passed for a laugh. "Your brand of comfort bears some similarity to your tactical offense."

"You've lost something," she said, "and you've every right to feel sorrow for what you've lost. They're not the same, sight and your Grace. Your Grace shows you the form of things, but it doesn't show you beauty. You've lost beauty."

His mouth tightened again, and he looked away from her. When he looked back she thought he might be about to cry. But he spoke tearlessly, stonily. "I won't go back to Lienid. I won't go to my castle, if I'm not able to see it. It's hard enough to be with you. It's why I didn't tell you the truth. I wanted you to go away, because it hurts to be with you when I can't see you."

She tilted her head back and considered his stormy expression. "This is very good," she said. "This is some excellent self-pity."

And then the rumble of his laughter again, and a kind of

helpless heartache in his face that caused her to reach for him, take him into her arms, and kiss his neck, his snow-covered shoulder, his finger not wearing its ring, and every place that she could find. He touched her face gently. He touched her lips and kissed her. He rested his forehead against hers.

"I would never hold you here," he said. "But if you can bear this—if you can bear me behaving like this—I don't really want you to leave."

"I'll not go," Katsa said, "for a long time. I'll not go until you want me to; or until you're ready to go yourself."

HE HAD QUITE a talent for playing a part. Katsa saw this now, because she saw the transformation now, whenever they were alone and he stopped pretending. To his brother and his cousin he presented strength, steadiness, health. His shoulders were straight, his stride even. When he couldn't hide his un-happiness, he played it as moodiness. When he couldn't find the energy to direct his eyes to their faces and pretend to see them, he played it as inattention. He was strong, cheerful—strangely distracted, perhaps, but healing well from grave injury. It was an impressive act—and for the most part, it seemed to satisfy them. Enough, at least, that they never had reason to suspect the truth of his Grace, which was ultimately all he was trying to hide.

When he and Katsa were alone, hunting, collecting water, or sitting together in the cabin, the disguise quietly fell from him. Weariness pulled at his face, his body, his voice. He put his hand out occasionally, to a tree or a rock, to steady himself.

His eyes focused, or pretended to focus, on nothing, ever. And Katsa began to understand that while some of his sorry state was attributable to plain unhappiness, an even larger part of it stemmed from his Grace itself. For he was still growing into it; and now that he no longer had vision to anchor his perception of the world, he was constantly overwhelmed.

One day beside the pool, during a rare break between snowstorms, she watched him notch an arrow calmly to his bow and aim at something she couldn't see. A ledge of rock? A tree stump? He cocked his head as if he were listening. He released the arrow, and it sliced through the cold and thwacked into a patch of snow. "What—" Katsa started to say, and then stopped when a spot of blood welled to the surface and colored the snow around the arrow's shaft.

"A rabbit," he said. "A big one."

He started forward toward his buried kill, but had taken little more than a step when a flock of geese swooped down from overhead. He put his hand to his temple and fell to one knee.

Katsa strung two arrows and shot two geese. Then she hauled Po up. "Po, what—"

"The geese. They took me by surprise."

She shook her head. "You could sense animals before, but the sense of them never knocked you down."

He snorted with laughter, and then his laughter fizzled into a sigh. "Katsa. Try to imagine how things are now. My Grace shows me every detail of the mountain above me, and the drop to the forest below me. I feel the movement of every fish in the pool and every bird in the trees. The ice is growing back over our water hole. Snow is forming fast in the clouds, Katsa. In a moment I expect it'll be snowing again." He turned his face toward her now, urgently. "Skye and Bitterblue are in the cabin. Bitterblue's anxious about me, she doesn't think I eat enough. And you're here, too, of course—your every movement, your body, your clothing, your every worry coursing through me. The sighted can focus their eyes. I can't focus my Grace. I can't turn this off. How exactly, when I'm aware of everything above, below, before, behind, and beyond me, am I supposed to keep my mind on the ground beneath my feet?"

He trudged away from her toward the red patch of blood. He yanked tiredly at the arrow in the snow. It came away in his hand, and lifted with it a large, white, bloody rabbit. He plodded back to her, rabbit in hand. They stood there, considering each other; and then flakes of snow began to fall. Katsa could not help herself—she smiled, at the fulfillment of his prediction. A moment later Po smiled too, grudgingly; and when they turned to climb the rocks, he took her sleeve. "The snow's disorienting," he said.

They set out across the slope, and he steadied himself against her as they climbed.

SHE WAS getting used to the new way Po had of considering her, now that he couldn't see her. He didn't look at her, of course. She supposed she would never feel the intensity of his gaze again; she would never again be caught in his eyes. It was something she tried not to think about. It made her stupidly, foolishly sad.

But Po's new way with her was also intense. It was a kind of attentiveness in his face, a concentration in his body, directed toward her. When it happened she could feel the stillness of his face and body, attuned to her. She thought that it happened more and more as the days passed. As if he were reconnecting with her, slowly, and pulling her back into his thoughts. He touched her easily now, too, as he'd done before his accident—kissed her hands if she was nearby, or touched her face when she stood before him. And Katsa wondered if it was true, or just her imagination, that he was paying them, all of them, more attention—truer attention. As if perhaps he was less overwhelmed by his Grace. Or less absorbed with himself.

"Look at me," he said to her once, on one of the rare occasions when they had the cabin to themselves. "Katsa, do I seem to be looking at you?"

They were working with their knives before the fire, shaving the bark from the branches of a tree to make arrows. She turned to him and met his eyes, full on, gleaming directly into hers. She caught her breath and set her knife down, flushed with heat; and wondered, briefly, how long it would be before the others returned. And then Po's failed attempt to keep from grinning snapped her out of her daze.

"Dear wildcat. That was more of an answer than I reckoned for."

She snorted. "I see your self-esteem remains intact. And just what were you hoping to achieve?"

He smiled. His hands returned to their work, and his eyes emptied again. "I need to know how to make people think, conclusively, that I'm looking at them. I need to know how to look at Bitterblue so she stops thinking there's something strange about my eyes."

"Oh. Of course. Well, that ought to do it. How do you manage it?"

"Well, I know where your eyes are. It's mostly just a matter of direction, and then sensing your reaction."

"Do it again."

Her purpose was scientific this time. His eyes rose to hers, and she ignored the rush of heat. Yes, it did seem as if he saw her—although now that she studied his gaze, she could tell that there were small indications otherwise.

"Tell me," he said.

She considered him. "The light of your eyes is strange enough, and distracting enough, that I doubt anyone would notice. But you don't seem quite . . . focused. You're looking at me, but it's as if your mind is elsewhere. You understand?"

He nodded. "Bitterblue picks up on that."

"Narrow your eyes a bit," Katsa said. "Bring your eyebrows down, as if you were thinking. Yes—that's pretty convincing, Po. No one you direct that gaze toward will ever suspect a thing."

"Thank you, Katsa. Can I practice it with you, now and then? Without fear of you throwing me onto my back and forcing me out of my clothes?"

Katsa cackled at that and threw the shaft of an arrow at him. He caught it, neatly, and laughed; and she thought for a moment that he looked genuinely happy. And then, of course, he registered her thought, and a shadow settled across his face. He withdrew into his work. She glanced at his hands, at his finger still missing its ring. She took a breath and reached for another branch.

"How much does Bitterblue know?" she asked.

"Only that I'm keeping something from her. She knows my Grace is more than I've said. She's known it from the beginning."

"And your sight?"

"I don't think it's even occurred to her." Po smoothed the edge of a shaft with his knife and swept a pile of bark shavings into the fire. "I'll look her in the eyes more often," he said; and then he withdrew again into silence.

Po AND SKYE teased Bitterblue endlessly about her entourage. It wasn't just the guards. Ror was taking the royal position of his sister's daughter very seriously. Soldiers were always arriving, leading horses piled high with supplies, especially as the winter storms began to wind down. Vegetables, breads, fruits; blankets, clothing, dresses for the queen; and always letters from Ror, asking Bitterblue's opinion on this or that matter, updating her on the plans for the coronation, and inquiring after the health of the various members of her party, particularly Po.

"I'm going to ask Ror to send me a sword," Bitterblue said one day at breakfast. "Katsa, will you teach me to use it?"

Skye's face lit up. "Oh, do, Katsa. I haven't seen you fight yet, and I was beginning to think I never would."

"And you imagine I'll make for an exciting opponent?" Bitterblue asked him.

"Of course not. But she'll have to stage a sword fight with a few of the soldiers, won't she, to show you how it's done? There must be a decent fighter or two among them."

"I'm not going to stage a sword fight with unarmored soldiers," Katsa said.

"What about a hand fight?" Skye sat back and folded his arms, a cockiness in his face that Katsa thought must be a family trait. "I'm not such a bad hand fighter myself."

Po exploded with laughter. "Oh, fight him, Katsa. Please fight him. I can't imagine a more entertaining diversion."

"Oh, it's that funny, is it?"

"Katsa could pound you into the ground before you even raised a finger."

Skye was unabashed. "Yes, exactly—that's what I want to see. I want to see you destroy someone, Katsa. Would you destroy Po for me?"

Katsa was smiling. "Po isn't easy to destroy."

Po hooked his feet to the legs of the table and rocked his chair backward. "I imagine I am these days."

"Returning to the question at hand," Bitterblue said, rather sternly. "I should like to learn to use a sword."

"Yes," Katsa said. "Well then, send word to Ror."

"Aren't two soldiers just leaving?" Po asked. "I'll catch them."

The legs of his chair clattered down to the floor. He pushed away from the table and went outside. Three pairs of eyes lingered on the door that closed behind him.

"The weather's looking less like winter now," Bitterblue said. "I'm anxious to go to my court and get started with things. But I don't like to until I'm convinced he's well, and frankly, I'm not convinced."

Katsa didn't answer. She ate a piece of bread absentmindedly. She turned to Skye and considered his shoulders, strong and straight like his brother's; his strong hands. Skye moved well. And he was closest in age to Po; he'd probably fought Po a million times growing up.

She narrowed her eyes at the remains of their meal. She wondered what it would be like to fight with no eyes, and distracted by the landscape and the movement of every creature close at hand.

"At least he's finally eating," Bitterblue said.

Katsa jumped. She stared at the child. "He is?"

"He was yesterday, and he was this morning. He seems quite hungry, actually. You didn't notice?"

Katsa let out a burst of air. She pushed her own chair back and headed for the door.

SHE FOUND HIM standing before the water, staring unseeing at its frozen surface. He was shivering. She watched him doubtfully for a moment. "Po," she said to his back, "where's your coat?"

"Where's yours?"

She moved to stand beside him. "I'm warm."

He tilted his head to her. "If you're warm and I'm coatless, there's only one friendly thing for you to do."

"Go back and get your coat for you?"

He smiled. Reaching out to her, he pulled her close against him. Katsa wrapped her arms around him, surprised, and tried to rub some warmth into his shivering shoulders and back.

"That's it, exactly," Po said. "You must keep me warm."

She laughed and held him tighter.

Po said, "Let me tell you something that's happened," and she leaned back and looked into his face, because she heard something new in his voice.

"You know I've been fighting my Grace all these months," he said, "trying to push it away. Trying to ignore most of what it shows me and concentrate on the little bit I need to know."

"Yes."

"Well, a few days ago in a fit of, well, self-pity, I stopped."

"You stopped?"

"Fighting my Grace, I mean. I gave up, I let it all wash over me. And you know what happened?" He didn't wait for her to guess. "When I stopped fighting all the things around me, all the things around me started to come together. All the activity, and the landscape, and the ground and the sky, and even people's thoughts. Everything's trying to form one picture. And I can feel my place in it like I couldn't before. I mean, I'm still overwhelmed. But nothing like before."

She bit her lip. "Po. I don't understand."

"It's easy, Katsa. It's as if when I open myself up to every perception, things create their own focus. I mean, think of us now, standing here. There's a bird in the tree behind me, do you see it?"

Katsa looked over his shoulder. A bird sat on a branch, plucking at the feathers under its wing. "I see it."

"Before, I would have tried to fight off my perception of the bird, so as to concentrate on the ground under my feet and you in my arms. But now I just let the bird, and everything else that's irrelevant, wash over me; and the irrelevant things fade away a bit, naturally. So that you are all of my focus."

Katsa was experiencing an odd sensation. It was as if a nagging ache had suddenly lifted and left her with a stunning absence of pain. It was relief and hope together. "Po. This is good."

He sighed. "It's a great comfort to be less dizzy."

She hesitated, and then decided she might as well say it, seeing as he probably already knew it. "I think it's time you started fighting again."

He smiled slightly. "Oh? Is that what you think?"

She rose nobly to the defensive. "And why not? It'll bring back your strength, improve your balance. Your brother makes a perfect opponent."

He touched his forehead to hers. His voice was very quiet. "Calm yourself, wildcat. You're the expert. If you think it's time I started fighting, then I suppose it's time I started fighting."

He was smiling still, and Katsa couldn't bear it, because it was the smallest and the saddest smile in all the world. But as he raised his fingers to touch her face, she saw that he was wearing his ring.

CHAPTER THIRTY-NINE

IT BECAME a kind of school. Katsa made up drills for Skye and Po that were first and foremost a challenge to Po's strength. Skye was satisfied, for the drills favored him. Katsa was satisfied, for she could see Po's progress. She set them always to wrestling, rarely to proper hand fighting, and reminded Po constantly, in his mind and out loud, to muscle rather than Grace his way out of every scrape.

Alongside the grappling brothers, Katsa taught Bitterblue to hold a sword, and then to block with one, and then to strike. Position and balance, strength and motion, speed. The child was as awkward at first with the sword as she had been with the knife, but she worked stubbornly, and like Po she made progress.

And Katsa's school grew. The guards and messengers couldn't resist the spectacle of the Lady Katsa teaching swordplay to their young queen, or the Lienid Graceling and his brother wrestling each other into the ground. They gathered round, asking this and that question about a drill she fabricated for the princes, or a trick she taught Bitterblue to compensate for the queen's lack of size and strength. Before Katsa knew it she was teaching the trick to a pair of young soldiers from Monsea's southern shore, and devising a drill to improve the opposite-hand swordplay of Bitterblue's guards. Katsa enjoyed it thoroughly. It pleased her to watch her students grow stronger.

And Po did grow stronger. He continued to lose at wrestling, but each time his defeat took longer, and still longer. His balance, his control, improved. The battles became increasingly amusing, partly because the brothers were so evenly matched and partly because as the snow melted the yard turned into a morass of mud. Of course they liked nothing better than to smear the mud in each other's faces. If it weren't for Po's eyes, most days the brothers would have been indistinguishable.

THE DAY CAME when one of the mud-covered princes pinned the other to the ground and shouted his victory and Katsa looked over to find that the brother on top was, for the first time, Po. He leaped to his feet, laughing, and shot a wicked grin at Katsa. He wiped mud from his face and crooked his finger at her. "Come here, wildcat. You're next."

Katsa leaned on her sword and laughed. "It took you half an hour to pin your brother, and you think you're ready for me?"

"Come mud wrestle with me. I'll flatten you like a spider."

Katsa turned back to the exercise she was teaching Bitterblue. "When you can beat Skye easily, then I'll mud wrestle with you."

She spoke sternly, but she couldn't hide from him her pleasure. Nor could he hide his own. He comforted his poor moaning brother, who recognized, from his vantage point on the ground, the beginning of the end.

KATSA FOUND HIM changed as an opponent—less because of the sight he'd lost than because of the sensitivity he'd gained with his growing Grace. When they fought now he could sense not just her body and her intention but the force of her blows before they struck, the direction of her momentum. Her balance and imbalance, and how to capitalize on it. He was not back to full strength yet, and sometimes his own balance still tricked him. But there were times now when he caught her by surprise, something neither of them was used to.

He was going to be as good a fighter as he'd been before, if not better. And this was important. The fights made Po happy.

Bitterblue did not stay long past the start of spring. Skye followed her sometime thereafter, summoned by his father to Leck City to assist with the imminent coronation. And finally Katsa and Po made the journey themselves to the city that was soon to assume Bitterblue's name. Po bore the traveling well, a bit like a child who's never traveled before and finds every experience fascinating, if slightly overwhelming. And indeed, when it came to traveling with his new way of perceiving the world, Po was an infant.

In their room in Bitterblue's castle, on the morning of the great event, Katsa suffered herself to put on a dress. Po, in the meantime, lay on the bed, grinning endlessly at the ceiling.

"What are you grinning at?" Katsa demanded for the third or fourth time. "Is the ceiling about to cave in on my head or something? You look like we're both on the verge of an enormous joke."

"Katsa, only you would consider the collapse of the ceiling a good joke."

There was a knock at the entrance to their room then, and Po actually began to giggle. "You've been in the cider," Katsa said accusingly as she went to the door. "You're drunk."

And then she swung the door open and almost sat down on the floor in astonishment, because before her in the hallway stood Raffin.

He was muddy and smelled like horses. "Did we get here in time for the food?" he asked. "The invitation said something about pie, and I'm starving."

Katsa burst into laughter, and then into tears, and once she started hugging him she couldn't stop. Behind Raffin stood Bann, and behind Bann stood Oll, and Katsa hugged them and cried over them as well. "You didn't tell us you were coming," she kept saying. "You didn't tell us you were coming. No one ever even told me you were invited."

"And you're one to speak of sending word," Raffin said. "For months we didn't hear a thing from you—until one day Po's brother appeared at our court with the wildest story any of us had ever heard."

Katsa sniffled and wrapped her arms around her cousin again. "But you understand, don't you?" she said to his chest. "We didn't want to get you mixed up in it."

Raffin kissed the top of her head. "Of course we understand."

"Is Randa with you?"

"He didn't care to come."

"Is the Council well?"

"It's moving along swimmingly. Must we stand here clogging the hallway? I wasn't joking about starving to death. You're looking well, Po." Raffin peered doubtfully at Katsa's short hair. "Helda's sent you a hairbrush, Kat. Much use it'll be."

"I'll cherish it," Katsa said. "Now come inside."

LIKE ANY EVENT requiring formal clothing, the crowning ceremony was tedious, but Bitterblue endured it with the appropriate gravity and poise. The rim of the great golden crown was padded with some thick purple material, to keep it from sliding down to rest on her nose. It looked, Katsa thought, as if it weighed as much as the girl herself did.

Katsa didn't mind the tedium, for Raffin was on one side of her and Bann on the other, and not five minutes passed without them amusing themselves in some way. When Bann whispered to her about Raffin's new medicinal discovery that cured bellyache but caused itchy feet, and his subsequent discovery that cured itchy feet but caused bellyache, Katsa giggled. Standing three rows ahead with his two sons, Ror whipped his head around to glare at her. "This is not a Sunderan street carnival," he whispered with great and dignified reproach. And Po's shoulders began to shake with laughter, and various voices whispered for Ror to shush but then realized whom they were shushing and issued an appalled stream of apology.

"Yes, all right," Ror was left saying, repeatedly and with

increasing volume. "Truly, it's all right." The interruption grew to something rather large and intrusive, causing a coronation attendant to stumble in his litany of the Monsean rulers across time. Bitterblue smiled softly at the attendant, and nodded for him to continue. After that, word passed through the crowd that the young queen was kindhearted, and not one to punish small mistakes.

"And how is Giddon?" Katsa murmured to Raffin once things had settled down. She was feeling kindly toward her old suitor because she was happy and surrounded by friends.

Behind her, Oll cleared his throat. "He gets a bit mopey whenever your name is mentioned, Lady. I won't pretend I don't know why."

Raffin spoke quietly. "Randa keeps trying to marry him off, and Giddon keeps refusing. He spends more time than he used to on his own estate. But he gives himself completely to the work of the Council. He's an invaluable ally, Kat. I daresay he wouldn't object to seeing you someday. If you wanted to visit us at court, you know, we'd find a way of sneaking you in without Randa knowing. If you wished it. You haven't told us your plans."

Katsa smiled quietly. "I'll go back to the mountains with Po after this." It was all she said of her plans, because for the moment it was all she knew.

She tilted her head and rested it against her cousin's tall shoulder. The coronation passed in a blur of contentment.

EPILOGUE

THEY SWAM through the tunnel, Katsa and Po, and burst into the black air of the cave. They hoisted themselves onto the rocks and wrung what water they could from their clothing.

"Take my hand," Po said. He led her up an uneven slope jutted with rocks. Katsa could see nothing in the darkness, not even the slightest shape. She tripped, and swore.

"Where exactly are we going?"

"To the beach," he said. He stopped and lifted her over some rock formation she couldn't see. When he put her down, her feet touched something gritty and soft. Sand.

Outside, the trees were green with spring's end and the sun thawed the world, but inside this cave was always a cold season. They sat on the sand and huddled against each other to keep warm; and shivering led to playful pushing, and pushing to roughhousing, and before too long they were laughing and wrestling full tilt on the ground, their wet hair and clothing full of sand. Finally, pinned against her, Po whispered his surrender, running his hand along the back of her leg in a manner that was distinctly uncombative. And the wrestling turned to something slow and gentle and yielding, and they were warm, and occupied with each other, for some time.

———

SOUND WAS STRANGE in the cave, wet and musical. They lay side by side, warm where their bodies touched. "I've inhaled some sand," Po said, coughing. "So have you, of course, but it doesn't seem to be bothering you."

"No," Katsa said absently, staring up into blackness. Her fingers felt along the scars on her shoulder, and then the scars on her breast. "Po?"

"Hmm?"

"You trust the men who'll be Bitterblue's advisers?"

"For the most part."

"I hope she'll be all right. She never talks about her mother's death, but I know she's still having nightmares."

"I don't see how she could help having nightmares," Po said. "She's so young, and she has so much she's trying to make sense of: a murdered mother, a father who was a madman."

"Do you think he was mad?"

Po hesitated. "I truly don't know. Certainly he was cruel, and perverse. But it's hard to tell where he ended and his Grace began, do you know what I mean? And I suppose we'll never know now where he came from. Or what it is he really wanted." He breathed in and out slowly. "At least people's feelings for him are shifting. Have you felt it? He won't be remembered kindly."

"That will be a help to Bitterblue."

"You know, she wonders if I'm a mind reader. She wonders it, Katsa, and still she trusts me and doesn't press me to spill my secrets. It's extraordinary."

Katsa listened to the quiet that came over the cave when

Po stopped speaking. "Yes," she said simply. "Bitterblue is not like other people."

"At the coronation Skye accused me of refusing to marry you," Po said; and now she heard a smile in his voice. "He was quite indignant about it."

Katsa sighed. "Oll came to me with the same point. He thinks it's dangerous for us to leave each other so much freedom and make these vague plans to travel together in the future, doing Council work, with no promises. I told him I'm not going to marry you and hang on to you like a barnacle, just to keep you to myself and stop you loving anyone else."

"It's all right, you know. Other people don't have to understand."

"I worry about it."

"Don't worry about it. We'll muddle through. And there are those who do understand. Raffin does, and Bann."

"Yes," Katsa said. "I suppose they do."

Po shivered, and she reached for him to warm him. A feeling swelled, suddenly, at the edges of her heart. She whispered. "You're determined to go to Lienid right away?"

He took a moment before answering. He couldn't quite manage to keep his voice light. "My mother will cry when I tell her about my sight. To be honest, I dread that as much as anything else."

"I'll come with you."

"No, Katsa, I'll be all right. I want to face this thing and be done with it. And I don't want you to change your plans."

Katsa was en route back to Bitterblue City to give fighting

lessons to girls. It was a thing she'd decided she wanted to do, in all seven kingdoms, and after the coronation Bitterblue had begged her to start in Monsea. Po had encouraged it, rather insistently, for it gave Katsa an excuse to keep an eye on Bitterblue's welfare for just a little while longer.

"I'll be in Monsea a few months at least," Katsa said. "But I promise the next lessons I give will be in Lienid."

"So I'll hope to see you by autumn's end. I'll pretend to myself it's not a long time."

"I'm going to take the land route west," Katsa said. She hesitated, then made an admission. "I'm going into the Middluns, Po. There's one more king I need to face."

Po released a small, surprised breath. "But you faced him already."

Katsa sighed. "Yes. But I was scared of myself then. I was scared of him. I'm not anymore. Po—I need Randa to know I'll come and go as I please. I won't hide myself like some kind of criminal, and I won't be afraid to visit my friends. I miss Raff so much already, and I need to see Helda—I want to convince her to go to Monsea. Bitterblue needs her."

Po's arms came around her and pulled her against him. His fingers brushed sand from her hair. "All right," he said softly. "Be careful. I'll look for you after you've faced your king."

They lay quietly together in the dark. Katsa settled her head against his chest. She heard lapping water and its echo. She heard the pulse of his blood through his skin.

"You know," he said, "I wish you could see this cave."

"What's it like?"

He paused. "It's . . . beautiful, really."

"Tell me."

And so Po described to Katsa what hid in the blackness of the cave; and outside, the world awaited them.

ACKNOWLEDGMENTS

A DEBUT NOVEL is a true team effort. With all my heart, I would like to thank my sister Catherine (and the guys), always my first reader(s); my stupendous editor, Kathy Dawson; my agent, Faye Bender, who is a rock star; Liza Ketchum, who taught me to think like a novelist; Susan Bloom, Cathie Mercier, Kelly Hager, Jackie Horne, Lisa Jahn-Clough, and everyone else who changed my life at Simmons College's marvelous Center for the Study of Children's Literature; my sister Dac, Dana Zachary, Deborah Kaplan, Joan Leonard, Mom, and Rebecca Rabinowitz, aka my fearless readers; Daniel Burbach, who offered loads of support; my uncle Dr. Walter Willihnganz, who answered a lot of silly medical questions with great patience; my uncles Alfio, Salvatore, and Michael Previtera, who answered a lot of even sillier questions about bows and arrows at the Previtera family Christmas party; and last, but far from least, both of my parents, for everything.

Read the companion to *Graceling*:
FIRE

It is not a peaceful time in the Dells. The young King Nash is clinging to the throne, while rebel lords—in the north and south—build armies to unseat him. War is coming. The mountains and forests are filled with spies and thieves.

This is where Fire lives, a girl whose startling appearance is weirdly irresistible and who can control the minds of everyone around her.

Everyone except Prince Brigan.

Exquisitely romantic, this companion to the highly praised *Graceling* has an entirely new cast of characters, save for one person who plays a pivotal role in both books.

Turn the page to read the prologue to *Fire*.

PROLOGUE

LARCH OFTEN THOUGHT that if it had not been for his new-born son, he never would have survived his wife Mikra's death. It was half that the infant boy needed a breathing, functioning father who got out of bed in the mornings and slogged through the day; and it was half the child himself. Such a good-natured baby, so calm. His gurgles and coos so musical, and his eyes deep brown like the eyes of his dead mother.

Larch was a game warden on the riverside estate of a minor lord in the southeastern kingdom of Monsea. When Larch returned to his quarters after a day in the saddle, he took the baby from the arms of the nursemaid almost jealously. Dirty, stinking of sweat and horses, he cradled the boy against his chest, sat in his wife's old rocker, and closed his eyes. Sometimes he cried, tears painting clean stripes down a grimy face, but always quietly, so that he would not miss the sounds the child made. The baby watched him. The baby's eyes soothed him. The nursemaid said it was unusual for a baby so young to have such focused eyes. "It's not something to be happy about," she warned, "a child with strange eyes."

Larch couldn't find it within himself to worry. The nurse-maid worried enough for two. Every morning she examined the baby's eyes, as was the unspoken custom of all new parents in the seven kingdoms, and every morning she breathed more easily once she'd confirmed that nothing had changed. For the infant who fell asleep with both eyes the same color and woke with eyes of two different colors was a Graceling; and in Monsea, as in most of the kingdoms, Graceling babies immediately became the property of the king. Their families rarely saw them again.

When the first anniversary of the birth of Larch's son had come and gone with no change to the boy's brown eyes, the nursemaid still did not leave off her muttering. She'd heard tales of Graceling eyes that took more than a year to settle, and Graceling or not, the child was not normal. A year out of his mother's womb and already Immiker could say his own name. He spoke in simple sentences at fifteen months; he left his babyish pronunciation behind at a year and a half. At the beginning of her time with Larch the nursemaid had hoped her care would gain her a husband and a strong, healthy son. Now she found the baby who conversed like a miniature adult while he drank at her breast, who made an eloquent announcement whenever his underwrappings needed to be changed, positively creepy. She resigned her post.

Larch was happy to see the sour woman go. He constructed a carrier so that the child could hang against his chest while he worked. He refused to ride on cold or rainy days; he refused to gallop his horse. He worked shorter hours and took breaks to feed Immiker, nap him, clean his messes. The baby chattered constantly, asked for the names of plants and animals, made up nonsense poems that Larch strained to hear, for the poems always made Larch laugh.

"Birdies love treetops to whirl themselves through, for inside of their heads they are birds," the boy sang, absentmindedly, patting his hand on his father's arm. Then, a minute later: "Father?"

"Yes, son?"

"You love the things that I love you to do, for inside of your head are my words."

Larch was utterly happy. He couldn't remember why his wife's death had saddened him so. He saw now that it was better this way, he and the boy alone in the world. He began to avoid the people of the estate, for their tiresome company bored him, and he didn't see why they should deserve to share in the delight of his son's company.

One morning when Immiker was three years old Larch opened his eyes to find his son lying awake beside him, staring at him. The boy's right eye was gray. His left eye was red. Larch shot up, terrified and heartbroken. "They'll take you," he said to his son. "They'll take you away from me."

Immiker blinked, calmly. "They won't, because you'll come up with a plan to stop them."

To withhold a Graceling from the king was royal theft, punishable by imprisonment and fines Larch could never pay, but still Larch was seized by a compulsion to do what the boy said. They would have to ride east, into the rocky border mountains where hardly anyone lived, and find a patch of stone or scrub that could serve as a hiding place. As a game warden, Larch could track, hunt, build fires, and make a home for Immiker that no one would find.

IMMIKER WAS REMARKABLY calm about their flight. He knew what a Graceling was. Larch supposed the nursemaid had told him; or perhaps Larch himself had explained it and then forgotten he'd done so. Larch was growing forgetful. He sensed parts of his memory closing up on him, like dark rooms behind doors he could no longer open. Larch attributed it to his age, for neither he nor his wife had been young when she'd died birthing their son.

"I've wondered sometimes if your Grace has anything to do with speaking," Larch said as they rode the hills east, leaving the river and their old home behind.

"It doesn't," Immiker said.

"Of course it doesn't," Larch said, unable to fathom why he'd ever thought it did. "That's all right, son, you're young yet. We'll watch out for it. We'll hope it's something useful."

Immiker didn't respond. Larch checked the straps that held the boy before him in the saddle. He bent down to kiss the top of Immiker's golden head, and urged the horse onward.

A GRACE WAS a particular skill far surpassing the capability of a normal human being. A Grace could take any form. Most of the kings had at least one Graceling in his kitchens, a superhumanly capable bread baker or winemaker. The luckiest kings had soldiers in their armies Graced with sword fighting.

A Graceling might have impossibly good hearing, run as fast as a mountain lion, calculate large sums mentally, even sense if food was poisoned. There were useless Graces, too, like the ability to twist all the way around at the waist or eat rocks without sickening. And there were eerie Graces. Some Gracelings saw events before they happened. Some could enter the minds of others and see things it was not their business to see. The Nanderan king was said to own a Graceling who could tell if a person had ever committed a crime, just by looking into his face.

The Gracelings were tools of the kings, and no more. They were not thought to be natural, and people who could avoid them did, in Monsea and in most of the other six kingdoms as well. No one wished the company of a Graceling.

Larch had once shared this attitude. Now he saw that it was cruel, unjust, and ignorant, for his son was a normal little boy who happened to be superior in many ways, not just in the way of his Grace, whatever it might turn out to be. It was all the more reason for Larch to remove his son from society. He would not send Immiker to the king's court, to be shunned and teased, and put to whatever use pleased the king.

THEY WERE NOT long in the mountains before Larch accepted, bitterly, that it was an impossible hiding place. It wasn't the cold that was the problem, though autumn here was as raw as midwinter had been on the lord's estate. It wasn't the terrain either, though the scrub was hard and sharp, and they slept on rock every night, and there was no place even to imagine growing vegetables or grain. It was the predators. Not a week went by that Larch didn't have to defend against some attack. Mountain lions, bears, wolves. The enormous birds, the raptors, with a wingspan twice the height of a man. Some of the creatures were territorial, all of them were vicious, and as winter closed in bleakly around Larch and Immiker, all of them were starving. Their horse was lost one day to a pair of mountain lions.

At night, inside the thorny shelter Larch had built of sticks and scrub, he would pull the boy into the warmth of his coat and listen for the howls, the tumbled stones down the slope, the screeches, that meant an animal had scented them. At the first telltale sound he would strap the sleeping boy into the carrier on his chest. He would light as powerful a torch as he had the fuel for, go out of the shelter, and stand there, holding off the attack with fire and sword. Sometimes he stood there for hours. Larch didn't get a lot of sleep.

He wasn't eating much either.

"You'll make yourself sick if you keep eating so much," Immiker said to Larch over their paltry dinner of stringy wolf meat and water.

Larch stopped chewing immediately, for sickness would make it harder to defend the boy. He handed over the majority of his portion. "Thank you for the warning, son."

They ate quietly for a while, Immiker devouring Larch's food. "What if we went higher into the mountains and crossed to the other side?" Immiker asked.

Larch looked into the boy's mismatched eyes. "Is that what you think we should do?"

Immiker shrugged his small shoulders. "Could we survive the crossing?"

"Do you think we could?" Larch asked, and then shook himself as he heard his own question. The child was three years old and knew nothing of crossing mountains. It was a sign of Larch's fatigue, that he groped so desperately and so often for his son's opinion.

"We would not survive," Larch said firmly. "I've heard of no one who has ever made it across the mountains to the east, either here or in Estill or Nander. I know nothing of the land beyond the seven kingdoms, except for tall tales the eastern people tell about rainbow-colored monsters and underground labyrinths."

"Then you'll have to bring me back down into the hills, Father, and hide me. You must protect me."

Larch's mind was foggy, tired, starved, and shot through with one lightning bolt of clarity, which was his determination to do what Immiker said.

SNOW WAS FALLING as Larch picked his way down a sheer slope. The boy was strapped inside his coat. Larch's sword, his bow and arrows, some blankets, and bundled scraps of meat hung on his back. When the great brown raptor appeared over a distant ridge, Larch reached for his bow tiredly. But the bird lunged so fast that all in an instant it was too close to shoot. Larch stumbled away from the creature, fell, and felt himself sliding downward. He braced his arms before him to shield the child, whose screams rose above the screams of the bird: "Protect me, Father! You must protect me, Father!"

Suddenly the slope under Larch's back gave way and they were falling through darkness. An avalanche, Larch thought numbly, every nerve in his body still focused on protecting the child under his coat. His shoulder hit something sharp and Larch felt tearing flesh, and wetness, warmth. Strange, to be plunging downward like this. The drop was heady, dizzying, as if it were vertical, a free fall; and just before he slipped into unconsciousness Larch wondered if they were falling through the mountain to the floor of the earth.

LARCH JACKKNIFED AWAKE, frantic with one thought: Immiker. The boy's body wasn't touching his, and the straps hung from his chest, empty. Larch felt around with his hands, whimpering. It was dark. The surface on which he lay was hard and slick, like slimy ice. He shifted to extend his reach and screamed suddenly, incoherently, at the pain that ripped through his shoulder and head. Nausea surged in his throat. He fought it down and lay still again, weeping helplessly and moaning the boy's name.

"All right, Father," Immiker's voice said, very close beside him. "Stop crying and get up."

Larch's weeping turned to sobs of relief.

"Get up, Father. I've explored. There's a tunnel and we must go."

"Are you hurt?"

"I'm cold and hungry. Get up."

Larch tried to lift his head, and cried out, almost blacked out. "It's no use. The pain is too great."

"The pain is not so great that you can't get up," Immiker said, and when Larch tried again he found that the boy was right. It was excruciating, and he vomited once or twice, but it was not so bad that he couldn't prop himself on his knees and his uninjured arm, and crawl across the icy surface behind his son.

"Where," he gasped, and then abandoned his question. It was too much work.

"We fell through a crack in the mountain," Immiker said. We slid. There's a tunnel."

Larch didn't understand, and forward progress took so much concentration that he stopped trying to. The way was slippery and downhill. The place they went toward was slightly darker than the place they came from. His son's small form scuttled down the slope ahead of him.

"There's a drop," Immiker said, but comprehension came so slowly to Larch that before he understood, he fell, tumbling knees over neck off a short ledge. He landed on his injured shoulder and momentarily lost consciousness. He woke to a cold breeze and a musty smell that hurt his head. He was in a narrow space, crammed between close walls. He tried to ask whether his fall had injured the boy, but only managed a moan.

"Which way?" Immiker's voice asked.

Larch didn't know what he meant, and moaned again.

Immiker's voice was tired, and impatient. "I've told you, it's a tunnel. I've felt along the wall in both directions. Choose which way, Father. Take me out of this place."

The ways were identically dim, identically musty, but Larch needed to choose, if it was what the boy thought best. He shifted himself carefully. His head hurt less when he faced the breeze than when he turned his back to it. This decided him. They would walk toward the source of the breeze.

And that is why, after four days of bleeding, stumbling, and starving, after four days of Immiker reminding him repeatedly that he was well enough to keep walking, Larch and Immiker stepped out of the tunnel not into the light of the Monsean foothills, but into that of a strange land on the other side of the Monsean peaks. An eastern land neither of them had heard of except for foolish tales told over Monsean dinners—tales of rainbow-colored monsters and underground labyrinths.

LARCH WONDERED SOMETIMES if a blow to his head on the day he'd fallen through the mountain had caused some hurt to his brain. The more time he spent in this new land, the more he struggled against a fog hovering on the edge of his mind. The people here spoke differently and Larch struggled with the strange words, the strange sounds. He depended on Immiker to translate. As time passed he depended on Immiker to explain a great many things.

This land was mountainous, stormy and rough. It was called the Dells. Variations of the animals Larch had known in

Monsea lived in the Dells—normal animals, with appearances and behavior Larch understood and recognized. But also in the Dells lived colorful, astonishing creatures that the Dellian people called monsters. It was their unusual coloration that identified them as monsters, because in every other physical particular they were like normal Dellian animals. They had the shape of Dellian horses, Dellian turtles, mountain lions, raptors, dragonflies, bears; but they were ranges of fuchsia, turquoise, bronze, iridescent green. A dappled gray horse in the Dells was a horse. A sunset orange horse was a monster.

Larch didn't understand these monsters. The mouse monsters, the fly and squirrel and fish and sparrow monsters, were harmless; but the bigger monsters, the man-eating monsters, were terribly dangerous, more so than their animal counterparts. They craved human flesh, and for the flesh of other monsters they were positively frantic. For Immiker's flesh they seemed frantic as well, and as soon as he was big enough to pull back the string of a bow Immiker learned to shoot. Larch wasn't sure who taught him. Immiker always seemed to have someone, a man or a boy, who guarded him and helped him with this and that. Never the same person. The old ones always disappeared by the time Larch had learned their names, and new ones always took their places.

Larch wasn't even certain where the people came from. He and Immiker lived in a small house, and then a bigger house, then even bigger, in a rocky clearing on the outskirts of a town, and some of Immiker's people came from the town. But others seemed to come out of crevices in the mountains and in the ground. These strange, pallid, underground people brought medicines to Larch. They healed his shoulder.

He heard there were one or two monsters of a human shape in the Dells, with brightly colored hair, but he never saw them. It was for the best, because Larch could never remember if the human monsters were friendly or not, and against monsters in general he had no defense. They were too beautiful. Their beauty was so extreme that whenever Larch came face to face with one of them, his mind emptied and his body froze, and Immiker and his friends had to defend him.

"It's what they do, Father," Immiker explained to him, over and over. "It's part of their monstrous power. They stun you with their beauty, and then they overwhelm your mind and make you stupid. You must learn to guard your mind against them, as I have."

Larch had no doubt Immiker was right, but still he didn't understand. "What a horrifying notion," he said. "A creature with the power to take over one's mind."

Immiker burst into delighted laughter, and threw his arm around his father. And still Larch didn't understand; but Immiker's displays of affection were rare, and they always overwhelmed Larch with a dumb happiness that numbed the discomfort of his confusion.

IN HIS RARE moments of mental lucidity, Larch was sure that as Immiker had grown older, Larch himself had grown stupider and more forgetful. Immiker explained to him over and over the unstable politics of this land, the military factions that divided it, the black market that flourished in the underground passages that connected it. Two different Dellian lords, Lord Mydogg in the north and Lord Gentian in the south, were trying to carve their own empires into the landscape and wrest power from the Dellian king. In the far north was a second nation of lakes and mountain peaks called Pikkia.

Larch couldn't keep it straight in his head. He knew only that there were no Gracelings here. No one would take from Larch his son whose eyes were two different colors.

Eyes of two different colors. Immiker was a Graceling. Larch thought about this sometimes, when his mind was clear enough for thought. He wondered when his son's Grace would appear.

In his clearest moments, which only came to him when Immiker left him alone for a while, Larch wondered if it already had.

IMMIKER HAD HOBBIES. He liked to play with little monsters. He liked to tie them down and peel away their claws, or their vividly colored scales, or clumps of their hair and feathers. One day in the boy's tenth year, Larch came upon Immiker slicing stripes down the stomach of a rabbit that was colored like the sky.

Even bleeding, even shaking and wild-eyed, the rabbit was beautiful to Larch. He stared at the creature and forgot why he'd come looking for Immiker. How sad it was, to see something so small and helpless, something so beautiful, damaged in fun. The rabbit began to make noises, horrible, panicked squeaks, and Larch heard himself whimpering.

Immiker glanced at Larch. "It doesn't hurt her, Father."

Instantly Larch felt better, knowing that the monster wasn't in pain. But then the rabbit let out a very small, very desperate whine, and Larch was confused. He looked at his son. The boy held a dagger dripping with blood before the eyes of the shaking creature, and smiled at his father.

Somewhere in the depths of Larch's mind a prick of suspicion made itself felt. Larch remembered why he'd come looking for Immiker.

"I have an idea," Larch said slowly, "about the nature of your Grace."

Immiker's eyes flicked calmly, carefully, to Larch's. "Do you?"

"You've said that the monsters take over my mind with their beauty."

Immiker lowered his knife, and tilted his head at his father. There was something odd in the boy's face. Disbelief, Larch thought, and a strange, amused smile. As if the boy were playing a game he was used to winning, and this time he'd lost.

"Sometimes I think you take over my mind," Larch said, "with your words."

Immiker's smile widened, and then he began to laugh. The laughter made Larch so happy that he began to laugh as well. How much he loved this child. The love and the laughter bubbled out of him, and when Immiker walked toward him Larch held his arms open wide. Immiker thrust his dagger into Larch's stomach. Larch dropped like a stone to the floor.

Immiker leaned over his father. "You've been delightful," he said. "I'll miss your devotion. If only it were as easy to control everyone as it is to control you. If only everyone were as stupid as you are, Father."

IT WAS STRANGE, to be dying. Cold and dizzying, like his fall through the Monsean mountains. But Larch knew he wasn't falling through the Monsean mountains; in death he knew clearly, for the first time in years, where he was and what was happening. His last thought was that it hadn't been stupidity that had allowed his son to enchant him so easily with words. It had been love. Larch's love had kept him from recognizing Immiker's Grace, because even before the boy's birth, when Immiker had been no more than a promise inside Mikra's body, Larch had already been enchanted.

FIFTEEN MINUTES LATER Larch's body and his house were on fire and Immiker was on his pony's back, picking his way through the caves to the north. It was a relief to be moving on. His surroundings and his neighbors had become tedious of late, and he was restless. Ready for something more.

He decided to mark this new era in his life with a change of his foolish, sentimental name. The people of this land had an odd way of pronouncing Larch's name, and Immiker had always liked the sound of it.

He changed his name to Leck.

A YEAR PASSED.